# THE INSIDE MAN

Also by Trevor Wood

**THE JIMMY MULLEN SERIES**
*The Man on the Street*
*One Way Street*
*Dead End Street*

**STANDALONE**
*You Can Run*

**THE DCI JACK PARKER SERIES**
*The Silent Killer*

# THE INSIDE MAN

# TREVOR WOOD

QUERCUS

First published in Great Britain in 2025 by

QUERCUS

Quercus Editions Ltd
Carmelite House
50 Victoria Embankment
London EC4Y 0DZ

An Hachette UK company

The authorised representative in the EEA is Hachette Ireland,
8 Castlecourt Centre, Dublin 15, D15 XTP3, Ireland (email: info@hbgi.ie)

A CIP catalogue record for this book is available
from the British Library

HB ISBN 978 1 52943 255 8
EB ISBN 978 1 52943 257 2

1

Typeset by CC Book Production
Printed and bound in Great Britain by Clays Ltd, Elcograf S.p.A.

Papers used by Quercus are from well-managed forests and other responsible sources.

For Amer Anwar, a true gentleman and a terrific writer.
Rest in peace, my friend.

# PROLOGUE

Do you want to hear a sick joke? It was April Fools' Day when I was told I was in the first stages of early onset dementia. Nice timing, eh? They really caught me out this time.

It was in the afternoon, which shouldn't count. My dad would have gone mad. Until he did go mad, that is. He was a stickler for the rules before he fell victim to this pernicious disease himself. After that, not so much. Maybe passing his rogue gene on to me was a posthumous slow-release prank of the worst kind.

I didn't notice the date at the time – as you can imagine I was a little preoccupied. It was only when, several months later, my consultant suggested I kept a diary to monitor my condition that I made the connection.

That was more than six months ago and I've recorded every little incident along the way, both good and bad, looking for a pattern of decline that, thankfully, hasn't yet materialised.

It's a random list of mishaps, forgetting the odd name,

the occasional fall, even the times I lost my temper – I'm a detective chief inspector, for God's sake, an ability to fly off the handle at the slightest provocation is in the job description. But back then I thought everything was a symptom. I like to think I've calmed down a bit since, or maybe I'm simply not noticing the signs – which in itself could be another sign I guess. And so it goes on, second-guessing has become second nature. Is that also a symptom? Is it starting now? Or am I just getting old and a bit clumsier?

There are other things in the diary. The day I vowed to stop drinking to try and slow things down. Then there are the days where I broke that vow, occasional enough not to be a bother. So far. The first time I successfully completed the *Guardian*'s cryptic crossword is written in capitals. I haven't managed to finish it since.

The day I left my wife is in there too. And the day she found out why. Some quite big stuff really – but symptoms of the disease? Probably not. Symptoms of my need to exert some control over my life and my subsequent failure to do that? Most definitely. I couldn't help thinking how much more fun it would have been if I'd kept a similar diary when I was a teenager; my first drink, my first kiss, the day I discovered masturbation. The list goes on.

Looking back at my notes, the one thing I can safely say so far is that I have a lot fewer fucks to give than I used to. I take more chances and it's not just the fools I can't be doing with, I don't suffer anyone gladly. No one at work seems to have noticed yet, so maybe I haven't changed that much, though one of my detective sergeants has been giving me the occasional side-eye so I may be wrong about that. If she has worked it out she doesn't appear to have shared the information with anyone. Perhaps she's keeping it for a trade-off of some kind? I'm certainly not in any kind of hurry to become the talk of the station – I don't know how many days I've got left before my brain starts to scramble but I'm not spending them sitting in the basement looking through cold cases.

I do worry that I'm getting reckless. I guess you could call that a symptom. Maybe I should think more carefully before I jump into things with both feet? If my boss got wind of that thought he'd know I was losing it; it took him two years to persuade me to do one of his ridiculous risk assessment courses and even then I disappeared on the first morning to take charge of a murder case. As motives go, my desire to get out of that room was probably as strong as the actual killer's hatred for their victim.

I guess my main take, going forward, is that I need to be more careful, apply the brakes a little more quickly, especially where my team are involved. I've got nothing left to lose, my days are numbered anyway, but I wouldn't want any of them to get hurt and if I carry on like I have they surely will be.

# 1

*28 October 2024*

Maria Groom stared out of her bedroom window at the shadow of a man hiding in her back garden.

She pulled the curtains closed, leaving a small gap to look through, and kept one eye fixed on the tree he was standing behind, while glancing to check her phone was still on the bedside table.

Was it her imagination? That's what they'd suggested the last time she'd said something. It was probably a cat, they'd said. But she knew what she'd seen. It was no cat. She was so sick of this shit.

It had been darker then but this time there was a full moon casting some light into the garden and she was one hundred per cent certain she'd seen a figure ducking behind the overgrown oak tree that stopped the light getting into her house all summer.

The shadow hadn't moved for minutes now. But she knew it wasn't 'her eyes playing tricks on her'. Or a damn cat.

Not unless Dr Seuss's Cat in the Hat had suddenly sprung off the page of Nicky's picture book and decided to hide in the garden.

Whoever it was knew she'd been watching him and was keeping still until he thought she'd gone to bed. Then he'd make his move.

'Alexa, turn the lights off.'

The bedroom went dark. She stayed as still as possible, keeping her gaze firmly on the shadow this time. Minutes passed. Then there was a flicker of movement and the man stepped out from the tree. There wasn't enough light to see him clearly and he was clad in black from head to foot, which didn't help; a baseball cap's visor keeping his face in the shadows.

'Alexa, lights on,' she commanded, throwing open the curtains so he could clearly see her staring down at him.

He stared right back then put his finger to his lips as if to tell her it was their secret, before turning around and clambering over the fence into next door. At least he was heading away from her now.

She scrambled for her phone before returning to the window, hoping to take a video of the man – despite the neutral clothing she had no doubts it was a man, she might even be able to name him – but he'd disappeared.

Without taking her gaze from the neighbour's garden she rang the usual number and waited a few moments for someone to answer. There was no further sign of the intruder.

'Emergency. Which service?'

'Police please,' she said.

## 2

*29 October 2024*

The last time I'd taken part in a drugs trial, the defendant got ten years for distributing cocaine across most of the north-east. That wasn't the kind of drugs trial my consultant was suggesting.

'It's your call, Jack,' he said. 'It's a new drug called donanemab. They've already run one trial and the results have been encouraging so they're running a follow-up, specifically aimed at pre-symptomatic people in the very first stages of early onset dementia. You're an ideal candidate.'

'How is it any different to the drugs I'm already taking?'

'All the drugs on the market at the moment only deal with the symptoms of the disease, this one attacks the causes. It targets the build-up of amyloid proteins in the brain. The earlier trial showed that seventy-five per cent of volunteers had amyloid removed entirely. And even for those who didn't, it still slowed down their decline.'

That perked my interest. Putting the brakes on this thing

was the only real hope I had until now. Discovering that Alzheimer's was inevitably coming my way, sooner rather than later, had been a bitter blow – to say the least – but I was doing all I could to delay it.

I guess in some ways I was fortunate. I'd been a passenger in a hit and run crash that had killed my detective sergeant, Laura Kemp, and in the ensuing treatment a scan had picked up signs of my condition far earlier than would normally be the case, giving me time to prepare for the worst.

'It's another tool to add to your toolbox,' the consultant continued. 'You've been doing everything right so far. Your last test showed no real decline in performance and I can see that you've taken my advice on diet and exercise, you're looking much healthier than the last time I saw you.'

'I've eaten so many sodding tomatoes I'm surprised I don't look like one and I've barely touched a drink since the last time we spoke. I've stopped driving too, just in case, as you suggested.'

'I thought we all stopped drinking and driving in the nineties,' he joked. Humour clearly wasn't his strong suit.

I wasn't in denial. Dementia was going to get me in the end but I wanted more time. There were things I needed to finish before it finished me.

Paramount amongst these was finding Laura's killer. I believed the crash was deliberate but the driver had never been identified. She had been my friend as well as my colleague and I couldn't let it lie. I wanted the killer nailed.

'D'you need a bit of time to think about it?' the doc said, clearly assuming I was thinking about the trial rather than losing focus. I didn't want to heighten his concerns by correcting his assumption. If concentration was becoming an issue maybe I wasn't still pre-symptomatic?

'What does it involve?' I didn't have the time for something that would take me away from work for long spells – especially as no one there knew about my condition – and I couldn't keep inventing excuses for my occasional absence. As far as my colleagues knew this was a routine appointment to follow up on the concussion I received in the collision.

'It's delivered intravenously through a drip bag so you'd have to attend the clinic once a month for at least an hour each time.'

I reckoned that was manageable without arousing too much suspicion.

'Count me in,' I said.

'Hold your horses, Jack, there are some possible side effects you should know about. They're serious enough that, although the drug has been licensed, it hasn't been approved for the NHS.'

'Like what?'

'Headaches, some swelling of the brain.'

'My whole life is a headache and last time you said my brain was showing signs of shrinkage so it could do with beefing up a bit.'

He laughed. 'You know that's not quite how it works. Around two per cent of the original participants suffered some serious swelling, including three who died.'

'That's one hell of a side effect.'

'You can't make an omelette . . .'

My consultant knew his stuff but his bedside manner left a lot to be desired. I shrugged.

'I'm dying anyway. And those odds look pretty decent to me. Where do I sign?'

Truth was, I'd do pretty much anything to buy more time to find Laura's killer. And all this talk of drugs had given me a new idea who that might be.

## 3

When I'd started my off-the-books investigation into Laura's death I'd been a lone wolf and had put all my apples in a basket case named Frankie Grant.

Frankie was the head honcho of one of the two biggest crime gangs in the city which was a good enough reason for targeting him, in normal circumstances. But there was a better reason I'd been after him this time – it was his car that had driven into Laura's – allegedly stolen off the man's drive an hour or so before the hit-and-run. He'd been the obvious suspect.

It was a strategy that crashed and burned when Frankie revealed that Laura had been taking pay-offs from him. I didn't believe it, at first, but the proof was overwhelming. And, as he gleefully pointed out at the time, if that was the case, why would he want her dead? I was back to square one.

My boss, Detective Chief Superintendent Bob Curtis had put the official investigation firmly on the back burner to try and protect her reputation – or so he claimed. I strongly suspected it was more to cover the force's back – and his own. He was an old friend but hugely ambitious and if the powers-that-be knew he'd had a rogue cop in his team his card would have been marked.

But I didn't give up that easily. Laura may have been bent but she was a friend, and her reasons had been entirely altruistic – her dad desperately needed the money. Fortunately, after realising what I was doing, Laura's replacement, Emma Steel (the one who'd been giving me the side-eye), and her fellow DS, Leon Johnson, had agreed to help me out on the quiet which gave me scope to spread the net a little wider.

'Could you check out Harry Connors?' I asked Emma when the three of us met up in my office after I got back from the consultant.

'I can do that,' Leon said.

Emma gave him one of her glares. My two detective sergeants were extremely competitive and neither liked the other one to steal their thunder.

'I think he asked me, not you,' Emma said.

'You wouldn't be so keen if you knew who he was,' Leon fired back.

Emma cupped her face in her hands.

'Oh no, is he a big, strong, scary man like you?' she simpered in her best schoolgirl voice. 'You do know what my nickname was back in Sussex, don't you?'

'Ball-breaker?' he suggested sarcastically.

I laughed. It was close but her actual nickname, Balls of Steel, fitted her like the proverbial glove – a chain-mail glove in her case.

Emma scowled and gave Leon the finger. No one outside our inner circle would have guessed they were in a relationship. I'd only discovered it by accident and had been sworn to secrecy to prevent any station gossip – relationships within the squad made things very complicated. It didn't stop them fighting though; if anything it seemed to make things worse. I gave Leon a chance to regain some ground by showing off his superior local knowledge.

'To be fair he is a lot scarier than Leon,' I said. 'D'you want to bring Emma up to speed?'

'The two main gangs in the city are the Grants, who you already know about, and the Connors,' Leon said. 'They've mostly kept out of each other's way, operating a variation on the divide and rule principle. The Connors had the bars, drugs and working girls covered, the Grants pretty much everything else, including armed robbery and theft – particularly car theft. The two kept to their own patches, by and large.'

'But that has changed in recent years,' I said. 'Stevie Connors, the family's patriarch, was jailed ten years ago for his role in human trafficking. In the meantime his oldest son, Harry, has taken charge of the family business and brought a certain amount of order and stability to it.

'Harry is more polished than his dad, a privately educated kid with a business degree from Durham uni, and he's managed to keep his nose clean in the intervening years, increasing the Connors' profits while avoiding any major scandals, unlike his dad. No one really knows if he's cleaned out the stable or is just better at hiding in plain sight.

'Unfortunately, Stevie is due out soon and I suspect his influence is already filtering back into the family's plans – and pinning Laura's death on Frankie Grant would have put a spanner in the works of his biggest rival.'

'It makes sense,' Leon said. 'If anyone would have the balls to nick a car from Frankie Grant's drive it would be the Connors lot. And in one move they could have got rid of Grant's inside woman and thrown a lot of shade over their only competitors.'

'So where do I come in?' Emma said.

'You're new here so he doesn't know you,' I said. 'The Connors clan run a lot of the bars in the city but Harry's base is Stevie's Bar, named after you-know-who. I thought you could hang out there for a bit, see what you can pick up.'

'I think I should go with her,' Leon said.

'No chance,' I said, before Emma could protest. 'They'd spot you in a heartbeat.' Leon was the only black cop in the city and he'd been around a lot longer than Emma. Every villain in town would know him and if Emma was seen with him they'd clam up around her.

'But if you have any doubts, Emma, then say so. I don't want you doing anything you're uncomfortable with.' I was more than aware that this was an off-the-books investigation which could come back to bite all of us on the backside if something went wrong. Which was why I couldn't use a trained undercover officer.

She shook her head. 'I'm fine with it.'

'I'm not.' Leon's doubts were written all over his face.

Emma put her hand on Leon's shoulder.

'Don't worry, handsome, I'll try and behave myself. Though this Harry Connors does sound like quite the catch.'

## 4

It had rained in the night but the evidence was still clear the next morning – there was a large footprint in the dirt around the back of the oak tree. Maria placed her foot gently beside it. She took a six and it was several sizes bigger. It was also too big to be her bastard of an ex-husband, what with his tiny feet. Not that he would sneak about like that – Evan was more the screaming-in-your face type.

She took out her phone and snapped off a number of photos from different angles. You could clearly see the pattern of the tread. Surely now the police would do something? She'd heard nothing since her call the previous night.

'You should get them tree surgeons back oot again.'

Rosie Lloyd was leaning over the fence that separated their gardens, looking up at the overgrown tree. Maria normally did her best to avoid neighbourly chats, the woman could talk for England.

'It's not that bad.'

'Aye, I knaa, I just wouldn't mind watching them again,

hanging off the branches with their tops off, swinging them chainsaws aboot.'

Maria laughed. For once the woman was right. They were pretty fit. If she hadn't sworn off men at the time she might have tapped one of them up.

'What are you up to anyway?' Rosie continued, nosy as ever. 'I saw you from the bedroom window, wandering around in the dirt.'

'I thought I saw someone in the gardens last night.'

'You did, pet. Bloody peeping Tom. I saw him nipping out through wor back gate.'

'I called the police but no one came.'

'Waste of time, love. They never do nowt.'

Rosie had been burgled the previous year and Maria knew that despite the woman making several calls no one had come to investigate. They'd sent her some crime prevention leaflets in the post, including an advert for a company that fitted doorbell cameras.

'I don't suppose you got a photo of him, did you?'

'Sorry, pet. My phone was dead. I'm always forgetting to charge it. D'you think it was one of your fellas again?'

Maria cursed herself for letting it slip that she'd thought one of her exes was harassing her online the last time she'd been trapped in a conversation with Rosie. She'd had another horrible argument with Evan and needed to vent to someone about her bad luck with men. Her neighbour happened to be the first person to come along.

'Maybe,' she said.

'It wasn't that husband of yours out there, surely?'

'Ex-husband. But no, he was taller than Evan.'

'Aye, that bastard's definitely got that small man thing-ummybob.'

'Syndrome.'

'Aye, that's it.'

It may not have been Evan but he could have sent one of his new-found business partners round to intimidate her; to make sure she kept her mouth shut about their dodgy partnership. She shook her head, no, she was pretty sure she knew who it was. Rosie was still prattling on.

'From what you told me last time it sounds like you have a few candidates to choose from, you lucky sod. Long time since anyone wanted to look through my curtains.'

'Stalking isn't funny,' Maria said.

'No, course not,' Rosie said. 'Ignore me. I was being daft. Just fantasising, ya knaa. You do that when you've been married as long as me. Not that I'm complaining.'

Rosie had been tied to Gerald, an accountant, for twenty-five years. He was as exciting as he sounded. But even he was better than some of Maria's choices had been. She was a terrible picker. No, not terrible, absolutely shocking. Somehow she always managed to choose style over substance; one bad apple after another, none of them able to cope with her fierce streak of independence.

That was why she'd kept on the move, she'd had to, to shake some of them off. Like blood-sucking leeches, they were. She was so sick of this city.

Maybe it was time to move again, start afresh, somewhere completely new this time. If only she could make sure that Evan wouldn't be able to find her.

# 5

*30 October 2024*

> *Feeling reckless when broke near a French city*
> *without you two (7,4,2,4)*

'I want you to help me die.'

Helen shook her head, her horror at the idea written all over her face.

'That's not going to happen.'

'Would you rather I asked someone else? A stranger, maybe?'

'I'd rather you didn't die at all, Jack.'

'We all die sometime. Some of us sooner than others.' I stopped there but continued to stare in the mirror. It was hopeless. I had rehearsed this same conversation several times and each time it ended with my wife unequivocally refusing to help me and I knew the same thing would happen in real life unless I found a different approach. Maybe I should start on a more positive note? I tried again:

'I think I'm ready to move back in.'

Helen smiled. 'That's great.'

'But I have one or two conditions.'

The smile faded. 'Me too,' she said. 'One: Don't keep anything from me again or I'll throw you out. Two: Don't pretend you have a girlfriend again or I'll throw you out. Three: Bin the saviour complex. I'm a big girl, I don't need protecting. Four: Lose the death wish, you could have years left yet.'

Better but no cigar. Even my imagination couldn't produce a positive outcome. Though, if Helen offered them, I could probably live with those conditions. I'd learned my lesson. When I was first diagnosed I'd thought the situation was simple: I was going to become a burden and, if my late father was anything to go by, a danger to Helen and our teenage son, Aidan. My dad had beaten the shit out of my mother and me when, in his confusion, he didn't have the faintest idea who we were or why we were in 'his' house. I would not let that happen to my family. Admittedly, my initial response was probably over the top; conning my wife into thinking I was having an affair so she'd kicked me out of the family home. At the time I'd thought that was for the best – I knew she'd sacrifice her own life to nursemaid me and I couldn't let that happen – but she'd since discovered the truth.

In the battle between her Florence Nightingale complex and my saviour complex Helen was on the verge of triumph. For now, our marriage was still intact and I'd agreed to consider moving back in. But there had to be conditions attached before my neural networks clogged up completely and I was unable to express my views – hence my rehearsals. Don't get me wrong – hopefully I had a few years of gradual decline to go through first in which I could enjoy family life to the full. I just wanted to make sure my eventual exit strategy was nailed down before then.

My chosen destination was Switzerland. The annual membership subscription with Dignitas was already bought and paid for. The difficulty was persuading Helen to help me.

I didn't know for sure she'd be against it. In fact, her view was completely untested and would remain so until my rehearsals in front of the mirror ended in a different conclusion. It was a one-time only conversation and I was prepared to wait until I was sure it would end the way I wanted. I had one final practice – maybe if I came at it from a different angle?

'What do you think of the move to introduce assisted dying into the UK?'

'I don't think about it at all. Should I?'

'We're supposed to be a liberal country. Belgium have it.'

A glimmer of a smile flickered across her lips.

'Well, if it's good enough for Belgium . . .'

'It's not funny, Helen. I think people who are facing a painful, inevitable death and have little quality of life should be able to decide where and when they shuffle off this mortal coil.'

'And that would include you, would it?'

'One day, yes.'

'And I would be the one doing the assisting?'

I nodded.

'I think then, on balance, I'm against it.'

I sighed. This was getting me nowhere. I picked up my crossword to take my mind off things. It was another thing my consultant had recommended to keep my brain ticking over and I was slowly getting better at them.

One across was a variation on a clue I'd seen before: *Feeling reckless when broke near a French city without you two.* The answer: Nothing left to lose. Toulouse without the letter U. Self-explanatory really. I scrawled it across the grid thinking how inappropriate it was.

I had everything to lose.

## 6

Maria shook the last of the Coco Pops into her bowl and poured a dash of milk on them. She waited to watch the chocolate spread through the liquid, turning her breakfast into a crunchy milkshake. One of the joys of being an adult was being able to eat what you like when you liked. Her parents had been fresh fruit and porridge fanatics and their food rules had really pissed her younger self off. Nicky didn't know how lucky he was to have a mam who wasn't obsessed with healthy eating.

This was her favourite time of the morning, the hour or so between her waking up and Nicky shouting for her. Peace and quiet. No incessant questions, why this, why that, what are you doing? She sighed. What a mess she'd made of things. Nicky may have been able to eat what he liked but that was about the full extent of his luck. He'd drawn the short straw where parents were concerned in every other way.

Maria had never really wanted to be a mother – her own mam had been such a rotten example that she'd always worried she'd follow in her footsteps – but, unlike her friend Sara, who ironically had always wanted kids, she seemed to get pregnant easily. The second time it happened she hoped that once she had that baby in her arms her instincts would kick in.

At first, she'd thought her inability to connect properly with Nicky was just the aftermath of a difficult birth. Evan, of course, was no help, either leaving her to it or screaming at her to get a grip, but eventually the doctor diagnosed post-partum depression. He suggested that once she'd got over the early stages she'd be fine and she and Nicky would bond like everyone else but three years had passed since then and despite her best efforts it simply hadn't happened.

Trouble was, Evan was an even worse parent than her. She could be selfish but next to an egotist like him she was practically Mother Teresa. The main reason she'd battled for custody when they inevitably split up was that the alternative was unthinkable. Evan would probably have killed the kid if he'd had him full-time.

She was about to tuck in to her breakfast when the doorbell rang. Maria glanced at the clock on the wall. 8.15 a.m. Who on earth would be calling on her at that time of the morning? None of her friends, that was for sure. The ones she still had after Evan had driven most of them away weren't morning people. Neither was she – but when you had a kid you didn't have a choice, did you? The doorbell rang again. Maybe the police were finally responding to her call about that peeping Tom in the garden.

Through the frosted glass she could see a delivery man

holding a large parcel in front of him but as she walked along the hallway he started to turn away. Not exactly patient, was he? None of them were. The number of times she'd come downstairs to find one of those 'we missed you' cards when she'd just been to the loo! Though one of her exes was a driver for one of these companies and he reckoned their schedule was so tight that he couldn't even stop for a piss. He used to keep a plastic water bottle in his cab to save time.

She moved a little quicker and pulled open the door before he could walk off completely.

'Hold fire,' she said.

The man turned around again, holding the parcel in front of him.

'You sure that's for me?' she said.

'It's not, but could you'd take it in for number forty-five across the road?' he said.

'The Wilsons?'

He nodded. Or at least she thought he did as the large parcel was obscuring all but the top of his head.

'Sure,' she said. He thrust it towards her and she grabbed it with both hands.

'I'll need you to sign for it,' he said.

'No bother.'

She turned around to put the parcel down in the hallway and when she turned back he was standing in the doorway blocking the light but there was no sign of the handheld device that she normally had to sign with her finger.

Maria looked up at the man's face and her heart nearly

stopped. What the hell? She stumbled back and tripped over one of Nicky's toys, falling backwards down the hallway, cracking her head on the radiator as she fell. Her last thought was a surprising one to her: *please don't hurt my baby.*

7

## 3 November 2024

Emma looked like a million dollars. Her hair was glistening, her make-up subtle with just enough lip gloss to draw the eye. And her little black dress showed off all the right bits in exactly the right quantities. She knew she was radiating an 'it's unlikely but you may as well give it your best shot' vibe to all the men in Stevie's Bar.

No one there would have guessed she was a policewoman. Even if they'd had dealings with her before, she doubted they would recognise her. She wasn't exactly undercover, not in any official capacity, more trying to shake a few trees to see what fell out.

She knew this was risky but now that the powers that be had finally approved DI Jenkins' early 'ill-health' retirement package there was a spot for a new DI on the team and she was desperate to get it. Detective Inspector Emma Steel had a nice ring to it. Jack was going to be on the interview panel and, even though this would have to remain on the QT with the big bosses, if she nailed it she reckoned she'd be in pole position in his eyes. She already had an ace up her sleeve to help secure Jack's vote but this would surely give her a complete winning hand.

Leon wanted the promotion too, obviously, and he was more experienced than her but he didn't fight dirty. She did. What that would do to their relationship remained to be seen. He was so unlike the bad boys, or bad girls, she normally went for, she found him hard to read. Still, if he couldn't handle her there were plenty more fish in the sea. And as the mirror behind the bar confirmed, she didn't half scrub up well.

It was her second visit to Stevie's Bar since Jack mooted the idea but the first had been singularly unsuccessful. A visiting hen party had turned the place into a circus and she hadn't been able to hear a damn thing anyone said to her. She'd left after one mocktail. It was quieter this time, just a gentle buzz of conversation and some chill-out music playing in the background.

She felt rather than saw someone park themselves next to her at the bar. Glancing in the mirror she realised she'd hit the jackpot. Harry Connors was perched casually on the adjacent stool. She recognised him from his photos, tall, blond and slim with a twinkle in his eye. Just her type – well, one of them anyway. Pity about his line of work. Unsurprisingly, the previously lacklustre barman seemed to wake up, dashing over to offer his services.

'An Old Fashioned and whatever the lady's having,' Connors said, without being asked. The barman looked at her for confirmation but Emma ignored him. Not least because he should have remembered – he'd only served her some fifteen minutes earlier and the bar was practically empty.

'What would you like, love?' the barman said.

'I'm not your love,' she said before turning to his boss. 'And I'm no lady either so I didn't realise you were talking about me.'

The gangster's son laughed. He had great teeth. Bought and paid for by his people-trafficking dad, no doubt. She'd have loved to smash them out of his mouth but would have to wait for that pleasure.

'You don't want that drink then?' Connors said, still smiling.

'I didn't say that. As you're paying, I'll have a gin and tonic, Hendrick's.'

The barman got right on it this time.

'I haven't seen you in here before,' Connors said. 'I'm Harry.' He held his hand out but she ignored it.

'Oh, I know who you are,' Emma said.

'And vice versa, DS Steel,' Connors said, with a wink. 'I don't think I've had the pleasure.'

'And nor are you likely to,' she fired back.

Emma cursed her bad luck. She thought the guy who'd gone into the back earlier had looked a little too long her way but had put it down to a combination of the outfit and the bar stool, which worked together to show her long legs off to best advantage. Clearly it had been a bit more than that. Maybe she didn't look quite as different as she'd believed.

'I'd heard you were prickly,' he said.

'I won't say what I've heard about you.'

'So you are a lady after all! I can promise you my reputation is entirely unwarranted and mostly down to jealousy. I'm just an honest businessman.'

'A contradiction in terms, surely.'

'Like a sexy copper?'

'Maybe.'

'You don't sound like you're from around here. How long have you lived in my wonderful city?'

'It's *your* city, is it?'

'In a manner of speaking.'

She let it go.

'I came here about four months ago. A vacancy came up and I fancied trying my luck in the north. My predecessor was killed in a hit and run incident.'

She was watching him closely but he didn't blink. A very cool customer.

'I think I read about that. Such a tragedy. She was too young.'

They were interrupted by the arrival of their drinks. Once the barman had disappeared again Connors picked up where they'd left off.

'Have you caught the driver yet?'

'Not yet, but I think there'll be an arrest any day now.'

'Excellent.'

He raised his glass in a toast.

'Here's to justice prevailing.'

Emma picked up her glass and clinked it against his.

'To justice.'

Leon had warned her that Connors had a reputation as a ladies' man and from the way his eyes flicked down to her heels and moved slowly back up again it looked like his information was pretty solid.

'I assume you're not on duty, given the drink.'

'You assume correctly.'

'Shall we grab a booth?' Connors said. 'It's much more comfortable than perching here. And your legs are distracting my barman.'

Emma looked across the room to the cosy cubicles at the back, where the lighting was a little more subdued. She guessed it was where couples headed for a little privacy.

'Why not?' she said. If you wanted to slay the dragon you had to enter his lair at some point.

4 *November 2024*

I'd spent the evening rehearsing my intended conversation with Helen again. After a couple of hours of staring at myself in the mirror I had a splitting headache so took a couple of paracetamol and went to bed early, hoping to get a good night's sleep for a change. A plan that worked perfectly until Leon rang me shortly after midnight, panicking.

'Emma's not answering her phone,' he said.

'Maybe she's asleep. Like I was.'

He ignored the barb.

'She said she'd ring me when she got back.'

'Come on, Leon, she probably just forgot.'

'I don't think so. Her flat's empty.'

'How do you know?'

'I'm standing outside. I've been banging on the door for ten minutes.'

'The neighbours will love you.'

'It's not funny, Jack, I knew I should have gone with her.'

'Calm down, Leon. Harry Connors is not going to do anything to Emma.'

'You probably thought that about Laura and look what he did to her.'

'We don't know that for sure.'

'You seemed pretty confident the other day.'

I took a breath. I liked to keep things informal but I had my limits. Leon was edging towards insubordination. He had a bad habit of letting his heart rule his head.

'Calm down, son,' I said. 'You know that Stevie's Bar has a late licence, she could still be there.'

'She went out about eight o'clock, why would she still be there?'

'I don't know, maybe she's having a good time. Maybe she's pulled!' He deserved a bit of mockery given his shitty attitude. 'Or, maybe she's doing what we asked her to do and getting valuable information.'

'I didn't ask her to do anything.'

I sighed. 'You know this is exactly why we discourage relationships between team members, don't you?' Then added, 'Look, I'll text her to make sure she's OK, will that stop you fretting so much?'

'I suppose.' He sounded exactly like Aidan when I told him off for having an untidy room. I could hear him grinding his teeth on the other end of the phone. 'Maybe I should go down there?' he added.

I could hear a siren disappearing into the night outside. Surely not?

'Please tell me you're not driving there now?'

'I'm not. Not yet anyway.'

'That would be a big mistake. Don't interfere. Let her do her job. If you barge in there you'll not only damage our investigation but you'll probably screw up your relationship too. She won't thank you for it, you know that. You'll be toast.'

'But—'

'No buts. I'm warning you, don't go there.'

The phone went dead.

It rang again at 7.15 a.m. I stretched out a hand and picked it up without looking at the caller. If it was Leon again he would be on school visit duties before the call had finished.

'Parker,' I said.

'Hi, boss, it's Emma.'

I knew it wasn't about the night before because I'd kept my promise to Leon and texted her. She'd said she was fine. I hoped he hadn't ignored me and gone to find her as she might well have kicked the shit out of him. I wouldn't have blamed her.

'We've been called to a crime scene in Gosforth,' she said.

'Crime scene?' As head of a murder team it normally took a body to get me interested.

'A missing person slash murder.'

'Well, which is it?'

'Possibly both,' Emma said.

The house was like a land-locked version of the *Mary Celeste*, stranded in a leafy street in Gosforth rather than the Atlantic Ocean. All of the usual household detritus was scattered around: washing up on the drying rack by the sink; a half-full cereal bowl on the table next to a carton of curdling milk; the radio still on, though barely loud enough to hear.

The rest of the house showed similar signs of life: a towel lying on the bathroom floor, a dressing gown discarded in the main bedroom; a handful of children's toys at the bottom of the stairs. But the people had vanished.

When I mentioned the famous ship to Emma she gave me a blank look.

'Sorry, did I wake you up there?' I said. I hadn't had the chance to quiz her on her late night yet but it was pretty clear she wasn't at her sharpest.

'I have no idea what you're talking about.'

'I thought you had a degree.' Emma was a direct-entry detective who'd been fast-tracked into CID because of her qualifications. It wasn't a route I was particularly fond of but she was a lot brighter than most.

'I do, but not in History.'

'Mindfulness, was it?' I said, and got an eye-roll that I probably deserved.

'Psychology, actually.'

'Same difference.'

'Regardless, I've never heard of her.'

My sigh echoed around the room. The detective sergeants were getting younger every year. Or I was getting older. Though given my condition I guessed I should probably enjoy that while I still could. The alternative wasn't great.

'Look it up,' I said.

She pulled her phone out of her pocket. Sometimes I forgot there was a world of knowledge at people's fingertips nowadays.

'Not now,' I said. 'Just trust me, it's a similar situation.'

There were reasons to be concerned. The day before, Maria Groom's estranged husband, Evan, had gone round to pick up his son Nicky for his regular monthly access, only to find there was no response to his knocks and rings. He'd returned early this morning at the crack of dawn, reasoning that she'd have to be in at that time but still no joy. Furious at what he thought was his ex-wife's refusal to answer, he'd woken another neighbour who often fed Maria's cat when she was away and, equally concerned, she'd let him into the house with her key.

The man and the neighbour had found the house in the same state it was now. But it wasn't the signs of a sudden departure that had caused the neighbour to call the police. It was what she found by the back door.

We walked back into the kitchen to take another look. I could sense Emma nodding her head next to me. There was no doubt about it. On the wall, right next to the door, was a bloody handprint that was so small it could only have come from a child.

# 10

Evan Groom was outside the house, bouncing from one police barricade to another like he was in a pinball machine. He'd been pacing around when we'd first arrived, had screamed at us for taking our time, and hadn't calmed down since.

The first uniform on the scene, a promising young PC, Sid Allan, had been doing his best to keep the man away from the house but Groom was as elusive as smoke, constantly slipping away from his minder.

The third time Groom was blocked at the door was the final straw. I understood that the man was upset – his ex-wife and child had disappeared under suspicious circumstances – but he'd already contaminated the scene when he broke into the house, so he wasn't exactly flavour of the month with me.

'If you attempt to get back into this house once more, I will have you arrested,' I shouted, as Sid Allan tried to move him away again. Beside me I heard Emma suck in a breath.

'Steady, boss,' she whispered, 'he's lost his kid.'

'Arrest *me*! For what?' the man yelled back.

'Obstruction,' I said, a little more gently, lowering the temperature a fraction. Emma was probably right, there were journalists around and the optics of me shouting at the father of a missing child weren't great – more of that recklessness that I'd vowed to stamp out surfacing again.

'Listen, Mr Groom, it's like this: the more you interfere with our investigation the longer it will take. And neither of us wants that. What I would like you to do is sit down quietly with the family liaison officer and allow them to take a full statement from you. I need you to tell us when you last saw your wife and child, anything you know about their last known whereabouts and exactly what happened when you came to the house on both the most recent occasions. Can you do that for me?'

'But—'

'But nothing. If I'm going to find out what happened here, I need to know what you know as soon as possible. Including the names of anyone who might have reason to hurt your family.'

'You think they've been hurt?'

There was no answer that wouldn't set him off again, so I ignored the question.

'I'll also need to know your precise movements over the last week or so and possibly for longer.'

'Am I a suspect?'

'Should you be?'

Something that looked a lot like guilt flashed across Evan Groom's face. I wasn't surprised. There was a reason why ex-husbands with custody issues were always high on our suspect list.

## 11

Detective Chief Superintendent Bob Curtis was one of my oldest friends, but he was also my boss, which meant it wasn't the easiest relationship these days.

If we'd been as close as we once were I would probably have told him about my diagnosis but his role meant he was more politician than policeman now and I couldn't trust him to have my back. If he decided to play safe my career would be placed on the back burner. I'd be lucky if they let me man the recruitment stall at the Northumberland county show.

We'd had a couple of disputes recently, mainly to do with Laura Kemp's hit-and-run accident, but I was pretty sure he'd be on my side for the Maria Groom case. Even though I was head of the murder team and we didn't have a body, I was intrigued enough to try and keep the case for the time being.

'It's not like you to want a missing person's case, Jack.'

'I think it might be more than that.'

He glanced at his watch.

'You've got five minutes, and then I'm off to a meeting with the PCC. Unless you'd like to take my place . . .'

Bob knew the answer to that one, just like he knew my views on the very existence of Police and Crime Commissioners. I tried hard to move with the times but didn't believe that unqualified civilians had any place in the management of the police force. I got straight to the point.

'Maria Groom and her three-year-old son, Nicky, were reported missing early this morning by her next-door neighbour. We've got uniforms doing a door-to-door and we're currently interviewing the ex-husband and a neighbour who was with him when they entered the house.'

'Any question marks over the ex?'

'Not sure yet. Sounds like there were issues over access to the kid. He was a pain in the arse at the scene but Emma is interviewing him now, so we'll see how that goes.'

'Anything else?'

'Two other neighbours have come forward to express concerns about her. One is a family friend who usually gives her piano lessons every Wednesday afternoon when Nicky is at nursery, but Maria didn't show up this week. When she went round to check on her there was no one there. Maria had never missed a lesson before and even messaged if she was going to be late but this time there'd been nothing. We've also spoken to a local childminder who usually looked after Nicky every Friday afternoon who had a similar story.'

'What else have you got?'

'We haven't yet found anyone who has seen Maria or

her boy since Tuesday night, nor even spoken to her. That's almost a week. There were signs of the house being abandoned suddenly, foodstuff left out, things all over the floor and more worryingly a child's bloody handprint on the kitchen wall. There were also bloodstains by a radiator in the hallway. The CSIs are there now. We've also found her phone in the house.'

For the first time Bob Curtis looked concerned. We both knew it was unlikely she'd have forgotten it if she left of her own accord. Somehow phones had become people's life-support machines in recent years.

'Amazingly, there was no password on it. Emma went through it this morning, but I haven't had a chance to talk to her about what she found yet,' I added.

'OK. But putting the murder team on the case rather pre-judges the issue, doesn't it? Especially in the media's eyes.'

'Maybe. That's more your concern than mine. But surely if we go the other way and we're wrong the fallout will be much worse.'

That clearly gave Bob pause for thought so I pressed the point home.

'The ex-husband was behaving a little erratically and I think he has a lot more to tell us which I'm sure Emma will get out of him. And there's one other thing.'

'Go on.'

'One of the PCs spoke to a neighbour who said, "It was probably that peeping Tom we've been telling you about." When he pressed her, she said that several of the people in the street had called about a peeper being seen in the gardens in the last couple of weeks, but they'd got no response.'

'Shit. That's not good. The press are bound to get hold of that if it's true. Or even if it's not, come to that.'

'Aye. Gary Coxon from the *Chron* was sniffing around the scene this morning and you know what he's like. Dog with a bone. I've got someone checking the call logs to confirm the truth of what the neighbour said. My guess is they sent a patrol car to cruise around but that was it.'

Bob Curtis closed his eyes and rubbed his forehead as if trying to erase any memory of this conversation. It clearly wasn't the news he wanted before a meeting with the PCC. He took a deep breath and nodded.

'Given that, I think we need to be seen to be taking this seriously. Body or no body, it's your job until Ms Groom turns up with a suntan from her last-minute trip to the Canaries wondering what all the fuss is about. But stay focused on the husband. Mark my words, Jack, in these cases, it's always the husband.'

## 12

Rosie Lloyd was enjoying being a witness a little too much. She had a big beaming smile and her eyes were darting around the room taking it all in. Not that there was much to see. Four bare walls, a table and four chairs. The only anomaly being the camera in the top corner of the room. Leon could tell she was storing up every little detail to tell her friends how she'd been 'helping the police catch a killer'.

Sid Allan told him she'd even been excited to get a ride to HQ in the back of a squad car. Normally witnesses were reluctant to get involved but Mrs Lloyd was clearly an exception.

'Tell me about what happened this morning, Mrs Lloyd. Right from the beginning.'

'Well, the first thing I heard was the banging and shouting.'

'And what time was that?'

'Just after six thirty a.m., I think. I remember cos I was listening to Zoe Ball on the radio and she'd not been on long.'

'What happened next?'

'I knew it was him straight away, like. Evan Groom.'

'Not the first time then?'

'Not by a long chalk. Last time I'd seen him they were having a screaming match about him bringing the bairn back late. He's a nasty bastard that Evan. I can see why Maria got shot of him.'

'Not a fan then?'

'No. I've met a lot of bullies in my time, so it doesn't take me long to spot them.'

You and me both, Leon thought. As the only black kid in his school he'd been the target of more than one or two.

'Did you ever see him get violent?'

She considered it for a while.

'Not physically, no, but it often seemed . . . imminent. He's got a very threatening manner.'

'Did he ever threaten you?'

'Aye! This morning! When he couldn't get any joy next door he banged on my door instead. Said if I didn't give him the key to Maria's house, he'd knock my effing block off.'

'But you didn't give it to him, did you?'

She smiled and seemed to grow a couple of inches taller.

'No, I bloody didn't. I know how to stand up to folk like him.'

'But you did agree to check the house out.'

'Aye. Despite his shouting he had a point. I hadn't seen Maria for a few days and she usually asked me to feed the cat when she went away, you see. I mean the poor creature lives round mine most of the time anyway but it's unlike her to forget.'

'So the two of you went to check the house out.'

'I went. He followed me. I couldn't stop him. As soon as I'd got the door open he barged past me, shouting the odds. I should have guessed, I suppose.'

'What happened next?'

'Well he charged all over the house, didn't he? Waste of time if you ask us, I could tell the place was empty right from the get-go. There's something about an empty house, a stillness, ya knaa.'

'And it was you who called the police?'

'Aye, that's right. It was that bloody handprint, wasn't it. Freaked me out. Funnily enough he seemed a bit annoyed with me when he realised I'd rang you lot.'

'Really?'

'Aye, thought I was overreacting, gave me dog's abuse. Soon as you turned up he changed his tune, acting all concerned and that. Like I said, he's not a nice man. I wouldn't be at all surprised if he's got something to do with this.'

Leon was inclined to agree with her but kept his thoughts to himself. He suspected the woman didn't need any encouragement to start the rumours flying.

'OK, now tell me about Maria. What's she like?'

A slight frown crossed her face.

'She's nice enough.'

'I'm sensing a but.'

'You're a sharp one, aren't you? Look, I don't like to speak ill of . . .'

Leon could tell she nearly said 'the dead' but had realised that would sound bad.

'... anyone,' she continued. 'But she can be a bit stand-offish.'

'How do you mean?'

'You know when you're chatting to someone but you can tell they'd rather be somewhere else and they're looking for a way out.'

Leon hesitated.

'Maybe it's just me,' she added. 'Gerald says I never know when to shut up.'

Leon had some sympathy for her beleaguered husband – and for her neighbour – but being chatty was a good thing in a witness so he pressed on.

'Anything else? What about young Nicky?'

'Sweet bairn but very quiet. He spent a lot of time in the back garden on his own.'

She leaned in closely as if someone else was listening in.

'I'm not sure Maria enjoyed being a mam. I mean she did her best, she didn't neglect him, like, he was always clean and dressed, but I never really saw her playing with the lad. I wondered if she'd had the baby blues – they call it summat else these days though, don't they?'

Leon had no idea.

'Anyway, she didn't spend much time with the poor mite. And she seemed to gan oot a lot. There were always young lasses coming round to babysit.'

'OK, we'll have to see if we can track them down. Can you tell me a bit more about what you told PC Allan earlier?' Leon asked. 'About the man you saw.'

'Ooh yes, about a week ago it was. I saw him clear as day,

walking across the middle of my back garden like he owned the place.'

'D'you know the actual date?'

'Yes, cos I'd just got off the phone to my son. It was his birthday. I bet you can't believe I've got a forty-year-old son, can you?'

Leon bit his tongue. Rosie Lloyd looked to be somewhere in her mid-sixties so it wasn't difficult to envisage her grown-up son being even older than he was. He frowned as if it was the most puzzling thing he'd heard all year.

'Really? What's your secret? You haven't made a pact with the devil, have you, Mrs Lloyd? A picture in the attic maybe?'

She giggled like a teenager.

'Rosie, please, you silver-tongued charmer, you. It's just good genes, lots of water and a proper skin care routine. Oh, and no smoking obviously.'

'Obviously. Well, it clearly works.'

The woman was positively beaming now.

'So when is it?'

She looked blank.

'Your son's birthday? The date you saw the intruder?'

'Oh, right, yes, silly me,' she laughed. 'It's October twenty-eighth.'

'And can you describe him?'

'Of course. He's my son! Typical Scorpio, like me, loyal, creative and passionate.'

'I meant the man in your garden.'

Rosie Lloyd laughed fit to bust.

'Ha! You must think I'm an idiot. I've never been in a police station before. I'm a bit overexcited.'

Leon sighed. This was going to take a little longer than he'd hoped.

'Let's start with his hair,' he said, pen poised.

'Oh, I couldn't see his hair. He had one of those baseball caps on.'

'Height?'

'Over six feet tall I'd say. His head was above my washing line and I have to stretch to reach that. I'm five foot four and my arms must add at least eight more inches, mustn't they?'

'What about his other clothes, apart from the cap?'

'Jeans, I reckon, hard to say in the light. I don't remember his shoes.'

'What about his face? Did you see that?'

For the first time Rosie Lloyd looked hesitant, nervous almost. She looked around as if there might be help somewhere.

'Mrs Lloyd?'

She was blushing now. He waited, knowing she wasn't the kind of woman who could stay quiet for long.

'I couldn't see that clearly but I think he was . . . coloured,' she said, almost whispering the last word.

'A black man?' he said, checking that his ears hadn't deceived him. It had been a long time since he'd heard anyone use the word 'coloured'.

She nodded, still avoiding his eyes. Leon tried not to react but couldn't help himself. He'd been spending too much time with Jack.

'Dreadlocks?' he asked. 'Smoking a giant spliff?'

'No, of course not, I would have mentioned that.'

'Then what? If you couldn't see his face why did you think he was a black man?'

'Well, you know, it was dark so it makes sense, doesn't it? A white face would have stood out.' She folded her arms across her chest as if that settled things. 'And there was something about the way he moved too.'

'The way he moved?'

'Yes. He lolloped.'

'Lolloped?'

She frowned. 'You know, like a Dalmatian.'

Leon prided himself on his control, but he could tell his anger was leaking out a little by the way the woman in front of him was behaving now. The eager witness he'd started with had gone, now she wouldn't look him in the eye. She glanced at the door as if planning a quick exit.

'And where did he "lollop" to?'

'He went out of my back gate into the alleyway and then disappeared down the lane.'

'Did any of the other neighbours see him?'

'Maria definitely did, we had a chat about it the next morning, but you can't ask her, can you? The ones on the other side were on holiday at the time so there's no point asking them either.'

'And what did you do?'

This time she did look at him. She knew she had a point to make.

'Well, I didn't call the police if that's what you're after. Waste of bloody time. Anyway, turns out I didn't have to because Maria had already called them, hadn't she? And guess what? They didn't turn up . . . again!'

## 13

Emma had met some sleazeballs in her time but Evan Groom was right up there. He had all the ingredients you'd need to make up the imperfect man: patronising, impatient, aggressive and arrogant. She could easily imagine him snogging himself in the mirror.

Jack had been right when he said the man wouldn't like being quizzed by a woman, not that Emma had needed any persuasion to take on the responsibility. She could tell that Leon was a bit miffed being palmed off with the next-door neighbour while she got the ex.

At first Groom had tried to be charming but when he'd realised it was wasted on her he'd dropped the mask and switched to combative mode. She would soon make him regret that. Emma had spent the previous hour going through his ex-wife's phone and had plenty of ammunition to fire at him.

'So, let me get this right, Mr Groom, the last time you saw Maria was just over a month ago, when you took your son, Nicky, back to his home.'

'His other home. My house is his home too.'

'OK. His other home.'

'Yes. We'd had a smashing day, even though I'd had to iron out some of the boy's bad habits. Maria lets him get away with murder.'

'Such as?'

'Eating sweets between meals. Picking his nose. Not looking at you when you speak to him. Not saying "please" and "thank you". It takes a while for him to start behaving properly but once I've re-trained him we have a great time.'

'What did you do?'

'We went for a walk in Leazes Park in the morning, fed the ducks and that. And then in the afternoon we watched the match in my local.'

'Likes pubs, does he, your three-year-old son?'

'He likes being with me, wherever that may be. And he loves football. Massive Newcastle fan, obviously.'

'I'm sure he is. What happened when you took him back to Maria that last time? Anything unusual?'

'Well, it's not exactly unusual, but she said I was late when I wasn't. He's never ready when I'm supposed to pick him up, she always has to get him dressed and pack his bag, and I'd had enough so I just extended his time with me accordingly.'

'You had an argument?'

'I wouldn't call it that. More a frank exchange of views.'

'One of the neighbours described it as "a screaming match".'

'That bitch next door, no doubt. She would, wouldn't she?

Women always stick together. Maria's no angel, believe me. She might have fooled the courts when they determined access but she doesn't fool me.'

'You don't seem to like your ex-wife very much?'

Groom seemed to realise where she was going and tried to head it off.

'Shouldn't you be out there looking for my son rather than going through ancient history?'

'There's a team of people out there doing just that, Mr Groom. And I'm trying to get information that might assist them. I assumed you'd want to help with that.'

He sighed. 'I do, obviously. I want to get my son back.'

'But not your wife?'

He laughed, humourlessly, and shrugged.

'What can I say? Things don't always turn out the way you hope. But I loved her once. I married her, didn't I? It wasn't my fault it didn't work out. After Nicky arrived, she had no time for me at all. Even though I was the breadwinner. I couldn't do anything right.'

Emma tried hard not to show her bemusement that he'd ever found a woman who'd put up with his bullshit. Maybe she succeeded as Groom didn't seem to notice. Or maybe he was just bad at reading the room.

'And have you seen the house she's in?' he went on. 'Costs me a small fortune in maintenance. Not to mention the endless parade of babysitters.'

'You're clearly a very generous man.'

'Yes, I bloody well am.'

'And yet Maria divorced you before you'd been married a year. Unreasonable behaviour, wasn't it?'

'Her words. Pots and kettles if you ask me.'

'The court agreed with her. How did you feel about only seeing your son one day every month?'

'It's a travesty. I tried to appeal but they wouldn't let me – said there was no grounds. The system's rigged in favour of women.'

'Tell me about what happened yesterday.'

'I turned up ten minutes early to pick up my son. I thought at first she was refusing to answer the door because I was early – it would have been typically small-minded of her – but it gradually became obvious there was no one home. Her car was gone for a start. I tried ringing her but it went to voicemail.'

'What did you do?'

'What could I do? I went home.'

'You weren't spoiling for a fight?'

'No, of course not. I'm a nice guy. Ask anyone.'

Emma pulled out a sheet of paper from the file in front of her and read from it.

'Sunday. Ten twenty: "Where are you, bitch?" Ten twenty-five: "Answer the fucking door or I'll break it down."'

Evan Groom had his head in his hands now. She carried on reading.

'Ten thirty: "I'll kill you for this." Ten forty: "You're dead."'

Emma looked back up again.

'Do I need a solicitor?' he said.

'I don't know, do you?'

'I haven't done anything.'

'"I'll kill you for this",' she repeated.

'It's just an expression.'

'Is it? Do you acknowledge that these are the messages you sent to Maria while you were trying to get into the house?'

He nodded. 'I was angry. I wanted to see my son.'

'There are plenty more – and not just from yesterday.'

She looked back up the transcribed list.

'This is from three weeks ago. "Don't try and fuck with me again or you'll regret it. You really won't like my new friends." Do you want me to go on?'

'No.'

'Who are your "new friends" that Maria wouldn't like?'

'No one. I was pissed off with her and wanted—'

'To frighten her?'

He shook his head. 'It wasn't like that. You don't know her. She loves to wind me up. You should have seen the ones she sent me.'

'I have. Not a death threat amongst them.'

'She threatened to cut my dick off.'

'Talking of which . . .'

Emma pulled a printout from her folder. One of many that she'd found on Maria's phone.'

'This yours?'

Groom picked it up and recoiled, dropping it back on the table.

'Jesus Christ! No, it isn't. Where did you get that?'

Emma glanced down at the dick pic. The engorged penis

practically filled the frame of the shot. Given that the man in front of her radiated small-dick energy she wasn't at all surprised that it was probably someone else. She ignored the question.

'So after you'd threatened to kill your wife, did you try to get back in the house again later that day? Is that when something happened between you and Maria?'

'No. Definitely not. I went to watch the football in the pub as I'd planned. Just without Nicky. The place was packed, people will vouch for me.'

'But you went back again today?'

'Yes. Why would I have done that if something happened yesterday?'

To muddy the waters, Emma thought. But was Evan Groom that bright? She didn't think so. When she didn't reply he carried on.

'It was Nicky's nursery day so I knew if I got there early I'd catch her in and at least I'd get to see my son.'

'But there was no answer again?'

'That's right. I wasn't letting her get away with keeping me away from Nicky so I woke up Roz next door to get the key. I'd tried yesterday but she wasn't in.'

'Her name's *Rosie*.'

'Whatever. She wouldn't hand it over but I persuaded her to open it for me.'

'She said you threatened her.'

He smiled. It wasn't a good look for him. Emma could only imagine what his sex face was like, then wished she hadn't, that was truly the stuff of nightmares.

'People are such snowflakes these days, don't you find?' he said. 'It would have saved a lot of time if she'd done what I asked.'

'But she didn't give you the key?'

'No, she insisted on coming with me, nosy cow.'

'Then what?'

'*Rosie* tried knocking too but got no joy. Eventually she agreed with me that something was wrong and opened the door. That's when we found the mess and the blood and called you lot.'

'Wasn't it Rosie who called the police?'

'I guess, but at my insistence. I'd left my phone somewhere. If it wasn't for me going into the house you wouldn't know they were missing at all, would you?'

He was right, Emma thought. But by entering the house he'd also made sure there was a good reason for us to find his prints all over the crime scene.

'Has Maria been worried about anything recently?'

'What's she got to worry about? She lives the life of Riley while I have to earn enough for both of us. I'm the one with all the worries. Who knows what goes on in the woman's head? If you want to know what Maria's been up to you should talk to her friend Sara, they're like a little witches' coven when they get together.'

Evan Groom pulled a face that Emma assumed to be his attempt at a witch. He was the kind of man you'd never get tired of slapping. Emma gripped the sides of her seat to stop herself from doing so. She'd read horror stories from back in the day about police 'fitting up' suspects and had never imagined that she would ever be tempted to do something similar but at that single moment – without wishing any harm to his poor ex-wife – she would have loved nothing more than seeing Evan Groom sent down. Even if he had nothing to do with Maria's disappearance, she was pretty sure he would hurt someone else one day – if he hadn't already.

Groom seemed to sense her misgiving. He held his hands up in apology.

'Look, DS Steel, we seem to have got off on the wrong foot here. I know I can go a little too far – and those text messages look bad – I admit that I'm quick to anger, but I was, and still am, worried about my son.

'Maria is a little, let's say *unstable* at times. When she first had Nicky she couldn't handle it – she kept wanting me to look after the baby even though she was at home all the time and I had a full-time job. I'm not sure she's ever recovered, to be honest. I tried my best, but she was never happy being a mother. I was surprised she fought so hard for custody.'

Emma still wasn't convinced. It was the nearest to a human response he'd shown so far but he still made her skin crawl. It was like watching a replicant from *Blade Runner*. He looked like a human and walked like a human but there was something off about him, as if he had seen other people behaving reasonably and was trying to copy it – basically the standard behaviour of a psychopath.

'What do you think has happened then?' she said, to bring things to a close for now. She needed to get away from this guy, maybe even take a shower.

Groom took a while to think about it, like he'd never considered it before, maybe because he already knew the answer.

'I'd check out her boyfriend before me, Sam Gallagher, works at that fancy restaurant on the Quayside, can't remember the name.'

'The Fork on the Tyne?'

'Aye, that's the one. Maria reckons he looks like a rock star but I always thought he was a bit of a perv.'

Takes one to know one, Emma thought.

'If not him then it'll be one of her many new *friends*,' he added. 'It's been like a revolving door since I moved out.'

'I was told she threw you out.'

'You say tomatoes. Maria loved nothing more than to badmouth me so God knows what she told the neighbours. In fact, you know what . . .' he added, leaning way too close to Emma, a mix of stale aftershave and sweat making her shift her chair back slightly. She would definitely need to have that shower. 'Forget about the dodgy boyfriend theory. It actually wouldn't surprise me at all if she'd set this whole thing up just to fuck with me.'

## 14

*Five days earlier*

Maria's eyes flickered open, a blurred shape above her blocking out most of the light, her head hurting like hell. She closed her eyes again, trying to gather her thoughts and hoping it might help the pain go away. Was it Evan? Had he hit her again?

She could hear someone speaking, chanting almost. She tuned into the words: '*Please wake up, please wake up, please wake up.*' A man's voice. As she opened her eyes slowly she could see he was leaning over her, holding her hand as he repeated his mantra. It took her a moment or two to remember what had happened and to realise, by the uniform, that it was the delivery guy. At least he'd taken off that fucking mask.

'Oh, thank God,' he said. 'I was getting worried it was worse than it looked. I was just going to phone for an ambulance.'

She sat up slowly. It didn't help, the pain shooting through her skull like an electric shock. She gasped and the man let go of her hand. She touched the back of her head and could already feel a bump coming on. When she pulled her hand away, she could see a fair bit of blood on it.

'Christ,' she muttered.

'It might not be as bad as it seems,' he said. 'I've done a bit of first aid training so I had a quick peek while you were unconscious. Head wounds can bleed a lot even when they're quite minor. I think you'll be fine.'

'No thanks to you,' she growled, wondering how she might give *him* a head wound to see how 'fine' he would feel. 'That Pudsey the Bear mask scared the crap out of me.'

'I'm sorry. I didn't think. I'm trying to raise some money for the kids.'

'Well just carry a fucking bucket around next time.'

'I do that too. I've got one in the van if you'd like to make a donation.'

'I think I'll pass,' she said, giving him a glacial stare.

He stepped back, finally seeming to realise he was being a dick.

'I understand. I really should get going. Are you going to be OK?'

She nodded, though she wasn't exactly sure. But she was embarrassed at her overreaction to the mask and wanted him to leave.

'You should probably get that checked out,' he added.

'I was going to be *fine* a minute ago,' she snapped, getting slowly to her feet. Her vision was slightly blurred but apart from that she felt OK, no nausea at least.

'Well, if you're sure, I'd better get off, the slave-driver bosses monitor our every move and I'll be getting hurry-up messages by now.' He turned and headed for the door.

'Haven't you forgotten something?' she said.

He turned back, confused. She pointed at the parcel.

'I think the least you can do is get someone else to sort that out, don't you?'

'But I've already left a card. I saw you through the window when I was getting out of the van and assumed you'd take it in for me like a good neighbour.'

'Well, that was before you pulled your mask stunt. I might have to go to the hospital to get checked out so won't be in anyway.'

'I thought you said you were fine.'

She glared at him. He looked suitably embarrassed but didn't give up easily.

'But the card . . .'

'You'll just have to leave another one, won't you?'

He shook his head as if she was the one in the wrong but then he picked up the parcel.

'I'm sorry,' he said but she wasn't in a forgiving mood.

'So you said.'

Once the man had left she sat on the floor again, hoping her head would clear. There was a small pool of blood underneath the radiator where she'd banged it. It looked like a murder scene.

The idea came almost instantly, like in Tom and Jerry where a lightbulb appears above Tom's head when he thinks of a cunning plan to catch the mouse. She was definitely watching too much kids' TV.

It needed more thought, for sure, but maybe, just maybe, it would work, not like in that grown-up movie she'd seen a few weeks back where the woman was too clever for her own good and it all fell to pieces because her husband wasn't as stupid as she'd believed. Maria knew she wasn't exactly a genius, but she was definitely smarter than Evan. She could make it work.

She smiled, even though the slight movement of her features caused her head to ache a little more. She could smell freedom.

It took her several hours to get ready to leave. The first hour or two of that was planning her next moves. Where would she go? How would she make sure that Evan, or even more importantly, his new friends, couldn't find her? Thank God she'd kept the bulk of her running-away cash in an account in her maiden name – it would take the police a while to track that down if for some reason they started searching for it. To muddy the waters even further she sat with her iPad creating new accounts and moving some of that money to those. Tracing all of that would give her the thing she needed most – time to get away.

Finally, she cut her hair way shorter – as near to a fashionable soft crop as she could manage on her own – and dyed the remains black so no one would easily recognise her. She'd bought the dye for the local pub's Hallowe'en night but Morticia Addams would not be making an appearance this year after all. It hurt to go anywhere near the tender bump on her skull but needs must and at least the bleeding had stopped now.

She packed the bare minimum she needed to survive: their passports, the card from her secret account, some simple outfits for her and Nicky and a handful of his favourite toys; things no one would notice were missing, certainly not Evan who never allowed Nicky to take anything with him on his occasional weekends – forcing the poor kid to play with the 'proper boys' toys' he'd bought for him but wouldn't let him bring home.

For her final trick she dropped her phone into the pocket of a coat she was leaving behind, removing the passcode requirement first. No one would ever believe she'd left it behind of her own accord and once the police read some of Evan's abusive texts he'd be suspect number one. They might even think he was responsible for all the dick pics, though if they checked out his tiny equipment they'd soon realise it wasn't him sending them. She'd like to see them set up an ID parade for that.

Nicky couldn't believe it when she let him make the handprint on the wall – he obviously thought the blood was paint – and he'd laughed his head off once he'd done it. Evan would have given him a slap if he'd tried that at his house – he liked things to be just so, hated any kind of mess.

The only time Nicky made a fuss was when he realised he wasn't going to nursery, which he loved, but the promise of an ice cream shut him up. Once he knew they weren't coming back for the rest of his toys he'd probably scream the place down but she'd cross that bridge when she came to it.

Evan would go mental when he worked out what was happening. Not because he was Superdad and couldn't bear to be separated from his kid but because he hated it when she bettered him – as she had in the custody battle. But he wasn't due to see Nicky for at least four days and by then, with what she had planned, he'd be so up to his neck in it that seeing his son again would be the least of his worries.

Maria topped up the cat's food before she left. She felt guilty about leaving Felix behind to fend for himself but he spent most of his time next door anyway so he wouldn't starve and Rosie would probably welcome the company. He could always come back into the house through the cat flap when he got tired of her incessant chatter.

She had a few other things to sort out but they could wait until she was in a safer place where no one would know her or Nicky. Her next move would be to get rid of the car and get a replacement that no one would be looking for. She had the ideal candidate to help her – though he might need a little persuasion.

## 15

4 *November 2024*

Bob Curtis had often accused me of being 'too hands-on' for a DCI, urging me to take more of a managerial stance. I'd fought him tooth and nail but these days, to his delight, I was mostly doing what he'd asked. He put it down to his powers of persuasion and I was happy to let him believe it. It wasn't quite the truth though.

I'd read that large meetings full of different voices could be confusing for anyone in the early stages of dementia. And though I wasn't at that point yet, embarrassing myself in front of the entire team wasn't a risk I was prepared to take. So I was happy for Leon or Emma to lead the main briefings – once the three of us had conferred over the way ahead, which we did after they'd finished interviewing the initial witnesses.

'OK, what have we got so far?' I asked.

Leon jumped in.

'The bad news is that none of the neighbours saw Maria either leave or get taken from the house. And none of them have seen her for almost a week. The last reported sighting is on the evening of the twenty-ninth when a neighbour saw her putting the bins out. There are still a couple to question who weren't in when the house-to-house team went around first thing.'

'What about family and friends, Emma?'

'According to her ex, she has no other family, other than her son,' Emma said. 'No siblings and both parents are dead. The only friend he could name was a woman called Sara Quinn, an old school friend, who now lives near the Scottish border. But he didn't even know her surname. We had to find her name and number in a phonebook in the house. He's a touch self-absorbed.'

'What did you think of him apart from that?'

'Gigantic prick, who probably wishes he had a gigantic prick.'

I smiled. My young DS had a way with words.

'A possible suspect?'

'Absolutely. Groom has a massive chip on his shoulder about their custody battle. He's a typical entitled man – says he's worried about his son but didn't seem to care a jot about what has happened to Maria. And his abusive messages put him right in the frame.'

'You don't think the dick pics are his though?'

'Not from his reaction, no.'

'It worries me that her phone was left behind,' Leon said. 'No one under forty does that any more.'

Sadly, he was probably right to be concerned by that. Ten years ago I probably wouldn't have thought twice about it but now phones were practically attached to people by an umbilical cord.

'What about Groom's alibi for the Sunday afternoon?' I asked Emma.

'It checks out to a certain extent. He was seen in the pub but he could have gone back to the house again later that afternoon.'

'Though it looks like Maria has been missing for longer than that,' Jack said. 'Did you get his whereabouts for the previous week?'

'Yes, some of it anyway. I've got Clive Andrews putting together a detailed list of where he's been and when. Groom claims to have been on a break in the Lakes for the last four days. He was a bit vaguer about the time before that – says he was busy working most of the time. Interestingly, he claims he's lost his phone so we might have to talk to his service provider to see if we can track his movements.'

'What does he do?'

'You'll like this; he was an Ofsted inspector.'

I smiled. When you were married to a headmistress the words 'Ofsted inspector' were equivalent to 'child molester'. Helen hated them all and that was good enough for me. Groom seemed exactly like the kind of man who would love telling other people how to do their job.

'When you say "was" . . .?'

'Gave it up a couple of years ago. He describes himself as a businessman now, all very vague, fingers in various non-specific pies, or so he claims. He was elusive when it came to details.'

'OK, let me know if anything doesn't check out. Bob Curtis is keen for us to pursue the ex-husband angle. Anything else?'

'He mentioned an ex-boyfriend called Sam Gallagher, who's a chef at the Fork on the Tyne, but it sounded like he was throwing shit to see if it stuck. Also, I've put a call out to her friend Sara but she hasn't got back to me. Hopefully she might be able to help us. Maybe Maria would have talked to her about the peeping Tom.'

'Talking of that,' Leon said. 'The news got a bit worse. At least four of the neighbours said they'd reported a man being seen around the back gardens recently but none of them spoke to an actual police officer. I think we might have dropped the ball on that one.'

'Any description?'

'Tall, black top, black jeans, black baseball cap. Your standard night-stalker get-up.'

'Would that fit that Gallagher guy?' I asked Emma.

'Maybe,' she said. 'Apparently Maria thought he had a bit of a rock-star look about him. I'll see if I can find a photo of him on the restaurant's website.'

'Check out his skin colour,' Leon said. 'Because according to ever-so-slightly racist Rosie Lloyd, the stalker looked like a black man because he "lolloped".'

'Lolloped,' Emma snorted. 'She really said that? Right to your face?'

'She did.'

'I mean, to be fair, you do lollop.'

'Black people, you mean?'

'No, course not, that would be racial stereotyping. I meant you personally. I've mentioned it to Jack once or twice.'

'I don't fucking lollop.'

They both turned to me for confirmation.

'Hey, don't get me involved in your little squabble,' I said. 'I've never said that you lollop.' I paused for two seconds. 'You do flounce occasionally though.'

I swear there was steam coming out of Leon's ears.

'I don't fucking flounce either.'

Emma's previously straight face cracked and I joined in the laughter.

'Racist bastards,' Leon muttered. 'I should report you both to the IOPC.'

'You might want to wait until after the DI panel has sat,' I said. 'I might be your only friend on there.'

'Hey, I hope you're not playing favourites,' Emma said. 'I was counting on your vote.'

Both of my detective sergeants had passed the national inspectors' exam and would be interviewed for our vacant post before the month was out. There were some external candidates too but they were a strong pair and I was slightly worried about the fallout if one of them got it.

'And you shall have it. As will Leon. Unless he flounces in.'

Even Leon laughed this time.

'Let's move on, shall we,' I said, once the laughter had died down. I got up and pushed the door closed. This was just between the three of us.

'What happened at Stevie's Bar last night?' I asked Emma.

'Oh, didn't I mention it? Harry Connors took me back to his place,' she said, with a grin.

## 16

Leon's face was like thunder. It was clearly news to him.

'Taking one for the team, were you?' he said, angrily.

'Relax, man, nothing happened.'

'Why did you go, then?'

'Because he asked me. And I had a job to do.'

Emma placed a manila folder on the desk.

'Nice work if you can get it,' Leon grumbled.

'At least *he* didn't make me pay for my own cab home.'

'What a gentleman. Saved you from doing the walk of shame in the morning, did he?'

Emma rolled her eyes. I tried to get things back on point.

'What did you make of him?' I asked.

'To be honest, I liked him. He's a funny guy.'

'For a human trafficker,' Leon said. 'Like father, like son.'

'Harry says—'

Leon screwed up his face. 'It's *Harry* now, is it?'

'That is his name.'

I sighed. It was like dealing with teenage kids.

'Enough! You two need to take it down a notch, the rest of the team can hear you out there.'

'I'm not the one shagging a gangster. It's her that—'

I silenced Leon with a glare.

'Emma was asked to find out more about Stevie Connors and it sounds like she's doing a great job so button it.'

She smiled while Leon sulked. You could almost see the angry heat shimmering around him. If they were like this when I was there I could only imagine how fractious it would get when they were alone together.

'What were you about to say?' I asked Emma.

'He claims to have cleaned up the organisation. Says they're all about the hospitality business now.'

'Wait a minute, does he know you're a cop?'

She hesitated for a moment.

'Aye, he knew immediately.'

'Your cover's blown then. You need to keep away,' Leon said.

'He's invited me out for a meal on Thursday.'

Leon's mouth dropped open.

'What about me? It's bonfire night.'

'I'm sure you'll find a party somewhere.'

'While my girlfriend makes goo-goo eyes at a gangster.'

'It might be ex-girlfriend if you don't grow up.'

I slammed my hand on the desk. I could see heads turn in the office outside.

'Last warning. Strictly business from here on or you can both forget the DI job.'

'But—'

It was Emma's turn to get the icy stare. She got the message and shut up.

'I'm not sure what game he's playing but I trust your judgement. Go to dinner, see what else you can get from him. But be careful. And keep your eyes open for anyone who looks like the driver from the hit and run.'

Two witnesses had seen the driver who took Laura's life. One of them was me but I was concussed and on the verge of passing out. The other, a young twocker who had seen the man running away. Our descriptions were similarly vague – tall, thin, and possibly with blond hair.

'I'm already on it, boss,' Emma said. She opened the folder and pulled out a photo, placing it on the desk in front of the two of us.

'This is Micky Chambers. One of Connors' boys. I managed to sneak a photo of him last night.'

'Any form?'

'Sadly not, so we don't already have his DNA on file, but we can't rule him out.'

'Him and about sixty million others,' Leon said, sarcastically.

The driver had been wearing a red cap when he fled the scene but it had fallen off and the twocker had picked it up and eventually handed it in. Sadly, the DNA we took from it wasn't on the system.

I studied the photo, trying to match the man to the image that flashed through my head all those months ago. Chambers seemed a little older than I'd thought but close enough for me to be interested.

'What does he do for Connors?' I asked.

'He's his chauffeur,' Emma said.

## 17

Sara Quinn was a storyteller, and she had lots of tales to tell about her oldest friend, Maria Groom.

After twenty minutes on the phone, Emma knew Sara's life history. She'd heard about her first day at school – the day she met Maria – and her first date, the friends had double-dated twins for a laugh. She knew about the music the two had listened to every night after school – mostly at Sara's house because Maria's mum was a cow – and the netball team they had both played for: Maria was Centre, Sara, Goal Attack.

And so on and so on. One of the problems with doing an interview on the phone was it was harder to interrupt people and Emma was struggling to get a word in edge-ways – until she found something that Sara didn't know about her friend. She had no clue what had happened to her. But she did have a theory.

'She'll have run off with a man, probably,' she said. 'The thing you need to know about Maria is that she's a romantic at heart. She falls in love at the drop of a hat. She always thinks she's met "the one". But with Maria love is blind, until it suddenly isn't. And the thing that none of these men have understood is that, when she realises that they're not Mr Perfect, she falls out of love almost as quickly. And drops them like a stone.'

'Including Evan Groom?' Emma squeezed in.

'You bet. They married within six months of meeting. Maria was already pregnant and she felt that the baby needed a father. It was all a bit of a shock, to be honest, I was the one who always wanted kids. Sadly, it wasn't to be for me.'

For the first time, to Emma's relief, Sara Quinn took a breath.

'I'm sorry to hear that, Sara. Maybe it's not too late.'

'I'm not sure about that, but at least Maria gave me the chance to be a godmother.'

'Was Evan a good father?'

'I doubt it, the man had an ego the size of a planet. And anyway he never got the chance to find out – by the time Nicky was three months old she'd thrown him out.'

'You weren't surprised that the marriage didn't last?'

'The only surprise was that she married him in the first place. The man's a nightmare – thinks he's the bee's knees. He couldn't believe it when she dumped him. But I could. Maria was struggling with the new baby and he was no help at all. And like I said she gets bored easily. Whoever she's gone off with this time better start counting the days.'

'Look, Sara, I don't want to worry you, but what if she hasn't gone off voluntarily?'

There was a long silence on the other end of the phone.

'Are you still there, Sara?'

'D'you really think she's been abducted?'

'We're not ruling anything in or out at this stage. Can you think of anyone who might do something like that?'

'Maybe. Look, I love her like a sister but she has left a trail of heartbroken men in her wake.'

'Including Evan Groom.'

'Well, I wouldn't say he was heartbroken – you need a heart for that.'

'You're not a big fan then?'

'Look, to be fair, I've only met him a handful of times but it was hate at first sight, though I should say the feeling was mutual. For various reasons I haven't seen as much of Maria in the last few years but some of that was because of him.'

'So you think he could have done something to her.'

'No question, especially if he was having problems getting his fair share of young Nicky. He wasn't happy with the access the court gave him, God knows why as Maria says he often doesn't turn up anyway. And he's got a nasty streak a yard wide. I found him intimidating, always seemed like he might suddenly do his talking with his fists, you know the type. But there's not just him, some of her other boyfriends were pretty pissed off with being dropped too.'

'What others?'

Sara hesitated again. Emma wondered if she was being selective with her name-dropping.

'There are too many to remember off the top of my head but she has a type. Good-looking, arrogant, superficially charming but when you dig down a bit deeper they're controlling and self-centred.'

Emma could feel herself nodding involuntarily, aside from the 'superficially charming' bit that described Evan Groom to a tee.

'It all goes back to that mother of hers, she's dead now, thankfully, but she was an awful woman. That's why we spent all our time round my house when we were bairns. One of the few times I went to hers she slapped Maria full in the face because she hadn't laid the table. And if Maria was ever late home her mum used to throw her tea in the bin and send her to her room.'

'What about her father? Didn't he have something to say about that?'

'Poor man was a right pushover, wouldn't say boo to a goose. He's passed too. Heart attack years ago. I think that wife of his just wore him out. That's why Maria goes for the type of men she does, I reckon. She's looking for someone with a bit more about them than her dad had but she mistakes arrogance for strength – and despite their macho posturing, they never come up to scratch.

'Though Evan's the first who's managed to get a ring on her finger so credit to him for that. The guy before Evan only lasted about half as long, and the one before that even less.'

'Was Sam Gallagher one of those?'

'Aye. We used to joke that he was the missing member of Oasis – he had that kind of look about him.'

'Was it an amicable break-up?'

'They never are with Maria. It's that arrogance, you see, they can't believe they've been dumped. And he clung on like a limpet. Turning up at her door in the middle of the night and all sorts. She had to get an injunction out on him in the end.'

Emma made a mental note to bump Gallagher up to the top of their list of people to talk to.

'Can you send me a list of names of any other boyfriends? And anything else you can remember about them?'

'Course. Might take me a while, mind. She never much liked being alone. Until Nicky came along, she replaced them almost as quickly as she dumped them.'

## 18

Since I first received my diagnosis, my brother had become my sounding board. As a former Catholic priest, he at least knew how to keep a secret. Now he seemed the perfect choice for a fallback option if Helen resisted my pleas. I'd even brought along a bottle of his favourite Irish whiskey to seal the deal. Sadly, it turned out he was a long way from perfect.

'Switzerland!' Phillip said. 'You want us to go to Switzerland!'

'Bro trip!' I attempted to high-five my older brother. He just stared at my hand until I slowly lowered it. 'You should never leave a man hanging,' I said.

'We're not six. And since when did we call each other "bro"?'

'Exactly. We've never had the chance to bond and this would be a good opportunity to get to know each other.' Phillip was twenty years older than me so had moved out of the family home before I could say my own name.

'By searching for cuckoo clocks?'

'That's borderline racist. Switzerland is much more than that! It's a stunningly beautiful country, mountains – we could go skiing – then there's the lakes . . . banks . . .'

'My knees are buggered, I can't swim and I don't have any money,' Phil said. 'Call me picky but I don't see the appeal. How about Dublin? Nice little distillery tour.'

I was well aware that Phillip was open to bribery and throwing in a free weekend of hard drinking would probably swing it. Sadly, the Irish didn't do euthanasia and, as far as I knew, the Swiss didn't do good whiskey.

'I know what you're doing,' Phil said. I knew this was going to be a serious chat because he put his glass of Jameson's down. 'I'm not helping you kill yourself.'

Phillip had many faults but naivety wasn't amongst them. My wife and brother agreed on very little but they both believed I was being unnecessarily alarmist about my condition. Helen's opposition to a Swiss trip would have been logical – Phillip's was more theological. My brother had firm views on the sanctity of life. Lord knows where he picked up that idea from. The Old Testament God I was brought up on had a higher kill count than Pol Pot.

'Not even if it saves my marriage?'

'You're the only one who thinks your marriage is the problem. Just move back in, for goodness' sake. You could have *years* before anything kicks in, yet you seem to want to spend all that time looking over your shoulder rather than enjoying what you have – a fantastic family.'

'You and I used to have a fantastic family and look what Alzheimer's did to that.' Phillip hadn't witnessed much of the violence that our father had inflicted on our mam when the disease had got a grip on him, but I had.

'Once it had started, yes, it was damaging. But you're not at that stage. There are thousands of people out there who are further advanced than you who are still in a meaningful, loving relationship.'

'Yes, but often one of them hasn't got the foggiest who they're in a relationship with. And how many of them would still be around if they'd had the same warning of what was coming over the hill that I have? Most of those poor sods didn't have a clue what was about to hit them.'

Phil sighed. We'd gone back and forth over this countless times. I sensed there might be some wriggle room this time though.

'Look, you were right when you told me not to move out. I thought I could cope without Helen and Aidan and I was wrong. But I need an escape route, Phil, I don't want them to become my carers. I need to know that someone will save them if I get to the stage where I don't know who they are or what the hell is going on.'

'And I'm that saviour?'

'Who else is there? You wouldn't have to press the button or anything, just help me get away if I'm becoming a burden.' That wasn't completely true. Someone would have to press it. The Dignitas people wouldn't do it for legal reasons and I might not be in any condition to do it myself but we could cross that bridge when we came to it.

I could see there was a chance. I reached into my bag and pulled out a document.

'It wouldn't be entirely your responsibility, Phil. I've laid it all out here – it's called Advance Decisions. It spells out all the circumstances in which I would like to end things. It's important that I've done this while I'm still compos mentis. All you would be doing is carrying out my wishes.'

'And breaking the law.'

He was right. But they rarely prosecuted anyone for assisting suicide.

'Not to mention the fact that Helen would kill me if I went along with it.'

'Not if you show her this. If anything, she should thank you. I broke us apart but you'd be the one who put us back together again. You're like a guarantor on our marriage.'

He took the document from my hand and skimmed through it. There was a lot of head shaking and a couple of frowns before he got to the end. I nearly tried to lighten the mood by saying something about Switzerland being the ideal place to go when you were on a slippery slope and going downhill fast but for once I managed to control my tendency towards flippancy.

'You make a convincing argument,' he said, when he finally put the thing down. 'And I am partial to a nice Swiss roll. But it's still no.'

## 19

## 5 November 2024

Leon woke up with a big cheesy grin on his face and started humming the Vaccines' banger 'Post Break-up Sex'.

It wasn't entirely appropriate – he and Emma hadn't broken up, just had the mother of all arguments before carrying that passion into her bedroom. He closed his eyes and watched an edited highlights reel on the back of his eyelids and could feel his grin go wider.

Compared to his previous serious girlfriends – all two of them – she was way more experienced. She led and he followed, as best he could. He'd never known anything like it, and truth be told, at times he was playing catch-up. He could feel his grin fading – maybe he wasn't good enough for her? He tried not to worry about it – the last thing he needed was performance anxiety – but he'd bet that Harry Connors had been around the block a few times and knew a lot more tricks than he did.

Leon had starred in *Othello* at school – as the only black

kid in the sixth form he was pretty much nailed on for the main part – and always remembered the line about being wary of jealousy: 'It is the green-eyed monster which doth mock the meat it feeds on.'

But such wariness was easier said than done, especially as Emma liked to press his buttons – she seemed to thrive on the tension – certainly if last night was any guide. Maybe he was out of his depth? The trouble was he was edging ever closer to saying the 'L' word. He'd had to bite his tongue more than once because he was pretty sure that she wouldn't say it back and, from bitter experience, he knew that could be the death knell for a relationship.

He glanced across the bed. Emma was gently snoring, blissfully unaware of his confusion. She didn't seem to do much in the way of agonising – he'd love to be that uncomplicated. Leon sighed and swung his feet out of bed. He'd never get back to sleep and they had a press conference in a couple of hours, so it was time to get a move on.

He wandered into her kitchen and put some coffee on. Maybe there was time to throw on some clothes and nip out to the local bakery on Pink Lane for some of their fantastic almond croissants? As he was mulling that over, the doorbell rang. There was no movement in the bedroom so he shuffled out to the front door and opened it.

A young guy was standing there with a large bunch of red roses.

'Emma Steel?' he said.

'Do I look like I'm her?' Leon said, already getting a bad feeling about this.

'Does she live here?'

'She's in bed.'

'Could you take these then?' the kid said, holding the bouquet out hopefully to Leon, who realised it wasn't fair to take out his fears on the lad.

'Sure,' he said. As he closed the door behind him, he could see an envelope stuck to the wrapping. He knew he shouldn't but he couldn't help himself. He opened the envelope and pulled out the card inside.

*See you tonight H xxx*

Before he could put the card back, he heard the bedroom door swing open behind him and Emma stepped out wearing a smile and nothing else. She reeked of sex.

'You shouldn't have,' she said, smiling broadly.

'I didn't,' Leon said, handing her the card.

She read it and looked back up at him, the smile fading.

'Don't overthink it, Leon. You've nothing to worry about.'

'Aside from the fact that Harry Connors, one of the biggest villains in the city, knows where you live,' he said.

## 20

Press briefings were a necessary evil. It was by far the quickest way for us to get information out to the public – though our Press Office manager Alan Gardner reckoned that Twitter (I refused to call it X) was fast catching up. Apparently, the Northumberland Police account had nearly 200,000 followers, way more people than read newspapers these days. I wondered how many of them were villains hoping to keep tabs on our operations – like murderers turning up at their victims' funerals.

The briefings were particularly good for missing persons and for the time being we were treating Maria Groom as exactly that. The bloodstains were a concern, obviously, though there didn't seem enough of the stuff to indicate anything worse than an injury so we were going to keep that to ourselves for now, not wishing to raise the alarm levels too high.

There were about eight journos at this one including the *Chron*'s latest Rottweiler, Gary Coxon, who was on my shit-list for the way he'd harangued me during our last investigation. He would eventually learn that he needed us more than we needed him. Leon had taken his usual place alongside me – Bob Curtis loved nothing more than showing off our one black policeman as if he was representative of what was still a primarily white force. It annoyed the hell out of Emma, who reasonably enough argued that a woman's presence would be equally valuable.

'Good morning,' I said. 'We're asking for your help to find a missing mother and child. Maria Groom, thirty-seven, and her three-year-old son, Nicky, from the Linden Road area of Gosforth, haven't been sighted by anyone for a week. She was last seen at home by a neighbour on the evening of Tuesday, twenty-ninth of October at around nine p.m.

'Maria is described as five feet six inches tall, of slim build, with shoulder-length blond hair. She was wearing a red fleece and black leggings at last sighting. Nicky also has blond hair and was wearing a blue denim jacket and jeans. There are recent photos of both of them in your press pack which may help jog people's memories. We are also searching for Maria's car, a white Ford Fiesta, with the registration NA15 BCW.

'You'll also find details of our 101 helpline number and other ways in which the public can contact us with information. I'd be very grateful if you can share all of these as far and wide as possible.

'Please also ask people who live or work in that area with dashcam footage, CCTV or a doorbell camera to contact us if they believe they have information that might help the investigation. Thank you. If anyone has any questions . . .'

Gary Coxon was, as usual, the first to pounce.

'Is there any reason to believe that either Maria or Nicky are in danger, Detective Chief Inspector?'

'Obviously we are concerned for their safety,' I said. 'Ms Groom has missed several recent appointments, and those who know her say that she is normally reliable and would always let them know if she couldn't make it.'

'Many of the neighbours I spoke to said there had been a prowler in the area.'

'There were some reports in the last few weeks but there is no reason, as yet, to link those to Ms Groom's disappearance.'

'Only some of the neighbours I've spoken to told me that the police didn't respond to those reports.'

I'd had no doubt that Coxon would have got all the gossip from the neighbours so I'd come prepared.

'That's not the case, Gary, patrols in the area were stepped up but no further sightings of a prowler were made or have been reported and, as I said, there's no evidence to link those reports to Maria's disappearance.'

'Just a coincidence, eh?'

'Any more questions?' I said, ignoring his snidey remark. There was no immediate response. I picked up my papers to try and head off a last dig from Coxon. Irritatingly, before I'd moved away, he dived in again.

'One more thing,' he said. I could tell from his face that I wasn't going to like it. 'You are head of the murder team and you don't normally get involved with missing persons.'

I waited for an actual question.

'You dismissed the prowler issue but is there any other reason to suggest they might have come to harm?'

He was positively grinning now. I could guess what he had up his sleeve but I wasn't biting.

'We have a team examining the house at the moment but we'll have to wait for the results from the CSIs,' I said.

'So there's no truth in the rumour that you found bloodstains in the house?'

## 21

The press was already having a field day with the bloodstains story. Local radio and the papers' websites had all led with it and I had no doubt that the print copies wouldn't be far behind. I had refused to confirm the story, falling back on my 'awaiting results' line, but they were all using a quote from an unnamed source. I had no doubts it was the neighbour.

Leon and Emma had been doing most of the legwork on the friends and neighbours so I called another meeting of the brains' trust to get me up to speed. I could tell from the way they sat further apart than normal on the other side of my desk that things were still frosty between them.

'What have we got?' I asked. Leon jumped in.

'We still can't find anyone who has seen Maria Groom in the last six days,' he said. 'We've spoken to most of her neighbours and her ex-husband. It looks like she disappeared sometime between the evening of the twenty-ninth, when Rosie Lloyd saw her putting her bins out, and late afternoon on the thirtieth when the music teacher went round to the house.'

'This bloody Rosie woman clearly likes a good gossip,' I said. 'D'you think it was her who spoke to the press?'

'I wouldn't be surprised.'

'Where are we with CCTV and ANPR on the car, Emma?'

'Nothing on ANPR. We've still got some CCTV to go through but zip so far. We're also checking footage from the train station, just in case, but that's drawn a blank up to now. I'm chasing her bank records too.'

'She can't just have vanished. What about the stuff her friend said about her dating history? It sounded like there were a lot of possible suspects from the past. Did you follow that up?'

'Sara Quinn sent me a list of ex-boyfriends.' Emma passed both Leon and me a copy of the email.

'It's fairly exhaustive,' Emma said. 'Some of them go back years. It's going to take a bit of time to track them all down.'

'She's been around a bit,' Leon said as he looked down it. 'I'm not that much younger than Maria Groom and she's beating me about twelve to two in the ex-partner stakes.'

I could see Emma bristling and didn't have to wait long for a reaction.

'Have you heard yourself? Is that what you say about me when I'm not around? If it was a man you'd be buying him a pint and slapping him on the back,' she said.

You really didn't need to be a detective to see that their relationship was starting to crumble. Was it my fault? Had I made a mistake letting Emma go after Harry Connors?

'What else do we know about this Sam Gallagher guy?' I said, changing the subject.

'I've already done a bit of background,' Emma said. 'Maria got a temporary injunction against him coming to one of her previous addresses. He kept turning up at her door at all hours apparently.

'It seemed to stop but Sara said she thought it had continued on social media. I did find a few weird messages on her Messenger app which were all clearly from the same fake account but the only really offensive things were the dick pics and until we get Gallagher in, it will be hard to confirm they're from him! No pun intended.'

'OK,' I said. 'Keep the pressure on the husband but, regardless of what Bob Curtis wants, let's not put all our eggs in one basket. Check out Gallagher too. Maybe he's the prowler all the neighbours have been talking about.'

## 22

The Fork on the Tyne was the only Michelin-star restaurant in Newcastle. Situated on the Quayside with great views down the river, it was a must for any foodies in the city, if they could afford it. Leon couldn't. This was the first time he'd ever set foot in the place.

The entrance was impressively chilled, a smattering of small tables overlooking the river, where the punters could have a pre-dinner drink before being taken to the upstairs restaurant. Maybe he should take Emma there? They'd never really been out on a proper date; it hadn't been that kind of relationship, more fuck-buddies than boyfriend and girl-friend. Not his choice but he was worried about scaring her off if he showed how keen he was. Maybe she was waiting for him to make a grand gesture? A table here might be just that.

'Can I help you?'

A smartly dressed young waitress, in a simple white blouse and dark trousers, was standing at the bottom of the stairs, tray in hand.

'I'm looking for Sam Gallagher,' he said. He took out his ID. 'Detective Sergeant Johnson,' he added, flashing the badge.

'Ooh, what's he done?' she said. Leon ignored her question.

'Is he around or not?'

The waitress looked like she desperately wanted to ask him again but managed to hold it in check.

'I think he's in today but I'll have to check with Benny,' she said.

'Who's Benny?'

'He's the head chef, he runs the restaurant. And he doesn't like his sous chefs being disturbed when they're preparing dinner.'

'Really? Tell Benny that I'm running a murder enquiry and I think that's slightly more important than . . .' he picked up a menu from the bar, 'glazing a kohlrabi, whatever that is when it's at home.'

'It's a type of cabbage. We glaze it in a home-made miso sauce and—'

Leon's glare stopped her in her tracks.

'I'll see if he's available,' she said, and quickly disappeared through a door which he could see led into the kitchen.

While he waited Leon studied the menu more carefully. The seven-course tastings menu was £135 a head, plus £85 per person for a recommended wine flight. Maybe he'd take Emma to his local Italian instead. They knew him there, it was two for the price of one on Thursdays and the spaghetti carbonara was great, as far as he could tell.

The kitchen door swung open and the waitress leant through.

'Follow me,' she said.

The kitchen was all shiny aluminium and busy-ness, several chefs, all in matching white T-shirts and aprons, rushed around, clattering pans and shouting instructions as they prepared that day's lunch. The heat was intense in places and Leon could feel a bead of sweat on his forehead; he was a little overdressed for this environment.

The waitress stopped and pointed him to a workstation in the corner of the kitchen, where a bearded, long-haired, undeniably good-looking guy in chef's whites was rapidly chopping vegetables, the knife moving so quickly that Leon feared for the man's fingers. He caught a fleeting glimpse of a tattoo around his wrist. Gallagher seemed entirely oblivious to anything around him and as Leon had approached him from the side he probably hadn't seen him coming so he coughed to get the man's attention. When he still got no response he tapped him on the shoulder.

Gallagher swivelled around rapidly, the knife way too close for Leon's comfort. The chef looked puzzled, clearly surprised at finding a fully suited and booted man he didn't know invading his kitchen space. He quickly dropped the arm holding the knife down by his side.

'Sorry about that,' he said, with a broad smile. 'You surprised me.'

Sara Quinn had described Sam Gallagher as looking like the missing brother from Oasis and Leon could see why – he was definitely rocking a pop-star vibe. He had great teeth and was tall, well over six feet, which fitted with the stalker Rosie Lloyd had described.

'Sam Gallagher?' Leon asked.

'That's me.'

'DS Johnson, Northumberland CID, just need to ask you a few questions.'

The smile dropped from Gallagher's lips and before Leon could move, the chef had dropped the knife and barged past him, crashing through a fire escape door to the outside. He sprinted after him, slipping slightly on some wet cobbles as he hit the outside, then dodging past several large communal waste bins to an alley that led back out to the main street. From there he saw Gallagher disappearing up a set of steps on the other side of the road that led towards the back of the railway station.

Leon sprinted across the road, dodging the traffic, and gained quickly on the fleeing chef who clearly wasn't a runner. Or maybe he was hampered by his long apron flapping in the wind. As Gallagher climbed near the top of the narrow steps his path was blocked by two huge bald-headed lads in Newcastle United tops heading down, side by side. They looked like the guys who famously put their bellies on show in the match crowd in the middle of winter. It looked like there was no way past for Gallagher but then the two men seemed to see what was happening and parted like the Red Sea for Moses to allow him through before closing again as Leon got close.

'Out of my way,' Leon shouted.

The men stared at him but didn't make way. As he got near one of them held up a large, meaty hand to stop him.

'Whoa, Linford Christie, what's gannin' on?'

Leon tried to squeeze past them but they blocked him off.

'Move it, I'm a cop.'

'Likely story,' the second man said. 'You'll have some ID on you then, won't you, bonny lad?'

Fuck's sake, Leon thought, reaching into his jacket.

'Steady, son,' the first man said, stepping back.

'Jesus Christ! It's not a knife, it's my badge.' He pulled out his ID and flashed it at the two lads who examined it far more closely than they needed to. 'One more second and I'm arresting you both for obstruction.'

Finally, they nodded and moved to one side. He brushed past them and ran to the top of the steps but it was too late. Gallagher had vanished.

What the hell had made him do a runner like that?

# 23

*Five days earlier*

Maria lay awake staring at the man in bed with her. He clearly couldn't believe his luck when she'd knocked on his door, bag in hand. It was no hardship to fuck him, it was the one thing he'd always been good for. And, to be frank, it helped her to let go for an hour or two, but she'd be gone as soon as she'd got what she was really there for.

She'd taken a chance spending the night but reckoned it would be at least another three or four days before anyone reported her missing and after leaving her house, she'd done plenty to muddy the waters since.

After a quick trip to Evan's house, knowing full well he'd be occupied elsewhere as usual, she'd abandoned her car at Walkergate Metro station. She left the keys in it, hoping someone might nick it which would throw anyone looking for her off the scent. If not, if it was there long enough, it would probably be reported to the police. That would be interesting. She almost wished she'd be there to see it.

And then to see Evan's face once he found out about the presents she'd left him in both places.

From there she'd taken the Metro out to Whitley Bay, trying hard to avoid any CCTV on the stations, keeping her hood up and sticking a baseball cap on Nicky's head. He was happy to wear it when he realised it was a Magpies cap. His dad had told him that Newcastle United were God's team. The man might be a gold-plated wanker but he could be persuasive – she'd give him that.

The walk to Sam Gallagher's house from there was straightforward though – she even found time to get Nicky that promised ice cream from Di Meo's, and more importantly, fling her iPad into the North Sea along the way.

Despite everything that had gone on between them, Sam was unbelievably pleased to see her. He even liked her new hairstyle and colour; typically he thought she'd done it just for him. He was great with Nicky though. He'd let him help with carving a face into a pumpkin for Hallowe'en. Then the pair of them had run around on his back lawn for ages until Nicky was exhausted and crashed out in the spare room. Thankfully the garden wasn't overlooked so nobody would remember her and Nicky being there when their faces were all over the media.

But this was a new dawn. Sam would be less happy this morning. She looked across at him, sleeping peacefully, completely unaware what was about to happen. He was a handsome bastard, though, there was no doubt about that. He opened one eye and caught her staring at him. A huge grin broke out across his face.

'Morning,' he said, reaching out and stroking her face.

'Morning. About the car—'

'Don't spoil it, I told you I need it.'

She bit her tongue, pretended everything was sweet. He'd had his chance. Typically he couldn't read her at all and went back to the stroking, tucking her hair behind her ear.

'I didn't expect this to happen again,' he said. His grin wasn't the only thing that grew bigger. Those dick pics really didn't do it justice. 'I'm ready to go again if you are.'

'I can see that. But I need a pee first.'

Maria leapt out of bed and strolled to the bathroom, giving him a final glimpse of her arse. It was the last time he'd have that pleasure. It was his fault. If the selfish bastard had agreed to lend her his car when she'd asked him – twice now – then she wouldn't have had to implement Plan B.

Once inside she took a good look in the mirror. Her lipstick was smeared all over her face from the frantic snogging of the night before, which also accounted for some of the stubble rash she could see when she leaned in closer to the glass. She smiled at her reflection – it was the best she would look for some time.

She pulled a hand towel from a rail on the wall and folded it twice for extra thickness, placing it carefully around her nose for protection. She needed to scare him but at the same time keep the damage to a minimum – blood and bruising was fine – a broken nose a step too far. She took one final glance, turned her head slightly and smashed it into the mirror.

The impact sent her reeling back towards the door. She

took a couple of deep breaths before gently easing the towel away and moving back to the newly cracked mirror. Blood was seeping from a split above her eye. There'd be some bruising for sure but nothing worse than that. Her nose was bleeding too – and tender to touch – but there was no other damage to it. Perfect.

A few minutes later Maria walked back into the bedroom with a white towel wrapped around her, the top of it already stained with the blood which was dripping from her eyebrow and nose.

Sam had his back to her. She could clearly see the fierce scratches she'd left all over it the night before. She'd made sure there were more on his arms too.

'What was that noise?' he said as he rolled over to face her. His smile disappeared immediately. 'What the fuck?' He sat up abruptly, confusion written all over his face.

'I need your car,' she said.

'What? What's that got to do with this?' Sam waved in the general direction of her damaged face. 'And anyway, I already told you, you can't have it. I need it for work.'

'You might not have a job once I've reported this,' she said, holding up a bloodied hand.

He opened his mouth to speak but nothing came out. She sat on the bed next to him, ignoring the pain coming from her damaged face.

'I don't understand,' he muttered.

'You never did. Listen carefully, Sam. I fled my house with my son because I was frightened of my violent ex-husband

and didn't know where to go. I thought my old boyfriend might help me, he'd always said he'd be there for me if I needed him. But instead of helping me, he beat me. With my three-year-old child asleep in the next room.'

Sam scrambled back on the bed until he came up against the headboard, getting as far away from her as possible, as if some of her crazy might rub off on him.

'You're barking mad.'

'Maybe I am. Look at my face, only a lunatic would do this to themselves. But the police won't think that. Check out those scratches on your arm. I managed to get quite a bit of your skin under these fingernails, I reckon. I was thinking of playing the rape card but a) I don't want to perpetuate the myth that women make this stuff up, and b) quite frankly there's a better chance of me duetting with Taylor Swift than getting a rape conviction these days.'

'They won't believe you.'

'Really?' She shifted into a helpless little woman voice. *'He attacked me when he couldn't get it up. I tried to fight him off but he punched me in the face repeatedly.'*

Maria grinned and switched back to her normal voice.

'And when they realise you've been stalking me again it'll be a slam dunk.'

'Stalking! What do you mean?'

'I know it was you in my garden the other day. My neighbours caught you on their private CCTV. The police might not have been interested then but they will be after this.' She pointed to her face. She was bluffing. There were no images caught on camera. She hadn't been sure it was him either until now, when, as usual, his face gave him away. He bowed his head in shame.

'I missed you. I just wanted to see you again.'

'Well now you have, but I'm taking the car in return. It's either that or you end up in court and lose your job at that fancy-pants restaurant. I know how much you love it. You never shut up about it on your Facebook page. Even if you get off, the stink of it will stay with you forever.'

'I'll just report my car stolen. They'll hardly believe all that happened and then I let you borrow it.'

Maria jumped back into character again.

*I was so scared that I waited until he fell asleep, then took his car keys. I was in a state of shock, had no idea where I was going, just wanted to get as far away from him as I could.'*

Sam shook his head, he knew when he was beaten.

'How long do you need it for?'

'Not sure. A week maybe.'

'A week!' He sat up. 'What am I supposed to do in the meantime?'

'Buy a Metro pass, you cheap shit. How about I talk to the police now, and then, when they've locked you up, I come back and take the car anyway?'

Sam shook his head and pulled the sheets around him as if they might protect him. For a moment Maria thought he was going to cry.

'And if anyone asks, you haven't seen me, OK?' she added.

'What's going on?'

'Trust me, you don't want to know. And, seriously, don't

even think about reporting this. One look at my face and they'll lock you up and throw away the key.'

Sam had his head in his hands now, shaking it from side to side. She almost felt sorry for him. Obviously, she'd never go to the cops but he didn't know that and now, even when news of her disappearance broke, he'd never talk to them either for fear that she'd stitch him up. He looked up at her again.

'You didn't have to blackmail me. I'd do anything for you.'

'Apart from lend me your car.'

'I didn't know it was that important to you.'

'Well, you do now,' she said.

## 24

*5 November 2024*

Leon's day went from bad to worse after losing Sam Gallagher. He tried to find him at his home address but got no joy there. Then Jack had bawled him out in front of a sniggering Emma for letting the chef escape his clutches at the restaurant. Now he was sitting in his car chewing a cheap takeaway burger while he watched her eating a piece of prime steak in another restaurant across the road from him.

Opposite her, Harry Connors appeared to be breaking open a lobster claw with a silver cracker. They looked like they were having a ball. Was this what Maria Groom's old boyfriends had felt like when they'd seen her having fun with their replacements? Not that he'd been replaced, not yet anyway.

The sky above him exploded with blue and green light as the latest rocket flew up above the River Tyne. He could hear the whoops from the crowd lined up along the Quayside. Was he the only man in town having a shit time? He took a bite from his burger and squirmed as a mixture of bright red ketchup and yellow mustard squeezed from the back of the bun and dropped onto his trousers.

'Goddammit,' he cursed.

He tried to use the flimsy serviette he'd grabbed off the counter of the burger place to wipe his lap clean but it just spread the mess around. He could see Emma laughing. At least one of us is having a nice time, he thought. There was a bang on the window. A traffic warden stood by the side of the door, peering in at Leon. He wound down his window.

'You can't park here, mate,' the man said. 'I'll give you two minutes to get out of here or I'll have to give you a ticket.'

Leon reached into his inside pocket and the warden flinched. Did everyone in this city think that if a black man put his hand in his pocket it would come out with a weapon?

'Relax, it's not a gun, I'm a cop, just getting my ID.'

He flashed his badge at the man who examined it carefully. It happened to Leon a lot. A black cop was like a unicorn in this part of the world. Eventually the man nodded and walked off without another word.

'No problem, officer, sorry to have done my best to blow your surveillance,' Leon muttered. 'Prick.'

Forty minutes later a black Mercedes pulled up right outside the restaurant and Connors and Emma came out and sat in the back. As the car passed him, Leon ducked down slightly but not enough to miss catching the driver's face. It was

Micky Chambers. He let him get to the junction a few yards away and started up the car to follow him. He hoped they would drop off Emma at her flat but could immediately tell they were heading in the wrong direction for that. He knew that Connors had a place near Ponteland and his heart sank when the car ahead took the turning towards the airport. She was going back with him again.

For a moment he considered putting his blue light on and pulling them over but he knew that Emma would go ballistic – and what would he say? No, he'd just have to wait it out. Knowing his luck he wouldn't even get to see any more fireworks. Or at least not the kind that you associated with Guy Fawkes.

Leon could feel that shitty burger threatening to make a reappearance. It was going to be a long night.

## 25

Emma could get used to the chauffeur-driven life. She lounged in the back of Harry Connors' Mercedes as Micky Chambers drove her home again. She would get him to drop her off a bit closer to her flat this time – clearly her attempts to hide her home address from Harry Connors by being dropped off at Central Station last time had failed miserably so she may as well save the shoe leather.

She'd tried to engage Chambers in conversation as they headed back to the city, hoping to steer the conversation around to his driving experiences, but he was clearly a man of few words so she gave up and instead thought about the events of that night. Harry Connors had again been the perfect gentleman, funny, interested in her and engaging. He didn't talk about himself, unless prompted, and was attentive, refilling her glass until she said she'd had enough and not trying to order food for her, like some men had done in the past. He even stood up when she went to the Ladies to powder her nose. Contrary to some of her recent nights in with Leon, it had been a nice evening.

She'd been happy to head back to his for a nightcap, sure that it would be no more than that unless she initiated it, which she wasn't planning to do. Though sometimes you never really knew what you were going to do, did you? Anyway, the moment hadn't arisen and Harry hadn't pushed it. When she'd said it was time to go he'd messaged Chambers and ten minutes later the car had pulled up outside the house. She had no idea where the driver went in the interim period but it couldn't have been far away. Maybe he just stayed inside the grounds of Connors' mansion? They were big enough for him to tuck himself away for a kip somewhere.

But what had she learned? Harry Connors played his hand carefully, that was for sure. She had tried to steer the conversation around to Laura's death but could never quite get there. He spoke about his dad coming out soon, but was clear that he was going to remain in charge of the business. He seemed convinced that Stevie Connors was going to spend most of his time trying to get his handicap back to a respectable state on the region's golf courses. His dad was apparently delighted with the books and saw no need to interfere. He accepted that the bad old days were over and that the family business was not only in good shape but strictly legal these days.

Did she believe him? She wanted to, but she wasn't born yesterday. The man was charismatic and he talked a good game but it wasn't easy to clean up a criminal enterprise and she suspected it would take a hard man to do so. She wasn't so sure that Harry Connors was a hard man.

The car suddenly slowed down and she could see flashing lights ahead.

'What's going on?' she said.

'I'm not sure, miss. The police are funnelling cars into a lay-by. There's only one in front of us though so we shouldn't be long.'

Emma sat up. The road ahead had been coned off and, as Chambers had said, they were forced to drive up to a checkpoint. The car in front moved off and he drove the Mercedes towards a uniformed officer who waved him forwards before giving him the standard palm up stop sign.

Chambers wound the window down.

'Can I help you, officer?' he said. The cop leaned towards the window, glancing at Emma in the back before he spoke. She didn't know him and didn't think he recognised her either.

'I hope so, sir. There was a road rage incident on this spot a couple of days ago and we're looking for possible witnesses. A man forced a blue Vauxhall off the road and attacked the driver of the car when he got out. The victim was badly concussed and all he remembers was that his assailant was driving a black car.'

'I think he'd remember this one. It's not exactly your average household motor.'

The officer hesitated for a moment. Emma was pretty convinced he was making it up as he went along.

'Like I say sir, he was badly injured and his memory is hazy.'

'What day was it?'

'It was on Sunday night, just before midnight. About this time of night, actually.'

'Well, I'm afraid I can't help you. I didn't see anything, and I wasn't anywhere near this area at that time anyway.'

'Do you have anyone who can confirm that?' the officer said, glancing again at Emma. She thought about identifying herself but given the fact that she was working off-the-books, it wasn't a good idea.

'I'm afraid not. I was at home on my own.'

The officer nodded. 'No problem, sir. I'll need to take your details in case the investigators want to follow up on anything.'

'That's fine.'

'And I was wondering if you'd be prepared to let us take a DNA sample so we can definitively rule you out of the incident. The attacker left his DNA all over the victim.'

Emma's ears shot up at the mention of DNA. This was no coincidence. They wanted Micky Chambers' DNA to compare to the sample they had for the suspect in Laura's death. They couldn't get it legitimately but Jack Parker loved to cut corners when he could and this had his fingerprints all over it. But how did they know that Micky Chambers would be driving down this road at this time of night?

'Well, sir?' the officer said. Emma leant forward, fascinated to see if Jack's plan worked. She had to admit it was clever even if it put her in a compromising position.

'This is strictly voluntary?' Chambers said.

'That's right, sir, there's no obligation but it would help eliminate you from our enquiries.'

'I think I'll pass,' Chambers said.

Emma saw the officer glance behind them and shake his head. It was subtle but she knew what she'd seen. She looked around. She recognised the car immediately. Leon had clearly been following her! Had he been doing that all evening? Watching her in the restaurant?

Maybe it wasn't just Maria Groom who had a stalker.

## 26

*6 November 2024*

The previous night's debacle with the traffic cops seemed to have jinxed us. We were having one of those days that you get in every investigation, a lot of legwork producing little in the way of results. The team had been working the phones all day and chasing down possible witnesses back at the scene, all to no avail. There'd been no sightings of Maria or her son and no other leads. Evan Groom had made himself scarce, hiding away somewhere so we'd been unable to quiz him further. By the end of the day my thoughts had turned back to something we could progress: our search for Laura's killer.

I decided to try something different. The trouble with having to resort to any Plan B was twofold. Firstly, it meant that Plan A – in this case Leon's half-arsed attempt to get Micky Chambers' DNA – had failed miserably. Secondly, if Plan B was any good it would probably have been Plan A in the first place. But beggars can't be choosers.

If you'd told me a few months earlier, just after I'd tried to punch Frankie Grant's lights out in Bob Curtis's office, for instance, that I'd be asking the gangster for a favour before the year was out, I'd have told you to give your head a shake. The fact that this approach was a big part of plan B worried the shit out of me but I was doing it anyway. Ever since my diagnosis I no longer worried about the longer-term consequences of anything other than my disease.

As I made my way to Grant's house, I was almost looking forward to seeing the look of astonishment on his pig-like face when I knocked on his door, but that pleasure had to be deferred when I looked up and unexpectedly found that I was standing on the corner of Helen's street.

I tried to persuade myself that I was so busy going through all the possible consequences of my new plan that I wasn't paying attention to where I was going but, while recklessness may not have been one of the recognised symptoms of my disease, getting lost or going to the wrong places was. I sat on the sign at the corner of the street. Was this the start of my cognitive decline? Or was I simply distracted and my homing instincts had kicked in? There'd been plenty of times in the past that I'd got home before remembering I was meant to be stopping off at the shops on the way back. Maybe this was just more of the same?

I chose to go with distracted this time. It had been a hectic, frustrating thirty-six hours. But as soon as I'd stood up and reprogrammed myself to head to Grant's house another problem came up. Aidan turned into the street and stopped right in front of me.

'You following me again, Dad?' he said, laughing. Earlier in the year I'd been worried that he was being bullied and tailed him home from school. He'd never let me forget it.

'I'm not clever enough to follow you from the front, son. We have to do special training for that kind of thing.'

'I didn't know you were coming round tonight.'

Nor did I, I thought.

'I like to keep you on your toes, make sure you're tidying your room properly.'

'As if. Anyway, you're lucky to catch me. I was supposed to be playing Minecraft at Bobby's but he's dumped me for his new girlfriend.'

'Young love, eh?'

'Pussy-whipped, more like.'

'I wouldn't let your mam hear that kind of talk. Mummy Bear didn't raise no misogynists.'

'I won't tell her if you don't. I know how good you are at keeping secrets now.'

My son had become a lot cockier since he discovered the Alzheimer's medication in my bathroom cabinet. If he'd been a bit cannier, he might have used that information to blackmail me but he was still an innocent in that regard and he'd snitched to his mam instead.

But he was right about my ability to keep secrets. A talent Helen shared. We both knew that my condition was genetic and there was a fifty-fifty chance that Aidan would get it too. We'd decided to wait until his sixteenth birthday to share that news with him. He was cynical enough about his future without that hanging over his head before he sat his exams. He could decide for himself whether he wanted to get tested after that. According to my consultant some people preferred not to know. I got that. Knowing was both a blessing and a curse.

'Earth to Dad,' he said, laughing.

'What?'

'I said, "Are you coming in then?"'

I looked up. Somehow, we'd made it another few hundred yards down the road. I saw my wife's puzzled face looking out of the front window at us standing at the end of her driveway. Our driveway, as it used to be. And maybe would be again. Perhaps it was time to continue that conversation. Frankie Grant could wait for another day.

'Aye, why not?'

## 27

### *Return to form (8)*

'I wasn't expecting you to pop in tonight,' Helen said, as she opened the door to let us in.

To be fair, neither was I, but there was no chance I was admitting I'd gone to the wrong house.

'I found him on the corner,' Aidan said. 'He looked a little lost.'

My son was becoming adept at blowing my cover. Having lit the fuse, he disappeared upstairs before the explosion.

'Not at all,' I shouted after him before turning back to Helen. 'I'm still not used to being a visitor to my own house, that's all,' I said.

'You know what to do about that, Jack,' she said.

I wondered how long her offer for me to move back in would stay on the metaphorical table. It was tempting to bite her hand off now but I still had to be absolutely sure that I wasn't already sliding down the slippery slope to confusion – and, if my dad was any indication, outbursts of violence. Helen was willing to take that chance but I wasn't. Not yet, anyway. Though there was light at the end of my tunnel vision.

'I'm working on it,' I said.

'I'll stick the kettle on and you can tell me the latest excuse.' Helen headed to the kitchen. I waited a second and followed her. It no longer seemed right for me to settle in the front room without her even though it had been our family home for years before I left.

'Biscuit?' she said, without looking back.

'No, thanks.' I dropped on a chair on one side of the kitchen table.

'They're Italian. Biscotti! Doesn't that count as a Mediterranean diet?'

'I wish. I'm sick of eating healthily, it's taken all the fun out of mealtimes.'

There was a newspaper folded open in front of me and I noticed the crossword had been filled in. The clue to 1 Across was *Return to form*. The answer felt like an omen: *Comeback*.

Helen brought over two cups of tea and sat opposite me.

'I didn't know you did the crossword,' I said.

'I didn't. But neither did you, you know, before. It's good for a husband and wife to share things, don't you think?'

I smiled. She had a way of making her point without banging you over the head with it. It was one of the things that made her a good headteacher.

'You know I do.'

'So go on then, what's stopping you from moving back in?'

'I'm just making sure I've got all my ducks in a row.'

'Last time you were crossing the t's and dotting the i's.'

'I know. I'm sorry.'

'No worries. It's not like I don't have options. There's a new departmental head who I'm pretty sure was flirting with me the other day.'

She knew how to wind me up but in return I knew how to cover up my reactions. We were a good match for each other.

'I'm hardly in a position to complain if you did find someone else.'

'You can say that again. Look, obviously it's your decision but it's like anything else: the longer you leave it the harder it will get.'

'I've got the chance to take part in a trial for a new drug and that might well be the final piece of the puzzle I've been waiting for.'

She gave me a quizzical look.

'You should be careful, some of these things have weird side-effects.'

Helen also had an uncanny knack of hitting the nail squarely on the head.

'I know. But my consultant thinks it's perfect for me. It attacks the causes rather than symptoms, unlike my current drugs. And if it goes well I think I'll be ready to move back in.'

'How long will that be?'

'I don't know yet. I'm not even sure they'll take me.'

Helen took a long drink from her cup. And gave me a look that I hadn't seen in a while.

'Why don't you stay tonight?' she said. 'Treat it like a trial run.'

This time I couldn't stop my reaction. I could feel a smile spreading across my face. Then Aidan ran into the kitchen and switched on the small TV Helen kept there to watch while she cooked.

'I think you should see this, Dad,' he said, turning up the volume.

**28**

Evan Groom was standing outside his house holding a piece of paper. At least I assumed it was his house. I'd never had the pleasure, though if he was about to do what I expected it wouldn't be long before I was knocking on his door. The banner running along the bottom of the screen read, *Live: Father of missing boy complains about police treatment.*

As the cameras clicked, Groom looked up and began speaking. His tone was measured and calm and he looked the part in a smart suit, his hair freshly cut since the last time I'd seen him, a tear in his eye that gradually made its way down his cheek. Having met the man, and heard Emma's reactions towards him, I wouldn't have been surprised if he had just hidden an onion in his pocket.

'Thank you for coming here this evening,' he said. 'I wanted to publicly express my anger at the way the police are investigating my beautiful son's disappearance. I have tried to talk to them about this, and wanted to speak at yesterday morning's press conference but they will not listen to me.'

This was his first lie. He would have been more than welcome but had ignored several calls and messages we had sent him asking him to attend.

'My son, Nicky, who is only three years old, has not been seen for a week now and instead of looking for him they are wasting valuable time trying to point the finger at me. I have no idea what is going on or why they don't seem to be mounting a nationwide search. Instead, they appear obsessed with trying to take the easy option. To pin it on the nearest person they can find.

'I have been nothing but open in my dealings with them.' Lie number two.

'All they have to do to confirm I have been nowhere near my ex-wife's house in the last week is to check my phone.'

Helen saw me pull a face. Lie number three.

'Lying bastard told us he'd lost it,' I growled as Groom continued with his bollocks.

'I also invited them to search my home. An offer they have yet to accept.'

I stopped counting.

'But I can assure everyone they will find no sign of my boy there. Why would I kidnap my own son?'

He lowered the paper and stepped forward, a clearly rehearsed move that saw a number of camera flashes from somewhere off screen. The enterprising TV cameraman closed in on his tear-stained face. Groom stared right into the lens.

'All I want is for my son to be safe and to be returned home to me. To that end I send a personal message to

Detective Chief Inspector Parker and his team. Please stop wasting your time on a vendetta against a terrified and deeply anxious father. Stop interrogating me and look for my son instead. I'm confident that if you would simply listen to me, I can help you find him.'

I suspected he was confident about lots of things. Not right, just confident. He moved even closer to the camera, as another tear squeezed out of the corner of his eye.

'My boy needs me. He's tiny and vulnerable. He will also be scared out of his wits and missing his dad.'

He paused for effect. I had no doubt we were in for a well-rehearsed punchline.

'If anything happens to my son, DCI Parker, it will be your fault and I will never forgive you.'

The screen went black. A voiceover said, 'If you have seen anything that may help the police, and Mr Groom, locate his missing son, please contact our helpline on 0191 4980111.

The TV channel cut back to its studio where the presenters were nervously shuffling around their papers. They knew there would be repercussions for allowing that outburst to go out. This was exactly why they rarely covered anything controversial live. Chancers like Evan Groom couldn't resist the opportunity to go too far.

'I see the wife barely got a mention, as per,' Helen said resignedly. She'd been a cop's wife for a long time and knew what would happen next. I turned around, already preparing my excuses, but I didn't need them.

'I guess that means you won't be staying after all.'

'I'm sorry.'

She sighed.

'At least, this time, you're leaving me for a woman who actually exists.'

## 29

*Three days earlier*

Maria stared out of the window at the sleeting rain. She hoped there'd be no problem with their flight, she couldn't wait to get out of this miserable country. It wasn't due to take off until 5 p.m. so hopefully the weather would have improved by then.

Nicky was still fast asleep in her bed. She didn't normally let him sleep with her but he'd been unsettled by the constant change in his surroundings so she'd caved for a bit of peace and quiet. In fact, she'd slept better than ever since they'd done their runner – more proof that it had been the right thing to do.

The drive up to their Airbnb in North Berwick had passed without incident though it took longer than normal as she'd stayed well within the speed limit and kept mostly on the back roads. Even though it wasn't her car Maria knew there was a small chance Sam would stitch her up when the shit hit the fan so she couldn't afford to trigger any cameras.

And she knew from watching all those fly-on-the-wall shows they could track the movement of cars on the bigger roads so she kept off the A1 as much as she could.

Nicky had barely noticed the damage to her face when she'd got him up at Sam's – she had no idea how egocentric little kids were until she had one – he'd just laughed and said that 'Mummy looks funny'. Obviously, Sam hadn't joined in the laughter. He'd handed over his car keys and told her that he hoped he'd never see her again.

They'd been holed up in their Airbnb for a day longer than Maria had hoped but she couldn't rush things. Having dumped her iPad and left her phone at home fearing they'd be able to trace it, she'd picked up a burner phone on the way but it didn't have internet capability. Fortunately, the local library had great access and she'd been able to dump Nicky in the kids' section with the picture books he loved while she sorted out their flights and some accommodation for when they landed.

Her escape had been so quick that she hadn't really thought about their final destination. But now she had her answer: Barcelona. She'd been there with Sara when they were teenagers and they'd had an absolute blast. Sadly the only direct flight the day before had been sold out when she tried to book it, hence the slight delay.

She knew she needed to get away before her disappearance was discovered as the police would probably contact the ports and airports straight away. It was tight as hell now but Evan wasn't due to pick up Nicky until that morning and she didn't think he'd raise the alarm straight away, if he turned up at all – he often didn't.

She'd been keeping a keen eye on the news but so far there'd been no mention of her disappearance. She knew it was only a matter of time before someone reported her missing. Rosie might be the one, being her usual nosy self, but more likely it would be Evan, when he didn't get his supposedly precious access – but by the time anyone took him seriously she should still be long gone.

The drive to Edinburgh airport was uneventful and she had no problems parking in the short-term car park. Poor Sam would get one hell of a bill when they eventually found his car.

Nicky had never flown before and he was getting increasingly excited about it, to the point of annoyance. 'Can I fly the plane, Mummy?' 'Will I see a spaceship when we're up in the sky, Mummy?' 'Where does the poo go when you flush the toilet, Mummy?' As they walked into the departure area she bought him a muffin from the Costa café there just to shut him up.

The agent on the check-in desk gave Nicky a big beaming smile as he tried to climb onto the baggage conveyor belt, scattering muffin crumbs all over it.

'I'm sure you'd rather be in the plane than the hold, young man,' she said, pushing him firmly back to the front of the counter.

'What's a hold?' Nicky said, but then he found a big chunk

of muffin caught up in his jumper and settled down on the floor to eat it, without waiting for an answer.

'Have you got your passports?' she asked Maria, still smiling broadly, though when she caught full sight of her barely concealed bruising the smile faded for a moment before returning. Maria wondered if the woman practised keeping it in place in the face of belligerent British travellers, trying hard to return the smile herself even though it wasn't her default position. Evan had endlessly harped on about her 'resting bitch face'.

'Oh,' the stewardess said, 'slight problem.'

'I know I look a little different. It's all cosmetic though. It's still me.' Maria returned her semi-fixed grin, hoping the reflection would win her over.

'It doesn't matter. That isn't the problem.'

'What is it then?'

'Your passport's out of date.'

'No, it isn't, I checked it earlier,' Maria protested. The expiry date isn't for another three and a half months.'

'True, but it was issued more than ten years ago.'

'And?'

'The rules changed recently. You're the third one today to get caught out. There is a warning on the website but you didn't fill in your advance passenger information form so you probably wouldn't have seen it. I'm afraid you can't travel until you renew your passport.'

'And how long will that take?'

'Normally it's three weeks but if you get to a passport office, I think you can pay extra to speed it up.'

'Is there a passport office in Edinburgh?'

'I'm afraid not. Glasgow is the nearest. And you'll need to make an appointment.'

'Fuck.'

'Fuck,' Nicky repeated. Somehow, he always picked up on the swears.

It took nearly two hours to reach Glasgow, another to find the passport office. She cursed Sam for not having satnav. Maybe she shouldn't have left her proper phone behind after all.

Dragging Nicky behind her, she walked in to find that, despite making an appointment, there was a queue of people in front of her. She plonked Nicky down in one of the chairs but he immediately started to wail. Thankfully there was a vending machine to the left of the reception where she managed to get some chocolate.

To her relief the queue moved quickly and within ten minutes there was only one person left in front of her, a large man who despite the weather outside, looked like he was already dressed for the beach, a matching blue T-shirt and shorts and a pair of sandals that showed off his bunions to hideous effect. Unfortunately, instead of sorting out his situation quickly, the man started to argue with the young woman behind the counter. And it was immediately bad news for Maria.

'A week! I can't wait a fucking week! My flight's taking off in four hours' time.'

'We do have a premium fast-track option which is quicker.'

'Of course you fucking do. How much do I have to fork out for that?'

'That will be £128.'

Maria smiled. That would be no problem.

'Christ, you people just love holding us to ransom, don't you? Sod it, I don't have much choice, do I? You'd better take Visa.'

The reception smiled. She was clearly used to the grief.

'That'll do nicely, sir. Your passport will be ready in two days' time.'

'Two fucking days! I can't wait two days. Didn't you hear me say my flight leaves tonight?'

Maria could feel herself nodding, glad that she was getting all of this second-hand as she'd have reacted the same way as the man in front of her – and drawn way too much attention to herself.

'Sadly, there's nothing I can do about that, sir. Would you like to arrange a fast-track passport or not?'

'There's nothing fucking fast about forty-eight hours.'

The receptionist's smile didn't even flicker.

'Is that a "yes"?' she said.

His howl of outrage made Maria step back a little. A security guard, who looked like he'd been carved from rock, appeared from nowhere.

'Do you need help, Janice?' he said.

'I don't know. Do I?' she asked the irate customer, who'd quietened down a little after seeing the size of the guard.

'No, lassie,' he said. 'You're fine. I'll take the fast-track.'

Good decision, Maria thought, and when it was her turn

she did the same. She now had forty-eight hours to wait before she could get away, which was cutting it fine. It was all in the lap of the gods now. If Evan kicked off about not getting his time with Nicky then there might be a problem but knowing him he'd be full of piss and vinegar but wouldn't do a damn thing. And she doubted he'd involve the police – not with his dodgy little sideline doing so well. She'd bet he wished she hadn't discovered what he was up to before they'd agreed on maintenance payments.

It was getting dark by the time they got out of the passport office so she found a low-rent hostel to kip down in where she could pay cash with no questions asked but, predictably, it was a dump so there was no way she was staying there a second night.

She needed somewhere to hide out for another thirty-six hours or so where no one would notice her. Or at least no one who would talk to the cops. Luckily, she knew just the place.

## 30

*7 November 2024*

Bob Curtis was on the warpath. He had made it clear when he was first promoted that our friendship ended at the door of the station; inside the building it was strictly business, especially when we weren't alone. The main target of his wrath this time, though, wasn't me, it was the other man in his office, our Press Office manager, Alan Gardner.

Curtis picked up a copy of that morning's *Evening Chronicle* and read out the opening paragraph in the snarkiest voice he could find.

"'Maria Groom and her son Nicky are still missing and the man leading the hunt for them doesn't have any idea where they are. Detective Chief Inspector Jack Parker is quite literally clueless.'"

I'd already seen it, of course, I'd caught the rest of the team giggling at the headline as I'd walked into the office that morning. *Inspector Clueless* practically filled up the entire front page. They must have used the biggest font they could find. It was accompanied by a photo of Maria and Nicky smiling at the camera, looking as wholesome as could be, and a small headshot of yours truly looking like I'd just got out of bed.

Bob hurled the paper at Alan who let it hit his chest and fall to the floor.

'This is down to you!' Bob yelled. 'What is the point of having a press officer if they don't know what's going on with the press? Why didn't you stop that interview going out? Don't you have any contacts at the TV station?'

To his credit, Alan didn't blink. He was always calmness personified, which probably came from his experience on the front line – he'd covered the Westminster beat in his previous life as a journalist so had to put up with entitled, arrogant politicians shouting the odds. This was probably a walk in the park in comparison.

'I knew about it at the same time you did,' he said, 'when Mr Groom appeared on screen.'

'Then you need to build more bridges,' Curtis said, a little less noisily, quickly realising he was being a bit of a twat. 'Make sure you tell them that if they ever pull a stunt like this again, they'll be off the press conference list for good.'

'Already done,' Alan said. 'In fact, I've gone one step further and withdrawn their privileges already. The BBC are delighted they'll now have exclusivity.'

Curtis turned his attention to me.

'And what about Groom? Does he have a point?'

'Not at all,' I said. 'He's just showboating. I get the impression he likes being in the limelight. Either that or he's got something to hide and is trying to get us to treat him with kid gloves. We're obviously exploring every avenue. But he and his ex-wife have a chequered history, and we wouldn't be doing the job properly if we weren't looking at him very closely – as you suggested, boss.'

He nodded, pacified by my note of respect. Bob and I were usually on first-name terms when we were alone but outside of that I knew how to play the game.

'Maria Groom has apparently had several tempestuous relationships in the past, though, so we're looking at some of her other previous partners as well, not just Groom.'

'What does your gut tell you?'

'Evan Groom's not a very nice man, that's for sure. He comes from a wealthy family – his late father made a lot of money in the property market – but Groom seems to have squandered most of it. Emma reckons he's deeply misogynistic – you should see the text messages he sent Maria – and until that press conference he'd barely expressed any concern for his son let alone his wife, who he didn't mention last night. One of Maria's old friends claims he wasn't much of a dad anyway. He's all about his own image, hence the grandstanding. Whether that makes him a murderer, or even a kidnapper, is another question. Leon's going to talk to him again this afternoon.'

'You should go with him. Read him the riot act. I don't want to see him shredding our reputation on TV again.'

'OK, I can do that. We should have finished checking all the CCTV footage in the area near the house today so hopefully we'll get something from that.'

'Forensics?'

'This afternoon, I hope. At least some of it. We found an old hairbrush in her bathroom so with a bit of luck we should at least be able to confirm whether the bloodstains in the house came from Maria or not. At the moment—'

My phone buzzed in my pocket.

'One moment, boss,' I said, pulling it out to check the caller. It was Leon. He knew I was in with Curtis so wouldn't call me if it wasn't urgent. I took the call.

'Make it quick,' I said.

'Sorry to interrupt, boss, but I knew you'd want to hear this. We've found Maria Groom's car.'

## 31

The car had been spotted by a sharp-eyed police community support officer. It was in Walkergate, to the east of the city centre, parked outside a house that had seen better days. Much better days, Leon thought, if the yellowing curtains in the only downstairs window and the peeling blue paint on the front door were any indication.

The PCSO hadn't attempted to talk to the occupant but he had spoken to a neighbour who'd confirmed that he had seen a man get out of the car and enter the house earlier that day, though he didn't know the man's name – it wasn't that kind of neighbourhood, apparently. The electoral register drew a blank too.

Leon and Emma stood either side of the car, peering through the filthy windows.

'See anything?' he said.

'There's an empty coffee cup in a holder between the seats and a CD case in the door pocket but that's about it,' Emma said. 'I don't think this thing's been cleaned since the old Queen died.'

'If ever,' Leon said. 'I can see a stain on the passenger's side. Could be blood, I guess, but could easily be from that coffee cup. We should get the CSIs to go over it.'

'D'you think?'

Leon stood up. Emma was staring at him over the roof of the car.

'Are you still mad at me?' She'd barely spoken to him for days.

'Hey, you're on fire today. That's two for two.'

'Because of the other night?'

'Boom. Three for three. You're smoking.'

'I said I was sorry.'

'You made me look a right twat. Chambers clearly thought I'd set up the road block. You should have at least warned me.'

'I realise that now. It was a spur of the moment decision. Once you'd gone back to Connors' house I knew there was a good chance Chambers would be driving you home. It seemed a good way to get his DNA without raising any alarms. Jack gave me the go-ahead so I called in a quick favour from a black rat I know.'

Leon saw Emma's frown and realised she had no idea what a black rat was. That was one of the troubles with fast-trackers, they hadn't learned the lingo.

'It's slang for traffic cop,' he said.

'Like I give a shit. What I do know is that if it isn't Chambers, we're screwed. I probably won't get another chance to find out what Connors knows.'

'Well, I can't say I'm entirely sad about that.' Leon tried to bite his tongue but failed. 'You looked like you were having a nice time in the restaurant.'

'I was. The food was great.'

'And the company?'

'He's very easy on the eye.' Emma laughed. 'Look at your face. You're like a kid who's been told his goldfish has died.'

'No. I'm like a man whose girlfriend has just been on a date with a gangster which she enjoyed a little bit too much.'

'It wasn't a date.'

'But you did enjoy it.'

Emma sighed. 'I've had enough of this bollocks. Are we going to talk to this guy or what?'

'Fill your boots,' Leon said.

She turned and walked up the path, Leon swallowed his anger and followed her. He was still a few feet behind when she knocked on the door so he had a better view of the front window than she did and saw the yellowing net curtains twitch.

'You're being watched,' he said, nodding towards the window.

Emma, to her credit, didn't look over; instead she knocked again.

No answer. She waited another few moments and knocked a third time. Leon tried the gate at the side of the house which led to the back garden. It opened, and the minute it did he heard shouting from the back of the house.

'He's done a runner,' he said, charging through the gateway. As he turned the corner he saw a half-naked man, wearing pyjama bottoms, pinned to the ground by Sid Allan, who had been sent round the back for exactly that eventuality. The runner was wriggling around like a maggot on a hot plate and Sid was struggling to keep a grip on him.

'Give us a hand, Leon, he's sweating like a pig. Stinks as well.'

Leon laughed and as Emma caught up with him she joined in.

Sid looked like he was trying to ride one of those bucking bulls you used to get in the wilder pubs like Buffalo Joe's, where pissed students would attempt to stay on for a cash prize. Clearly the young cop had never been one of those wannabe cowboys as he suddenly flipped to one side when his slippery charge shrugged him off.

'Shit,' Leon said, as the man leapt to his feet and ran for the back gate. Leon was too quick for him though, grabbing him by his left arm before he could escape. The man swung round quickly and caught Leon with a wild right hook that made his ears ring. He kept a firm grip until another punch caught him in the same spot.

As he fell to the ground Leon heard Emma shout, 'One more step and I'll use this.' He glanced up and saw her pointing a Taser at his assailant. He was surprised as he knew she didn't carry one. Sid Allan, however, did and the look of shame on his face told its own story; he must have dropped it in the fight.

Emma pressed the trigger gently and the electric charge arced between the two contacts. That warning sign was more than enough for the man in the pyjama bottoms.

He sank to his knees and put his hands on his head. Leon breathed a sigh of relief – if she'd actually used it on him without having done the training it would have caused a heap of trouble. Turned out he had an even better reason to be grateful.

'I wouldn't shoot if I were you, pet,' the man said. 'The last time someone zapped me with one of those I shat myself.'

The pyjama-clad man was a certain Vic Kendall. Sid Allan, who'd gone back to the station to clean himself up, had previous with Kendall, having nicked him for being drunk and disorderly just a couple of months earlier.

They took him back into the house where a quick check showed he was a regular offender, minor league stuff, some shoplifting and a bit of trespass. He'd once been found fast asleep in a pub bar when the live-in landlord came down in the morning. Vic had hidden in the loo at closing time and then come out and drunk himself into a stupor through the night. He'd never done jail time but there were several fines outstanding and judging by the pile of red bills stacked up inside his front door he probably had no intention of paying them.

Vic was surprisingly chatty under the circumstances.

'If this is about the betting shop thing, I can explain,' he said, before they'd even asked him a question.

'What betting shop thing?' Leon said.

Vic grinned. 'Nothing. Pretend you never heard that. It's that lying sod in the corner shop then. You can't believe a word he says, black bast—' He stopped, abruptly, clearly realising that a bit of blatant racism wasn't going to win Leon over any time soon.

'Black what?' Leon asked.

'Nothing,' he said again. 'I misspoke.'

'What did you mean to say?' Emma said.

'You can't catch me out like that, love, I'm not that stupid.'

'The jury's out on that, dipshit. And, to be clear, call me "love" again and I'll light your balls up like a Christmas tree,' she said, squeezing the Taser's trigger again. Vic flinched at the flicker of light she produced.

'Sure thing, Chief. Is Chief OK?'

Emma pretended to think about it.

'It'll do fine. How do you know Maria Groom?'

'Maria who?'

'Groom. Like at a wedding.'

'I wouldn't knaa about that. I'm not married.'

'I'm astonished.'

'You're quite mean, you, aren't you? Anyways, I've never heard of her.'

'Then whose is that car outside?'

'Which one?'

'The Ford Fiesta.'

'Not the foggiest.'

'Your neighbour saw you driving it.'

'Not me.'

'OK,' Leon said. 'Let's take him down to the station. Grill him properly.'

'Hey, no need for that,' Vic said. 'But one good turn and that. What's it worth to tell you where I found the car?'

Leon leant forward, resisting the urge to pull a face at the man's hideous body odour.

'We might not arrest you.'

'For what?'

'Resisting arrest. Assaulting a policeman . . .'

'I didn't knaa you were polis. I thought you was robbers.'

'PC Allan was in uniform.'

'Could have been a clever disguise.'

The man was incorrigible.

'Car theft then.'

'I just telt ya. I didn't steal it. I found it.'

'When was this?'

'About a week ago, I reckon.'

'Can't you be more precise?'

'Perhaps. I'll check my appointments diary.' He grinned at Emma, though the image was spoiled by the many gaps in his teeth.

'Where?'

'In a car park. Near Walkergate Metro.'

'But you didn't steal it.'

'No. The door was open and the keys were in the ignition. So I borrowed it.'

Emma laughed. 'It's a car, not a library book. When were you going to return it?'

'Today, probably. I'll be glad to get rid. Piece of shit anyway. Barely got any gas left in it and I'm not paying good money to top up someone else's tank.'

'OK, we'll need you to come down to the station with us

and make a statement about all this. And you know we'll be checking CCTV, don't you?'

'Good luck with that. The kids round here love nowt more than lobbing rocks at the cameras. If it was an Olympic sport there'd be gold medals all round.'

As they escorted Kendall out the front door, Leon picked up a couple of the bills on the floor.

'Hold on a second. Who's Mrs D. Flowers?'

Kendall hesitated a moment too long.

'She's my auntie, on my mother's side.'

'What does the D stand for?'

'You what?'

'What's Mrs Flowers' Christian name?'

More hesitation.

'You don't know it, do you?'

'Course I do. She's my auntie.'

'And?'

'Doreen, isn't it! Auntie Doreen.'

'So why is this addressed to Deborah?'

'Must be a mistake. 'Appens all the time now the computers have taken over.'

'This isn't your house, is it?'

'No. I never said it was. It's my auntie's.'

'Doreen.'

'Yes. No. Deborah.'

'Where is this auntie of yours then?'

'On holiday. I'm housesitting.'

'Of course you are, Vic. Fine upstanding lad like you – who

wouldn't want you to look after their home? What have you done with her?'

'What! Nothing.'

'I'll look around upstairs,' Emma said.

Leon took Kendall into the living room and sat him on the sofa.

'Looks like you're in a lot more trouble than for just nicking a car, Vic.'

'It's not what you think.'

'What is it then?'

'I just wanted a roof over my head for a change. I'm not doing any harm.'

'I'll be the judge of that.'

'Look, my mate's a taxi driver and he took the woman to the station a few weeks back. She was going to look after her sister down south somewhere for a month or two. It's amazing what people will tell a cabby once they've got chatting.'

'And you thought you'd do her a solid by looking after the place?'

Kendall smiled. 'Aye, that's right. Be a shame to leave the place empty, wouldn't it? There's a lot of scallies round here who'd have all the woman's furniture away if I hadn't stepped in. Mind you, I had to tidy it up a bit first. Place was a right tip.'

## 32

Good news had been rare lately but maybe my luck was changing. A call from the consultant confirmed that I had a place on the drug trial. I would have to attend the clinic once a month for about an hour each time. I could manage that without having to explain any prolonged absences. Though it was possible there could be some short-term side effects from the sessions, dizziness perhaps, he assured me that I should be able to work around it easily.

There was a downside though and one which I hadn't anticipated. The trial was to last eighteen months. There was no way Helen would wait that long for me to make my mind up about returning home. I was going to have to bite the bullet and make a decision.

While I was still thinking about that Leon returned to the station with the guy who'd been driving around in Maria Groom's car. Sadly, it looked like he'd had nothing to do with her disappearance but we decided to let him stew in the cells for a bit while his story was checked out and the CSIs had a good look at the car. Which gave us the perfect window to renew our acquaintance with the newly-minted star of the local TV news, Evan Groom.

Groom was sitting in the club bar at Close House, a luxurious golf course in the Tyne Valley, about twenty minutes from the city. He was nursing what looked like a large gin and tonic. It was a step up from the station's interview rooms and even though it was a cold morning the winter sun was streaming through the large glass windows as we sat opposite him. Normally we'd have dragged him down to the station but Bob Curtis's political antennae had been twitchy about that – he didn't want any more bad publicity – so we'd let him choose the venue.

Groom had taken advantage of his local knowledge to position himself with his back to the window, which meant the sun was in our eyes from the minute Leon and I sat down. I suspected that was deliberate.

'Nice of you to join me, gentlemen,' he said. He looked remarkably relaxed. Either he had nothing to do with his ex-wife and child's disappearance or he was arrogant to the point of complacency. Or, despite the earliness of the hour, that wasn't his first G and T.

'There are worse places to carry out a vendetta,' I said, pointedly referencing his comments on the TV.

'Exaggeration for effect,' Groom said. 'I assume you're Detective Chief Inspector Parker? I don't think you introduced yourself to me the other morning, you were too busy telling me off. It's amazing how a little bit of bad publicity can change people's attitudes, isn't it?'

'I wouldn't recommend pulling a stunt like that again.'

'Noted, Chief Inspector. Got you here though, didn't it?'

'As you know, we'd already been trying to talk to you anyway. Apparently, you were too busy, no doubt preparing for your performance on the telly last night.'

'Well, you're here now.'

'Pretend I'm not. I'm just observing. Detective Sergeant Johnson is leading the interview.'

Groom turned to look at Leon.

'Keeping an eye on you, is he?'

Leon ignored him. I didn't blame him, it was clear the man was a wind-up merchant and wanted to provoke a response.

'I have to say I'm disappointed that I'm still getting the monkey rather than the organ grinder,' Groom added. There was a stunned silence around the table and Groom's mouth opened in horror as he realised what he'd just said.

'I apologise, Detective Sergeant, that wasn't intended the way it seemed. I don't have a racist bone in my body, I can assure you.'

'You'd be surprised how often I hear that, Mr Groom. But I'll give you the benefit of the doubt for now. Anyway, monkey is so last year where racial insults are concerned. But if you start using the "n" word, you and I are really going to fall out.'

Groom bristled a little. 'If this is going to be adversarial, perhaps I should have a solicitor present?'

'It's not necessary at this stage. But if you have one to hand that's fine.'

Groom looked around and pointed out of the window.

'That's him, over there, in the blue Argyle jumper, practising on the putting green. Shall I give him a shout?'

I recognised Reggie Taylor, one of the more capable briefs around, his lawyering a lot better than his golf if his latest putt was anything to go by.

'Entirely up to you, sir,' Leon said. 'Though it looks like he might need the practice.'

Groom smiled. 'Let's leave him for now and get on, shall we?' he said, sighing. 'I was rather hoping to renew acquaintances with the bonny lass I chatted to a couple of days ago. I wouldn't kick her out of bed for eating crisps.'

Leon made a note on his pad. I couldn't read it but could tell by how hard he was pressing down that he was already irritated. His body language radiated the same emotion. Groom completely failed to read the room.

'I bet she goes like a steam train, eh!'

Leon's pencil snapped but Groom continued, obliviously.

'Did she miss something? Is that why I've got the A team this time? Women, eh?'

'Detective Sergeant Steel is a highly competent officer,' Leon growled. 'I'm just here to follow up on a couple of things.'

'And I'm happy to assist your enquiries. Anything that will help you find my son.'

'And your wife.'

'Ex-wife. But yes, of course, Maria too. I'm worried about both of them.'

'But you have no idea where they might be?'

'None at all. Though . . .'

Groom pretended to be thinking about something but he was a lousy actor, he clearly had a seed he wanted to plant.

'Any information you have would be very valuable, I'm sure,' Leon said.

'OK. I don't like to badmouth anyone but Maria used to be a right slapper, different bloke every week. Probably still has but you should check out some of her exes. Especially the last one. Very weird fella.'

'Aren't you her last ex?' Leon said. Groom laughed.

'The one before me. Sam Gallagher. I told your girl about him the other day but I'm not sure she was paying attention. Really fancied himself. He couldn't accept that she dumped him for me. I had to chase him away from the house a couple of times back in the day.'

'We're already planning to talk to Mr Gallagher,' Leon said, deftly sidestepping the fact that he'd done a runner the first time we'd tried. 'Did Maria have any other friends you think might be involved in her disappearance?'

'How long have you got?' Groom asked. 'Most of her "friends" were men and most of them had been there, if you get my drift. She wasn't great at shaking off old boyfriends. Couldn't say "no", I guess.'

His repeated use of finger quotes was irritating the hell out of me but I did my best to hide it.

'Do you remember any of their names?' Leon asked.

'There was a delivery driver. Rob something.' Groom looked down at his feet for a moment. 'Gibson, I think, Rob Gibson. I never met the man but he was an old schoolfriend, bit of a hanger-on. They went way back, I remember. One of those old friendships that somehow drifted into a relationship that one of them quickly regretted. Or at least that's the impression Maria gave me. I think he had drug issues.'

'Drug issues?'

'Aye, I mean Maria likes to dabble a bit—'

I jumped in. 'Are you saying your ex-wife is a drug user?'

'Nothing heavy, just a bit of weed occasionally.'

'Did you bring that up in your custody battle?'

He looked a little sheepish and shook his head.

'No. Too much of a gentleman, I suppose. I'm kicking myself for it now.'

I didn't believe a word of it. I suspected she wasn't the only one in their relationship who 'dabbled' so he hadn't wanted to open up that particular can of worms.

'But I think Gibson's habits were a bit more hardcore, acid and that,' he added. 'Feel a bit sorry for him now, truth be told; sounded like he was a nice guy apart from that. Maria has a habit of dropping her men without any warning. She even did it to me, if you can believe that!'

'Strangely, I don't actually find it that hard,' Leon said, without a flicker of a smile. I couldn't help thinking that he was now enjoying the rally, and it was probably advantage Leon.

'Touché,' Groom said. Another pet hate of mine. He deserved locking up just for that.

'Any idea where we'd find Gibson?' I asked.

'Not a clue.'

'OK, thanks, Mr Groom,' Leon said. 'We'll look into both

of those two men. In the meantime, you told DS Steel that you would provide a more detailed account of your movements over the last week. Do you have that handy?'

For the first time Groom looked rattled.

'Ah, sorry, I'd forgotten about that.'

'But I understand from your TV interview that you've now found your phone?'

'Ah, little white lie, I'm afraid.'

'Do you lie a lot, Mr Groom?'

'No.'

'So you haven't found it after all?'

'I'm afraid not, been a little busy lately.'

'Doing what?'

'I'm not sure that's any of your business.' Leon's cold stare prompted him to continue waffling. 'This and that,' he added.

'Perhaps if you didn't do so many television interviews you could find the time to do something that might actually help us find your wife and child,' Leon said. 'Try and get us that timetable by tomorrow, would you?'

I suspected we'd be waiting a lot longer than that. Groom had something to hide, though whether it concerned his ex-wife and child I wasn't sure.

As we stood up, Groom caught my eye. 'Well, Mr Observer, how did he do?' he asked, nodding at Leon.

'A lot better than you,' I said.

We were about to get back in the car when Emma rang me.

'Where are you?' she said.

'Just finished with Groom. We'll be back in half an hour.'

'You might want to bring him with you,' she said. 'The CSIs have found something in the car that puts him right in the frame.'

## 33

'I'm arresting you on suspicion of the kidnapping of Maria Groom. You do not have to say anything. But, it may harm your defence if you do not mention when questioned something which you later rely on in court. Anything you do say may be given in evidence.'

Evan Groom's face was a picture as Leon read him his rights, somehow keeping the smile off his own face. Groom had laughed when we'd walked back into the clubhouse as he was raising a glass with his solicitor, thinking we'd forgotten something. He wasn't laughing now.

Reggie Taylor looked equally shocked. The bottle of Champagne the two men had just opened was going to be extremely flat by the time we'd finished with them. Ignoring Groom's protests and the solicitor's instruction to him to keep his mouth shut, we escorted him down the steps of the clubhouse and bundled him into the back of the car.

As we pulled away I saw Reggie throwing his clubs into the boot and getting into his Bentley to follow us. Somewhat surprisingly, Groom had finally decided to take the man's advice and didn't say a word to us on the journey back to the station. If he'd known that Emma had already got a warrant to search his house I suspect he'd have been a little more vocal.

It was no skin off my nose. He'd be singing like a canary pretty soon, I was sure of that. We'd let him sweat for a while once we'd got him locked up, waiting to see if Emma found anything incriminating at his home. The evidence that the CSIs had found in his ex-wife's car was pretty damning though.

It would take a while to confirm that the bloodstains they had found on the passenger seat were from Maria Groom – forensic results weren't quite that quick – but I had little doubt they would be. Not just because it was her car but because I believed that whoever had sat in that seat had managed to send us a message, written in their own blood, on the underside of the glove compartment. It was a little ragged, clearly due to the duress they were under, but nevertheless it was readable.

It said: IT WAS EVAN.

## 34

Emma stood back from the doorway as Sid Allan and his fellow PC Tim Carmichael smashed through Evan Groom's front door with a battering ram. She wished the man himself had been there to see it – he wouldn't be quite so cocky now.

As soon as the entrance was clear she walked into the house with DC Clive Andrews close behind.

'I'll stay down here, you check upstairs,' she said, heading straight into the lounge. The place looked as clean as a whistle. Not so much as an empty coffee cup on the table. All a little anodyne for her taste, more like a show home than an actual home.

She wandered through another door into the kitchen. Again, the thing that stood out was its sterility. There was no sign of any disturbance. Almost as if it had been thoroughly cleaned up recently. No one is this tidy, she thought. She opened the fridge door. Aside from a bottle of gin, a carton of milk and a couple of lemons, it was empty. Did the man never eat?

'All clear upstairs,' Clive said, as he appeared in the doorway. 'It's spotless. The main bedroom looks more like a hotel room. Even the pillowcases look freshly laundered and pressed – looks like he's had some deep cleaning done to me.'

'Same down here,' she said. 'He's either a neatness freak or something's happened in here that he's had to hide. Or maybe he spends most of his time somewhere else – like stalking his ex in her back garden.'

A door to the side led into a double garage. Groom's car was still at the golf course, she guessed, so it was relatively empty. There was a workbench at the back of the garage but nothing on top of it. To the side there was a lawn mower and a handful of gardening tools but little else. She walked across to check out the tools but it looked like they were fresh out of the box. Emma doubted they'd ever been used. He probably paid a gardener who brought his own equipment.

As she went to move away she noticed something under the bench, tucked behind one of the legs in the far corner, right up against the wall. She bent down but couldn't quite see what it was and it was too far away to reach.

'There's something at the back, Clive,' she said. 'Be a love and scuttle under there, will you? Don't want to bugger up my tights. Stick some gloves on first though, just in case.'

Clive laughed. 'No bother. But if I screw up my back again you can pay for the physio.'

Clive pulled out a pair of disposable gloves, and put them on, got down on his hands and knees and crawled under the bench, reversing back up as soon as he had hold of the object.

'Bingo,' he said, as he stood up holding out the find with a big grin on his face. It was a lady's white, high-heeled shoe, with what appeared to be a bloodstain on the toe.

35

If it ain't broke don't fix it was one of those rare maxims that I concurred with. Evan Groom had so clearly hated being questioned by Emma the first time that it was a no-brainer to let her have another go.

And she was doing a great job of pressing his buttons a second time. He already looked like he wanted to rip her head off. It was almost fun to watch and I was glad I'd decided to take a rare seat alongside her for the interview. I'd been keen to see his reactions first-hand.

'Why do you keep asking me the same fucking questions over and over again? I told you before, I hadn't been to Maria's since the last time I dropped Nicky off there.'

Reggie Taylor tapped him on the arm and leant in to counsel him. I was sure his brief was telling him to 'calm down'. Those hours spent in a cell had wound him up nicely.

'OK, thank you, Mr Groom,' Emma said, smiling sweetly at him. I could tell how much she was enjoying provoking him – and I had no doubts that Groom could too but he couldn't control himself. 'And what about the last time she came to your place? When exactly was that?'

'For God's sake,' Groom said, to Reggie's obvious dismay. 'Another stupid question. She's never been to my house. The lazy cow rarely gets off her fat arse. Always makes me do the fetching and carrying. I have to collect Nicky and bring him back.'

'Right. And what about your other lady friends? How many of them have stayed at your house recently?'

'Quite a few, actually. Most women are very happy to spend time with me.'

'I'm sure they are,' Emma said. 'Big man like you. So no specific girlfriend at the moment we could talk to?'

Groom hesitated, blinked a little. I could sense a nervousness that hadn't been there before. I made a mental note to add a search for the man's former girlfriends to our actions. Then he seemed to pull himself together and a smile crossed his lips.

'No. It wouldn't seem fair for one woman to get all the attention. I could put you on the waiting list if you like?'

'I think I'll pass,' Emma said.

'Where are you going with this, Detective Sergeant?' Reggie asked. 'It appears to me that you're simply trying to provoke my client.'

I gave him a look which told him to wind his neck in. We both knew it was part of the game.

'I'm just wondering whose this might be?' Emma said, pushing a photo of the woman's shoe she'd found in Groom's garage across the table.

Groom grabbed it. His brow furrowed in confusion.

'A shoe? What is this? *Cinderella?*' He laughed at his own sorry wit. 'Who do you think I am – Prince Charming?'

Emma shook her head, clearly wondering what planet the guy was on. She pushed the photo closer to him.

'Do you recognise it?'

'Of course I bloody don't! Where did you find it?' Groom said.

'In your garage.'

'Bollocks,' he said. 'I've never seen it before in my life. And no woman's ever set foot in there.'

'Maybe you carried them in,' Emma muttered quietly.

'What the fuck are you implying?'

Another arm tap from his brief and a whispered consultation. I took the chance to quietly tell Emma to ease off a bit and move on. I knew she was trying to tip him over the edge but that last comment had been a little too much and wouldn't look good on the transcript. If Reggie hadn't been more concerned with calming his client down, he would have challenged her.

'Let's move on, shall we?' she said, taking my lead. 'When's the last time you were in your wife's car?'

'Not for a very long time. We've been apart for more than three years.'

'So you won't have seen this then?'

She pushed another photo across the desk.

Groom glanced down then did a double-take.

'What the fuck is this?'

It was a photo of the underside of the glove compartment. With the words IT WAS EVAN clearly visible.

'It's a message written in blood. Probably Maria's blood.'

Groom was shaking his head and I could hear his foot tap-tap-tapping on the floor. He was rattled. He screwed up the photo and threw it across the floor before glaring at Emma.

'One of you bitches is trying to set me up,' he growled. 'I can't decide if it's you or Maria.' He started to get to his feet but his brief put his hand on his client's shoulder and forced him back into his chair.

'I'd like to consult with my client in private, please,' Reggie said.

## 36

Evan Groom didn't say another word that evening aside from 'no comment' despite us stressing how important it was to find his ex-wife and son quickly, so, much to his irritation, he'd been packed off to the cell block. An uncomfortable night's sleep might well loosen his tongue.

I sent the team home, urging them to get some much-needed rest before we had another go at him the next morning.

Unlike Groom I'd, ironically, decided to start talking. Having discovered how long the drugs trial would go on for, I realised it was time for me to finally have that much-rehearsed conversation with Helen.

This time she knew I was coming for dinner, but she wasn't expecting the bag at my feet. Helen looked down at it for longer than normal then looked back up.

'Really?' she said, with a half-smile.

'It depends.'

'On what?'

'I have a proposal.'

'Well let's hope it goes as well as your first one.'

When I'd asked Helen for her hand in marriage all those years ago she'd put me out of my misery quickly, saying 'yes' before I'd got past 'Will you—' She wasn't psychic or anything, I was already kneeling down with a ring box in my hand. I didn't think it would be that easy this time.

'Let's eat first,' I said.

Aidan joined us for dinner; a simple chicken cacciatore. It wasn't one of her normal repertoire so I knew that our son had told her all about my new lifestyle. My consultant had suggested a Mediterranean diet might help slow down my condition and I was doing my best to stick to it. My own shop-bought ready meals weren't at her level though. It was delicious. I really hoped that this would become the norm again.

'Shall we talk?' I said, once we'd finished and I'd loaded the dishwasher – which always used to be my job . . . before. Aidan immediately got up from the table to head upstairs. 'No, you too, son, this involves you as well.'

They both looked concerned but I tried to lighten things.

'Don't look so worried, it might never happen.'

'It already has, Dad, hasn't it?'

I reached across the table and took Aidan's hand.

'I'm ready to move back in,' I said. 'I just need to make sure we're all on the same page. Let me say a few things first and try not to interrupt because it's taken me way too long to have this conversation. If I stop I might lose my nerve and we'll be back to square one.'

Aidan looked at Helen who nodded. I carried on. I'd tried

this out on Phillip on my way over and, with a couple of tweaks, he'd approved so I was feeling hopeful.

'I've let my fear of what's happening in my head interfere with enjoying the here and now. When I left I was so focused on how this will end that I forgot about the rest. I wanted to exert some kind of control over events but that was wrong-headed. You know I'm doing everything I can to slow this thing down to buy more time but I've realised that I've also got to make the most of each extra moment with you both too.'

I squeezed Aidan's hand and got a glimmer of a smile from him. I suspected he would be the hardest nut to crack still.

'However, I can only do that if I know for sure that I won't end up hurting both of you in the long run. So I need certain guarantees.'

Despite my earlier plea, Helen interrupted my flow.

'Why do I feel I'm not going to like this?'

'Just hear me out, love, I've spent a lot of time thinking about this. Too much, if the truth be told, it's been getting in the way of everything else.

'The fact is that at some stage this disease is going to start erasing me. Bit by bit. And for a while – maybe even years – that will be fine, there will still be enough Jack left for everyone, including me. But at some point I'll tip over the edge – I won't be me any more.'

'You'll still be my dad though,' Aidan said. 'And you're the only one I've got.'

'You're right, son. But I won't be the kind of dad you need. I'll be more of a burden than a bonus. The best way to think about it is that it's not about quantity of life but quality. I've accepted that my life isn't going to be as long as I would have hoped. But as long as the quality is right that's fine – it's when the quality drops that the problems start, and I'm not just talking about my life but yours. Someone described Alzheimer's as "coming to take your soul" and I think that's spot on.'

'But how do you know when that will happen?' Helen said. 'It's so arbitrary.'

'But it doesn't have to be. That's why I've written this,' I said, pulling a folder out of my bag. 'It's my Advance Decisions. It lays out the conditions that I think will be unbearable for me, where I won't be Jack any more. The outside will look the same but the man inside will be gone.' I put the folder on the table. 'This outlines the way I'd like to handle it when that's the situation. I know this seems premature but I had to get this down on paper now as one day I simply won't be able to and by then it will be too late.'

'But what about what *we* want?' Aidan said.

'I know what you want, Aidan, you want to keep me alive. But there are circumstances where I don't think that's the best thing for any of us.'

They were both frowning but Helen spoke first.

'Give me an example.'

'I think it would be better for you to read it. Together. Take your time over it. I'll go into the front room while you do. I can answer any questions after that. Then, if you're OK with all of this and you're prepared to sign it, I'll stay. If not, at least I tried.'

Neither of them looked convinced.

## 37

## JACK WILLIAM PARKER – ADVANCE DECISIONS

*There will come a time when I am no longer a competent, rational, loving man capable of making my own decisions. There could be many signs of this. I may not be aware of my surroundings, unsure of where I am, or unable to be allowed out on my own for fear of getting lost. I may not always, or possibly ever, recognise my family and friends. I may not remember who is dead or alive, mistaking one friend or relative for another long gone. I may not be able to carry out simple tasks like dressing myself or taking care of my personal hygiene. I may become over-emotional, unnecessarily agitated or even violent. I may even experience hallucinations and become delusional.*

*This is not the man I want to be.*

*When any of those symptoms are displayed I want you to let me go. I don't wish to be a burden to you when I am no longer the real Jack, when the core of me, the inside man, has disappeared. Please do not confuse that version of me with the one that you love now. That man will be long gone.*

## Medical Care

*When my condition starts to worsen in any of the ways I have indicated above, I don't want medical treatment for anything that is related to my Alzheimer's Disease:*

- *No hospital treatment*
- *No care home*
- *No care AT home by either visiting nurses/doctors or my family*
- *I don't want to be put on a respirator for breathing difficulties*
- *No feeding tubes if I am struggling to swallow*
- *No hydration*
- *I do not want to be resuscitated if my heart stops*

*To be clear, when the effects of this disease worsen I don't want to go into care. Nor do I want anyone in my family to become my carer. I don't want anyone to have to watch me 24/7 because they're worried I'll walk off and never find my way back. I don't want to be fed through a tube if I can't eat properly. I don't want to be a burden to anyone.*

*When the time comes that any of those are likely, I want to end my life. Ideally, I'd like that to happen with my family near me. Sadly, that's not currently possible in this country. Maybe it will be in the future. If not, then I have joined Dignitas who will assist me to leave this world peacefully, though I would have to go to Switzerland. When that time comes, I'd like my wife and son to accompany me, if that's what they want.*

I checked my watch. It had been twenty minutes since I'd left the kitchen. After about ten of those I'd heard a low buzz of conversation which was still going on.

'No.' Aidan's voice. A shout. I heard a crash, maybe a chair hitting the floor, then the sound of a door flying open as someone ran up the stairs. I had no doubt it was my son, I'd been sure he would find it too difficult, I just hoped Helen would get it. Still I waited. A few minutes later the living room door slowly opened and Helen walked in holding the folder. She'd clearly been crying.

I stood up and pulled her in for a hug.

'I'm sorry to put you through this,' I said.

'It's not your fault,' she said.

I held her, terrified that this wasn't going to go the way I wanted it to. Eventually I couldn't wait any longer. I stepped back to give her some room, taking her hands as I did.

'Well,' I said. 'What do you think?'

'OK,' she said.

'You're sure?'

'I've signed it.'

'I didn't think you would.'

She shrugged. 'If it's the only way to get you back here . . .'

'You know there's a small chance you could get prosecuted if you go to Switzerland with me? It's ridiculous but sometimes the law is an ass.'

Helen smiled. 'That's the first time I've ever heard you say that. You've always been a "letter of the law" kind of guy.'

'Maybe I'm starting to see the light.'

'It's about time.'

'Seriously, that doesn't worry you?'

'I hope it won't come to that.'

I was pretty sure it would but I quit while I was ahead.

'No other questions?'

She shook her head. 'It's pretty self-explanatory.'

'What about Aidan?'

Her hesitation seemed endless.

'He'll come round,' she said, eventually.

## 38

*8 November 2024*

*Give your nephew a start? (5,8)*

I was completely disorientated when I woke, sitting up immediately my eyes opened. Where the hell was I? Then I saw Helen's dressing gown on the back of the door. I was home again. I hadn't slept in that bedroom in almost six months.

The house was very quiet. I checked my watch: 8.30 a.m. Helen would have already gone to work, probably dropping Aidan off on the way. I went downstairs to make a cup of tea. To my surprise I saw Aidan standing in the yard in his school uniform, smoking. He had his back to me so had no idea I was there.

I yanked the back door open.

'What the hell, Aidan?'

He swung around quickly, desperately trying to hide the cigarette.

'Since when have you been a smoker?' I said, angrily.

'I didn't know you were still here.'

'That's not what I asked.'

'Since my dad left home, if you must know.'

It was like having a bucket of cold water thrown over me.

'Does your mam know?' I asked quietly.

'No. Well, not really. She caught me once but I promised it was a one-off. Please don't tell her, she'd go crackers.'

'I won't, but it stops now. OK?'

He looked like he wanted to protest but eventually he nodded, dropped the cigarette on the ground and stubbed it out with his foot.

'You'd better get rid of the evidence if you don't want your mam to know.'

He picked it up and grumpily threw it over the back wall. It wasn't quite what I'd meant but I'd given him enough grief for my first morning back in the house.

'Now hand the rest over and get yourself to school.'

He reluctantly pulled a packet out of his blazer pocket and tossed it over to me before turning and leaving through the back gate.

I went back into the house and finally got my morning cuppa. The newspaper was lying on the kitchen table, the crossword half completed. Maybe Helen and I could do them together from now on?

I picked it up and scanned the gaps, wondering if she'd mind if I finished it off. One down looked the most likely, two words, the second beginning with an R and ending with an N. It mentioned a nephew in the clue so it looked like *Relation* to me. I found a pen and filled it in just as my phone rang. It was Leon.

'Where are you, Jack? I've been sitting outside for five minutes.'

Shit. I'd forgotten he was picking me up.

'Whoops,' I said, 'my bad. I'm at home, my old home.'

'Oh, right. You moved back in?'

'I think so,' I said. 'One day at a time, I guess.'

'Glad to hear it. I never understood why you guys split up in the first place. You'll not do better than Helen.'

'You saying I'm punching?'

He laughed. 'I would never be so bold ... but aye, I am. I'll pick you up in five. Have another go at Groom, eh! I'm sure he'll crack this time.' He ended the call.

I hoped he was right; that a night in the cell would have made our prime suspect realise what a bad position he was in. Hopefully he'd be a bit more forthcoming this time around.

Before I could return to the crossword my phone rang again. It was Laura's dad, Gordon. After her funeral I'd rashly promised him I would find his daughter's killer but had signally failed to do so. I couldn't ignore his call.

'Hi, Gordon. How are you holding up?'

'As well as can be expected.'

'And Liz?'

His silence spoke volumes. Their daughter's death had sent his wife spiralling into the depths of depression and she'd not come out of it. I knew that she'd barely left the house since.

'Much the same,' he said, eventually.

'These things take time.' We both knew I was spouting empty platitudes but Gordon was kind enough not to say so.

'I'm sorry to bother you again, Jack.'

'It's never a bother, Gordon, I should have kept you in the loop.'

'Nonsense, lad, I know how busy you are. I saw you on the telly the other day.'

'Aye, it's non-stop. That doesn't mean I have forgotten Laura though.'

'I never thought you had, son. Any news?'

Should I mention Micky Chambers? Not by name, obviously, I didn't want a vigilante situation on my hands – but the man needed some hope.

'Maybe. We've got a new lead on a possible suspect. I should know something concrete within a day or two.'

'I knew you wouldn't let me down, Jack. It would be lovely if you could pop round sometime. It always cheers Liz up.'

It was his turn to lie. The last time I'd been there she'd stayed in bed and the time before that she'd been practically catatonic.

'I'll see what I can do,' I said.

'You're a good man, Jack.'

He ended the call.

His faith in me was misplaced. I'd kept much of what I'd found from him. Primarily because it would break his heart again if he knew that he was partially responsible for his daughter's death. Many years before, he'd had a short-lived affair which unbeknown to him had produced a child. More recently the woman had turned up on his doorstep and blackmailed him for financial support. Desperate to keep the affair from his wife he almost bankrupted himself and had to ask Laura for help. He was the reason she'd started taking back-handers from Frankie Grant, which I still believed ultimately led to her death. He had no idea that was the case and I certainly wasn't going to tell him now. The man had more than paid for his one mistake and if Liz ever found out I was sure it would kill her.

I sighed. A small part of me longed for the black and white world I used to inhabit but that was long gone. Instead, I went back to another black and white place where the rules still applied: the crossword. *Give your nephew a start?* Two words, the first five letters long, the second one probably *Relation.* But what was the other one?

It was obvious now. And something that would be writ large in our notes when we resumed our interrogation of Evan Groom that morning.

I picked up the pen and filled in the first word: BLOOD.

## 39

Blood was even more prominent than I'd imagined that morning. The CSIs had rushed through the tests from the car. They confirmed what I'd known in my gut, that the stains on the passenger seat and, perhaps more significantly, the writing on the bottom of the glove compartment, came from Maria's blood. If she'd written her message in the way we imagined, she had quite literally pointed the finger at her ex-husband.

Evan Groom was not his usual polished self as he was led into the interview room. A night in the cells had done its work and left him dishevelled and distracted. His hair was plastered to his skull and his shirt showed distinct sweat patches under the arms. Unfortunately, Reggie Taylor wasn't so discomfited. He grabbed me before he went in to consult with his client.

'I hope you've managed to get some actual evidence of Mr Groom's wrongdoing this morning, Jack? Otherwise, my client will be heading home in a few hours.'

'Not necessarily,' I said.

It was true that we usually had twenty-four hours to charge someone or release them from custody but if there was a possibility of more evidence coming to light then we'd get another twelve hours on top of that. As Clive Andrews and the CSIs were still tearing apart Groom's house looking for clues as to what he might have done with his wife and son, I was pretty confident one of Bob Curtis's fellow superintendents would sign that off if we needed him to.

The brief raised an eyebrow.

'He could speed things up considerably by telling us where he's been for the last week,' I said. 'He's promised several times to give us his whereabouts during that period but somehow keeps forgetting. I mean, if he's got an alibi, I don't really understand why he won't tell us what it is.'

Reggie patted me on the shoulder.

'I'll see what I can do. I'm sure he'll be happy to cooperate when he realises the error of his ways.'

I sat this one out again as Groom continued to take umbrage at being interviewed by my younger colleagues. Anything that got on a suspect's tits was worth trying. I was sitting in a nearby room watching the interview on a live video feed.

After going through all the preliminaries Emma started where she'd finished off the day before by producing another copy of the photo of the accusation written in blood in the car.

'Now that you've had a good night's sleep, I'm hoping you'll be able to explain why your wife wrote this message on her car's glove compartment.'

'Because the bitch is trying to stitch me up.'

I could see Reggie wince. Any advice he'd given Groom to tone down his abrasiveness was clearly being ignored.

'Really?' she said.

'Yes. There's no other explanation. I had nothing to do with her abduction.'

'You think she's been abducted?'

Groom hesitated, obviously wondering whether he was wandering into a trap.

'You clearly do, otherwise I wouldn't be here.'

'Where do you think she's been taken?'

'How the fuck would I know?' His voice was getting more strident now.

'How about your garage? It's where we found her shoe after all. Remember?'

She passed over the second copy of the photo he'd screwed up and thrown away the night before.

'Maybe, when you were lying awake in the cells last night trying to calculate how long you'll be spending in prison, you remembered how this shoe ended up underneath your work bench.'

'I have no idea.' Groom's accompanying smirk would have upset most people but not Emma.

'D'you think this is funny, Mr Groom? Your wife and child are missing and you seem to think it's a cause for humour.'

'I'm smiling at your incompetence. I've never seen that shoe in my life before. If you want to find Nicky and Maria you should spend more time looking for them and less time interviewing me. It's probably not even hers.'

'You've never seen your wife wearing a shoe like that?'

'No.'

'Only we found some photos of the pair of you in an old photo album in her house, dressed up for a night out, and the shoes she had on look remarkably similar to the one we found in your garage.'

She passed across one of those photos. Groom barely glanced at it.

'I'm not in the habit of obsessing over a woman's shoes. I'm not a foot fetishist.'

'OK, let's move on. Where were you on the morning of October the thirtieth?'

'I don't know.'

Groom's brief leaned over and whispered in his ear. Groom whispered back.

'My client would be happy to furnish you with full details of all his movements both then and in the last ten days as soon as you release him from custody and he is able to check his calendar,' Reggie said.

'I thought he'd lost his phone.'

Groom rolled his eyes.

'I have. I'm old-school – my calendar is on my office wall.'

'Thank you. You might have avoided a lot of this if you'd given us this information earlier.'

I quickly texted Clive Andrews to look for the calendar Groom had mentioned, thinking it would provide some of the answers we were looking for. Meanwhile, Reggie Taylor was giving Emma grief.

'I didn't hear a question there, Detective Sergeant Steel. If you've run out, I suggest you let my client go so he can carry on with his life.'

'I have a question,' Leon said, picking up the reins. 'Why did your wife kick you out of the house before your child was three months old?'

'I have no idea. Why don't you ask her?'

'I hope I'll be able to do that soon. In the meantime, I've spoken to her solicitor who tells me that in the custody battle she claimed you were abusive and controlling.'

'She would have said anything to get custody.'

'And what would you do to get your son back?'

'No comment.'

'One of her friends has confirmed Maria's accusations. And the neighbours claim to have heard regular screaming matches coming from her house recently. Do you like to get your own way, Mr Groom?'

'Doesn't everyone?'

Another whisper from his brief. Even on video you could feel Groom's frustration coming off him in waves – Leon was getting to him and both Reggie and I could tell he was close to cracking.

'How did you feel when the court only gave you custody of Nicky for one weekend a month?'

'No comment.'

While the interview continued, I felt my phone buzz in my pocket. It was Clive Andrews.

'Have you still got Groom in custody, boss?' he said.

'Yes. Emma and Leon are grilling him now.'

'Great. I think I've found something which will definitely buy us another twelve hours.'

'Go on.'

'I went to look at that calendar, like you suggested. I'll bring it back with me. But on the noticeboard next to it there was a piece of paper with an address on it. I've checked with the Land Registry and it looks like he's got another property, inherited from his parents, I think. An old farm cottage over Belsay way. Pretty remote by the looks of it. I've had a look on Google Maps and it appears to have some outbuildings too, so could well be where he's stowed his missus and kid if he's taken them.'

'Top work, Clive. Pick me up on the way, will you? I'd like to take a look at this myself.'

I made a couple of calls to sort out the formalities and, as I expected, got approval to hold Groom for another twelve hours. I then texted Leon to let him know what was happening. I watched him absorb the information on the screen and then he hit Groom with it.

'Have you got any properties other than the house in Jesmond, Mr Groom?'

Groom blanched, his body noticeably tensing.

'What's that got to do with you?'

'Yes or no?'

Groom turned to his brief and clearly asked him a question as the man nodded. Groom sighed and turned back to Leon.

'Yes.'

'A farm cottage in Belsay?'

Groom looked surprised, maybe even worried, shaking his head as if he couldn't believe the direction this was taking.

'How did you know that?'

'You left the address on your noticeboard.'

Groom looked bemused.

'I didn't. Why would I do that? I know where it is.'

'When was the last time you were there?' Leon pressed, ignoring his question.

'I'm not sure.'

'Have you been there any time in the last three weeks?'

Groom looked hesitant, glancing at his brief again.

'Well, Mr Groom? Have you?'

'Yes,' he said.

'How about your wife and child?'

'They've never been there so there's no point looking.'

'Thanks for the advice but our team are already on their way.'

Groom went even paler. I thought for a moment we might have to call a paramedic.

'You can't do that! Can they?' The latter question was directed at his solicitor. Reggie knew fine well that as Groom was already in custody, we wouldn't need another search warrant, just my approval. He turned to Leon.

'I assume you can provide written authorisation for this.'

'You can have a copy as soon as this interview is over.'

Reggie turned back to his client.

'I'm afraid they can,' he said.

'This is bullshit,' Groom said, rising to his feet and leaning threateningly towards Leon.

'We'll see about that, won't we?' Leon said with a smile.

## 40

*Four days earlier*

Maria wasn't having much luck finding her new destination, just a fraction back over the Scottish border into Northumberland. She'd only been there once before and it was so off-grid that even if she'd had satnav it probably wouldn't have shown up.

There'd still been no reports of her disappearance, thank God. Once that happened she hoped that the police would find Evan's secret hideaway a little easier to track down than this place was – she'd handed it to them on a plate so they shouldn't have anywhere near as much bother as she was having. Sticking the address on his noticeboard had been a stroke of genius – she knew that Evan would never spot it but was sure the cops would be a little more observant than him.

In contrast, Maria didn't know the exact address she was looking for and had got lost twice. The nearest bit of civilisation was a small hamlet called Byrness, just over the border, so she had back-tracked to there and started again. She finally got lucky and found the right road; then it was just a question of finding the rough track which led to the house. After missing it twice she spotted it, partially hidden by a sign which promised 'Eggs for Sale' which she was sure hadn't been there the last time. God knows why anyone would want to live in such a secluded spot but it was perfect for her to hide away for a day or two while she waited for her new passport.

As she came around the final bend, she could see a woman feeding animals in front of the cottage. There were a couple of sheep and some chickens surrounding her – which explained the eggs sign. Maria had no idea what the attraction was in looking after filthy animals – give her a cat every time, as long as you fed them, they took care of the rest – but she knew Nicky would love them.

The woman turned as she heard the car approaching, looking a bit puzzled by her unexpected visitor. Maria breathed a sigh of relief. It was Sara. At least she didn't have to turn around and carry on driving. Sara would never have seen Sam's car before and he had those tinted windows that make it hard for people to see in, so she clearly didn't have a clue who had come to see her.

Maria watched as her friend put her hand to her forehead to shield the low winter sun from her eyes, trying to see who was driving up her track. She laughed – not at the woman's confusion but at the scene in front of her. One of the chickens had jumped on a sheep's back and the pair were headed towards the car. Nicky caught sight of them and giggled loudly.

'Look, Mam, a chick-sheep,' he shouted.

She pulled up in front of the house and got out of the car. Sara was clearly confused for a second by the new hair but then a smile lit up her face and she marched across to greet her friend, only switching to a frown when she saw signs of the bruising on Maria's face. Maria made a vow to buy some better concealer when she got the chance.

Thankfully, Sara didn't mention it immediately but Maria knew she'd be after chapter and verse as soon as they were out of Nicky's hearing.

'Is everything OK?' Sara said, pulling her in for a hug. As soon as she was close enough, she whispered, 'I had the police on the phone earlier.'

Fuck. That was sooner than Maria had hoped. How had they got on to her so quickly? Sara was looking at her questioningly, concern all over her face. Maria glanced at Nicky, who had opened his window to look more closely at the animals, and shook her head. Sara took the hint and changed the subject.

'Why didn't you tell me you were coming?'

'Spur of the moment thing, you know,' Maria said, which was mostly true. Swapping her old phone for a burner had meant she didn't have a clue what Sara's number was so she couldn't ring her in advance, but little ears were still listening so she would explain that later.

'Let me look at you.' Sara held her at arm's length. 'Love the hair but not so keen on those bruises.'

'Long story,' Maria said.

'Can't wait to hear it. Cup of tea?'

'Absolutely. I'll just get Nicky out of the car.' She opened the back door, unfastened his car-seat belt and pulled him out.

'Oh my God, look at the size of you,' Sara said. She went to hug him but Nicky shied away. Sara pretended not to care but Maria could tell she was hurt. 'Well, you can't blame him, I am a stranger these days, it's ages since I've seen the bairn.'

'He'll drive you mad within an hour.'

'I don't mind that. It's lovely to see him again, I barely see any kids these days.'

Sara smiled, before a shadow passed across her face. Maria was reminded how hard it was for Sara when she discovered she couldn't have children.

'You remember your Auntie Sara, don't you, Nicky?'

He stared at her for a moment then shook his head.

'She's your godmother! Say hello like I showed you.'

Nicky walked over to Sara and held his hand out to shake.

'Hello, Sara, I am Nicky, please to meet you,' he said.

'Well, isn't my lovely godson a proper gent,' Sara said, laughing and taking his hand firmly. 'Pleased to meet you too, Nicky. Would you like a chocolate biscuit?'

'Yes, pleeeeeaase.'

'Just the one,' Maria said. 'He'll eat the packet if you leave it lying around.'

'In one afternoon? I don't think so. Luckily I've only just done a big shop.'

'I was hoping to stay tonight. Would that be OK?'

'Of course,' Sara said, without much conviction. The expression on her face didn't support her words.

'You sure?'

Sara hesitated but before she could answer Nicky burst out laughing as the chick-sheep nudged him with its nose, making the hen on its back flap off into the air before landing on the ground.

'As if I would send my godson packing,' she replied, though Maria could tell there was an issue of some kind.

'Have you got plans? We can go somewhere else if it's a bother.'

She prayed that Sara wouldn't send her away, she was dog tired. She'd barely slept in that dodgy B&B – a combination of a crap mattress, Nicky's squirming and the stress over the passports – and she desperately needed a place to bed down and hide for one night before she tried to leave the country.

Sara shook her head. 'No, don't be daft, pet, be my guest.' She held out her arm to escort Maria and Nicky into the cottage.

'Your biscuit awaits, young sir,' she said. Nicky didn't need telling twice. He ignored the arm and practically sprinted to the door.

'What brought this on?' she asked Maria as they walked together to the door with Nicky out of hearing distance.

'I need your help,' Maria said. 'It's a big ask though.'

'You know I'd do anything for you and Nicky,' Sara said.

Maria watched through the cottage window as Sara made a phone call in the yard. Nicky was still chasing the chickens outside but he was clearly wilting. She had never seen him so happy, or so tired. Sara had spent hours playing with him, teaching him the names of all the animals. She'd even taught him a song to remember them which he chanted repeatedly, marching around the yard: 'Blue, Stu, Little Poo, Cuthbert, Dribble, Stub.'

It was nearly eight o'clock before they managed to get him into bed in the tiny box room at the back of the house but he was asleep as soon as his head hit the pillow and finally they could talk. Maria sat on the sofa while Sara opened a much-needed bottle of wine in the open-plan kitchen behind her.

'You're a natural, you know,' Maria said. 'He loves you. I never make him as happy as he was today.'

'Ach, no, I'm sure that's not true. It's easier to put the time in when you don't see them very often.'

'I'm sorry about that. I should have been in touch.'

'Water under the bridge,' Sara said, as she brought in the bottle and a couple of glasses and poured the wine. She seemed about to say something else about the thing that had come between them but then let it go. 'Did you recognise that song?'

Maria laughed. 'Yes, I think so, wasn't it from that weird video your mam used to sit us in front of when we wouldn't shut up?'

'Yes! *Trumpton*. I named all the animals especially so they'd be easier to remember.'

'Well, it clearly worked. Trouble is, I'm going to have to put up with Nicky singing it repeatedly for the next week or two.'

Sara smiled. They seemed back on track.

'Now you need to tell me what the hell is going on – in detail this time.'

Maria had given her the short version earlier, putting off the rest until Nicky was in bed. 'What did the police tell you?' she asked.

'Just that you'd gone missing under mysterious circumstances. They wanted to know if you were in any kind of trouble or if there was anyone who might hurt you.'

'And what did you say?'

'I bad-mouthed Evan, obviously. And I threw Sam's name into the pot too.'

'Shit.'

'What's the problem?'

'That's his car outside.'

'Look, Maria, if you want me to help, you really need to tell me everything.'

So she did. Maria knew she was rambling, banging on about her bad choices, the mess she'd made of her life and about the difficulties of being a single mum – which she knew was insensitive in view of Sara's history, but she was on a roll. Sara did what she always did, soaked it all in, storing everything up until she had something sensible to say. By the time she was done it was gone midnight and they were on their second bottle.

'But why now?' Sara asked.

'Because Evan's violence has escalated recently. He slapped me the last time we argued about Nicky. I'm pretty sure he's been hitting Nicky too. There have been marks on his arms when he's brought him back home. Since he got involved with his new friends, he seems to think he's above the law. Maybe he is.'

'Well, it certainly sounds like you've screwed him now,' she said, laughing. 'Even that slippery bastard will struggle to talk his way out of this.'

'D'you think?'

'For sure.'

'But do you reckon they'll be looking for us yet? That our names will be on a list at the airport and that?'

'Maybe not. I looked all over the internet while you were having a shower and there's no mention of you. What time's your flight tomorrow?'

'Six p.m. Provided my passport is ready in time.'

Maria had rebooked a flight to Barcelona but from Glasgow this time to save herself some travelling time.

'So you'll probably be fine. If I was you, if there's no more news tomorrow, I'd get the hell out of here toot sweet.'

'But what if there is? Even the passport office might be in the loop.'

Sara looked like she was about to say something but then didn't.

'What is it?' Maria asked. 'If you've got any ideas, I'm all ears.'

'Maybe there's another way you can get a passport.'

'It doesn't matter how I get it, does it? It's getting through security that's the issue. My name will be in the system, alarms will go off the minute they check me in.'

'Not if it's someone else's name in the passport.'

'That's fucking genius, Sara, call up that master forger

you know and get him to knock up a couple of fake passports for me and Nicky and we'll be out of your hair.'

Sara glared at her. 'I'd forgotten how sarcastic you can be when you've had a drink.'

'Well for God's sake, how do you expect me to get a fake passport?'

'Haven't you ever heard of the dark web?'

'Of course, but passports?'

'You can get anything on there. My friend gets all his drugs there.'

'Your "friend"?'

Sara laughed, though she looked a little uneasy.

'Whatever. I'm saying I bet he could help get fake passports for you and Nicky. It'll cost you but I'm sure he could do it. My phone's got a great camera so the photos will be no problem and you can stay here until they're ready and then disappear like that.' Sara clicked her fingers to indicate the speed with which she'd be away.

Maria closed her eyes, imagined lying on a beach, drinking cocktails, Nicky building sandcastles in front of her, a handsome, muscular stranger eyeing her from the edge of the sea. She could almost taste the piña colada. She opened them again. It couldn't be that easy, could it?

'Look, I'm sure it'll be fine, I probably won't need them, but if I did why would he take the risk of doing that for me?'

'To be honest, I'm not sure he would.'

Maria sighed. She knew it was too good to be true.

'But he'd definitely do it for me,' Sara added.

## 41

## 8 November 2024

I pressed firmly on the doorbell of Evan Groom's other property for a second time. Still no answer. I listened carefully but the house seemed quiet. I stepped back and looked around.

The farm cottage was surprisingly small, given the amount of land it had, just two windows downstairs and one upstairs at the front, all with shutters on. Clive Andrews came round the side, shaking his head.

'Nothing round the back, boss,' he said. 'The door's locked and all the windows are shuttered.'

I looked across at two outbuildings about fifty yards away from the house. Old barns by the looks of them but there was no sign that Groom kept any livestock. He didn't seem the type, more city boy than gentleman farmer. We'd check those later but first came the cottage.

Sid Allan and Tim Carmichael walked over to the front door of the cottage with the battering ram – it was fast becoming their speciality. Groom was going to have a lot of fixing up to do if he ever got released.

They smashed the lock in two goes. Practice makes perfect.

'You take downstairs, I'll go up,' I said. Clive nodded. I headed up the stairs. It was still deathly quiet. There were no pictures on the walls, nor on the landing above. The place showed very little sign of being lived in. There were two doors upstairs, a bedroom and a bathroom, I guessed.

I opened the first door, a small sink and a loo with an old bath set against the wall, a shower hose attached to the tap. No mod cons – and no sign of life, though there appeared to be some hair trapped in the plughole.

The second room was more interesting. It wasn't locked but there was what looked like a newish mortise lock fitted to the door. The shutters were closed so I put the light on but on closer inspection realised they weren't just closed they were nailed shut. A double bed with a bare, stained mattress on it took up much of the space. There were clear scratches on the bed frame at both ends of the bed.

'Jesus, boss, it reeks in here.' Clive appeared in the doorway, grimacing.

'Of what?'

'Sex.'

'What do you make of those scratches?'

He took a closer look.

'I dunno. Handcuffs maybe?'

'I bow to your greater experience of these things.'

He laughed. 'Not me, boss, I've got two young kids, I'm

practically celibate these days. It's not just sex though, there's other stuff, disinfectant maybe . . .' He took in a deep breath. 'Shit as well, I think. Feels like it's been cleaned up but not very well.'

'We'll get the CSIs out here to check it out. Anything downstairs?'

'Nothing much. There's a bed sofa in the front room that looks like it's been slept on recently and off there is a tiny kitchen with a fridge which is surprisingly well stocked, there's some fresh milk in there too. I think someone has been living here – not least because the washing machine has some damp washing in it – looks like sheets and a duvet – from this bed, I suppose. There's also a filing cabinet off to one side, next to a desk which has an ancient-looking printer on top of it. The cabinet's locked but it will be easy enough to crack it open. I did find this though.'

He held up a mobile phone.

'It was on the table by the sofa. Doesn't seem like Groom looked very hard for it, does it? And look at these.'

He held up a big bunch of keys.

'If there's anything or anyone being hidden here it'll be in those outbuildings, I reckon.'

We were about halfway across the grass towards the outbuildings when Clive stopped.

'Bloody hell,' he said. 'Smells like a hippy festival round here.'

I had no idea what he was talking about but before I could ask he was off again, rattling the keys in his hand.

After a couple of false starts he found a key that fitted the large padlock on the biggest of the buildings and unlocked it with a triumphant shout.

'Open sesame!'

As soon as he'd pulled the door open I understood his earlier comment. The space was crammed with cannabis plants. I'd lost my sense of smell after a bout of Covid but maybe it was coming back because even I could smell it now. There were huge UV lights and hoses running all over the place. No wonder Groom had been reluctant to tell us where he was spending most of his time, there was enough here to earn him some serious jail time.

While I looked around the barn, to make sure that Groom's ex-wife and child weren't tucked away anywhere, Clive went across to the other, smaller building where he found it had been converted into a drying room for the plants. It was clear why Groom had been dismayed that we were coming here but, much to my disappointment, there was no sign of Maria or Nicky.

## 42

Evan Groom seemed to have aged several years in the relatively short time since I'd last seen him. I'd thought his panicked reaction when we discovered his other property was because his ex-wife was being held there but clearly he just knew what we would find and what it would cost him. As well as a possible ten years in prison, he faced having his property and all of his cash confiscated.

He barely even reacted to Emma and me entering the room – it seemed a lifetime since he'd been lusting after her in the golf club bar. That was a little annoying as I'd brought her purely for provocation – she hadn't been at the scene so it was obvious that I should lead the way this time. After going through the preliminaries, I went straight for the jugular.

'When did you start producing cannabis?'

Groom lowered his head and sucked in a long breath before glancing back up and exhaling. He looked relieved, if anything, like a man who'd had a weight removed from his shoulders. I'd expected denial or possibly silence but I was wrong. He seemed surprisingly keen to fess up. I wondered why.

'Just over three years ago. When I left my job with Ofsted.'

'Why didn't you just sell the farm?'

'It had been in my family for years. My father would have turned in his grave.'

'Still would, I reckon.'

Groom shrugged. 'Maybe. Needs must and all that.'

'Did Maria know what you were doing there?'

He hesitated, perhaps knowing it would give him a strong motive for getting rid of her.

'Unfortunately, yes, I had a few too many and let it slip one night. Bitch used it to blackmail me over the custody of Nicky. She threatened to tell you lot if I made a fuss.'

'Did she ever go there?'

'No. Never. Nor Nicky.'

'Not even on his weekends with you?'

'No. Absolutely not. I made sure of that.'

'So we won't find any of their DNA up there.'

'No. I told you that before.'

'For your sake, I hope you're right. Who do you sell the cannabis to?'

'No comment.'

'There's really not much point in keeping quiet. We'll have a team of people going through those records of yours.'

'Good luck with that. You won't find anything.'

'It might help reduce your sentence.'

'It might help get me killed.'

I could see he wasn't going to budge. I didn't blame

him – cannabis production was big business now and there were some vicious people involved. In the past I'd have been looking at Stevie Connors but since he'd been locked up I suspected others had moved into his territory. I changed the subject. Even though we'd got Groom bang to rights for one thing he still wasn't off the hook for his ex-wife's disappearance.

'Tell me about the bedroom.'

Groom frowned. He glanced at his brief but didn't speak. If anything, he seemed more worried than he had been about the cannabis.

'What about it?'

'It looked like someone had cleaned it up recently.'

'What can I say? I'm a tidy guy?'

'And yet it still reeked of sex.'

'I like sex. It's not a crime now, is it?'

'Not at all. Assuming there's consent. My colleague thought there may have been handcuffs involved.'

He smirked at Emma and kept his gaze on her as he answered. 'Very observant. You're not all vanilla then. What can I say? I like a little light bondage.'

To her credit she didn't react.

'It looked like someone had been kept in there.'

'Never happened.'

'Then why put a lock on the door and nail the shutters closed?'

'Security.'

'There was nothing in there other than the bed.'

'I used to keep all my records in that room but they're downstairs now.'

'In a room that doesn't have a lock.'

'I can see how you made detective.'

I ignored the obvious sarcasm.

'Why the change?'

'I got fed up traipsing up the stairs to get things. I realised no one was going to break in, it's in the middle of nowhere.'

'So it wasn't because you were keeping your ex-wife in that bedroom?'

'No!'

'Why had you washed all the bedding?'

'Why do you think?' He looked at Emma again. 'I bet you could tell him.'

I could see her clench her fist under the desk but when she still didn't respond to him he seemed to get bored of trying to taunt her and turned back to me.

'Bodily fluids can get a little messy.'

'We have a forensic team heading out there now.'

'You're wasting your time. I've already confessed to running the cannabis production. What else are you trying to stitch me up for?'

'We'd better not find Maria's DNA in that bedroom.'

'You won't.'

'Whose will we find then?'

'A gentleman never tells.'

'I wasn't asking a gentleman. I was asking you.'

He mimed zipping his lips.

'When's the last time you were at the farm?'

'That's easy. November the fifth. I remember all the fireworks going off as I drove up there after that debacle of a press conference you held. I was outraged that you hadn't asked me to be there. I rang the TV station while I was there and told them I wanted to do a piece with them. The signal was terrible and our conversation kept breaking up so I drove down again later that night to discuss it with one of the producers.'

'That seems a bit of a rush. Why dash up there at all?'

He leant across to Reggie Taylor who nodded.

'I needed to take care of the product.'

'Or you needed to remove any trace that you'd been keeping your ex-wife in that bedroom.'

'I can assure you it was the former. You've seen the place, it's a lot of work.'

'And you don't have anyone to help you?'

There was a slight hesitation before he answered. I made a mental note to get the CSIs out there to check for any evidence of other people having been in the barns and the cottage.

'How long do you spend there?'

'I'm there 24/7 usually. And I'm sure you already know that. I bet you've checked my phone and the satnav on the car by now. Why do you think I was keeping my phone away from you? Even though it would have helped prove I didn't go anywhere near Maria.'

He was right. We had checked and he did seem to have spent the entire week before his ex-wife disappeared at the farm. Unless he'd left his phone there and had another vehicle he could use. But if he did it wasn't registered to him and it wasn't on either of his properties. Was it really possible that he had nothing to do with the disappearance of Maria and Nicky?

'We'll be handing you over to our drugs team after this interview, Mr Groom. If you know where your ex-wife and child are this is your last chance to tell me.'

'I haven't the faintest idea,' Groom said. 'But seriously, who do you think put the address of the farm on my notice-board? Because I'm telling you it wasn't me. Maria stitched me up like a kipper. And now she's out there somewhere and she's taken my son with her.'

## 43

*Crashed biplane that's missing?*
*Is there another way to find it? (4,1)*

I headed home, only to find an empty house. Helen was out for a meal with her management team and Aidan was sleeping over at a friend's house. I attempted to do the crossword but my head wasn't right, a clue about a biplane had me mystified, even though the first word was only four letters and began with a P.

We had hit a dead end looking for Maria Groom and her son and would start again in the morning. I wasn't buying Evan Groom's story about the bedroom but would have to see what the CSIs found in there before we could press him further.

The break gave me a last chance to briefly focus on our off-the-books investigation into Laura's death. Leon's obvious concerns had me questioning if I was doing the wrong thing in encouraging Emma to get to know Harry Connors. She was a confident young officer who could handle herself but I was putting her in a tricky situation with little or no backup. I'd never minded bending the rules if I thought the benefits outweighed the negatives but I might have got the sums wrong this time – and it wasn't me who was taking the biggest risk.

Maybe I could flush out Harry Connors in a different way? Then I could stand Emma down and everyone would be happy. I'd intended to do it a couple of days earlier but had got sidetracked; there was nothing to get in my way this time.

I headed out for a gentle stroll around the area. An area that happened to include Frankie Grant's house. If anyone had a reason to clear this up it was Connors' main rival; if the attack on Laura had been a way of getting at Frankie, I reckoned he'd be quite keen on finding out who was responsible.

After the hit-and-run I'd spent a fair bit of time keeping an eye on the Grant household, deliberately trying to provoke Frankie into doing something reckless as I was convinced he'd been responsible for Laura's death. I knew better now and my harassment hadn't exactly made me popular with the man and his family. His teenage son Lee was particularly vexed at the time so it was unfortunate that he opened the door this time.

'Will you lot never leave my family alone!' he said, immediately trying to shut the door. I used the old coppers' trick of putting a foot in there but forgot I had brogues on rather than the boots I used to wear and only managed to pull it out of the way a second before he slammed it closed.

'I've got some information for your dad,' I said, just as it shut. 'About the car crash,' I added to the closed door. A few seconds later it opened again.

'What is it?' Lee said, looking around nervously. 'He's got company.'

Maybe he was worried about disturbing his dad but I wasn't.

'I think he'd like to hear it himself, son.'

'I'm not your son. If you tell us, I'll pass it on. He trusts me. We tell each other everything.'

'I doubt that.'

Lee Grant wasn't much older than Aidan, about seventeen I guessed, but as far as I knew Frankie kept him out of the family business – much in the way Stevie Connors had with his son until the old man was locked up and had little choice but to let Harry take over the reins. I was pretty sure that Frankie had no intention of following suit, whatever the kid seemed to think, but he continued to guard the entrance.

'He doesn't want to speak to you.'

'I think you'd better check with him, just to be on the safe side. Tell him it's about Harry Connors.'

The kid's eyes opened wide at the mention of Connors. He looked terrified.

'What's it got to do with him?'

'That's between me and your dad.'

He seemed frozen for a second, unsure what to do.

'Is there something you want to tell me?' I asked. That woke him up.

'I don't have to tell you anything.' He pointed at my chest as he spoke. His sleeve rode up and I could see scars on his right wrist. They looked fairly recent. He saw me looking and put his arm down quickly. 'I just don't want you getting my dad involved in some kind of gang war,' he added.

'I think it's you who shouldn't be getting involved here, kid, now run along and get your dad before I arrest you for obstruction. You won't get to university with a criminal record.'

'Who said I wanted to go to university?'

'Don't you?'

'None of your fucking business.' Without another word he turned and disappeared into a room off the back of the hallway, leaving the front door open. I knew I'd been a bit hard on the lad, but he needed to be discouraged from following in his dad's murky footsteps. If those scars on his arm were what I thought they were he had enough problems without going down that road.

A few moments later Frankie Grant came out of the same room wearing what can only be described as a smoking jacket.

'Fuck me, I wasn't expecting Oscar Wilde,' I said. 'Though he was an ex-con, wasn't he?'

He saw the smile spreading across my face and pointed at me.

'Not a fucking word about this to anyone, right?'

'There is only one thing worse than being talked about and that is not being talked about.' The Oscar Wilde quote flew straight over his head. To be fair I only knew it from a Monty Python sketch.

'Marion bought me this jacket and I like to keep her happy. Which also means not doing business when we have friends round for dinner.'

'You have friends?'

Frankie sighed. 'Do you ever take a day off? What did you say to my son anyway? He looked like he'd seen a ghost.'

'I was just discouraging him from joining the family business.'

If looks could kill I'd have dropped down dead on the doorstep.

'I don't need your help to raise my son. He's got nothing to do with you. Leave him out of this.'

For once, I couldn't argue with him. I was being a hard-arse for no good reason except habit. I held my hands up in apology – I couldn't quite bring myself to say 'sorry' but he got the message.

'So now that my son's off the agenda, what did you actually want? My dinner's getting cold and I'd much rather be talking to my friends than the likes of you. And it better be good as I'm pretty sure your boss told you not to come within a country mile of me after the last time you lost it and I reckon he wouldn't be thrilled to know you've ignored him.'

He was right about that. Bob Curtis would have my balls if he knew I was having this conversation. I needed to tread carefully.

'It won't take long but I think you'll want to hear this.'

Frankie sighed but nodded. 'Fine. Not here though. Come into my office.'

He turned around and walked back down the hallway. I followed him, closing the front door behind me. Frankie's office was basically a spare bedroom with a nice desk, an old-school vinyl record player and a large-screen TV. He sat behind the desk, leaving me standing. I didn't mind him playing his Bertie Big Bollocks games as long as he listened. I closed the door again. No need for anyone else to hear this.

'We're still looking for Laura's killer,' I said.

'If you hadn't spent ages trying to pin it on me, you'd have found them by now.'

'Possibly, but I think we're getting close now.'

'Really? What's that got to do with me?' He tried his best to look uninterested but I could tell he was faking it. Maybe he already had an idea where I was going with this.

'I think they were trying to get at you. Killing your inside woman and putting you in the frame for it.'

He laughed. 'Who'd have the balls to do that?'

'Stevie Connors.'

'He's been locked up for ten years.'

'Aye, but Harry hasn't.'

Frankie's furrowed brow told me how unlikely he found that.

'That show pony? He wouldn't dare.'

'He would if his dad sanctioned it.'

'What do you expect me to do about it?' Frankie said with a shrug.

'Nothing. But I thought you should know.'

'Aye, right.' Frankie looked unusually thoughtful for a moment. 'You never do anything for nothing. What's in it for you? It would suit you fine well if the two families went to war over this, wouldn't it?'

'No one wants a war, Frankie. I just want to know who killed Laura.'

Frankie was looking over my shoulder and I thought I heard a noise at the door, but no one came in.

'Well maybe you should come back when you have some fucking evidence,' he said. 'Can I get back to my dinner now?'

'Of course.' Seed planted, I turned and left. As I walked out of the room, I saw a door to the left of the hallway closing. I had a real sense that someone had been listening, maybe young Lee was being a bit too nebby. I hoped he wasn't trying to prove himself to his dad, he seemed way too soft for that.

The visit had served its purpose. I knew that Frankie was being disingenuous. There was no way he'd sit on his hands waiting to discover if Harry Connors had stitched him up. I'd pulled the pin out of the gangster's grenade and I reckoned he wouldn't waste much time before he threw it at someone.

44

Emma didn't do boredom. Jack had told her to get a good night's sleep before they reconvened the next day and started afresh in the search for Maria Groom but she was way too wired to just sit at home.

Leon had suggested a drink after work but she wasn't in the mood. She pretended she was going out with a friend and he'd gone off in a sulk. Truth be told, she was still pissed off with him over that traffic cop stunt, which had messed up her situation with Harry Connors; she hadn't heard a word from him since. From flowers to radio silence. Was Leon deliberately sabotaging her hard work as she was his only realistic competition for the DI job? She gave herself a slap; it was the kind of thing she might do but not him.

Why were relationships so hard? And why did some men feel they had to protect you? She could look after herself, thanks very much, she didn't need a minder. Leon's behaviour wasn't that different to men like Sam Gallagher. Following her to the restaurant was the kind of thing Gallagher would have done. She sighed. That was probably a bit harsh but sometimes Leon really got on her nerves. If she wanted to see another man, that was her choice. She'd never promised him exclusivity, and thankfully the dreaded 'L' word hadn't been mentioned – it was always the kiss of death as far as she was concerned.

Emma flicked through the TV guide but there was nothing she fancied; like most cops she couldn't bear watching crime dramas and that was all there seemed to be these days. Sod it, she thought. She threw on a frock, grabbed her coat and headed to Stevie's Bar. If the mountain wouldn't come to Muhammad and all that.

It was seven thirty and the place was still quiet. Micky Chambers was sitting at a table nursing a can of Coke. He nodded to her as she came in but didn't attempt to make conversation. He wasn't much of a talker anyway so she didn't read too much into that. She'd only just reached the bar when Harry came out of the back office. He'd probably seen her come in on the CCTV screens they no doubt had in there.

'Nice timing,' he said. 'I've been down south for a bit but got back last night. I was going to call you.'

'That's what all the boys say.'

'How many boys do you have on the go at any one time?'

'I like to keep my options open.'

'Smart girl. There are very few of us princes around so it's best to kiss as many frogs as you can.'

'You're a prince now, are you?'

'If the crown fits . . .'

She laughed. Harry Connors was so much more relaxed

than Leon ever seemed to be. Emma knew that sometimes she could be a little too intense, but she also knew when to kick back and have fun, unlike some.

'I suppose you are the heir to a throne of sorts.'

'Indeed. Speaking of which, my dad was released today and we'll be having a little party on Sunday if you fancy it? As my guest?'

'I'm not sure what my boss will think of that.'

'You don't strike me as a yes woman.'

'Maybe not but I doubt your dad will be all that thrilled at having a cop rock up as soon as he's out either.'

'If I'm happy, he's happy.'

Emma wasn't convinced that was strictly true, but it would be an opportunity to get on the inside a little more. And if she could help Jack find the driver who killed Laura, she was certain the promotion would be hers.

And, to be totally honest, she liked spending time with Harry. He was funny, self-deprecating and seemed remarkably considerate for a putative gangster. She found herself wondering if he was as considerate in bed too but shook that thought from her head immediately. She wasn't going there. But she would go to the party – even though Leon would go apeshit when he found out.

He glanced at his watch.

'I've got to be heading off. Don't take too long to decide though, I've got a few backup options of my own.'

'I'd love to come,' she said.

'Excellent. See you then.'

Over Harry's shoulder she saw Micky Chambers knock

back his Coke and get to his feet. The pair of them left the bar together. Almost immediately she heard shouting and a cry of pain. To her surprise, Vic Kendall, the man who'd nicked Maria Groom's car, came flying through the doorway into the bar, landing on his back. He jumped up and flew back towards the door, crashing into Micky Chambers and the pair tumbled to the pavement outside, both trying to throw punches but too close to each other to get any purchase.

What was Kendall doing there? The last time she'd seen him Leon had been taking him down to the cells while they considered what to do about his car theft and house-napping.

She got off her stool but was only halfway across the bar when she saw two uniforms run up and separate the two men. As she drew closer she realised it was Sid Allan and his usual sidekick, Tim Carmichael, so she ducked back into the shadows, not wanting them to see her in Stevie's Bar. Jack was very clear that this was an off-the-books operation and they'd be shocked to see her hanging out with gangsters. Cops normally kept away from this place, for obvious reasons. In fact, it was pretty strange they'd been right outside at the moment Kendall and Chambers started fighting.

Or was it? Emma shook her head. This had Leon's fingerprints all over it. She'd bet that he'd done this deliberately to pay her back for not wanting that drink. To be fair, it was clever. They wanted Chambers' DNA on record and if they arrested him now they'd get it. She'd bet big money on Leon having persuaded Kendall to come here and cause trouble with Chambers, probably promising him a free pass on the car theft and the house-breaking stuff if he helped them out.

She watched through the window as the two PCs frog-marched both brawlers up the street to a couple of waiting cars. All very convenient. Harry Connors stormed back into the bar.

'Some drunk barged into Micky,' he said, angrily. 'The two of them got into a bit of a rumble and your bloody pals have nicked both of them. Can you do anything?'

'How do you think that would look, Harry? You know I can't interfere.'

He stared at her for a moment, his eyes flashing darkly, but then sighed.

'You're right. Sorry. I wasn't thinking. I'm just pissed off. I've got to be somewhere in fifteen minutes and I'm going to have to get a cab now or I'll be late.'

He took out his phone and flicked through his screens.

'Can't you drive?'

'Long story,' he said, without taking his eyes off his phone.

'I could give you a lift,' Emma said.

Harry Connors stopped what he was doing and looked up.

'I don't want to ruin your night out.'

'You wouldn't be. I only came to see you.'

He looked a little surprised at that. He wasn't the only one, the words were out there before she'd had a chance to filter them.

'Well, if you're sure you don't mind.'

'Of course not.'

'You're an angel.'

Emma smiled. Jack would be pleased with her. Despite Leon's best efforts she was back in Harry Connors' good books.

## 45

'I've just got to grab something from the Merc,' Connors said, as they left the bar. They walked around the back of the building to some private parking spaces where he ducked into the car, emerging with a large bunch of flowers and a card.

'It's Mam's birthday,' he said.

'I'm not sure we're at the "meet the parents" stage,' Emma said.

'Don't worry. She probably won't have a clue who you are. It's a toss-up if she knows who I am these days. She's got Alzheimer's.'

'I'm sorry to hear that. It must be hard.'

'It is.'

Emma's car was parked in the Central Station car park. As they got there she noticed him glance at his watch again.

'I hate being late for her,' he said. 'She needs routine and surprises aren't good for her.'

'I know the drill,' Emma said. 'My uncle had it.'

And I'm pretty sure my boss is in the early stages of

it, she thought. She'd recognised some of the signs in his behaviour changes and, earlier that year, when Jack had been laid up in hospital, had inadvertently discovered that the consultant treating him was a dementia specialist. She still hadn't told a soul, including Jack, of her suspicions. And she certainly wasn't going to say anything to Harry Connors.

'I'll get us there as fast as I can,' she said.

'Maybe you could put your blue light on.' His smile made it clear he was joking.

The private care home was fancy as hell, which she might have guessed when he told her it was in Ponteland. She'd heard Leon refer to the place as Posh-eland because it contained some of the area's most expensive houses – footballers' wives' territory, he reckoned.

The contrast with her uncle's home couldn't have been starker. He'd ended up in a shitty private facility, run by a profiteering company that didn't give a toss for their patients' welfare. The staff were great but there were nowhere near enough of them and the patients spent most of their time in seclusion in their tiny, bare rooms with little help or company.

Harry's mum's room was a complete contrast to that. A large bed sat to one side of the room, with a separate seating area in a bay window on the other side, which looked out to the manicured lawns outside. There was an en-suite bathroom too. Her uncle had to use a shared bathroom which he often couldn't find, which for a man with incontinence problems wasn't funny. His last few years were a miserable existence and it was hard to watch a once proud man deteriorate so badly.

There seemed no danger of that with Harry's mum. She was asleep in an armchair near the window when they got there. A paperback book on the floor by her side.

'She always loved reading,' Harry said, 'you know, before ... She still tries, God bless her, but she ends up reading the same opening chapters every day as she can't remember what she's read before. That book hasn't changed in months.'

When the care assistant woke her up to tell her they were there she beamed widely, slowly getting to her feet and turning towards the pair of them.

'Happy birthday, Mam,' Harry said, handing her the flowers.

'Oh, is it today?' she said. 'How nice.'

'I'll put them in water for you, shall I, Mrs C?' the assistant said. 'I'll leave you to have a chat with your son and his girlfriend.' Harry didn't correct her and the description was the first time his mum seemed to realise Emma was there. Mrs Connors looked over Harry's shoulder and stared her straight in the eyes.

'Who's this?'

'This is Emma.' He turned and took Emma's hand. 'And Emma, this is my mam, Brenda.'

Brenda let her gaze run down to the floor and back up again. It was so similar to the way Harry had looked at her the first time they met that Emma couldn't help laughing.

'She's new, isn't she?'

'Aye,' Harry said. 'And she's not my girlfriend ... yet.'

'That's a shame, son, she's prettier than the last one. And she's got a bit of meat on her, unlike that skinny lass.'

'She is. And she has.'

Emma could feel her cheeks reddening.

'Are you saying I'm fat?' she said.

'No. You're perfect,' Harry said.

I'm really not, she thought, but left it unspoken.

'I should give you two some space, let you catch up.' She'd offered to wait in the car but he'd insisted she came in to say hello.

Harry shook his head. 'No, stay. Mam loves company and she sees me every week.'

'Don't believe him, love, I haven't seen hide nor hair of him for months. His brother's the only one who comes to see me most weeks.'

'I didn't know you had a brother,' Emma said.

Harry was already shaking his head. *I don't*, he mouthed.

'I'm going to bring Dad to see you next week,' he said.

The woman looked at him as if he was mad.

'Don't be ridiculous, son, your dad's been dead for years.'

Harry sighed and took her hand.

'Let's sit down, Mam, you're a bit tired.'

'Don't treat me like a child, son, I'm not remotely tired, I've just woken up, that's all.'

She let him lead her back to the chair anyway.

'You come and sit down next to me, Chrissie,' she said to Emma, who frowned at Harry as if to say 'who's Chrissie?'

*Old girlfriend*, he mouthed.

'Are you still running that pub?'

Harry closed his eyes. 'I do a bit more than that, Mam, I

have four pubs, and three nightclubs, plus a couple of restaurants and a number of other businesses.'

'He was always a show-off,' she said to Emma. 'He needs a good woman to set him right. Is that you?'

'I don't know,' Emma said. 'I can be bad sometimes.'

Brenda snorted with laughter.

'You should snap this one up, son, I like the cut of her jib.'

Harry turned to look at Emma, a question in his eyes.

'I'm trying, Mam,' he said. 'But I don't think she'll have me. She's probably too good for me.'

'Nonsense,' his mum said. 'You might be past your best but you're still quite a catch.' She turned back to Emma. 'You're not too good for him, are you, love?'

Emma looked from Harry to his mum and back again.

'No, I'm not,' she said.

## 46

*9 November 2024*

I liked hospital appointments about as much as I liked post-mortems, which was not at all. If it wasn't for losing my sense of smell I'd have blamed it on that weird disinfectant aroma that permeates both of them. So I was a little nervous about my first donanemab trial session that morning.

Helen insisted on taking me to the hospital so at least I had company. Typically, she'd devoured all the reports from a previous trial and was well versed in the possible side effects.

'You could be nauseous, dizzy or worse,' she said. 'I hope you've booked the afternoon off. I know what you're like, you'll still try and go back to work even if you're feeling sick.'

'I am involved in a murder enquiry, love, it's kind of important.'

'So's your health. And you're always telling me how good Leon and Emma are so I'm sure they can survive one afternoon without you.'

'Of course. But what's my excuse for not going back? I made up some bollocks about Aidan playing football this morning but I can't stretch that out all day even with extra time and penalties.'

I was determined to keep my condition a secret until it was affecting my work and there was no real sign of that yet so no one there had a clue I was doing this trial.

'Tell them you had a rare opportunity for some afternoon delight.'

I raised my eyebrows theatrically. 'Is that offer actually on the table?'

'It's not your birthday for another month or so. And I don't think we've done it on a table since Aidan was born,' she wisecracked. 'And I've some shopping to do, so no, it isn't. But I'm sure your colleagues will be impressed that you've still got some life in you. Even if it is imaginary.'

'I'm only fifty-three!'

'Which seems ancient to anyone under forty.'

She was right. It was another reason I wasn't saying a word about this – a lot of the team already thought I was a dinosaur and if they heard about my condition they'd make sure I was extinct.

Helen waited in the café while a young nurse escorted me to the treatment room. She got me to sign all the consent forms and told me what to expect.

'The drug is administered intravenously through a drip. You OK with needles?'

I nodded. Helen had warned me not to make any jokes about 'a little prick', especially if the nurse was a young woman, and, despite my natural inclination to glibness, I managed to follow her instructions.

The nurse sat me in a comfy chair next to a stand which held an IV bag. She sanitised the back of my hand with a wet wipe before inserting a cannula and connecting that to the IV with a tube.

'I'll just set this running and wait for a couple of minutes to make sure everything's working then I'll leave you to it. Holler if you need anything and someone will pop in. I'll nip back every fifteen minutes or so to make sure you're OK but I'm sure it'll be fine.'

I used the time to refresh my memory on the Maria Groom case. It was looking increasingly likely that Evan Groom hadn't abducted his wife and child. But if not him, then who? I had brought a pile of witness statements and transcriptions to read through to make the hour go a little more quickly. I skipped quickly through Rosie Lloyd's interview; the neighbour had told us very little that we hadn't heard from other witnesses. Maria Groom's old school friend Sara Quinn had been the most talkative, giving us a clear picture of their relationship and Maria's proclivity for changing her partners. She'd also sent Emma the list of old boyfriends that had led us to Sam Gallagher – a possible suspect that Evan Groom had suggested as well.

But as I read through the ex-husband's statements I noticed a contradiction between their thoughts on Maria's exes. Sara's list looked fairly comprehensive, covering most of the period between her and Maria leaving school until the present day. As Leon had already suggested, Maria

Groom hadn't been short of men friends. But there was one anomaly.

Evan Groom had only named two specific ex-boyfriends that he knew about. The first was Sam Gallagher and, despite his escape from Leon's clutches, I was confident we'd track him down pretty soon to wherever he was hiding. The other was a man called Rob Gibson, a bit of a junkie, apparently.

I rechecked Sara Quinn's list. There was no mention of him.

## 47

*Four days earlier*

Maria had barely slept a wink. She'd tossed and turned all night, exhausted by the stress of the previous few days but unable to get to sleep as she imagined all kinds of scenarios, each of which ended in disaster – a combination of being charged with wasting police time and losing custody of Nicky to Evan.

She'd eventually fallen asleep just as the light started to filter through the window, and slept in late, only woken by her burner phone buzzing on the bedside table next to her with some good news at last – a text from the Glasgow passport office to let her know her new passport would be ready for collection from 1 p.m. With a bit of luck, she'd be miles away in Barcelona that evening. She jumped into the en-suite shower and by the time she was dressed she was feeling a lot more positive.

Her good mood didn't last long. The minute she walked

into the kitchen and saw Sara's face she knew there was something wrong.

'What is it?' she said. 'Is Nicky OK?'

'He's fine. He's been fed and watered and is making the chickens' lives a misery by chasing them round the yard again.'

'There is something though, isn't there?'

Sara seemed about to tell her but then changed her mind.

'You'd better have a look at this,' she said instead, heading into the lounge where the TV was on with the screen frozen. 'I'm always amazed that you can pause live TV,' she said, 'can't really get my head around it. It's like making time stand still, but sometimes it comes in useful.'

She picked up the TV buttons and hit play. The next thing Maria saw was her own face staring out at her from the screen. It took her a moment or two to tune in to the words of the newsreader: '. . . haven't been seen for a week. Police have described their disappearance as suspicious. They are also searching for Maria's car, a white Ford Fiesta, with the registration NA15 BCW. Anyone who thinks they have seen either Maria or Nicky, or their car should ring the 101 helpline number.'

Another photo of her, with Nicky this time, came up on the screen as the newsreader finished reading before the news moved on to a story about Greggs opening a Champagne bar in Fenwick department store.

'I'm screwed,' Maria said, slumping onto the sofa.

'It's not as bad as it might have been,' Sara said. 'Your new hairstyle and colour makes you look much different and they don't know that you aren't driving your own car.'

'Someone might recognise Nicky though. And how long before Sam folds and tells the police about me?'

'He might not. He's obsessed with you, and he'll still probably be scared that you'll accuse him of beating the crap out of you.'

'It's a bit too late for that now.'

'But he won't realise that, he was never the sharpest tool in the box.'

'Maybe, but what do I do now? There's no point in me going to collect my passport. The police will have notified all the airports and ports. I'll get stopped before I've got past the check-in desk.'

'Not if they think you've been abducted by Evan like you planned. They won't treat it like a missing persons' case then.'

'It sounds to me that that's exactly what they're doing at the moment. And I don't really think the Evan stuff will stand up to much scrutiny in the long run. He'll probably have an alibi or something. He's a lucky bastard – his friends used to say that if he fell down the toilet he'd come back up with a gold watch.'

'He'll be screwed when they find the cannabis farm though.'

'*If* they find the cannabis farm. I can't take the risk of going to the airport, can I? When did the news get out?'

'I heard it on the radio first, about ten o'clock, then switched on the TV a bit later to see it was on there too.'

'Shit, shit, shit.' Maria put her head in her hands. It was just like she'd dreamt it – her plan was unravelling.

'Maybe it's time to think about my suggestion,' Sara said.

'Suggestion?'

'The fake passports.'

Maria suddenly remembered their conversation from the previous night. She'd been a bit pissed by then, but it was something about a friend and the dark web. She'd thought it was mad but maybe it was now her only chance to get away.

'D'you think your friend might help us?'

'I know he will.'

'You've already asked him.'

She nodded. 'But it'll cost you.'

'How much?'

'You'll have to ask him.'

'He's coming here?'

'Tonight.'

Maria shook her head – maybe this was going to work out after all.

'I don't know how to thank you.'

'I wouldn't thank me just yet.'

'Why not?'

'This friend of mine . . .'

'Yes?'

'It's Rob.'

'You're joking.'

'Don't look so scared,' Sara said, 'he's much better now. Wouldn't hurt a fly.'

# 48

*9 November 2024*

I came into the station with a renewed sense of purpose. The treatment at the hospital seemed to have gone well – with no immediate side effects – and I believed I had a new lead.

That head of optimism I'd been building up was decapitated when I called Leon and Emma into the office for a briefing and they both traipsed in with faces like a wet weekend.

'A horse walks into a bar,' I said. 'The barman says, "Why the long face?"'

Not a flicker.

'For God's sake, liven up the pair of you. What have you got for me now it looks like Evan Groom is off the hook where Maria is concerned?'

Their lack of response was a little disappointing. They glanced at each other and scowled.

'Right. I'll go first, shall I? Emma, you need to talk to Sara Quinn about Rob Gibson.'

'Who's that?' Emma said.

'He's the boyfriend before Sam Gallagher,' Leon said, clearly pleased to get one up on her. 'I remember Evan Groom mentioning him at the golf club.'

'Exactly. But when I was going through the interviews, I noticed that Sara Quinn didn't include him on her list. Which seems strange. Can you have another word with her, Emma, see if she remembers him?'

'Course.'

I waited for some more bright ideas but there was nothing.

'I swear that if no one opens their gob in the next thirty seconds the DI job will be a shoo-in for an external candidate.'

Leon was the first to react. 'I was looking at the dick pics on Maria's phone.'

'I wondered why you were in the bathroom so long,' Emma said.

'You're hilarious,' Leon replied. 'I'm pretty sure it's Sam Gallagher.'

'Why?' I asked.

Leon pulled out a photograph from a folder he'd brought in with him and put it in front of me. I tried hard not to laugh. It was a close-up of a large erect penis.

'It's like a penis, only smaller,' I said.

Emma rolled her eyes.

'Ignore the dick and look at the hand at the side,' Leon said.

That was easier said than done but I did my best.

'What of it?'

'You see there's a tattoo on the guy's wrist, it looks like a wristband with an S in the middle – a bit like the Superman logo.'

'S for Sam?' I said. 'Could be but there must be thousands of people with that initial and I bet a few of them have the tats to prove it.'

'Aye, but when I saw Gallagher in the restaurant kitchen, I noticed he had a wristband tattoo. I didn't see it quite as clearly as this but I'm pretty sure it's the same one.'

'Where are we with tracing him?' I asked.

'He's gone to ground,' Leon muttered, barely catching my eyes for fear of what he might see in them. He always took his mistakes way more seriously than I did – we all made them, it was what you did to repair them that counted. 'He doesn't appear to have gone back to his house after he fled from the restaurant. I've spoken to his mam who swears she hasn't seen him in weeks.'

'Have you been to her house to check she's not hiding him?'

'No. But I will. I checked his place first and he's clearly not there. There's junk mail behind the letter box and the neighbours haven't seen hide nor hair of him. His colleagues at the restaurant claim they don't have any time to socialise so don't know anything about any friends he might have or where else he might have gone.'

I thought about the bloody message we'd found in Maria's car.

'Do you really think Gallagher might have the where-withal to set up Evan Groom in the way someone seems to have done?'

'Until I can speak to him, I don't know. However, and I know you're going to laugh, when I was chasing him, I noticed he had a strange running action. I thought it was because he had his chef's gear and big boots on. But you remember Rosie Lloyd's description of the stalker in the garden?'

'The one who "lolloped?"'

'Exactly. Gallagher's a lolloper, which made it doubly annoying that those fat bastards got in my way.'

'So you let a chef in an apron and kitchen boots who lollops outrun you,' I said, noticing Emma smirk.

'He would have caught him if it wasn't for those pesky racists,' she said.

'Or if you hadn't been too busy swanning around with gangsters until the small hours to help me,' he fired back.

'Just doing my job,' she said. 'And doing it better than you by the sound of it.'

'Maybe if I could just flash my tits to get on, I'd be doing well, too,' he said.

'Maybe if you didn't spend most of your time finding half-arsed ways to get Micky Chambers' DNA you'd be better prepared. And I wouldn't have to play nice with Harry Connors all over again.'

Now I understood where the bad attitudes had come from. They were right up in each other's faces and if I hadn't been in the room I think they might have come to blows.

'Cool it!' I shouted. 'Let's take a moment, shall we?'

They moved apart again. Sometimes I felt more like a referee than a DCI. The temptation to literally bang their heads together was almost overwhelming. Something was going to have to change with them but for now I took a deep breath and tried reason.

'I signed off on the Chambers idea, Emma,' I said. 'Leon found some CCTV from the station that clearly showed Vic Kendall discovering Maria Groom's unlocked car in the Walkergate Metro car park and driving it away, and when pressed he had a concrete alibi for the time of her disappearance. So it seemed obvious he was nothing to do with our main case. We could have charged him with twocking, I guess, or even burglary of the old lady's house, but he hasn't really done any harm and persuading him to help us with Chambers seemed like more of a result for us.'

Emma was clearly embarrassed at inadvertently criticising my decision, but I bailed her out.

'To be fair, we should have told you what was happening. But I didn't know you were going to be in Stevie's Bar at that moment otherwise we wouldn't have timed it that badly so maybe we should all improve our communication. I'm not blaming you for being there, I'm happy that you used your initiative to re-establish contact. Also, though Leon's plan worked and Kendall did exactly what we asked, I'm afraid trapping Chambers was a waste of time.'

'How do you know that already? We can't have got his DNA test back yet. They only brought him in yesterday.'

'A bit of luck, really. Turns out "Micky Chambers" is an alias. Chambers is actually Patrick Corgan, who's got quite a record, as well as a lengthy driving ban, which probably explains the alias. We got a fingerprint match and Corgan's

DNA was already on the system – sadly it didn't match the DNA on the cap.'

'So, you can keep away from Connors now,' Leon said.

'Well, maybe not,' Emma said.

'Do you think someone else from Connors' gang might have been driving?' I said.

'Yes. Because of your little trick with Chambers, I had to drive Harry Connors to see his mum.'

'You're meeting his parents now!' Leon couldn't keep the contempt out of his voice.

'Not exactly, well, not yet anyway. His mum's in a care home – she's got Alzheimer's. I doubt she'll even remember I was there.'

I couldn't help notice Emma's eyes flick towards me quickly then away again when she mentioned Alzheimer's. It wasn't the first time I'd felt she knew something about my condition. But how? And why hadn't she said something? I would have to keep a close eye on her.

'Anyway,' she continued, 'I asked Harry why he didn't drive himself and he avoided answering me, just said it was a "long story". I think it might be worth hanging around to find out what that story is. Killing a young woman might put anyone off driving for a while. Even if they are the head of a crime gang.'

'You think Connors might have been driving himself?' I said.

'He's not a million miles from the description. Tall, slim, blond hair. Maybe a bit older than we were expecting but he looks younger than he is.'

'You should know,' Leon muttered, 'you've been staring into his baby blues often enough. What did you mean when you said "not exactly" – about meeting his parents?'

'Well, I don't think meeting his dementia-ridden mum counts but his dad was released from Durham prison on Friday and I've been invited to the celebration tomorrow.'

Leon stared across the desk at me. I don't think I'd ever seen him so angry.

'This is getting ridiculous, Jack. Aren't you going to say something?'

'Good work, Emma?' I suggested, pouring oil on the fire.

Leon pushed his chair back and started to walk out.

'Where are you going?' I asked.

'To find Sam Gallagher. Someone's got to do some real police work around here,' he said, slamming the door of my office behind him.

## 49

Leon could see where Sam Gallagher got his looks from. His mother, Olivia, was equally striking, piercing blue eyes with a dash of freckles across her nose the highlights of a perfectly proportioned face. Unfortunately, the eyes were glaring at him with an anger she was doing nothing to disguise.

'Why are you persecuting my son?' she yelled as he stumbled back down the steps outside her front door.

Leon held his hands up, partly as an 'I come in peace' gesture but also to try and stop her closing the gap between them as it seemed she might take a swing at him.

'I'm not. I just wanted a word. I take it you know he ran away when I tried to talk to him before?'

'You can't blame him for being wary of the police. You lot have already stitched him up once with that ridiculous restraining order.'

'That wasn't anything to do with me, Mrs Gallagher, well before my time. And anyway, it's pretty clear that it wasn't so ridiculous. It looks like he's been harassing Maria Groom on social media for years.'

He was going to try and avoid showing her the dick pics. It wasn't like she could identify her son from his penis. Or at least he hoped not.

'Nonsense. Why would my Sam do that? That bloody woman made his life a misery. She's a total head-case.'

'She's also missing and possibly in danger.'

Olivia Gallagher looked briefly ashamed but she soon seemed to get over it.

'Well, it's nothing to with my Sam,' she said. 'It can't be, he's been—' She put her hand to her mouth, apparently realising she was about to say something revealing.

'He's been what?'

'Nothing.'

'If he's got an alibi I need to hear it,' he said. 'She and her young son, Nicky, haven't been seen for well over a week. I thought Sam might have some idea where they could have gone in that time.'

'How the hell would he know? He hasn't seen her in ages. He's had two other girlfriends since she dumped him without any warning. The poor lad was mystified at the time but it's ancient history now.'

'She did report him for harassment back then and he was given a temporary restraining order.'

'Aye, but it was a travesty. He just went to collect his things and get some kind of explanation – she owed him that. When he first met her she'd been a wreck, bit of an addiction problem. Her previous boyfriend had got her hooked on all sorts.'

'Would that have been Rob Gibson?'

'Aye, that sounds about right. Sam said she reckoned he was well dodgy. Though she could have been making that up too, I guess. Maybe that's her thing, playing the victim? Anyway, true or not, my Sam helped her get back on her feet. But as soon as she got her mojo back she ran him ragged, out on the town every other night, looking to trade up.'

'To Evan Groom?' Leon tried to imagine a situation where that constituted trading up but couldn't. He must have given that thought away with his expression.

'Exactly,' she said. 'I saw him on TV the other night. What an arsehole! Not in the same league as my boy, is he?'

Leon couldn't help smiling. Olivia Gallagher reminded him of his own mam, fiercely protective, a proper Mama Bear, who thought the sun shone out of her son's arse.

'Ha! You know it's true,' she added. 'I can tell from your face.'

He tried hard to restore straight-face mode, the woman was too good at reading him.

'Regardless, I do need to talk to him, Mrs Gallagher. It doesn't look good that he ran away the other day – for him or me – and my boss won't let it lie. The longer Sam's in hiding the higher up the list of suspects my boss'll put him.'

'He won't know anything,' she said, much calmer than she'd been a few minutes ago and definitely shifting towards helping. He'd always had a way with older women. Maybe the old Leon charm could help turn things around and get him back in Jack's good books.

'Even so . . . the sooner he comes forward the sooner we can take him off our suspects list. And I'm sure he wants to get back to work. I would imagine there are plenty of chefs who'd give their right arm to take his place.'

'You're not wrong there. He loves that job.'

'His boss – Benny, is it? – had nothing but praise for him, said it was completely out of character for Sam to leave his post like that. But I'm not sure how long he'll be prepared to hold the position open.'

That was mostly bollocks. The boss at the restaurant had been more concerned about getting the service sorted with a chef missing than with giving a character reference but she didn't need to know that.

'Give me a moment, I'll give him a quick call, see if I can get him to talk to you. Wait there,' she said and went back inside the house, without shutting the door properly.

Leon waited a few seconds then moved up the steps to the doorway, listening carefully. Olivia Gallagher had done what she said and made the call. He could hear her urging her son to talk to him. Leon gave himself another pat on the back for winning the woman over.

However, after she'd finished pleading Leon's case, to his surprise, Sam Gallagher replied. And he could tell it wasn't on speakerphone. Leon nudged the door open slowly. The Gallaghers were standing at the end of the corridor by the entrance to the kitchen. The woman had played him like a cheap fiddle. Olivia had her back to him but Sam was facing towards the front door and he must have heard the door creak open. He looked up and saw him by the front door but before Leon could say anything he was haring off again, through the kitchen and out of the back door.

Not again, Leon thought, giving chase for the second time that week. Olivia Gallagher looked back over her shoulder and saw him coming but held her ground so there was no room to get past her.

'Out the way,' Leon shouted but she ignored him. In the distance he could see her son leg it out of the back gate into the alley behind the house. Leon turned and ran back out through the front door, tearing down the street in the same direction that Gallagher had headed. At the top of the street he flew left, cutting off the only obvious exit from the back lane but there was no one there. He searched up and down the lane but it was no use. He'd lost him again.

Jack was going to nail his balls to the wall for this.

## 50

Sometimes, in this job, humour was all we had left. Emma could barely contain her laughter as Leon slowly explained to me how Sam Gallagher had escaped him again – despite his lolloping.

'I think you'd better send me next time, Jack,' she said. 'If Leon goes for the chef a third time it'll be a recipe for disaster.'

'Ha-bloody-ha.' Leon screwed up a piece of paper lying on Jack's desk and threw it at her but she ducked under it. Emma had promised to leave their arguments at the door of the station and I could tell she was trying.

'I think your goose is cooked, mate,' she continued.

'Enough of the food puns,' I said, pausing for effect. 'It does sound like you had him on a plate though, Leon.'

Emma snorted with delight at that. Leon looked like he'd rather be anywhere else. I was pleased the mood had lightened from earlier but enough was enough.

'Did you at least find out something about Rob Gibson?' I added, to get us back on the straight and narrow.

'Yes,' Leon said, clearly pleased that the conversation had moved away from his mistakes. 'Olivia Gallagher said he'd got Maria involved in drugs, though she got that second-hand via Sam. I don't think either of them ever met the guy.'

It was progress of a sort. I reminded Emma to chase up Sara Quinn to see what she had to say about it when we were interrupted by my phone buzzing. It was the front desk. One of Maria Groom's neighbours had come in claiming to have some information pertaining to the case. Maybe we were finally getting a break. I sent Emma down to collect them.

Darren Wilson had spent two weeks in Tenerife and had been rewarded with a nut-brown tan which made Emma and me look pasty-faced. He radiated sunshine and had found a present for us on his return.

'Sorry I'm a bit late contacting you,' he said, once he'd been brought up to the squad room. 'I was away when all this stuff with Maria going missing happened, didn't know anything about it until I got back yesterday. I wasn't sure about contacting you, but Rosie was telling me about how she was a key witness and when I told her about this, she told me in no uncertain terms to get my arse down to the station.'

I wasn't sure how Darren was going to be any help at all given that he'd been away at the time of Maria's disappear-ance but then he reached into a small bumbag he had round his waist and pulled out two pieces of card.

'I had a parcel turn up while I was away – a set of new covers for my three-piece suite – but thankfully there was a card saying that one of the neighbours took it in for me. It's a bugger when you have to gan to the office to get it.'

He pushed over the card to Emma.

'Look, see, he left it at number forty-seven.'

'What's this got to do with Maria?' I asked. 'She lives at number sixty-two.'

'Aye, I knaa that. And nothing, on the surface. I picked up the parcel from next door and didn't think anything of it. But when I got home, I found a second card in amongst some other junk mail. Look.'

He pushed over the second card to me.

'I got that other card at eight forty-five in the morning, but this one came a bit earlier – at eight fifteen. Look at the address! It's number sixty-two.' He paused before the punchline. 'On the thirtieth of October, the day everyone says she disappeared.'

'I think he's on to something, Jack,' Emma said. 'If the time and date are right, there's a good chance the driver saw something that morning. He could be a key to this whole thing.'

'He could be more than that,' Leon said. 'The one thing that Evan Groom remembered about Rob Gibson is that he was a delivery driver.'

## 51

'Hello?'

'Hi, is that Sara? It's Detective Sergeant Emma Steel from Northumberland Police, we spoke on the phone a few days ago.'

There was a long pause and Emma thought she'd been cut off but then Sara spoke again.

'Just a minute.'

Emma could hear a jingling tune in the background. It sounded familiar but she couldn't quite identify it. Then she heard a door shut and the phone was picked up again.

'Sorry about that, had to turn the TV down. What can I do for you?'

'I wanted to ask you about Rob Gibson.'

There was another long pause.

'Are you still there, Sara?'

'Yes, sorry, I was just trying to remember the name.'

'Did you know him?'

'No, not really.'

Emma was surprised, given what Evan Groom and Sam

Gallagher's mum had said about him, especially as Sara had claimed to be Maria's best friend. She pushed her a little harder.

'You did or you didn't?'

'Hardly. I mean we were at school with him about a hundred years ago, but we were never that close.'

'You were old school friends?'

'Not friends. Never that. We might have had the odd class together but that was it. He was very quiet back then.'

'And he's not now?'

'No. I don't know. Is he a suspect in Maria's disappearance? Is that why you're asking me about him?'

'We're following up a number of leads.'

'Have you arrested him?'

'No, it's nothing like that.'

There was an odd sound on the other end of the phone, almost like a sigh of relief.

'Why did you think that?' Emma added.

'Oh, I don't know, I remember he got into trouble at school once. I think he went to a young offenders' institution.'

'He's not in trouble. He's what we would call a person of interest.'

'OK. I'm afraid I can't help you though.'

'Why wasn't he on the list of ex-partners you sent us?'

There was yet another long pause before she answered.

'I'd forgotten all about him until you mentioned his name. I'd moved up here by the time Maria began seeing him – I was surprised, to be honest, as he was a bit of a dork when we were younger – but it didn't last long at all, just a brief fling.'

'So you don't know where we might find him?'

There was no answer this time.

'Sara?'

'Not a clue, sorry. I'm sure Maria said that he'd gone off travelling or something.'

'What about family? If you were at school together you must have known his parents?'

'Do you know how big our school was? I mean obviously he was a Newcastle lad but people came from all over to that school so he could have lived anywhere in the city. I think Maria said he'd fallen out with his family anyway.'

Emma was starting to have serious doubts about Sara Quinn. She seemed to know plenty about a man whose name she claimed to barely remember just a few minutes earlier.

'We've been told that he may have had a drug problem.'

Another delay. Perhaps it was a ropey connection. Emma had spent a fair bit of time walking in Northumberland and knew the signal could be a bit hit and miss.

'I don't know anything about that,' Sara said.

'Was Maria into drugs? Her ex-husband suggested she had some kind of habit.'

'No. Well, I mean, we all dabbled a little when we were younger, didn't we? But these days, no, I don't think so.'

Emma couldn't help wondering if Sara Quinn knew her friend as well as she thought she did. Or maybe she was lying through her teeth.

## 52

*Four days earlier*

Maria sat on her bed waiting for Rob to turn up. She was beginning to think she'd made a huge mistake. Her failure to get out of the country before her disappearance was discovered had changed everything. The story about her and Nicky vanishing had been repeated on the evening news at the top of the running order. She hadn't expected it to escalate so quickly. Maybe she should just go home and pretend it was all a big misunderstanding? Evan was going to do some serious jail time when they found the cannabis farm anyway. Unless the police were totally incompetent, of course. But how would she explain the message she'd left in the car? And the shoe in his garage? They'd know she'd set it all up – at the least she'd be charged with wasting police time, wouldn't she?

The last thing she needed now was a reunion with another ex. Their last conversation had ended with Rob slapping her so hard she'd got whiplash. To be fair, he'd never laid a hand on her before, but he'd just discovered that she hadn't *lost* the baby she'd been expecting – *their* baby as he called it – she'd had an abortion. Her insistence that it was her body, her choice, had fanned the flames. There was no way back for them after that. She'd expected Sara to at least understand that but judging by the row they'd just had she really didn't. She replayed it in her head.

'There's no way I could have had a baby with Rob – he was a full-on junkie then.'

'Well maybe you should have thought about that when you slept with him!'

'It was just a bit of fun.'

'Not for him. He'd loved you since we were at school. He thought he'd won the lottery dating you.'

'Dating? We were never seriously dating. You can't honestly think I should have started a family with him.'

'Maybe not, but why tell him you were pregnant in the first place? If you'd just got rid of it or taken the bloody morning-after pill, he'd have been none the wiser. He was a wreck when he appeared on my doorstep looking for a place to stay.'

With the benefit of hindsight Sara was probably right. Maria had booked the abortion the same day she told Rob, after she'd realised how serious he was. When they had that last horrible fight, he'd accused her of being a hypocrite but there was a big difference between being an addict and having an occasional bump to liven things up, wasn't there? And now she was relying on him to help her. How messed up was that?

She'd known that Sara had been angry with her for the way she'd dealt with it – that was why their friendship had cooled a little. She'd still agreed to be Nicky's godmother but, on reflection, that was probably because she knew by then that she couldn't have her own kids and wanted the connection.

But Maria had no idea that Rob had not only gone running off to the Borders to heal his wounds but that he'd settled down up there. Sara insisted they weren't a couple, just good friends like they'd always been, but Maria suspected they were a bit more than that. She heard his car pull up outside the cottage and watched through a gap in the bedroom shutters as he walked straight in like he owned the place – there was definitely something going on with those two.

She wasn't going to run in there pretending she was glad to see him even though she needed his help. Instead, she rummaged around in her bag and found her concealer and her lippy – she had a feeling he'd be more inclined to help her if she looked good, and she hadn't been taking care of herself much recently – for obvious reasons.

She could hear Sara talking nineteen to the dozen. She couldn't make out what she was saying but the woman was clearly nervous, her constant chatter only occasionally interrupted by a grunt from Rob. Maria checked her face in the little compact mirror she'd brought with her – not perfect but it would have to do. She took a deep breath and headed for the door.

She saw Rob before he saw her, mainly because he was

sitting on the floor with his back to her, playing Lego with Nicky. Sara was perched on the sofa behind them, looking anxious.

'I see you two have met then,' Maria said.

'Nice kid,' Rob said, without even turning around to say hello. She knew he was making a point. He was a master of passive aggression. What he was leaving unsaid, but making sure she knew it, was 'like ours would have been'.

Maria walked past him, picking up Nicky on the way, and went and sat on the armchair in Sara's front room, intending to keep Nicky on her lap, though, of course, he squirmed so much that she had to let him go and he headed straight back to his Lego. And to Rob. She couldn't miss the smirk on the man's lips when he saw her irritation. He'd cleaned himself up since she'd last seen him. His hair was as wild as always, but he'd put on a bit of weight and it suited him.

'What happened to your face?' he said.

She really needed to up her game on the concealer front.

'A pathetic man took his anger out on me. Seems like I attract them.'

There was a flicker of guilt in his eyes but no more than that.

'You probably deserved it.'

'Nice.'

'I'm not the one who needs to be nice here. Sara said you wanted new passports for you and the kid.'

'His name's Nicky.'

'Not any more, unless you want people to find you. D'you want the passports or not?'

So much for the lipstick. He was clearly not going to make this easy for her. She tried to put her strictly-business head on.

'Yes, I do.'

'It's going to cost you.'

'I have money.'

'Ten grand for the pair.'

Maria tried not to show her shock but clearly failed. She wondered how much of that was a surcharge for the abortion.

'Not got it, huh?' he said. 'I'll be off then.' He got to his feet as if to leave.

'Wait,' Maria said. 'I can do eight.'

'It's non-negotiable. The people who do this don't piss around, Mar, it's their way or no way.'

She sucked up his use of his pet name for her. He knew that she'd always hated the way he abbreviated Maria but it had never stopped him doing it.

'Can't you get it a little lower, Rob?' Sara said, speaking for the first time. 'For old times' sake.'

'Don't see why I should help her after, you know . . .'

'You used to be friends.'

'Friends don't fuck each other over like she did with me, do they?'

Sara sighed. 'Do it for me then. You owe me that much.'

'No dice. It's ten or it's not happening.'

Maria closed her eyes, mentally running through what she had in her various accounts. She could cover it, but it wouldn't leave her as much as she needed to set up some-where else. And there was no way she could get that much quickly – most of the accounts she had needed some notice to withdraw. When she opened her eyes again, Sara was staring at her.

'What?'

'I asked you if you had it.'

'Sorry, never heard you. But the short answer is no. I can do eight but that's a stretch.'

'I'll cover the rest,' Sara said.

'Seriously?'

'Why wouldn't I? I can afford it. I know we've had our ups and downs recently but you're my oldest friend. And Nicky's my godson. It'll give the pair of you a fresh start. Even if Evan somehow evades justice, he'll never find you if you're careful.'

Maria glanced over at Rob who looked completely pissed off with Sara but when he saw her looking at him, he pulled his face into something approaching satisfaction.

'Looks like we have a deal. You're a lucky woman.' He looked across to Sara. 'Did you get the photos I asked for?'

'Yes. I sent them to you.'

It hadn't been easy to get Nicky to sit still but the promise of helping Sara collect the eggs from the hens had eventually won him over.

Rob pulled his phone out of his pocket and flicked through to the photos, nodding as he saw them.

'They should be fine. Have you chosen new names?'

'Christine and Nicky Smith.'

'Smith is smart. Lots of them about. Not sure about keeping the kid's real name though.'

She looked over at her son but as usual he was paying absolutely no attention to the grown-ups.

'I don't want to confuse him any more than I already have. It's bad enough that I'm uprooting him. If I tried to change it I think he'd probably forget and tell people his real name if they asked.'

'I guess. Seems like I've got everything I need then.'

Sara clapped her hands. 'We should have a drink to celebrate.'

'I don't think so,' Rob said.

'Come on, Rob, just one drink. What do you say, Maria?'

She could certainly do with a drink. If this worked out it was the start of the new life she wanted for herself and Nicky, far away from the toxic men who'd made her life a misery for much too long. She could see that Rob was keeping one eye on her, probably expecting her to be a bitch about it. He'd never been able to read her.

'Aye, why not,' she said. 'Just let me get Nicky to bed first.'

## 10 November 2024

The delivery depot was near a large industrial park about twenty minutes from the centre of Newcastle. Leon and Emma headed there to try and track down Rob Gibson – if he was the man who had left those cards.

The traffic out of the city was unusually busy for that time of day. First of all there were long delays going over the Tyne Bridge – there'd been some major maintenance going on for ages to restore it to its former glories but that wasn't the problem this time; there'd been yet another jumper, apparently. They'd seen Sid Allan helping to control a crowd of people and he'd discreetly mimed someone diving off the side. Then they got stuck in a second jam on the Felling bypass, which only increased Leon's foul mood.

'You could always use your blue light,' Emma said, with a sly smile.

'It's hardly an emergency,' Leon muttered, wondering what that smile was all about.

'OK, Mr by-the-book. Does Jack know you're such a stickler? I thought he liked us to bend the rules?'

'Give it a rest, will you?' Leon knew he was being a dick but he and Emma had been snapping at each other for days now and though he'd just about managed to keep a lid on it in the office he couldn't seem to break the cycle when they were alone.

'Is this about tonight?' she said.

'What do you think? You're going out with Harry Connors to celebrate his human-trafficking dad being released from prison. Maybe you'd like me to buy you a new dress or something?'

'Grow up, Leon, I'm not celebrating anything. Just doing my job.'

'Aye, that's what the working girls tell their boyfriends.' As soon as the words were out of his mouth, he wished he could pull them back in.

'Are you calling me a whore?' The temperature in the car seemed to drop below freezing. He knew he should apologise but it was too late. He tried anyway.

'I didn't mean it like—'

'Just shut up and drive,' she said.

Neither of them spoke for the rest of the journey.

The depot was huge with a car park outside that was almost as big. There were a number of delivery vans parked to one side and Leon reasoned they must be close to the place where the drivers picked up the parcels so he parked in amongst them. The pair got out of the car, still not speaking, and headed towards the nearest door. There was a counter inside but no one was behind it. Leon pressed a buzzer on the wall. He heard it sound in the back office but still no one appeared.

Emma tried the handle on a door that led into the main warehouse and it opened. She looked back at him and he nodded, following her through the doorway. A man in orange coveralls saw them come in and shouted something but he was too far away to be heard. The man walked rapidly towards them.

'You can't just walk in here, love,' he said, once he was a little nearer, 'it's staff only.'

'Police,' Emma said, reaching into her inside pocket and pulling out her ID.

The man glanced at it and sighed. 'I hope this is going to be quick, we're way behind this morning.'

Leon pulled out the two delivery cards that Maria Groom's neighbour had brought them earlier that day.

'We need to talk to whichever driver left these.' He handed them to the man, who examined them.

'This is from nearly two weeks ago.'

'I know. But presumably you can still identify them.'

'I take it it's urgent.'

'What do you think?' Leon said.

Another big sigh and a shrug. 'All I needed. Follow me.' He took them into a back office where he logged on to a computer and flicked through various screens, swearing occasionally as the machine seemed to be reacting slowly.

'Do you know a driver called Rob Gibson?' Emma asked him as he searched.

'Have you any idea how many drivers come through here, love?'

Leon expected Emma to kick the man's arse for patronising her but was relieved when she bit her lip. No point pissing off someone who was helping them.

'It's a lot. And I probably know the names of about three of them,' he continued. 'You'll need to ring HR to ask about specific individuals. Ah, here you go.'

'Is it Gibson?' Leon asked.

'No. I'm afraid not. The driver was someone called Larry Bright.'

'Do you know where we might find him?'

'Nope, sorry. You'll have to talk to—'

'HR?' Leon said.

The man smiled. 'Aye, HR. I'll get you a number.'

The man disappeared and took an age to come back. Emma didn't say a word to Leon while he was gone. Eventually he returned, gave them a number and let them use the office phone. The call to HR yielded two pieces of information. Larry Bright was on a walking holiday in the Lakes. In fact, the day he dropped off those delivery cards was his last day at work before his break. He wasn't due back into work until the following morning. They did pass on a phone number but there was no answer.

They obviously needed to talk to Bright and he'd leapt above Gibson on their to-do list as the other bit of info was that Rob Gibson hadn't worked there for nearly five years. Another dead end in a case that was loaded with them. The search for Maria Groom was proving far more complicated than he'd originally expected. As was his relationship with Emma. He needed to talk to someone about the latter problem and, sadly, there was only one candidate.

## 54

A new red flag against Evan Groom's name came through a call to the 101 switchboard. I had zero expectations. Most people that came via that route were either attention seekers or lunatics. Gina Dawson didn't seem to be either. She refused point-blank to come into the office but agreed to meet me in a café near the ticket machines at Central Station.

I was there early. In my experience you can learn a lot by watching the way people approach you. In Gina's case she may as well have carried a neon sign spelling out ANXIOUS. She looked over her shoulder at least three times as she walked along the concourse, at one stage walking straight into a *Big Issue* salesman who was hoping to flog her a magazine. She actually bought one – which I took as a good sign.

She spotted me immediately when she got to the edge of the café, still looking around as if she was being followed. There was no one in sight and I was the only customer. Nevertheless, she did a 360 degree tour of the place with her eyes before heading over.

'DCI Parker?'

'That's me.'

She was younger than I'd expected, early twenties I guessed, small and so thin that the words 'eating disorder' popped into my head. I didn't stand up or attempt to shake hands, or, God forbid, go in for a hug. I try to keep up with current trends but hugging strangers and pecking cheeks like an over-exuberant Frenchman is not something that should be encouraged. It's a hill I'm prepared to die on. Luckily Gina seemed to share my view and sat down quickly, though I noticed she made sure she had a good view of the entire concourse.

'Can I get you a drink?' I said.

'No thanks, I can't stay long.'

'No problem.' I was glad I'd already got a coffee. The office vending machine was shite so I always tried to enjoy the good stuff when I was out and about.

'You said you knew Evan Groom.'

'Unfortunately, yes.'

I gave her room to expand on the subject.

'We dated briefly.'

'When was this?'

'About six months ago.'

'How did you meet?'

'A dating site.'

'What did you think of him?'

'Charming, at first. A little full of himself but he seemed generous, always paid for meals and that.'

'How long did the relationship last?'

'I wouldn't call it that. A fling maybe.'

'OK. Same question though.'

'About a month.'

'Did you end it?'

'Yes.'

'Can I ask why?'

She looked over to the concourse and then at the barista who was busy topping up the coffee grinder before replying.

'He strangled me,' she said.

Now she had my attention.

'Did you report it?'

'No.'

'Can I ask why?'

The colour rose quickly in her cheeks. She practically whispered the next bit.

'It was when we were having sex. He said I would like it. I got the impression he'd seen it on Pornhub.'

'So it was consensual?'

'No! I mean the sex was, initially, but then he started to squeeze my neck. Gently at first but then harder and harder. I tried to get him to stop but I could barely speak. Then I passed out and I woke up to him slapping me.'

'Jesus.'

'I know, right? And the worst of it was he seemed aroused by it. He said I'd fainted with the excitement but it wasn't like that. You should have seen the marks on my neck, you could see where his hands had been. He could have killed me!'

## 55

After hearing Gina Dawson's grim story I needed a drink but I was trying to stick to my vow so I opted for the much less satisfying substitute of fresh air and exercise. My consultant reckoned that increased physical fitness was another thing that could help delay the symptoms of dementia and I was happy to give it a go. Well, not happy, perhaps, my body wasn't built for running, but it was better than joining a gym.

My son may not have been speaking to me but he did agree to take in a gentle jog around Jesmond Dene. I didn't like to talk when I ran anyway, I needed all the breath I had to get through it without wasting it on someone who wouldn't listen to me.

The only time he spoke for most of the run was when a rat ran across the path right in front of us, almost tripping Aidan. I asked him if he was OK and got an 'aye' in return. Communication between us had been so bad that, ridiculously, I actually cherished that tiny morsel.

I tried once again as we got within range of the house and I thought I had enough breath left to get home.

'Can I ask you something?'

He glanced across at me and I thought I saw a slight nod.

'Put yourself in my position. If you had this condition, would you want to make everyone else's life a misery?'

'By killing myself?' he shot back. 'Anyway, it's not my problem. I don't have it. You do.'

*But you might have it too.* I so nearly said it out loud but managed to hold the thought back. It was still too soon to lumber Aidan with something so huge.

'And I'm not a mortal sinner like you,' he added, speeding up so I couldn't respond, knowing that I couldn't keep up with him if he forced the pace. A mortal sinner? Had Aidan been talking to Phillip? It had my brother's fingerprints all over it.

I slowed down a little, feeling a headache coming on. Aidan's attitude hadn't helped but my bigger fear was that it was a side-effect of the drug trial. By the time I got back my son was sharing a complicated handshake with Leon who must have been waiting on the doorstep. It was one of their things that I was nowhere near cool enough to attempt or even understand. At least my son was engaging with someone.

'Can I have a word, Jack?' Leon said, as I trotted up the drive. Aidan took the hint and shot straight into the house. 'It's about Emma,' he added, as soon as Aidan had disappeared.

He looked a little nervous and I prayed he wasn't looking for relationship advice. I'd got enough problems getting my marriage and family back on track without playing Agony Uncle in someone else's life.

'Sure,' I said. I really needed to learn to say 'no' sometimes.

Leon followed me into the kitchen.

'I can't offer you a drink, I'm afraid, I don't have anything in.' I hadn't declared my almost teetotal status to anyone as I didn't want to lie about the reasons behind it. Helen may have found out about my condition but I didn't want to give my colleagues any clues – they were supposed to be good at solving them, after all. Though our latest case was perhaps disproving that idea.

'It's fine, I'm driving anyway.'

We settled for a nice fennel tea, not a word I'd have used to describe the herbal drink before my diagnosis. I snuck a couple of aspirins in to ease my aching head when he wasn't looking.

'What's the problem?' I asked.

'I called Emma a whore and now she's not speaking to me.'

'Well, as long as it's nothing serious.'

He lowered his head.

'What were you thinking? You can hardly blame her for being angry.'

He raised his head again and looked me straight in the eye.

'I don't. I blame you.'

'Don't push your luck, son.'

He held his hand up in apology.

'Sorry, my head's all over the place. I didn't mean it like that. But this thing with Harry Connors is getting out of hand. I'm concerned about her meeting his dad. I don't think she's ready to deal with the likes of him.'

'Because she's a fast-tracker, you mean.'

'No. Because she's a young woman. You know why he was locked up. He was trafficking girls for sex and not averse to sampling the merchandise himself. He's a predator. And we're sending her into his world without any support.'

He was only echoing my thoughts from the previous day, but I'd decided the pros outweighed the cons for the moment.

'It's a party in a public place. She'll be fine. I've spoken to her about this and offered her some backup, but she said she didn't need it.'

'She's just trying to show you she's got the balls to be the next DI.'

'Balls of Steel, eh! Is that what you're worried about – the competition?'

'No. Well, a bit. But mainly I'm worried about her. She doesn't have to know if we watch her back, does she?'

Maybe he had a point.

'I'll think about it,' I said.

Leon scratched his head, clearly reluctant to say something else.

'Spit it out.'

He sighed heavily, still hesitating.

'Now or never, mate.'

'I don't know how to say this. I guess my question is: is it all worth the risk? I mean, it's all pretty speculative and Laura was on the take, wasn't she?'

'She had her reasons. I don't agree with what she did, but she didn't deserve to die for it. Also, she was our friend.'

'I know. But she's dead and it's probable that was because she was too close to Frankie Grant. Now we're putting Emma in a similar position, just with a different gangster.'

Again, he wasn't wrong.

'Maybe it's time to call it a day and spend more time on our proper cases,' he added, 'especially now the Maria Groom case is so much trickier than we expected. She hasn't been seen for twelve days and we still have no idea what's happened to her.'

I shook my head. Although Leon had logic on his side, I couldn't let it go. I didn't often let my heart rule my head but Laura was killed on my watch, in my car, her death was my responsibility. And I believed we had enough resources to continue both investigations, even if one of them was off the books. Unfortunately, I wasn't sure I could convince Leon that we were doing the right thing. But I knew someone who could.

'Let's go for a walk,' I said.

'Now?'

'Aye. Give me ten minutes to have a quick shower.'

He looked at his watch.

'You can't be in a hurry,' I said. 'I know you haven't got a hot date because your girlfriend's going out with another man tonight.'

Leon looked torn between anger and laughter at that but thankfully the latter won out, even if it was bittersweet.

'Jesus, Jack, that was brutal, even for you.'

Fifteen minutes later we were on our way. On foot, even though I'd just finished a run. I was a great believer in marginal gains so anything that might stave off this disease for a bit longer was worth a try.

'Where are we going?' he asked.

'You'll see.'

Gordon Kemp was always pleased to see me, even though I kept disappointing him. Since I'd last seen him the light in his eyes had dimmed as his hopes of us finding his daughter's killer had done likewise. Even so, he greeted the pair of us with enthusiasm. Particularly Leon.

'Good to see you, Leon, lad, it's been far too long,' he said, giving him a huge hug as soon as he'd opened the door to let us in. 'Come in and have a cuppa.'

'Don't get your hopes up, Gordon,' I said. 'That lead I mentioned to you didn't pan out. We have got something else we're working on, but I mainly just came to touch base.'

'You'll get there, Jack, I'm sure. Laura said you were the best cop she'd ever known and she was rarely wrong. Like her mother.'

I could see his enthusiasm dip a little at the mention of Liz.

'How is she?'

'She's fine, having a little lie-down at the moment.'

It was a regular excuse when I visited.

'Really?'

'See, I said you were a good cop. You know when someone's pulling the wool over your eyes. OK, she's not fine, but she's a little better than she was. Until recently I could only get her out of the house to visit Laura's grave once a week. But yesterday we had a little drive up to St Mary's lighthouse, some chips in the car park overlooking the sea. Not exactly a holiday, but progress nonetheless.'

'That's encouraging.'

'Aye, I guess. I think the news that you had a new lead perked her up a bit. So, if she makes an appearance, maybe don't mention that it didn't go anywhere. She needs hope, Jack, we both do.'

They say it's the hope that kills you, but I could see that Gordon's desperate need was having the required effect on Leon. He was looking distinctly guilty about his earlier suggestion to drop our investigation.

'I know I can rely on you two to bring us some closure,' Gordon continued, putting his hand on Leon's shoulder, looking for reassurance that he was right. It wasn't long in coming.

'We'll get the bastard, Mr Kemp, don't worry about that,' Leon said. 'Excuse my language.'

'Call me Gordon, lad. And don't worry about the language, I've called the fucker a lot worse than that.'

They both laughed.

'Now let's talk about something a bit jollier, shall we?' Gordon suggested. 'Isn't it time you settled down, Leon? Have you got yourself a nice girlfriend yet?'

## 56

Emma stepped out of the car in front of Jesmond Dene House, a swanky hotel on the edge of the Dene. She took Harry Connors' arm as they paraded through the front door, each grabbing a glass of Champagne from the waiter who stood there with a tray in his hand.

'Cheers,' Harry said as they clinked glasses. They wandered into the anteroom to the right of the entrance where the guests were gathering before they took over the restaurant. Emma couldn't imagine how much that would cost but Harry had assured her it was all free for guests – a welcome-home present for his dad.

Stevie Connors stood in the centre of a group of dodgy-looking geezers, all big, bald, red-faced and musclebound. Emma tried hard not to laugh at the stereotypical image. What do you call a group of bouncers? A punch? Or maybe a gammon? She smiled at the thought.

'Penny for them,' Harry said.

'I hope my name's down on the list or that lot might not let me in,' she said, nodding towards the men, the biggest of whom was glaring across at them like he'd smelt something terrible.

'I'd like to see them try,' Harry laughed. 'But seriously, you looked worried.'

'It's nothing,' she said. 'I'm just feeling guilty that I'm partying while Maria Groom and her boy are still missing. I feel like I should be doing something to help find her.'

'You can't do it all, Emma. Everyone deserves a break some time.'

'Do they?' She realised she was being churlish. 'Look, I'm sorry, I've had a couple of bad days, perhaps I shouldn't have come.'

'I'm happy you did,' he said, taking her hand.

She smiled. Maybe she did deserve a night off.

'I really didn't think you would, you know?' he continued.

'Why not?'

'Well, partly because I knew you'd be all chewed up about taking some time off. But mainly because you're a detective sergeant in Northumberland Police and my dad over there is a convicted sex trafficker. Never the twain shall meet and all that.'

'Don't they say "know your enemy"?'

'Is that what I am to you? An enemy?'

She was going to laugh but he looked so hurt that she held it back. His eyes stayed firmly locked on hers and she couldn't look away.

'No,' she said.

'A friend then?' There was an intensity in his gaze that rattled her a little.

'Maybe.'

One of the posse of men around his dad said something and they all burst out laughing; the spell was broken. She could have sworn she heard Evan Groom's name but perhaps that showed how much the case was playing on her mind.

'You'd better come and meet the old man then,' he said, taking her free hand to lead her across the room.

Emma gulped down the last of her Champagne and imagined flinging it into the large fireplace to make an impact. Sensibly she resisted the temptation and placed it on the empty tray of a passing waiter instead. As they approached the group, one of the men saw them coming and made room for them to join in the circle.

Stevie Connors didn't take his eyes off her as she came alongside Harry to complete a bigger circle surrounding him. There was a hunger in his look that scared her a little, or maybe that was just his reputation preceding him. He looked good for his age but was way too thin. A diet of prison food could do that to a man, she guessed, though he probably held enough sway to get what he wanted inside. She noticed that everyone in the group had gone silent, waiting for him to speak.

'And who's this bonny lass?' he said, as the silence was becoming awkward. 'I don't think I've had the pleasure.'

And nor will you, Emma thought. It was a disturbing echo of something Harry had said to her the first time they'd met. Like father like son?

'This is the friend I told you about, Dad. Emma, this is my dad, Stevie.'

'Only my friends call me Stevie, son. Mr Connors to you, love,' he added, his eyes still firmly fixed on Emma. There was no indication in them that he was smiling, even though his mouth suggested as much. His retort drew a laugh from his acolytes, but she felt Harry's hand twitch.

'Only my boyfriends call me "love", Stevie,' she said, 'but maybe we can do a deal. I'll call you Mr Connors and you can call me Detective Sergeant Steel.'

She could feel the tension in the crowd rise, especially amongst this inner circle – but it felt like everyone in the room was listening in. The huge guy who'd glared at them when they entered looked particularly pissed off – but Stevie Connors barked out a laugh and the air came back into the room.

'I think you've got a good one this time, Harry. She's got a mouth on her. I like a girl who uses her mouth.'

That brought smirks all round and Harry's hand gripped hers tightly – maybe he was suggesting she backed down but that wasn't going to happen. She may have been trying to gain Harry's confidence but she had her limits. Anyway, she half suspected he'd brought her to show his dad who was the boss now.

Stevie Connors put his hand on the big guy's shoulder and nodded towards the bar. 'Give us a minute, will you, Dusty, get the lads a beer. We need a bit of family time.'

The circle of thugs dissipated before he'd finished speaking. She made a mental note to check out 'Dusty' who was giving her the heebie-jeebies. He wasn't a contender for

Laura's killer – too old and too fat – but there was something off about the guy.

'Excuse the ogling, my dear, they're a bunch of oafs who'd jump a scarecrow given half the chance and I haven't seen a good-looking woman in a very long time. Most of the female guards looked like Eastern European shot-putters in comparison to you.'

He put his hand on his son's arm.

'Grab me a proper drink, Harry, would you? Bourbon on the rocks, if you don't mind. It'll give me a minute to get to know your new girlfriend a little better.'

Harry looked reluctant but in the end he followed the other men to the bar. She noticed that Dusty was already holding court there and made no attempt to let Harry through. Maybe his takeover of the organisation wasn't as clear-cut as he had suggested. She was sensing a lot of resentment from the troops. His dad closed the gap to Emma, not quite in her personal space but right on the edge.

'You know, before I went inside, when Harry was a student at Durham, he used to pass on his rejects to me. They loved a bit of rough, those posh southern tarts. Maybe I could get him to reinstate that routine once he's finished with you, eh? What do you think?'

'I think I'd rather eat my own feet,' Emma said.

He gave her one of those smiles again, like he'd been programmed by a work experience kid who had got some of the code wrong.

'Can't blame a man for trying.'

'Probably not Brenda's view on the subject.'

His eyes went cold. 'Leave my wife out of it.'

'You certainly seem to. Have you been to see her yet?'

'Don't push your luck, sweetheart.'

'And vice versa. I'm sure Harry will be thrilled to hear about your proposition.'

'I wouldn't try and get between us, *love*,' he said, emphasising the final word. 'We're tighter than a gnat's chuff.'

'I think you'll find he's matured a bit since you went inside. Probably did him good to escape from your shadow, for a while.'

'Maturity is overrated,' Stevie said, 'though to be fair to Harry, I never managed to snaffle my own pet pig so he has that on me. Mind you, it didn't do Frankie Grant much good, did it?'

## 57

Gordon Kemp's chat with Leon had done the trick for the moment. By the time we'd walked back to my house he seemed fully committed to finding Laura's killer. There's no better motivator than a bereaved parent.

Aidan had taken advantage of my absence to disappear to a friend's house, knowing full well that I'd want an explanation for his 'mortal sinner' jibe as soon as we were on our own. As I couldn't get it from him, I thought I'd go straight to the horse's mouth – my gobshite of a brother.

I banged on his door with the righteousness of a wronged man. By the time he'd opened it I swear I'd taken some of the paint off.

'Keep your hair on,' he said, glancing down at my hand, clearly expecting to see my customary bottle of whiskey and screwing up his face when he saw I was empty-handed.

'I need a word,' I said.

'How about Jameson's?'

I ignored him and brushed past him into his kitchen.

He sighed and shut the door slowly, taking a moment before he turned and joined me.

'Everything all right?' he said.

'No, it bloody isn't. My case is stalling in the water and my son thinks I'm a mortal sinner.'

'Oh.'

'Yes, fucking "oh" is appropriate. It's down to you, I suppose.'

'Well, I can't take the blame for the case.'

'Not funny.'

'Sorry, you're right.'

'But Aidan?'

'Mea culpa.'

Fucking Catholics and their Latin hogwash. Given that I'd foresworn my religious upbringing years ago and to the best of my knowledge Aidan had never even been in a church, let alone given a toss about religion, there had only really been one possible culprit for this mortal sin claptrap.

'Of course it was you. Who else does he know who'd fill his head with such bollocks? I've no idea why he listens to you anyway. I bet you wouldn't try telling him that masturbation is a mortal sin?'

'Well, um, no, obviously.'

'Because he wouldn't fucking listen to you then, would he? So why is he listening to you now? The only mortal sin that's going to be committed around here is fratricide. That biblical enough for you? A bit of Cain and Abel.'

'Look,' Phillip said, 'let's calm down and talk about this rationally.'

'What's rationality got to do with religion? Sod all, that's what. How dare you turn my son against me?'

'I didn't. He was already against you. The boy's heart-broken because his dad wants to die. How do you expect him to feel? He thinks that you're abandoning him.'

'That's bollocks.'

'Is it? He's just turned fifteen and still believes in his bones that both he and the people he loves will live forever. And you've not only blown that belief out of the water, you've made it clear you're happy to bring your natural end a lot closer than God intended.'

'One: you haven't the foggiest what God intends. Why would he tell you? You're a defrocked priest.'

'I was never def—'

I held up my hand to stop him.

'Two: I'm not "happy" about it at all but it's for the best.'

'Says you.'

'Jesus, Phil. How dense are you? D'you want me to remind you once again what happened to me and our mam when Dad was at his worst? There is no way I'm putting Helen and Aidan through that. Helen gets that, why can't you?'

'Does she "get it?" I suspect she would have agreed to anything to get you back home. Mark my words, she's going to spend the next however many years trying to persuade you to change your mind.'

'Is that right? Have you spoken to her?'

'No, but Aidan has and he's crystal clear what his mother's strategy is for dealing with "the Jack problem".'

I could see he regretted saying that as soon as the words were out.

'I think you've just broken the seal of confession,' I said.

'For God's sake, for the last time, I'm not a Catholic priest any more.'

'Blasphemer,' I shouted back as I stormed out of the room.

When I got home there was a patrol car parked right outside the house and Aidan was sitting in the back of it.

## 58

A uniformed officer, who hadn't yet seen me, was ringing our doorbell.

As I reached the car I tapped gently on the window. Aidan looked up then straight back down again. I tried the handle but it was locked. I tapped again, a little louder this time but he ignored me. The noise alerted the officer at the front door and he turned around.

'DCI Parker?' he asked.

I nodded.

'PC Graham French. I don't think we've met.'

'What's going on?'

He went to say something then clearly hesitated. 'It might be better if we talk inside.'

'What about Aidan?'

'Him too.'

We sat at the kitchen table. Aidan still hadn't spoken. I'd put the kettle on but didn't move when it boiled.

'Nice place you've got,' PC French said.

'Can we get on with it? What's he done?'

He opened his notebook and read from it.

'Driving without due care and attention. Driving without a licence. Driving on the pavement. Driving while under the influence of alcohol.' He looked back up at me. 'And that's just for starters.'

'Driving what? He's only fifteen.'

'An e-scooter.'

I must admit I felt a slight relief. At least it wasn't a car. Hundreds of Orange e-scooters had appeared across the city about three years earlier, a rental trial that delighted some and exasperated others, myself included. The bloody things were everywhere around Heaton and Sandyford, loved by the students, of course, who often left them lying on the pavements after a night out.

'He crashed into a tourist on the Millennium Bridge,' French added.

'I didn't crash into him. He walked right in front of me,' Aidan said, speaking for the first time.

'That's hardly the point,' PC French said.

'But he was shit-faced.'

'It's probably best if you keep quiet for now, son,' I said, putting my hand gently on his arm. He pulled it away angrily. I turned back to French. 'I thought you had to be eighteen to hire them.'

'You do.'

'How did you end up on one of those, Aidan?'

My son kept his head down and his mouth shut, taking my advice a bit too literally.

'He was with another lad who ran off after they crashed into the pedestrian.'

'The drunk,' Aidan muttered.

'Is he hurt, the victim?'

The young cop shook his head.

'He's fine, too pissed to notice the pain probably. Last I saw he was stumbling along the Quayside, heading back to the Malmaison for a lie-down.'

'I told you,' Aidan said, glaring at me.

'So what now?' I asked.

French looked a little sheepish.

'Well, given that the man hasn't made an official complaint . . .'

I know it wasn't right but occasionally the privilege of rank earned me some favours.

'Thank you.'

Aidan looked at the cop and back at me.

'I'm not being charged?'

'Not charged,' I said. 'But, believe me, you'll definitely be punished.'

Once French had gone I finally made the tea, taking the chance to gather my thoughts, and trying hard not to fly off the handle. My headache was back again but under the circumstances that wasn't particularly surprising. I pushed that to one side – maybe this was a chance to build a bridge or two with my son. I plonked a mug in front of him and sat back down at the table.

'Good job you know a policeman,' I said.

He half-smiled. 'It's like being a nepo baby, only not so cool.'

'It's not cool at all, Aidan, you could have badly hurt that man.'

'We were only going about five miles an hour.'

'That's not the point.'

He sighed. 'I know. I'm sorry. Can I go to bed now?'

'Not yet. Why did you do it?'

'Just bored.'

'You could have been killed.'

He stared at me, his laser-beam eyes boring two holes in my already aching head.

'At least I'm not planning to die. Not like you.'

'Is that what this is about?'

Aidan blinked a couple of times. I could see he was on the verge of tears.

'I don't know. Maybe.'

'This disease is going to kill me, you get that, don't you?'

I thought he wouldn't answer but he surprised me.

'I guess,' he said quietly. I put my hand on his arm and this time he didn't move it away.

'But you know I'm taking part in this new wonder drug trial?'

'Yes,' he said, quietly.

'It's given me a horrible headache but I'm doing it because it might give me more time with you and your mam.'

The hope I saw in his eyes nearly broke me.

'Dementia is still going to shorten my life though, you understand?'

A small nod.

'I just don't want it to shorten yours and your mum's too,' I added.

The tears started to flow. Mine as well as his.

'Could I have a hug?' I said, leaning over towards him. He didn't respond but when I wrapped my arms around him he didn't resist either.

A moment later I felt him hug me back and we held each other until our arms got tired. Even then neither of us wanted to let go.

## 59

Leon drove towards Jesmond Dene House with a surprising new enthusiasm for the job Emma was doing with Harry Connors. She may have been enjoying it a bit too much but his chat with Laura's dad had made him realise how important it was. The man deserved to get some closure. That didn't mean that Leon couldn't keep a close eye on her though, did it? The hotel was a big place and he was pretty sure he could find a suitable spot to make sure there was no trouble. Emma might not like it but surely she'd eventually realise he was trying to keep her safe.

He was about to hit the Blue House roundabout, a couple of minutes from the hotel, when his phone rang. For a moment he imagined that either Jack or Emma had discovered what he was doing and were calling to tell him to back off – so he ignored it – but then he realised how ridiculous he was being and worried that he'd missed something important. He turned right at the roundabout and pulled in at a bus stop on the left of the road to check who had been calling. He didn't recognise the number but it was his work phone so thought he'd better ring them back.

'Hello,' a male voice at the other end said.

'This is Detective Sergeant Leon Johnson, from Northumberland Police. Returning your call.'

'Ah right, that's funny cos I was returning your call, so we're equal now. It's Larry Bright, I just got back home. You left me a message earlier.'

Bollocks, Leon thought, it was the delivery guy. He urgently needed to talk to him. It looked like Emma was on her own. She'd be OK, wouldn't she?

'Thanks for ringing me back, Larry. Where can I find you?'

Larry Bright lived in a small flat in the Byker Wall, one of the most recognisable landmarks in the city. It had been much lauded when it was first designed and won a few awards for its architect. The locals had mixed views about it though its residents seemed to love it. Leon leaned strongly towards the positive end, maybe because it reminded him of the pretend houses he used to make from Lego when he was a kid.

Fortunately, Bright lived in a ground-floor flat which was relatively easy to find. Despite his liking for the building, Leon usually struggled to navigate his way around the various walkways that led to the upper floors. Bright was a young, smiley black man who opened the door before Leon had even had a chance to ring the bell.

'Been keeping an eye out for you,' he said. 'Is this about my form? I've been waiting for someone to contact me for ages.'

'Huh?'

'My application to join the police? You're here about that, right?'

'You want me to put in a good word for you? I could do with some other brothers to keep me company amongst all the white trash.'

Bright looked shocked at first but Leon's grin brought a huge burst of laughter from him.

'You nearly got me, there, man,' he said. 'Come on in, I've put a brew on.'

It was a small flat but tidy except for a couple of buckets with Children in Need stickers on them in the corner of the front room and a Pudsey the Bear mask resting against them.'

'Excuse the mess, won't you?'

'It's a lot tidier than my flat, Mr Bright.'

'Call me Larry, please. How d'you take it? Your tea?'

'White, no sugar, thanks.'

Larry disappeared for a couple of minutes then reappeared with a couple of mugs and a packet of chocolate Hobnobs.

'You trying to bribe me to put in a good word for you?' Leon joked, grabbing a biscuit.

'Ha! You rumbled me. I can see how you made detective sergeant so young.'

Leon decided that he liked Larry Bright and was really hoping that he had nothing to do with Maria Groom's fate, though he couldn't help remembering Maria's neighbour and her description of the lolloping black man.

'Look, Larry, cards on the table, I'm not here about your

application. I didn't know anything about it until you mentioned it.'

The man's face fell a little.

'But you know how it works, mate, I'm hoping you can help me with something else – you scratch my back etc.'

Larry's smile returned immediately. It was bollocks, obviously, Leon had absolutely zilch to do with recruitment and whoever did wasn't going to listen to the likes of him, but he needed the man's full cooperation.

'Anything for you, Detective Sergeant.'

'Call me Leon, please.'

Leon hadn't thought the man's grin could get any wider but he'd been wrong.

'It'll be Detective Sergeant once you're on the team though, obviously.'

'Of course. What is it you need from me?'

'It's about one of your deliveries.'

'Right. You know I've been on holiday for a week or so though? Only got back today and found your message on my phone. I left it at home while I was away so my boss couldn't call me back in. They're always messing with your time off, you know.'

'Sure. But this goes back almost a couple of weeks, before you went away. You left a parcel card at a house on Linden Road in Gosforth, quite early on the morning of thirtieth of October. Any chance you remember that morning?'

Larry's face fell again. He was one of those people who couldn't hide his emotions.

'I didn't mean to do it,' he said suddenly. 'It was an accident.'

'What was?' Leon was hoping he hadn't seriously misjudged the man. Surely the neighbour hadn't been right all along? He wished he'd paid more attention to the way Larry Bright had walked into the kitchen.

'The woman just fell. It wasn't my fault.'

'Can we start from the beginning? I'm a bit lost. Are we talking about Maria Groom?'

'I guess. I don't think I knew her name. Pretty woman but a bit mean.'

Leon felt himself grimace a little. He hoped Larry hadn't done anything stupid.

'Talk me through what happened, can you?'

'Sure. I had a parcel to deliver to one of the other houses but there was no one home. I saw this woman, Maria, I guess, through the window and thought she could take it in for me. I didn't mean to scare her.'

'What did you do exactly?'

Larry nodded at the buckets and mask in the corner of the room.

'All that week I'd been collecting for Children in Need while I was on my round. People were being very generous, it was great until then. She took the parcel from me but I hadn't realised it was so big that she couldn't see my face. When she turned back she got a right shock because I was wearing the Pudsey mask. She stumbled backwards and tripped on one of her kid's toys. She fell and banged her head on the radiator and passed out. I was fucking terrified I'd killed her.'

'But you hadn't?'

'Course not. She came round quite quickly, a bit dazed and very angry but all right apart from that. There was a bit of blood, right enough, but scalp injuries can be like that – I volunteer with the St John Ambulance, thought it might help with my application.'

'Then what happened?'

'She made me take the parcel away again. And because of all the trouble, I was almost late finishing my round. I got a bollocking for it.'

'I meant to Maria.'

'Nothing. She was fine. Apart from being angry, that is. Why? I really didn't think she'd report me. It's not a criminal offence, is it? I'll never get accepted into the force if I get a criminal record!'

'Chill out Larry, no one has reported anyone and you're not in any trouble. Let me get this straight though. When you left her that morning, Maria Groom was fine?'

'Yes, for sure.'

'And there was no one else with her.'

'I don't think so. I mean, I never got further than the hallway. Like I said, there were some kids' toys on the floor, so I assumed she had a kid tucked away somewhere.'

'And you didn't see anything else suspicious that morning?'

'No, nothing at all.'

'And you'd never seen her before?'

'No. At least I don't think so. Why are you asking me all this?'

'Don't you watch the news?'

'I sometimes look at the BBC site on my phone, but like I say, I haven't had it while I've been away and I haven't had a chance to look at it yet. I rang you soon as I got back.'

'Maria Groom vanished off the face of the earth some time that morning.'

'You're joking.'

'No. It would seem that you were the last person to see her before she disappeared.'

'Really? Shit. I'm not a suspect, am I? That would scupper my application.'

'No, I told you, you're fine. As long as you've told me the truth.'

'I have, honest. She made me take the parcel away and I was out the rest of the day finishing my round. You can check with my bosses, they watch my every move.'

Leon could tell the kid was telling the truth. It looked like Evan Groom had been right all along. Unless something else had happened later that morning – which was a coincidence too far for his liking – the supposed crime scene was a combination of accident and artifice. Maria had set her ex-husband up and gone into hiding. While they'd been worried about her safety, she'd probably been tucked up somewhere safe and warm without a care in the world.

# 60

*Four days earlier*

Maria woke up in almost total darkness, disorientated, a rank smell overwhelming her senses. Her head was aching like hell. She tried to sit up but immediately felt sick and rolled to one side to throw up. Thankfully, despite the gloom, she could see there was a bucket on the floor by the side of her bed. She leant over more fully, almost falling out, but managed to get one hand on the bed frame to steady herself. The sight of what was in the bucket set her off again as she quickly added to its contents. She'd never felt so sick in her life. No wonder the whole room smelt sour. When she'd finally finished vomiting, she rolled onto her back and closed her eyes. Her throat felt raw and her head was heavy, like she was underwater. What had happened to her?

Then a more urgent thought: where the hell was she? And where was Nicky? She sat up quickly, wide awake now, and immediately wished she hadn't, flopping straight back down as the walls revolved around her. Could she make it to the door? Had she already tried? No idea. She closed her eyes and started to mutter the Lord's Prayer. Fuck knows why, she'd never believed in that stuff. But she needed someone to save her and God was the only candidate she could think of.

A minute or so later she tried again, opening her eyes gradually this time to try and reduce the nausea. Eventually her vision adjusted to the gloom and she could see shutters on the window and a small sliver of light coming in under the door. There was a cabinet next to the bed with a light on it. She tried to sit up again and this time got halfway without wanting to throw up. She managed to turn the light on and leant back on her elbows to look around the room.

A burst of recognition calmed her a little. She knew this room, the bookcase stacked with games and the painting of animals playing cards on the wall. There was a half-packed case on the opposite side of the bed from the bucket. Was that hers? She shook her head and immediately felt dizzy so lay down again. Looking straight up she was pretty sure she also remembered the damp patch that looked like a map of Italy in the corner of the ceiling.

She steeled herself to get out of bed but a wave of dizziness kept her tight to the mattress. She took a handful of deep breaths, trying again to remember how she had ended up there, hoping the nausea she was feeling would soon disappear. She'd had a bang on the head, hadn't she? She put her hands up to her face and flinched with the pain from around her cheekbone and eye. She felt around some more and found a small lump on the back of her skull, still a little tender to the touch. For some reason the image of a bear came into her head. Had she been attacked by a bear? Don't be stupid, she thought. You live in Newcastle, not fucking Wyoming, or wherever it is that bears are.

Maria breathed in deeply and held it, counting to ten before releasing the breath. She repeated this until her head became clearer. She tried to sit up again, much more slowly this time. That was better. She swung her legs off the bed to the right, avoiding the bucket, and put her feet down on the floor, waiting for the dizziness to return. Nothing. Maybe she could make it to the door this time. She rose to her feet but then stopped, putting her hand on the side of the bed to prevent herself from falling. Somewhere in the distance she heard a child crying. Nicky!

'Hello,' she shouted. Or at least she tried to shout. Her throat was so raw it came out as a croak. The crying continued but there was no response.

She tried once more, croaking 'Nicky', but still there was nothing other than the child's sobs. Maria took another couple of steps, keeping hold of the bed, reached out and twisted the handle on the door; it turned but when she tried to pull the door it wouldn't open. She tried harder but it held firm. She slowly knelt down, wincing at the pain in her skull, and glanced through the small gap between the door and the frame. She could see a bolt holding it in place.

She was locked in.

Maria woke up again, lying on the floor by the door. A sound outside interrupted her thoughts. Was that a car?

She climbed to her feet but immediately wished she hadn't, falling to her knees by the bucket and retching again. All that came out this time was bile. As she leant forward to spit into the bucket she overstretched and collapsed on the floor. She just wanted to die. Then, somewhere in the house, a telephone started ringing.

She dragged herself up again. She could hear voices now, not clear enough to make out what they were saying though. She crawled along the floor towards the door, hoping she could hear a little better, but it was no use. She tried to bang on the door but she was so weak that her efforts barely made a sound. Her voice was shot away too. What the hell was wrong with her?

Maria desperately tried to clear her head, to remember something, anything. Various images floated through her mind like butterflies: a shadowy figure behind her front door, an angry Evan screaming in her face, a teddy bear, a radiator, a strange car, Sara dancing around a room, someone else trying to kiss her; but they were so slight that they flew off almost as soon as she tried to pin them down. She could feel herself sinking into the floor, losing any sense of who and where she was.

An engine noise disturbed her thoughts. Had she fallen asleep again? The sound faded, the vehicle getting further and further away until she could hear nothing. The voices had gone too. Whoever had come to the house had gone again. Did that mean she was alone here? She edged closer to the door, straining to hear something, anything.

At first it was no use but then she heard a door open,

footsteps, another door opening, or closing, it was hard to be sure. She summoned up every bit of strength she had, raised herself up into a sitting position and thumped the door again, this time with more effect. Surely whoever was out there would have heard that. The effort exhausted her. She sank back down onto the floor, despair clouding out any other thoughts.

She thought she heard the footsteps again but was so confused that it could well have been her mind playing tricks. Then another sound, a click. Was that a key turning? The door began to open, only a fraction at first as she was blocking it with her legs. Maria rolled away to make more room.

Sara Quinn stuck her head around the edge of the door, screwing up her face at the stink.

'Oh, my darling,' she said. 'Thank God you've come round. I was so worried about you.'

Maria burst into tears.

A hot bath worked wonders for her. The sight of her bruises in the bathroom mirror had been a shock but it looked a little better once she'd cleaned herself up and she'd stopped feeling sick. Tea and toast on the sofa helped too. Maria was still feeling extremely fragile but at least she now knew where she was and had remembered how she got here – well, most of it anyway. And Nicky was fine. He was happily running around in the yard outside, terrorising the sheep, oblivious to the state his mother had been in.

When he'd first seen her, as Sara helped her towards the

bathroom, he'd wrinkled his little nose at her. After the bath she at least got a hug before he disappeared off to play again. Whatever had sent her over the edge last night didn't seem to have affected him at all. Sara had the knack of making him smile, she was much better with kids than she was. As if Maria had wished her into the room, Sara came in from the kitchen.

'I've put some soup on, should only be about half an hour, let's see if we can get you feeling yourself again. I'm so relieved you're back with us again. I'm going to kill Rob!'

Rob. His face looming above her. He'd been the one trying to kiss her, hadn't he? And then it flooded back. The passports, the drinking. Fuck, how much had she had?

'How long have I been out of it?'

'Pretty much since Rob slipped that ket into your drink, stupid bastard.'

'He did what?'

'I think he thought he was being funny. Or after some kind of revenge for . . . you know.'

'What a dick move.'

'Aye, don't worry, I've read him the riot act. I mean, we were all a bit worse for wear but I don't think he expected you to react quite so badly given that it's not exactly your first time.'

'Bloody hell, Sara, don't put me in his class! Aye, I dabbled a bit but that was mainly down to Rob. I haven't touched the stuff since I had Nicky. It's no wonder I had a reaction. What exactly happened?'

'At first you were funny, a little manic perhaps, and

dancing like a loon. But later on, you switched completely. Said you were going to be locked up, that you should wake Nicky up and go home, tell them that you'd had a breakdown. You even went and tried to pack your case, said you were going to drive home despite the fact that you were off your head already.'

'Jesus. I'm glad you stopped me doing that at least. I wouldn't have made it out of the yard.'

'That's why I locked you in the bedroom. I was worried you'd wake up while I was asleep and try and drive away again. I got Rob to hide your car in case you somehow managed to get out anyway. You've been in and out of consciousness ever since. At one stage I wanted to get a doctor out to see you but in a rare moment of lucidity you said you'd kill me if I did, said that I'd ruin everything.'

Maria shook her head. She'd got into some states in the past but this sounded like a new low.

'What time is it now?'

Sara checked her watch. 'It's nearly four p.m. But it was probably about five a.m. when we managed to get you into bed.'

'We?'

'Me and Rob, obviously.'

'He's not still here, is he?'

'No. But he rang earlier. Reckons the passports should be ready tomorrow. Express delivery. It'll not be long before you and Nicky are starting afresh. I must admit I'm going to miss the lad.'

'He's going to miss you too.'

Maria looked out of the window. Nicky was still charging around outside, but this time the hens were his target. He was laughing his head off as he ran. She'd never seen him so happy. He'd barely left the house when they were at home – her fault mostly. She just didn't seem to have the energy to take him out. And Evan wasn't any better – she knew he often took Nicky to the pub on his occasional weekends. Poor kid had barely had a childhood so far. He'd be better off without either of them.

Sara was outside now, joining in with the fun and games, pretending to try and stop the hens from running away but then stepping aside at the last second like a matador before Nicky could grab them. Maria could hear the gales of laughter coming from the pair of them. It hurt her to admit that if she gave Nicky the choice of coming with her or staying there with Sara she was pretty sure he'd pick the latter. And who could blame him? She was a lousy mother – not as bad as her own had been but that was a pretty low bar.

The final clincher for Maria was when Nicky asked if Sara could read him a bedtime story that night. He used to love being read to but a couple of months back one of his lazier babysitters gave him an audiobook to listen to, *The Gruffalo and Other Stories*, and that was the end of that. He said he didn't need anyone to read to him any more. She pretended it was a sign of him growing up, called him her 'big boy'. Now she understood that what he meant was that he wasn't bothered about *her* reading to him any more.

Sara was delighted to be asked and had been in there

way longer than Maria used to be. She was on her second cup of hot chocolate and could still hear the mumble of voices from the bedroom and the occasional giggle. She'd gone to the fridge to look for some snacks when Sara finally appeared, closing the bedroom door quietly behind her.

'He's fast asleep now, sorry it took so long, I'm clearly a bit rusty.'

'No, I think he was enjoying it too much to sleep.'

Sara smiled at the thought. 'He's such a sweetheart.'

'Not so much with me. You have the magic touch.'

Maria could see a cloud of sadness pass over Sara's head. Her friend had had three miscarriages in the past and after that seemed to have stopped trying. Then, to add insult to injury, her husband had left her for a younger model. He had two kids now. Maria knew how much that had hurt her. It was why Sara had fled to the Borders to live – she couldn't stand seeing those kids around.

'You'd be an amazing mother, you know. Why haven't you tried again?'

Sara sighed. 'I just couldn't. The first miscarriage ripped a little hole in my heart and each one after that made the hole way bigger. The odds against a successful pregnancy were going up all the time and I couldn't bear it happening again – I think it would have killed me. That's why I was so angry with you when you had the abortion. It wasn't really because of how it hurt Rob, it was because you had the chance of a child and chose to get rid of it – while I was desperate to have one and couldn't.'

'God, I'm so sorry.'

'Don't be silly, obviously it was your decision to make. I understand how crazy I was at the time. I think that's one of the reasons why Clint left. I'd gone a bit doolally. He desperately wanted kids and realised it wasn't going to happen with me.'

'You could have adopted, surely.'

'He didn't want to, he wanted his own – you know what some men are like, they need to keep the family line going. It's such macho bullshit, isn't it?'

'You didn't feel like that though, did you?'

'God no, I begged him to rethink but he wouldn't. For a while I was one of those women who see a pram outside a house or a shop and think, "I could just take that baby and no one would know. It would serve them right for leaving their baby unguarded."'

Sara laughed bitterly.

'You know, at first, when Rob told me what you'd done, I actually thought, "Why didn't the selfish bitch give it to me?"'

'Maybe I should have done that second time around. You've already bonded with Nicky better than I have and we've only been here a couple of days.'

'Don't be silly, love, you had post-partum depression. It can take an age to recover from that.'

'What if I never do? I genuinely don't know what I'm doing half the time.'

'That's hardly surprising given the mother you had. She wasn't exactly a role model.'

'Maybe it's genetic.'

'You're nothing like her. She would have dumped you in a heartbeat given half a chance – she kicked you out as soon as you hit eighteen – but you fought for custody of Nicky.'

'Only because Evan is even worse than me and I couldn't leave the poor kid with him.'

'I'm sure that's not true.'

Sara's face didn't match her words. 'I think you know it is.'

There was a long silence before Sara spoke again.

'Where are you going with this, Maria?'

It seemed so obvious to her now. Nicky had been like a different kid since the moment they got there, happy, lively and carefree. And none of that was down to her. Maria took a deep breath and plunged in.

'This has all been about escaping a life I hated and finding a better one for me and Nicky, but he deserves more than just a change of scenery. We both know I'm not a great mother but you would be. Maybe it could be about giving all of us a fresh start.'

Sara was staring at her now, her hands digging into the sofa cushion. Maria could feel the tension in the room.

'I don't think you should joke about this kind of thing unless you mean it,' Sara said eventually.

'I do mean it,' Maria said. 'How would you feel about me leaving Nicky with you?'

## 61

*11 November 2024*

Larry Bright's story had changed the narrative we'd been working on. Had Maria Groom fooled us all? The evidence had clearly pointed to an abduction but if that wasn't the case we needed to review everything. If she had disappeared of her own accord, where did she go?

For me there was also one other big question to answer. I had promised myself that I would quit the moment I thought my condition was affecting my ability to do this job – if I had got this so wrong, was that time now?

I pulled Leon and Emma into my office first thing that morning for a brainstorming session. I am conscious that 'brainstorm' was one of those words that has become frowned upon, but I was an old dog and 'thought shower' was a new trick I had no intention of learning. And, from my personal perspective it was a pretty good description of what was going on in my head.

'Are you sure that Larry Bright was telling the truth?' I pressed.

Leon nodded. 'Yes. I checked with his boss and their records back up his story. He was behind on his deliveries for a while but pretty much caught up by the end. He was working until late in the evening and finished his round. There's no way he could have done that if he'd abducted Maria – not to mention young Nicky.'

'Much as it makes me sick to think that Evan Groom was right, I'm starting to wonder if she chose to disappear,' Emma said.

'Go on,' I said.

'Well, we know she had a difficult relationship with her ex, getting lots of grief over access to their son and some pretty horrible abusive messages. And if that ex-girlfriend you spoke to is anything to go by, he can get physical too. On top of that she had a stalker – maybe the elusive Sam Gallagher, given his history and his reluctance to talk to us. She also had someone sending her dick pics on a regular basis. Though until we can get Gallagher in for questioning it's hard to know if that's him too.'

Leon held his hands up.

'Yes, OK, my bad, I'm going back out there today and this time I'm not coming back until he's in cuffs.'

'So,' Emma continued, 'after the accident with Larry Bright, maybe she took a look around at the bloody hallway and thought that, if she disappeared right then, everyone would think she'd been attacked or abducted and blame one of her exes and she could escape her crappy life and start afresh somewhere.'

'OK. It makes some kind of sense. D'you think she left her phone behind deliberately then? So we'd see the dick pics and the abusive messages from Evan Groom?'

'I hadn't thought about that, but why not? It worked, didn't it? As soon as I saw those, I was all over her ex in that first interview.'

'But we found her car at Walkergate Metro. Why would she leave it there if she wanted to get away?' I said.

'Perhaps she took the train after all?' Leon suggested. 'To make it harder for us to trace her movements.'

I shook my head. 'We've had people trawling through CCTV from the Metro station and Central Station and there was no sign of her.'

'Then maybe she's a smart-arse,' he continued. 'There's so much police drama on the telly these days, and all that true-crime stuff on Netflix, that everyone knows about CCTV and even ANPR. She might have realised that we'd trace her car wherever she went so she abandoned it and found another way to disappear.'

'And don't forget, according to Vic Kendall, the keys were left in it. Maybe she wanted it to be stolen and found else-where, just to muddy the waters,' said Emma.

'What about the message implicating Evan Groom – and the shoe in his garage, perhaps even the steer towards his cannabis farm on the noticeboard? D'you think she was setting him up?' I pressed.

'He's going to be unbearable if that's the case, but it looks a lot more likely now,' Emma said.

'But if she didn't get the train then where did she go?'

'She could have borrowed someone else's car?' Leon said.

'Whose, though? We've spoken to her neighbours and the few friends she seemed to have.'

'Not all of them,' Leon said, getting up.

'Where are you off to?'

'To find out if Sam Gallagher has a car,' he said.

'Do the same for Rob Gibson, will you? We know he can drive so that's a start.'

It was as good a plan as any and a pretty good working theory to begin with. It might be another reason why Sam Gallagher had been evading us. Leon left the room like a man on a mission and I was happy to let him go. I wanted to speak to Emma in private anyway.

'Did you speak to Sara Quinn about Rob Gibson?'

'Aye. She seemed to think he was harmless. Reckoned that he and Maria had a brief fling but that was it,' Emma said.

'Did you believe her?'

'Not entirely. She was a little evasive.'

'Have a look for her on the system, will you? See if there are any red flags there.'

'No problem.' Emma nodded towards the door. 'You don't think I should go with Leon, hold his hand?'

'No. He needs to do this himself. Get some self-respect back. And I'd like you to see if you can back up your theory about Maria's deception. Maybe recheck her bank accounts, see if there's any clues there. Perhaps she's got an account that we haven't discovered yet?'

'We did alert the airports, didn't we?'

'Definitely, standard procedure when there's a missing kid. Double-check it though, will you?'

'Sure,' she said, barely stifling a yawn.

'Late night?'

'Not really, just didn't sleep well.'

'Anything you want to tell me about?'

Leon's fears over Emma's role in our off-the-books investigation had been playing on my mind all night. And my doubts had grown now it was clear I'd completely misjudged the Maria Groom case. Maybe I was equally wrong about the Connors' involvement in Laura's death.

Emma shook her head but it wasn't convincing. Despite her sharpness this morning she looked tired.

'Look, cards on the table, Emma, I'm having doubts about whether this thing with Harry Connors is safe.'

'Leon been chipping away in your ear, has he?'

'A little, I admit, but I think he's right to be concerned.'

'I can handle it.'

'It's not about that. I have a duty of care and I'm not fulfilling it.'

I brought her up to speed on my conversation with Frankie Grant and could see the concern on her face.

'Jesus, things could escalate then. If he makes a move on the Connors family it would spark a gang war.'

'To be honest I'm surprised that it hasn't happened already. Knowing how volatile he can be I expected Frankie to react a little more quickly. You didn't hear anything at the party? Or see anyone from Grant's mob hovering around?'

She shook her head.

'Strange. Look, I know I've put you in a bad situation, tossing Grant into the mix. It was tricky before but now that Stevie's back on the scene, and with Frankie hovering in the background, it's much more dangerous. And, to be honest, I'm worried that you are getting a little too close to his son.'

'I'm not fucking him, if that's what you're thinking. Not that it's any of your business who I sleep with.'

'Generally, I'd agree with you but not when the man concerned is Harry Connors.'

'You know that Leon's just trying to make you doubt my judgement.'

'That's unfair and you know it. He's concerned about you, as am I.'

'Yes, OK, that was harsh. But I can handle Harry Connors.'

'What about his dad though? How did the big welcome home party go last night?'

She hesitated. 'Fine.' Her body language was telling me something completely different.

'You have to be honest with me, Emma.'

'Is that right?' Yet again I wondered if she somehow knew about my condition.

'What do you mean?'

'Nothing, I'm just tired.' She sighed. 'Harry's dad made a pass at me.'

'In front of Harry?'

'No, he's a psycho but he's not an idiot.'

'What did Harry say about it?'

'Nothing. I didn't tell him.'

'Why not?'

'Because I don't think his dad is quite as cautious as Harry and we might learn something if he keeps mouthing off in front of me. He's already let it slip that he knew Laura was on Frankie Grant's payroll.'

'You're kidding?'

'Nope. He told me straight out. Called her a "pet pig".'

'That's incredible.'

'I know. Still think you should pull me out?'

She had me there. It felt like she might be close to a breakthrough. If the Connors clan knew about Laura's link with Frankie Grant, they had every reason to get rid of her.

'A couple more days. But be careful. And don't give Leon a hard time. He's worried about you. Love can do that to the best of men.'

She looked surprised. Or maybe horrified, it was hard to tell.

'You think he loves me?'

'Don't you? Jesus, Emma, I thought you were a woman of the world. It's bloody obvious. He's smitten. Why do you think he's been behaving like a dick lately?'

Emma looked bemused. She seemed about to say something when my phone went off. I was going to ignore it but when I glanced down, I saw it was from Leon.

'Talk of the devil,' I said, taking the call. 'What's up? You can't have even left the building yet.'

He started to speak but I stopped him.

'Hold on a minute, Emma's still with me, let me put you on speakerphone.'

I pressed a couple of buttons on my phone and Leon's voice seemed to fill the room.

'Sam Gallagher does have a car. A Mini Cooper.'

'Well, that settles it, he's our man!' Emma said with a laugh. 'Nearly everyone has a car, Leon.'

'Yes, all right, smart-arse, but they haven't all been found abandoned recently, have they?'

'What do you mean?' she said.

'You remember that jumper from the Tyne Bridge yesterday, the one that caused that traffic jam we got stuck in?'

'Of course I remember,' Emma said. 'I'm not senile yet.'

I winced a little. Was that what people would think of me once the disease kicked in and my memory started to fade?

'Well Gallagher's car was found abandoned near the foot of the Tyne Bridge yesterday afternoon. About a minute away from where the jumper went in.'

'You think it might be him?' I asked.

'It's possible, isn't it? He's clearly been feeling guilty about something.'

'I'll get Emma to see if they've found a body yet but you need to tread carefully. If it is him, we'll need to inform the IOPC because of your recent contact with him.'

It was a formality for sure but another buggerance factor in the investigation that we could do without.

'Noted,' Leon said. 'I'll go and see Olivia Gallagher again. Maybe she'll be a little more helpful if I suggest she might have to come down to the mortuary and identify a body.'

'I'm not sure that's "treading carefully".'

'Maybe not,' Leon said. 'But in these situations, I always ask myself, "What would Jack do?"'

## 62

With Leon and Emma working on our mystery jumper and Sam Gallagher, possibly one and the same person, I turned my attention back to Rob Gibson. I was still puzzled by his omission from Sara Quinn's list of Maria's exes, especially given what Evan Groom had said about the man. Even though Emma said Sara had downplayed Gibson's relationship with Maria, surely she'd have considered a drug addict worth mentioning? Given his predilection I wondered if he had a record of some kind.

It didn't take me long to find Gibson on the PNC. As a fifteen-year-old he'd been convicted of possession with intent to supply a class B drug – he'd been caught selling weed to his classmates at school and they'd found a bagful of the stuff in his locker. The court had taken into account his youth and the fact that it was a first offence and sentenced him to four months in a detention centre. He'd spent two months there before being released under supervision. I read down the report and smiled. The three degrees of separation that operated in Newcastle had come to my aid again. I knew his social worker very well.

It was unusual for me to visit my brother during the day-time, so I didn't know what to expect when I knocked on his door. I'd tried to ring to tell him I was coming round – and to apologise for being a bit of a twat the last time I was there – but there was no answer. Phil was old-school. He didn't use a mobile, just a landline, mainly because he rarely left the house. Any time after 7 p.m. and I could be reasonably sure he'd have settled into drinking mode. It would be fair to call him a high-functioning alcoholic – his intake was way beyond the norm but he could handle it better than most. I suspected it had something to do with finishing off the communion wine in his priestly period. I had no idea what he did during the day but, for his sake as well as mine, I hoped it wasn't the same as the evenings.

Turned out, he liked to garden. Who knew? I'd never been out the back of his house. When he opened the door, he was dressed in an old baggy jumper with what looked like moth holes on the shoulder, some manky jeans, with muddy knee pads strapped over the top, and thick gar-dening gauntlets on his hands that almost went up to his elbows. He had a trowel in one of those hands and a small fork in the other. Don't ask me how he'd managed to open the door. I couldn't help laughing at the sight of his manual labour persona.

'What?' he said. I wasn't sure if he wanted to know why I was there or why I was laughing. I went with the latter.

'Sorry, Phil,' I said. 'I didn't know you were Newcastle's version of Alan Titchmarsh.'

He looked down at his chest and laughed.

'More like Charlie Dimmock with these moobs of mine.'

He may have been able to handle his drinking but he couldn't stop the inevitable weight gain from all the booze. He seemed to get bigger every time I saw him. Even though I'd asked him for help with my planned Dignitas trip I'd wondered at the time whether he'd still be around when I needed him. I made a vow to make this the last time I brought a bottle of Jameson's with me.

'Peace offering, is it?' he said, glancing at the bottle in my hand.

'Sort of. I need your help.'

'Do you now? Even though I'm a blasphemer?'

'Takes one to know one.'

That raised a small smile.

'I'm busy in the garden at the moment.'

'Good that you're getting some exercise,' I said. 'Wanna hand?'

Phil gave me a quizzical look.

'It must be important if you're willing to get your hands dirty.'

I couldn't argue with that, so I didn't. He pulled the door fully open and nodded me in.

'We can talk while we work,' he said.

He led me through the house to the back garden which was a little haven of peace. Gardens are like hen's teeth in certain parts of Newcastle where most houses have small back yards instead. Potted plants are generally the best that people can do, but Phil had clearly got someone in to dig up most of the concrete as he had a neat lawn and flower beds along the sides and back.

'You can give me a hand with planting these,' he said, pointing at a handful of sticks lying on the path that led between the lawn and the beds to the back gate. 'It'll make a change from you planting evidence.'

'Very funny.' I looked down at the path. 'It's a good idea to plant sticks – when they grow you can sell them to all the dog walkers around here.'

'Pillock,' Phil said, gruffly. 'They're gooseberry and black-currant plants. They might look like nothing now but in a sunny spot like this in a couple of years, three at the most, they'll be full of fruit. If you're nice I might let you buy some at a discount.'

I admired his optimism. Firstly, Newcastle wasn't exactly famed for its hours of sunshine. And then there was the other thing.

'I don't tend to think that far ahead these days.'

He rolled his eyes. 'If you're here to wallow in self-pity again then don't bother. We've all got crosses to bear. I have to take so many pills these days that I sound like a maraca when I walk.'

'That's not why I'm here.'

'Fine. Then watch what I do and copy me. You can pay for whatever help you want with good, honest toil.'

He placed one of the plants in a hole in the soil and padded it out with some nearby compost, patting it down until it was fairly solid. Then he trimmed the shoots with a pair of secateurs, before dousing it with the watering can. I followed suit. It was strangely fulfilling.

'I wanted to talk about Rob Gibson.'

He picked up another plant and went through the same routine, but I could see he was running the name through his head.

'Young kid? Caught selling weed?'

'That's right. How do you do that? It was more than twenty years ago.'

Phil had a prodigious memory, whereas, ironically, mine had always been a little sketchy.

'Unlike some of my colleagues, I actually cared about the kids I was involved with.'

'What do you remember about him?'

He moved across to the compost bin again.

'Quiet lad. No bother. Bit naive though.'

'Doesn't sound like your average weed dealer?'

'He wasn't. I got the impression he'd taken the blame for someone else. Or he'd been talked into selling it by his friends.'

'I don't suppose you remember who those friends were, do you?'

'I remember he hung about with a couple of girls who seemed much more streetwise than he was.'

'Names?'

He stopped patting down the soil and looked back at me, clearly intrigued.

'Let me think. Why do you ask?'

'Gibson's name has cropped up a couple of times in an investigation I'm running. It might not be anything, but my spidey senses are tingling.'

'Shit, I hope you're wrong. He seemed like a good kid back then, just needed steering onto the right path. I was hoping I'd done that.'

'People change. What about the girls? Were they nice?'

Phil took his time, picking up another plant as he thought about it.

'Not particularly. Though I barely knew them.' He put the plant in a hole and picked up his trowel. 'One of them might have been called Mary maybe,' he added, then shook his head. 'Though that might be bollocks.'

'I thought all you priests were infallible.'

'That's only the Pope, you philistine.'

'Could it have been Maria?'

'Possibly. I can't be certain though.'

He could see my obvious disappointment.

'But it might be in the file.'

'You kept your files?'

'I took copies of everything. Not supposed to, obviously, but I'd seen plenty of good colleagues shafted in case reviews carried out way after the event and I wasn't letting that happen to me. I wanted all the information at my fingertips if they ever came for me.'

'Can I have a look?'

'No, of course not, that would be unprofessional of me.'

Then he grinned.

'But I can look for you.'

## 63

Phil disappeared into the house and came back a few minutes later, parking his arse on a small bench in the corner of the garden while he thumbed through the file. I sat in front of him on an upturned metal bucket that I'd found by the gate. The file seemed pretty thin, which I guess wasn't unusual for a youth offender who'd apparently had no other offences.

He flicked through to the end then back again, clearly refreshing his memory, so I got up and went back to the planting, anything to keep on his good side. A few minutes later he spoke up.

'Aye, pretty much as I remembered it,' he said as I finished tapping down another plant – blackcurrant this time, according to the tag on it. I went back to my bucket.

'Young Rob got four months for selling weed to his schoolmates; bit harsh perhaps but there you go. He served two months in Low Newton, no bother at all there apparently, then landed up in my lap.

'Single parent family, his mam died in childbirth, dad was

a taxi driver with Ouseburn Taxis, worked all hours so left the kid to his own devices and—'

'Hold on, did you say Ouseburn Taxis?'

Phil looked down at his notes.

'Aye, that's what it says here.'

Small world, I thought. Ouseburn Taxis was controlled by the Connors family back then. Harry may have cleaned up the business – though not entirely, I suspected – but in Stevie's day they used the cabs to move drugs and girls around. Maybe Rob Gibson's dad was one of those drivers? Under those circumstances it was easy to imagine the younger Gibson getting caught up in dealing.

'D'you want me to go on?' Phil asked. I nodded.

'Young Rob didn't seem to have many friends, just those two girls I remembered.'

'Are their names in there?' I said, standing up slowly and feeling every inch of it in my back. People my age should not sit on buckets.

'Aye, of course. I always kept comprehensive notes.'

I waited. I could see he was enjoying keeping me in suspense.

'You were right, it was Maria, not Mary. Maria Evans and Sara Quinn. Why are you interested in them?'

'Maria Evans is now Maria Groom. She's gone missing.'

'You're doing missing persons now? They haven't found out about your condition, have they?'

'No, not yet. She disappeared in suspicious circumstances with her young child. We thought she might have been taken by someone though we're now more doubtful about that. What do you remember about her? About any of them?'

'It's a long time ago, Jack.'

'Try, will you? Anything you've got might help.'

He skimmed through his notes again.

'Well, like I said, Rob Gibson was my responsibility so I saw a fair bit of him but he didn't cause me any problems. When I spoke to the head at their school, he agreed that it had been a surprise and suspected the two girls were involved. He'd had problems with them before, especially Maria. Reckoned her home life was a bin fire, a sharp-tongued, domineering mother and an ineffectual father.

'Apparently the police had spoken to both girls but they'd denied any involvement. In essence the head reckoned they were shit-stirrers, that they loved nothing more than pushing the boys' buttons. They had most of those lads wrapped around their fingers – you know how it can be with adolescent boys, all those hormones bouncing around, sex on the brain, wanting to impress the lasses.'

'So, you didn't have much to do with the two girls?'

'No. I had one conversation with them, nothing official, they just happened to be at Rob's house when I paid him a visit. In my notes it says: "Cocky little madams, almost felt like they were flirting."'

'Flirting with you?'

He rolled his eyes. 'Cheeky bastard. I was a bit better-looking then and not carrying so much weight. I remember it being really awkward – they were way too young for that sort of shit – so I only stayed long enough to make sure Rob was fine. I heard them laughing as I left the room so maybe they were just taking the piss. Why are you asking about this now? Is Sara Quinn still around? Do you think she has something to do with your case?'

'Who knows? It's possible. Sara Quinn lives a lot further north now, somewhere up near the Borders, but is apparently still friends with Maria. I don't know what Rob Gibson has been up to recently. It seems that he and Maria had a relationship for a short while and it's been suggested he supplied her with drugs.'

'That would seem a little ironic given their history.'

'Indeed. The only other thing we know about him is that he worked as a delivery driver for a while.'

'Sounds like driving runs in the family.'

'Aye, maybe. Other than that, we knew very little about him until I saw your name on his record.'

Phil flicked back through his file.

'I've got his dad's address here. Might be out of date, obviously, but worth a shout. If anyone knows what Rob has been up to it will be him, surely?'

## 64

Leon rapped firmly on the front door, three times, like Black Rod demanding entrance to the House of Commons. There was a long delay while he imagined Olivia Gallagher standing just behind it, making plans to mess with him again.

Eventually the door opened, and she peered out.

'You again?' she said. 'This is harassment, you know. I could report you.'

'That's your prerogative. Is Sam here?'

'No. I'm on my own as usual. I haven't seen Sam since you chased him out of the house the other day.'

If she was telling the truth they were one more half-step towards identifying the jumper.

'Have you spoken to him? Do you know where he is?'

'No. He hasn't been in touch since.'

Maybe another half-step.

'Why should I believe you? You lied to me the last time I was here.'

'That's not how I recall it. I was just helping prevent another miscarriage of justice.'

She was brazenly unapologetic, he had to give her that. Maybe it was time he brought her down to earth. Emma had messaged him to say there was an unidentified body in the mortuary that had been fished out of the Tyne that morning – almost certainly the jumper from the day before.

'Now if we're done,' she said, closing the door. Leon stuck his foot in the gap to force it open again.

'That's assault,' she shouted. He decided it was time to play hardball.

'I need you to come to the mortuary with me,' he said. 'We pulled an unidentified body out of the Tyne today, I have reason to believe it might be Sam.'

He was expecting shock, instead he got disdain.

'It's not.'

'How can you be so sure?'

'Trust me, I'm his mother, I would know if he was dead.'

The door at the end of the hallway behind her was closed this time so Leon couldn't see all the way to the back kitchen but he clearly heard the sound of a door opening and closing inside the house somewhere. He could tell that Olivia Gallagher heard the noise too as her eyes had flick-ered to the right to see what was happening. Perhaps Sam Gallagher wasn't the jumper after all.

'Big mice you've got round here,' Leon said.

She leaned closer to almost whisper in his ear.

'Look, I was just being discreet,' she said. 'I have a gentle-man friend staying who's trying to keep out of this. He's quite a bit younger than me.' She stepped away, glancing around to make sure no one was listening. 'And he's married so please don't make a fuss. The neighbours round here are very judgey.'

She was good, but he was pretty sure she was lying.

'I know it's naughty but a woman my age can't always pick and choose—'

Her bullshit was interrupted by a shout from behind her and the crashing open of a door as Sam Gallagher burst through from the kitchen into the hallway. Leon brushed past his mother and blocked her son's path. Clive Andrews came running up behind Gallagher and pulled his arms behind his back. Leon had made sure he had backup this time and stationed Clive at the back gate. It had worked with Vic Kendall and now it had worked again. Leon heard the click of the cuffs around the chef's wrists.

'You're nicked,' Clive said, in time-honoured fashion.

Leon walked back into the office to a round of applause from the rest of the team, led by a grinning Emma.

'Piss off, you lot,' he said. 'Sarcasm is the lowest form of wit, you know.'

Once the hubbub had settled down they returned to more serious matters.

'Has Gallagher said anything?' Emma asked.

'Not a dicky bird. Said he wants a solicitor.'

'Jack said that if you found him you were to leave him in the cells overnight, see if that loosens his tongue.'

'Aye, he's already there.'

'Do you really think he's involved?'

'Why else would he have done a runner? Twice. Three

times if you count his aborted effort today. Where is Jack, anyway?'

'He's gone to see Rob Gibson's dad. Apparently, he knew Maria and Sara Quinn from back in the day, when the three kids were at school together. He still lives in the city.'

'It's a good job Jack's taken up jogging then. The witnesses in this case seem to have a habit of running away.'

## 65

Ben Gibson was a dying man. I knew as soon as he opened the door. Sometimes you can just tell. At least I wasn't going to have to worry about him doing a runner.

'Mr Gibson?'

He nodded.

'I'm Detective Chief Inspector Jack Parker, Northumberland Police. I was wondering if I could have a word about your son.'

He held a hand up as if asking me to wait then turned and walked back into the house. I stood on the doorstep, hoping I'd interpreted his sign correctly. After a minute or two I thought that maybe I should have followed him but then he reappeared. He had taken his high-necked jumper off and was holding his fingers against his throat.

'Sorry,' he said. 'I had to wash my hands before I could talk.' His speech was stilted and croaky but clear enough to hear. 'I have a stoma.'

'I'm sorry to inconvenience you.'

'Not a problem.'

'Can I come in?' I asked.

'Sure,' he said.

I followed him into the kitchen where he turned around again.

'Tea? There's one in the pot.'

'If it's no bother that would be lovely.'

When he'd poured my tea we both sat at a small table at the far end of the kitchen.

'D'you mind me asking about your stoma?' I said.

He shook his head. 'Throat cancer. Had my larynx taken out.'

'Did that help?'

'Did it fuck. It had spread too far.'

'How long have you got left?'

'God knows. Months rather than years, they say.'

'I'm sorry.'

'Not your fault, son. We all have our cross to bear, don't we?'

His attitude put me to shame. I remembered Phil telling me to stop wallowing in self-pity about my condition, that there were people worse off than me. Ben Gibson was one of those people.

'Can I ask you about your son?'

'My son's dead.'

Shit. Another suspect had bitten the dust. We were fast running out of them.

'I'm sorry.'

'You do a lot of apologising.'

He was wrong about that. Helen was always telling me I

needed to apologise more, especially given my recent propensity for ruining things for everyone.

'Anyway,' he continued, 'you can save it. When I say he's dead, I mean he's dead to me. Has been for years. Selfish little bastard.'

I tried to imagine thinking this way about Aidan in the years to come. I simply couldn't. Rob Gibson must have done something pretty damn bad.

'So you don't know if he's actually dead?'

'Don't know. Don't care.'

'Can I ask why?'

'I told him never to use drugs. Lying sod used drugs. My house, my rules.'

I was surprised he seemed so hardcore given what Phil had told me about his employer.

'I heard you were a cabbie.'

'I was. Stopped when this bastard disease got too much. What of it?'

'For Stevie Connors' firm?'

'Aye.'

He seemed less happy to talk about this than he did about his cancer. Or his sort-of-dead son.

'He used his taxi drivers to transport drugs and girls.'

'What's your point?'

'Wasn't that a bit hypocritical of you?'

'Look, I drew the line at transporting those poor girls, that wasn't right at all, and Stevie respected me for that, I think, or at least he never gave me too much grief about it. But if people are stupid enough to stick shit up their noses or inject it into their veins, that's on them, not me, so I had no bother shifting the stuff around from pillar to post. Stevie paid well and the more I did that work the less time I had to spend trying to get pissed-up posh students back to Jesmond from the Toon, before they threw up in the back of the cab. Entitled twats. But my own son, putting that crap into his body? Fuck that!'

'You're admitting to helping supply drugs?'

'I'm fucking dying, mate, what are you going to do? I'd probably get a bit more medical support inside so if you want to arrest me, fill your boots. But if you think I'd testify against Stevie then you're off your head.'

'I'm not here to arrest you.'

'More trouble than it's worth, eh? The, um, what do they call it these days? Optics, isn't it? The optics would be terrible.'

I smiled. There was something likeable about the man. And he was right. I could see the *Chronicle* headline right now. *Inspector Clueless strikes again. Dying man, dragged to jail.* I needed his help way more than I needed that kind of grief.

'When did you last see Rob?'

'Well, until recently, it must have been about five years ago, I reckon. And even then it was brief. His lass had thrown him out and he reckoned he didn't have anywhere to go. He told me he was clean so, soft shite that I am, I let him move back in. Caught the lying toad shooting up in my bathroom three days later.'

'And you don't know where he moved to?'

'Last I heard he was living near Scotland somewhere. Christ knows why he'd want to move there.'

Hadn't Emma said that Sara Quinn lived somewhere near the border? Had Rob Gibson lived there too? If you wanted to be off-grid the Borders were a good place to start.

'Does the name Sara Quinn mean anything to you?'

'Not a thing.'

He shook his head and took another sip of tea but then started coughing, quietly at first, then a full-blown hack. It looked exhausting. It took a good couple of minutes for him to stop.

'Can I get you some water or something?'

'I'm fine now.'

'You OK to answer a couple more questions?' I said.

'Of course.'

'How about Maria Evans? Was that the lass who threw him out?'

'Aye, that sounds about right.'

'Do you know why?'

'He told me he'd hit her.'

I was surprised. Phil had suggested that Rob had been a mild-mannered kid, under the spell of girls like Maria. I didn't have him pegged as the abusive type. Evan Groom hadn't suggested he was violent and Sara Quinn had told Emma he was harmless.

'Do you know why?'

'Aye. He said she'd got rid of his baby.'

'Maria had an abortion?'

'I can see how you made chief inspector.'

I smiled. I probably deserved that. I'd kept the poor man long enough.

'Thanks for your help, Mr Gibson. I'll leave you in peace.'

'Do you not want to know about the other day then? When Rob turned up at my door again.'

'I thought you said it had been five years since you'd seen him?'

'I said "until recently".'

Had he? How had I missed that? I hadn't noticed any slips in concentration or memory lately and had begun to hope that my lifestyle changes and the new drug were having some effect but perhaps that was wishful thinking. Maybe they'd given me a placebo instead of the real thing?

'He came here again?' The man nodded. 'When was this?'

'Friday morning. I remember because I was off to buy some fish for my supper when he turned up at the door. He looked like shit, I nearly didn't recognise him. He was all over the place. Said he'd been sleeping in his Mini, but his legs were too long, wanted a bed for a couple of nights.'

'He slept here?'

'No chance. He was worse than when he stayed the last time, rambling, practically incoherent, clearly off his face on drugs again. I told him to get back in his Mini and get out of my life.'

It took a moment for the penny drop.

'A Mini?'

'Aye, that's what I said.'

Like Sam Gallagher's car. The one abandoned by the Tyne Bridge around the same time that somebody jumped into the river. I had a sudden horrible feeling I was going to be seeing Ben Gibson again before too long. I wondered if he'd have any regrets.

'Did you see the car?'

'Of course, it was right outside my house.'

'Colour.'

'Red.'

I made a mental note to check with Leon.

'I don't suppose you noticed the registration?'

'You'd be right.'

'And he just drove off? He didn't say anything else?'

'He kept saying he was sorry. "I'm sorry, I'm sorry, I'm sorry", over and over again.'

'Anything else?'

'Aye. I probably should have mentioned this earlier. But he was rambling, ya knaa, he probably didn't mean anything by it.'

'Go on.'

'Before he got into the car, he turned back and said, "I didn't mean to kill anyone."'

## 66

*Four days earlier*

Maria was packing her suitcase in the bedroom when she heard the news on the radio that Evan had been arrested. Things were finally going to plan. He really was an idiot holding that ridiculous press conference of his own – she'd bet the police loved nicking him the next day. As she closed the case, she heard the front door open.

Sara had taken Nicky on a walk through the woods to see the waterfall at Hindhope Linn but they'd only just left so, at first, Maria thought she must have forgotten something but then she heard heavy, clumping footsteps in the hallway. It wasn't Sara.

She pulled the bedroom door open and saw Rob disappearing towards the kitchen. She'd hoped that she wouldn't have to see him again after the shitty doping trick he'd pulled on her two days before. He'd rung Sara earlier to say that the passports were ready but her friend said she'd pick them up so Maria could avoid another confrontation with him. Problem was she needed the passport if she was to catch her flight to France later that evening. She still intended to get to Barcelona eventually but Paris was the first available flight to mainland Europe she could get and she had to get away before everything went to shit. If that meant having to talk to Rob for a few minutes, then so be it.

'Hello,' she said, as she walked into the lounge. Rob reappeared from the kitchen. He had an envelope in his hand.

'Is that for me?' she said.

'What do you think?'

'I wasn't expecting you. Sara said she'd pick it up for me,' she added.

'Did she? I must have misheard.'

'She's out at the moment but she'll be back in a moment.'

'Really? I could have sworn I just saw her heading the other way with your boy. Looked like they were going to Hindhope Linn. Sara loves it there, it's her happy place. Be gone a while, I'd have thought.'

He flopped onto the sofa, keeping the envelope in his hand.

'I'm parched,' he said. 'Stick a brew on, will you.'

Maria could feel her patience seeping out, like a slow puncture, but she tried to keep a lid on it.

'Sure.'

Once she was in the kitchen she took a deep breath and gave herself a talking-to.

Don't rise to his bait. Give him a cup of tea. Get the passport and send him on his way. Be nice. Or as nice as you can.

She turned to grab some teabags from a box in the cupboard and Rob was standing in the doorway.

'Shouldn't you be packing? I thought you were in a hurry to get away.'

'I am.'

'Your face is looking better,' he said.

'Good.' She'd keep conversation to a minimum to avoid conflict. He was still holding on to the envelope like it was treasure. In a way, it was. She noticed his hand was twitching a little and he was way more talkative than normal. Was he on something? In her experience he usually was.

'I'm sorry about the ket, it was a stupid thing to do. Not my finest moment.'

'I hope it made you feel better,' she said, and immediately regretted it. *Don't poke the fucking bear!*

'Not really. I haven't felt great since you murdered my baby.'

She closed her eyes. This was her worst nightmare. She just wanted a quiet moment to herself before she left this place forever. When she opened them again, he'd moved nearer to her, like one of those weeping angels off *Doctor Who*. It was creepy as hell. Despite the cottage being a little cold, she could see sweat forming on his brow. Probably been on the nose candy again then. Behind her she could hear the kettle reach boiling point and click off but she didn't want to turn her back on Rob.

'I said I was sorry.'

'Did you? I don't remember that.'

'Well, I am.'

'So sorry that you're getting rid of another kid now?'

After she and Sara had talked for hours yesterday, her friend rang Rob and asked him if his contacts could make a slight change to Nicky's new passport. His new name would be Nicky Quinn. It cost Sara an extra grand but she didn't seem to care.

'I'm not "getting rid" of him. I'm giving him to someone who'll be a good mother.'

'Better than you, that's for sure.'

'Don't you think I know that? That's why—'

She managed to stop herself but it was too late.

'Why you killed my baby?'

'Can we not do this again, please, Rob? You know we'd have been terrible parents.'

'You speak for yourself. I could have been a great dad. You could have just given him or her to me.'

'I didn't think so.'

'Yet you had a baby with fucking Evan Groom. You clearly thought he was better than me.'

She shook her head. She'd walked straight into that. How could she explain to him that Evan had seemed a safer bet? He had money and, at the time, a decent job. It had taken a while to realise he was even more self-centred than she was.

'He wasn't a junkie.'

It was like flicking a switch. A blaze of hatred flared in his eyes as he moved towards her.

'Are you for real? A couple of nights ago you were banging on about him being the cannabis king of the north-east! He has a whole fucking farm of the stuff, apparently.'

Had she? She barely remembered a thing about that night. Rob was right in her face now, getting increasingly angry. She tried to move away but her back was against the counter so she couldn't retreat any further. She reached behind her – wasn't there a knife block there somewhere?

As she fumbled around with her left hand he grabbed her by the throat.

'You've always been a selfish bitch, Mar,' he said.

'Let go of me,' she screamed, trying to pull his hand away but his grip was too strong. She could feel the pressure growing on her neck and started to choke. She tried to knee him in the balls but he'd pressed right up against her, forcing her head back towards the cupboards behind her. She could feel his erection against her thigh, the sick fuck.

Rob was sweating profusely now, and Maria could see the beads rolling down his cheeks as he squeezed harder. Her hand found something behind her and she grabbed at it. It was the knife block. She pulled it closer so she could reach the knives but was too hasty and it tumbled off the counter. She looked down in despair as all the knives scattered on the floor by her feet, one of them nicking her bare foot as it fell.

Rob now had two hands around her throat. She hit out at his arms but she could feel herself losing consciousness and her blows were completely ineffective.

'Don't ... please,' she croaked but she could see in his eyes that he was beyond reason.

# 67

*11 November 2024*

Who had Rob Gibson killed? Maria? Nicky? Both of them? Or no one at all? Maybe it was just the delusional ramblings of a drug-addled mind. Maybe we'd never find out, given that it was looking more than likely that his was the body that had been fished out of the Tyne that morning. I'd arranged for Ben Gibson to go down to the mortuary to be sure. The old man hadn't seemed at all surprised at the possibility.

In case I was mistaken I'd covered my bases and asked Alan Gardner to put out a press release describing him as a 'risk to the public' with a photo that his dad had given me – it was about ten years old but better than nothing – and made sure all the PCSOs and patrol officers were briefed too. If he wasn't dead yet I wasn't optimistic about finding him though. We had a lot fewer boots on the ground than we used to have.

It was time to interview Sam Gallagher. Leon had confirmed that his car was red – it was surely too much of a coincidence that Rob Gibson had been driving something very similar. Were the pair of them somehow both involved in Maria's disappearance? Two ex-boyfriends with grudges? It seemed more like the plot of a schlocky paperback thriller than real life but following the first rule of the ABC of investigations, I wasn't going to assume anything.

I was ready to go when I got a call from Patrick Styles, who was managing the crime scene at Evan Groom's farm. It had been a long job, what with the big acreage, the two large cannabis barns and my concerns with what I'd found in the bedroom.

'Hi, Pat, you finished there now?'

'Not quite. After your suggestion yesterday I thought I'd finish off by doing a sweep of the entire area.'

I'd given Pat a bell the minute Groom's former girl-friend had told me her story. I remembered the state of that bedroom and the various smells that Clive Andrews had described and could practically hear the alarm bells sounding. I'd suggested that Pat looked around the grounds.

'I think we've found something,' he added. 'I've asked Scott Parkin to drive over and thought you might want to come with him.'

'I do.'

'Good job, he'll be outside the station in five minutes. I've got to get back to the scene. I'll fill you in when you get here.'

It looked like Leon would have to deal with Sam Gallagher on his own. I put the phone down, grabbed my coat and headed for the stairs. Scott Parkin was the most experienced cadaver dog handler in the area and he and his current dog,

Star, were the best in the business. The only reason Pat would get him involved was if he thought there was a body buried up there.

Pat met us at the end of the farm track that led to the cottage. Most of the area around the house had been taped off so we couldn't park right in front. Scott grabbed Star from the back of the car.

'Where do you want me?' he said. He may have been great at his job but good company he wasn't. He'd barely said a word to me on the journey over. I had no doubt that he liked dogs more than people.

'Follow me,' Pat said.

'No problem,' Scott said.

Like I said, he didn't do small talk. And there was no call for Pat to tell him why he was there – he had one job and Pat wouldn't have brought him in if he wasn't pretty sure he was needed. Nevertheless, as we walked Pat filled us in, for my benefit more than Scott's.

'We've got a ton of potential DNA from the bedroom and bathroom. There's obviously been an attempt to clean the place up but it was pretty amateurish, it just took a long time to collect everything, with the two barns to do as well. Obviously, we concentrated on the buildings but it looks like you were right that the real pay dirt – excuse the pun – was elsewhere.'

We circled around the cottage until we were about forty yards directly behind the house at the edge of a small apple orchard.

'Over here,' Pat said. He led the way through the orchard, closely followed by Scott, Star pulling slightly at his lead, with me at the rear.

'Don't take us all the way there,' Scott said to Pat. 'Let Star do his work. If there's anything here, he'll find it, trust me.'

Scott released the lead and the Springer Spaniel sprinted through the orchard, disappearing past the final line of trees. He immediately started barking and when we finally caught up with him, he was sitting next to a large pile of loose dirt which, even to my eye, looked like it had been disturbed fairly recently.

'Well, that didn't take long,' Scott said as we caught up with the dog. 'I think you'd better get digging, Pat. This lad very rarely makes a mistake. I think we can be pretty certain there's a body under there.'

## 68

Sam Gallagher looked concerned as Leon shuffled through some papers on the table in front of him. He had every right to be, Leon thought, not least because he'd opted for the duty solicitor, Gavin Sanders, a notoriously casual brief who genuinely didn't seem to give a toss about his occasional clients.

That wasn't even the biggest of his problems.

'You're a hard man to find, Sam,' Leon said after they'd gone through the preliminaries. 'Is it OK to call you, Sam?'

'That's fine.'

Leon passed over a photo of a red Mini Cooper.

'Can you confirm that this is your car?'

Gallagher looked briefly at the photo and nodded.

'For the tape please, Sam.'

'Yes,' he said. 'It's mine.'

'When did you last see it?'

'I'm not sure. I don't use it that often. I work in the city.'

'On the Quayside, yes?'

'Fork on the Tyne. It's a Michelin star restaurant.'

'Yes, I know that too, Sam, I came to see you there, remember? You ran away from me.'

'I'm sorry about that. I panicked.'

'Let's come back to that. Tell me a bit more about the car. When did you last drive it?'

'Um, a few days ago.'

'Can you be a bit more precise?'

'Maybe a week ago. Bit more, perhaps.'

'And where is it now?'

Sam glanced at the photo which Leon had left on the desk, as if looking for a clue.

'I'm not sure. In my garage, I think. Like I say, I haven't driven it for a while.'

'So, would you be surprised to learn that this photo was taken on the Quayside late last night? About thirty yards from where you work, in the car park near the old Fish-market.'

He certainly looked surprised but he kept his mouth shut this time.

'Any thoughts what we might have found in it?'

Gallagher shook his head vigorously.

'You have to speak, Sam.'

'S-sorry. No. I don't have a clue.'

'Why not?'

'Because I lent it to a friend.'

'So it's not in your garage then?'

Gallagher's brief rolled his eyes in despair. He'd get no help there.

'No,' he said.

'Which friend might that be?'

Gallagher turned back to his brief again and whispered something. Gavin Sanders pulled a face.

'Don't see why not,' he said, without even attempting to whisper back.

'It was Maria Groom.'

'The same Maria Groom who has been the subject of a police search since her disappearance nearly two weeks ago.'

Gallagher was growing increasingly pale.

'Yes.'

'The same Maria Groom who took an injunction out against you.'

'That was a long time ago.'

'But it was her.'

'Yes.'

'And yet you still lent her your car.'

'Yes.'

'Why?'

'Because she needed it.'

'What for?'

'I don't know.'

'Do you often lend your car to people who've taken legal action against you? Or to anyone else for that matter?'

'No. I don't.'

'Then why this time?'

'Like I said, she needed help.'

'Was she frightened of someone?'

'I wouldn't say that, no.'

Leon reached into his folder.

'I'd have thought she must have been a little scared if the only person she could turn to for help had been sending her dick pics.'

He passed over two of the photos they'd found on Maria's phone.

'That is you, isn't it?'

Gallagher stared down at the photos, shaking his head slightly.

'No comment.'

'I mean I can't comment on the dick – though I'm sure we can get an expert of some kind to help with that – but that looks very much like your hand. It's the same tattoo that I'm looking at across the desk.'

Gallagher moved his wrist below the desk. Leon laughed.

'The tattoo's still there, mate, you can't hide it forever. What have you done with Maria?'

'Nothing. I told you. I just lent her my car.'

'Why did you run away from me at the restaurant then?'

'Like I said, I panicked.'

'And again from your mother's house.'

'Same reason.'

'Innocent men rarely panic in those circumstances.'

Gallagher shrugged.

'Why didn't you come forward when we were looking for her?'

Gallagher again leaned towards his brief for a short conversation then sat up again.

'No comment.'

Leon sighed. Once the no comments started they tended to continue ad infinitum and that was strike two. Even though a failure to answer questions in an interview often annoyed juries if the case came to court, it was still bloody irritating. Luckily, he received a text from Clive Andrews who said he needed to speak to him urgently, which gave him space to keep his cool. Leon closed down the session temporarily and found Clive waiting in the corridor outside.

'Sorry to interrupt you,' Clive said, 'but I thought you'd want to know that Ben Gibson has identified the body in the mortuary, it's his son, Rob. And there's a match on some of the fingerprints we found in the car. Gibson junior had definitely been driving Gallagher's car.'

'How about Maria?'

'Yep, her too. Her thumbprints were found on the interior mirror.'

Now things would get interesting. Once the interview was restarted, he shook things up straight away.

'How do you know Rob Gibson?'

'I've never heard of him.'

'Really? Then how come he's been driving your car around?'

Gallagher was clearly startled by the sudden change of direction but quickly recovered.

'I have no idea. Who is he?'

'Like you, he's another of Maria Groom's ex-boyfriends. The one immediately before you, I believe.'

'The junkie?'

'That's the one. So you do know him?'

'Never met the man but I knew of him, just didn't remember his name. She told me he had beaten her up.'

'She's not the best picker, is she? A domestic abuser, a stalker and now a drug dealer.'

Gallagher lowered his head. 'I guess not.'

'Rob Gibson was fished out of the Tyne this morning. Not far from the Tyne Bridge. One witness thought he might have been pushed.'

This time Gallagher's shock was palpable.

'What? You don't think it was me, do you?'

'Was it?'

'No! Like I said, I've never met the man.'

'Your car was found about ten yards away from the steps that lead up to the bridge.'

'It wasn't me who left it there.'

'I'm going to ask you again. Did you kill Maria Groom?'

'What? No! Of course not.'

'What have you done with her son?'

'I haven't touched him. Well not—'

'Well not what? You should know we currently have a team searching your house. I hope for your sake we don't find a trace of the pair of them there.'

Gallagher looked alarmed.

'It wasn't like that, I—'

Gavin Sanders put his hand on his client's arm but Gallagher shook it off.

'It's fine. Look, Maria and Nicky came to see me on October the thirtieth. I remember the date because it was the day before Hallowe'en. I was carving a pumpkin for my mum when they turned up. Maria wanted somewhere to hide away for a day or so.'

'Handy for you if we find their DNA in your house.'

'Maybe so, but it's also the truth. The next day she asked if she could borrow my car.'

'And you had no problem with that. Despite the difficulties that the pair of you had in the past.'

'Let's say we, um, made up.'

'You slept with her?'

Sanders was shaking his head but Gallagher couldn't help himself.

'Yes.'

'Also very convenient.'

'Again, maybe so, but that's what happened. She and Nicky left the same day and I haven't seen either of them since.'

'And you didn't report any of this to the police, despite the fact that she was missing.'

'She wasn't missing. She was running away.'

'Where to?'

'I have absolutely no idea.'

## 69

I watched as Patrick and his team of CSIs started to remove the soil from around what everyone seemed sure was a recently dug grave.

With darkness setting in, they'd had to put up some lights so they could see what they were doing around the site. Scott and Star had checked the rest of the area but found nothing else. I'd called Ray Barron, the pathologist, and put him on standby to head up here if we did find a body.

I'd also told the rest of the team what was happening. Thankfully Evan Groom was already being held on remand so if there was a body there, we didn't have to go into panic mode as our main suspect was already under lock and key. It was no wonder he'd looked relieved when cannabis production was all he was charged with.

The CSIs were doing their usual painstaking job, making sure they didn't disturb any evidence, but it meant a lot of standing and watching. Not only was I cold and tired, but starving. I'd asked Ray to bring chips with him if he got the call. Sod the Mediterranean diet for one night. At least Scott had his cigarettes to keep him occupied. He dropped his latest one on the ground and pressed his boot on it to make sure it was out then picked it up and put it in his pocket with all the others to make sure they weren't considered evidence – though we were outside the cordon and a long way from the grave it was better to be safe than sorry.

'Those'll kill you, you know,' I said.

'Got to die somehow. Better this way than being buried in a shallow grave.'

I did say his chat wasn't the best.

'Hope it's not the kid,' he added, 'they're the worst.'

I nodded. We all felt the same. Any dead body was bad but seeing a dead kid took a chip off your heart that you could never replace. I'd probably seen about half a dozen in my career, including four-year-old twins who'd been trapped in a house fire, and I vividly remembered every single one of them. Memories of their faces, or what was left of their faces, hovered in the back of your mind just waiting to pop out – sleepless nights were a roaming ground for their restless spirits, which I suspected was why so many cops drank too much; less chance of you waking up with dead babies in your head.

'Over here, Jack!' Patrick shouted, waving me towards the scene. As I got closer, I could see something pale glinting in the moonlight in the middle of the grave. The closer I got the more obvious it became that it was a hand, and not a child's as far as I could see. A small mercy but a mercy nonetheless.

'Looks like a woman,' Patrick said as I reached the tape

that bordered the grave. 'The nails are quite long and you can see traces of nail varnish. There's what looks like a small tattoo on the webbing by her thumb.'

I made a mental note to ask Leon to see if they'd found any photos of Maria Groom that clearly showed her hands.

'Anything else?'

'There are some marks on her wrist that look consistent with her being tied up.'

I thought about the bedroom with the mortise lock on the door and the scratches on the bed frame. It wasn't a stretch to imagine this poor woman being held in that room.

'The grave seems pretty shallow too,' Patrick continued. 'So, on the plus side, I think there's only one body in there.'

I breathed a sigh of relief, though if it was Maria, it raised the question of where the hell young Nicky was.

'And it's not entirely my forte, I'm sure Ray will have a better idea than me, but I'd say, from the condition of the hand, that it hasn't been there long, there's barely any deterioration. Though it has been pretty cold recently which might account for that.'

'How much longer before we can see the rest of it?'

Patrick glanced over at his team, beavering away, methodically but slowly.

'At least another forty-five minutes I'd say.'

It was actually just over thirty. I'd stayed by the tape staring at the scene as they slowly uncovered the rest of the body, only leaving briefly to put on my space suit, overshoes and gloves so I could get a much closer look when the time came. I watched from a distance as a second hand appeared and then most of the naked torso. Whoever had buried her had got rid of her clothes first, which was probably sensible given the traces they may have contained.

Eventually the legs were revealed and then, finally, and very carefully, the face. Patrick called me inside the scene. I leant over the body and stared into the face of a woman who'd been battered beyond recognition. Was it Maria Groom? She seemed about the right height. There were no obvious wounds on her torso that I could see but there was some pretty severe bruising around her neck.

Regardless of the woman's identity, it was pretty clear that Evan Groom was in deep shit.

## 70

*12 November 2024*

Ray Barron was a happy man which didn't always mean I would be. He liked nothing more than to lead me down the garden path and then deliver a denouement that undermined everything I was thinking. Fortunately, I'd got used to this approach and had learned not to get too carried away early on. The man gave me a lot of leeway, knowing fine well that I didn't like to stand around while he got elbows deep into a corpse. It wasn't that I was squeamish, I just didn't want to lose sight of the fact that the victims had very recently been living, breathing people. Our arrangement suited him too; he hated cops hanging around while he worked, cramping his style.

'You took your time,' he said when I entered his empire, about fifteen minutes after getting his early-morning text that he'd finished the PM. I couldn't fault his dedication, I didn't think he'd been to bed at all.

'Had to wait for an Uber,' I said.

'Surely you can drive again now? It's been months since the crash.'

I'd given up driving after my dementia diagnosis, even though it probably wasn't yet a problem. One day it would be and I didn't want to be behind a wheel when that happened. I'd told everyone, including Ray, it was because of the concussion I'd suffered in the crash that killed Laura but that excuse was wearing a little thin now.

'Better safe than sorry. I still get the occasional headache.'

Obviously, I couldn't tell Ray that I was concerned it was a side effect from the drugs trial. He seemed worried anyway.

'Seriously, Jack, I'd get that checked out if I was you. I know a few doctors, as it happens.'

'Aye, but not many of them speak to you any more.'

'Beware of jealousy, my friend, not everyone can make it to the top like me.'

'Any chance you could get on with it? I'm a little busy at the moment, what with having a murderer to catch.'

'Patience, young man, I have gifts to pass on. But you might want to write some of this down, it's a bit sciencey for your prosaic copper's brain and you might need it for a murder trial.'

'So we're ruling out suicide?'

'Hmmm,' he said. 'In my experience bodies rarely bury themselves. But that doesn't exclude assisted suicide, of course.'

I'm not sure if he saw my grimace. I managed to hide it pretty quickly so I hope not. There was no way I was explaining how personal that felt.

'Can you cut to the chase?'

'It's not Maria Groom.'

I wasn't sure how to react. Hopefully it meant she and her son were OK but in some ways it made my life more difficult. If it wasn't Maria, then who the hell was it?

'You sure?'

'Absolutely. The woman on the table appears to be at least ten years younger than Maria and, more importantly, it's highly unlikely she's ever given birth.'

'You can tell that?'

'Educated guesswork. There are normally marks on the pelvis, scars, craters even. This woman has nothing like that.'

'So it's a best guess. It could still be Maria?'

'Yes and no. It is a best guess because it's one of mine. But, no, it's not Maria.'

'You seem very sure.'

'Did you ever hear the story about David Bowie?'

I was used to Ray's diversions but this was a new one.

'What?'

'David Bowie. You know, Ziggy Stardust and all that.'

'I know who David Bowie is.'

'Well, legend has it that one of his eyes changed colour when he was punched at school and I guess that's possible here.'

'You're saying her eyes are the wrong colour.'

'I am. But she was clearly beaten so . . .'

'You don't believe that, though.'

'Not really. Unless being beaten can change your blood group too.'

'So wrong eye colour and wrong blood group.'

'Exactly.'

'So it's definitely not Maria Groom.'

'Eureka. I believe I started at that point but for some reason you doubted me, so I thought I'd walk you through it.'

'Cause of death?'

'Firstly, she wasn't beaten to death as you may have originally suspected from her injuries. She has a broken cheekbone and one of her eye sockets is badly damaged. Her nose is busted and there are at least two teeth that appear to have snapped off but none of that was fatal.'

He often delighted in telling me which causes of death he'd ruled out before cutting to the chase, but I wouldn't give him the satisfaction of asking twice. Instead, I raised one eyebrow. He took the hint.

'Spoilsport. It's no fun if you don't join in. She was strangled. There were clear fingermarks around her neck. The soil had hidden some of them but once we'd cleaned that away they were obvious. And she had a fractured hyoid bone – always a dead giveaway, if you'll excuse the pun.

'Any idea if she was conscious at the time?'

'I think it's very likely.'

Ray clearly wanted to show off but I kept shtum and waited for his explanation. He didn't need any encouragement.

'I'm glad you asked though. There were none of the usual signs of a struggle, she has no skin under her fingernails, for instance. But they seemed remarkably clean under the circumstances. I suspect our murderer scrubbed them before he buried her.'

I sensed a 'but' coming.

'But he forgot to scrub her feet too. When someone is being strangled, they have a tendency to kick as well as scratch and I found skin under several of her toenails.'

'Any signs of sexual assault?'

'Hard to say but there was evidence of vaginal tearing, which could certainly indicate that.'

I remembered Clive Andrews saying the room reeked of sex. Was this girl being held on that bed in Evan Groom's cottage? The man had been in custody for four days so I was hesitant about asking Ray the obvious question, but I couldn't delay forever. If she'd died very recently then it couldn't have been Groom.

'Any chance of a timescale?'

Ray smiled. It was always the hardest question to answer. Even a recent death could be hard to pin down. Once a body had been buried the problem increased tenfold.

'It's not going to be as precise as you'd like.'

'No change there then.'

'Your gratitude is noted. I'd say with a degree of confidence that it's somewhere between a week and ten days. The skin discolouration isn't as pronounced as I would expect if it was longer. From the level of bloating and the release of liquids I'd put it closer to the more recent end of that window though the fact that the body was buried and it's been pretty cold out there may have slowed the process down slightly.'

That was better news for me. Not so much for Evan Groom. It still didn't answer the question of who she was, though.

'I don't suppose you've found anything that would help identify her, have you?'

'I thought you'd never ask. Come and have a look at this.'

'Do I have to?'

Ray knew my views on getting too close to a body in the mortuary.

'On this occasion, I'm afraid so. I've covered the poor woman up, so don't worry, it won't trouble you too much.'

He pushed open the doors into the mortuary. There was only one corpse on a trolley and it was lying face down. Ray had drawn a sheet up over her body almost entirely, leaving only the head uncovered. When we got to the trolley he walked around to the other side and gently, tenderly almost, lifted her hair up.

There was a small symbol on the back of her neck, just under the hairline. I did a double-take. It couldn't be, could it? I leaned down for a closer look. My first thought was bang on. It was a bar code.

'I don't understand,' I said.

'Neither did I at first,' Ray said. 'I thought it was some kind of fashion thing I'd never heard of before, but then I looked it up.'

'And?'

'There are reports of tattoos like this being found on girls who've been sex trafficked from Eastern Europe. Apparently, the number underneath the bar code is how much they have to earn to get their freedom. Basically, she's been branded.'

## 71

It wasn't that often that we found a body and already had our main suspect under lock and key. Evan Groom was going nowhere, which helped ease the time pressures we normally faced, not least because the press hadn't picked up on it yet.

We'd managed to keep a tight lid on the news – it helped that the farm was out in the sticks and out of sight of any of the neighbours. In a busier location the influx of CSIs, police and a cadaver dog would have been the talk of the neighbourhood and any journalist worth his salt would have heard about it.

We had DNA samples from Groom's farm cottage and the girl's neck and toenails, and Bob Curtis had authorised making them top priority so I had been promised results within thirty-six hours. Of course, he'd moaned about his budget, but it looked pretty open and shut and he loved a quick clear-up more than anything.

We were still no nearer to finding Maria Groom and her son, but, with her ex-husband locked up, the heat from him had obviously disappeared – no more impromptu press conferences for Mr Groom. And, much to my chagrin, it was becoming increasingly clear that she had disappeared of her own accord and stitched her ex-husband up like a kipper. The delivery driver's account of the incident where she banged her head and Sam Gallagher's story backed up the idea, and Groom's protest about the address of his farm being on the noticeboard had seemed one of the few times he'd been telling the truth.

We weren't giving up the search, obviously, she could still be in danger. I was concerned about Rob Gibson's claim to have killed someone – given the link with Gallagher's car, Maria seemed the most likely victim. Most of the team had been running through CCTV from all over the city centre trying to track the movements of that car from the time it left Ben Gibson's house up to when it was parked under the Tyne Bridge, hoping we might be able to confirm who was driving.

In addition, Leon was already working his way through ANPR sightings of the car elsewhere. It had been picked up several times but the pattern was unclear and he'd yet to find a photo that clearly showed the driver. Assuming Gallagher was telling the truth, we still had no real idea where Maria had gone once she'd left his house or how Rob Gibson had ended up driving the same car to his dad's house.

One of Bob Curtis's mates had authorised us to hold Gallagher for another twelve hours while we tried to find evidence to back up his story. In my view, the dick pics alone were enough to merit keeping the pervy bastard locked up for as long as we could get away with.

While we waited for a breakthrough on the car, I had an early appointment with a gravestone. Ray's crack of dawn autopsy meant I was up well before the rest of the team, and I tried to visit Laura's grave at least once a month. I'd missed the previous month and wasn't prepared to miss another despite the strains that the Groom case and my own personal problems were putting on me.

Laura's parents had wanted a permanent memorial to their daughter so, despite her being cremated, they had buried her ashes in a small cremation plot at the Hollywood cemetery in Gosforth. Gordon had told me he found it comforting to have somewhere specific that he could go and talk to her and I understood that. It was a peaceful spot, and I found some of the same comfort that he did. Sometimes I even told her about the case I was working on and she helped me figure things out. I wasn't hearing voices or anything like that, but I could imagine her take on things, which was often more incisive than mine. I even told her about my condition and my responses to it – let's just say she was less judgemental than my brother.

I took a cab out to the cemetery and, as the place didn't open until 9 a.m., I climbed over the gate. It wasn't the first time I'd done that. The opening hours in the winter months didn't fit in with mine, so I'd learned to take a thick blanket with me to throw over the spikes on the top. Obviously, as it was officially closed, the place was quiet but as I landed on the other side of the fence and started to walk towards the grave, I saw there was someone else standing over in the far corner, not far from where I was heading. I was both surprised and a little annoyed as I much preferred to have the place to myself. I didn't want anyone overhearing my conversations with Laura.

I was about halfway across when I realised that they were standing right next to her headstone. I could see them a little more clearly now, it looked like a young man, tall and slim, dressed mainly in black. I flashed back to the crash, the driver taking off and running down the street. Could it be him? I started to move more quickly but as I did, they turned around and saw me and took off in the other direction, running towards the far corner much faster than I could despite my recent attempts at jogging.

'Stop,' I shouted but it was pointless. As I approached Laura's grave I saw a small bunch of roses lying in front of it, garage-bought by the looks of it but it's the thought that counts. The gap between me and the fleeing visitor was growing. I almost gave up the chase but there was no gate in that corner and to get out they'd have to climb over a metal fence, complete with more spikes – that would be my chance to catch them up. I stepped up my pace and saw them stop in front of the fence and look back again before taking a leap at it, just managing to get their hands on the top. They hauled themselves up but lost their footing a little and almost fell off, catching themselves on the spikes. I closed the gap as they tried desperately to pull themselves over. I was only about twenty yards away as they managed to finally clamber to the top and swing their legs over the other side. I was too slow and too late to catch them but before they dropped down completely, they looked back at me through the railings.

I knew that face. But it didn't make any sense.

If anything, Frankie Grant looked even less pleased to see me than the last time. There was no smoking jacket this time, just a Newcastle United shirt, a pair of jeans and a worried look – which he had every right to be wearing. It was clear I'd been expected though, he didn't even ask me what I wanted, simply stepped to one side and let me in.

We went straight into his office where, despite the early hour, he'd already started on the whisky. He offered me a glass; it would have been churlish to refuse under the circumstances. I'd vowed to give up drinking but one glass wasn't going to make my condition any worse. I went straight for the jugular.

'I didn't know Lee was adopted,' I said.

'Why would you? It's no one's business but ours.'

He was right but it explained why I'd been bemused when I realised the kid running away from me was Lee Grant. If he was the hit and run driver, then his DNA from the baseball cap should have brought up a familial match with Frankie and I knew it hadn't. After leaving the cemetery I'd gone back to the station to double-check the test results and when I confirmed there was no match, I made a few discreet enquiries and discovered that Lee wasn't Frankie's birth son.

'I'm going to need his DNA.'

'No chance.'

'If I have to arrest him to get it I will.'

Frankie sighed. 'You're always such a hard ass. Can't we come to some arrangement?'

He barely looked at me, knowing that he was wasting his breath.

'What if I confess to driving the car?' he added, getting desperate now.

'You know that won't work, Frankie. We've got his DNA on a cap, and two witness statements, including one from me. You'd need to be about forty years younger and five stone lighter.'

'Witnesses can change their statements.'

'Not this one.'

Ultimately, he knew better than to try to bribe me.

'Where is he?'

He nodded towards the ceiling.

'Upstairs. Bawling his eyes out. I told him he was a fucking idiot going to the grave every week. Soft shite has never got over it really.'

'Why did he do it?'

Grant sighed. 'He thought I was having an affair with Laura.'

The idea was so ridiculous that I almost laughed. Grant caught my reaction.

'Yeh, OK, I know, but the kid looks up to me, you know, he thinks I'm a catch.'

'Seems an extreme reaction.'

'Not if you know his background. His mother drank herself to death after her fanny-rat of a husband left her for another woman. That's how he ended up in care in the first place.'

'But why Laura? You weren't having an affair with her.'

'He saw us together a couple of times, once in a café and another time in the yard, and then he followed me one night when I was meeting up with her in a hotel. I use a room there for meetings when I don't want to be seen. The kid got the wrong end of the stick.'

'But you reported the car stolen. Why would you do that if it was Lee?'

'He'd asked if he could borrow the car and I'd said no but he took it anyway. I wanted to teach him a lesson. Thought if you lot picked him up, he'd never do it again. I wouldn't have pressed charges, obviously. I didn't know what he planned to do with it, did I?'

His eyes were pleading with me.

'He didn't mean to kill her, just frighten her. He lost control of the car.'

'And I lost a friend. And her mam and dad lost their only child.'

That wasn't strictly true, but Gordon's secret son was between me, him and his conscience.

'How long have you known?' I asked.

'I found out as soon as he got home. Lee was in a terrible state, I'd never seen him so upset, crying and bawling. It spilled out of him. The kid's never been the same since. He's terrified of going to prison. Every time you rocked up outside the house he panicked, thought you knew it was him.'

'Is that why you told us Laura was taking bribes from you? To deter us from investigating her death properly? Even though you could have been prosecuted?'

'Aye. I'd do anything for the boy. You've got a son, haven't you? You'd do the same.'

He was right about that.

'I should have known you'd never let it go,' Grant added.

'I wondered why you didn't do anything when I fed you the Connors family as suspects.'

'I did think about kicking off just to throw you off the scent, but it would have been like self-harming. And there's been enough of that happening around here already.'

I remembered the scars I saw on the boy's arm and tried to imagine how I'd feel if that were Aidan.

'He's going to do time for this, you know?' I said.

'I should have sent him away, out of the country somewhere, out of reach.'

'Why didn't you?'

'I'd miss him too much. You know how it is. You lock horns with the little bastards every day but wouldn't have it any other way.'

I couldn't help smiling. It was as good a summary of a father–teenage son relationship as I'd heard. Frankie Grant saw it as a sign of hope.

'You can't bring Laura back. Do you really want to ruin a young lad's life for one mistake? He's only a year or so older than your lad.'

'He killed my friend.'

'An eye for an eye would make everyone blind, Jack. It was an accident. Don't do this to get back at me, visiting the sins of the father and all that.'

He had a point. Was there anything to gain in bringing

in the kid? What would I do if it was Aidan? He could easily have killed the tourist he hit on that e-scooter a couple of days earlier. Frankie seemed to sense me wavering.

'You saw him at the cemetery, he's been there every week since the funeral. I told him not to go, that someone would see him, but it's been like a what's-a-name ... a penance. Can't you give the lad a chance? He's barely eighteen, got his whole life in front of him to make up for this. And he will. You can take that to the bank.'

He'd almost convinced me, but I remembered my last chat with Gordon, and how much Laura's mam, Liz, had been affected. How much they needed closure.

'It's not my decision to make,' I said.

# 72

Emma had been avoiding Harry Connors since she'd made an excuse to leave his dad's party early. She knew that he'd wanted it to be some kind of rite of succession, where his dad handed over the family crown to his benighted son but, even though she'd done a runner, she was fairly certain that wasn't how it had turned out. Stevie Connors had not seemed to be winding down towards retirement and she was worried that Harry would be dragged into the mire by him.

And then there was the discovery of the dead girl – who appeared to have been a sex-trafficking victim – something that the Connors family had previous for. She thought she'd heard Evan Groom's name mentioned by one of the crowd of gammons at the party. At the time she'd put it down to her imagination but now she wasn't so sure. Could there be a connection there? Was Harry involved in trafficking?

The continuing publicity surrounding Maria Groom's disappearance had made it much easier for her not to return his calls or answer his many messages – hoping he'd assume she was too busy. But she'd eventually cracked and agreed to meet him outside the café in Exhibition Park for a very early breakfast. When she arrived, he was already waiting there with two cups of coffee. He greeted her with a peck on the cheek.

'You've been playing hard to get,' he said.

'Not really, busy with the Groom case, that's all.'

'No luck with finding her?'

She didn't want to talk about the case with him so nodded towards Cow Hill, on the other side of the Town Moor.

'Let's walk and talk, shall we?'

Harry looked down at his footwear, a nice pair of brogues, and laughed. 'Sure, though I might have worn something more suitable if you'd told me in advance.'

'It's a poor walker who blames his shoes,' Emma said, taking one of the cups from him before heading off towards a gate which led into the large, deserted open space between the park and the hill. In the spring and summer it was full of grazing cattle, belonging to the city's Freemen, but in the winter months they were packed off to the market or taken back to their farms for breeding.

'Do you want to tell me what happened between you and my dad at the party?' Harry said.

'Who said anything happened?'

'Come on, Emma, you were fine when I went to the bar and when I got back you couldn't get out of there quick enough.'

'I told you. I'd been called back to the station.'

'I know that's what you said but the atmosphere was

like the Arctic between the two of you, I know something happened.'

'OK, if you must know, he made a pass at me.'

'Seriously?'

'He suggested that you passed on your cast-offs to him when you'd finished with them, and he'd be happy if that tradition continued.'

'And you believed him?'

'Maybe.'

'No wonder you did a runner. It's not true, obviously.'

'Not even an element of truth?'

Harry sighed. 'Look, there was one girl I brought home from uni who had a weird thing about hooking up with dangerous men.'

'Is that what you are?'

'No. Of course not. But maybe she thought that at first. When she realised that I was a pussycat she latched on to my dad. If anything, she cast me off. And the old man was only too happy to oblige her.'

Emma couldn't hide the look of distaste on her face.

'I warned her she was playing with fire but she was a classic posh girl wanting a bit of rough. She spent one weekend with him and unsurprisingly that was enough for her. After that she ignored me. I was just a means to an end, obviously.'

'You don't seem to think your dad did anything wrong.'

'He didn't really. He pushed on an open door. It wasn't like I was in love with the girl.'

Emma glanced across at him. Was he saying he was in

love with her? God, she hoped not, her life was complicated enough as it was without that. She tried to move the conversation away from the subject.

'There was something else.'

'What?'

'He made a disparaging remark about my predecessor.'

'The woman who died in that car accident?'

'It was no accident.'

Harry stopped. She didn't notice at first and walked on a few yards before she sensed that he wasn't just behind her. When she looked back, he was staring at her.

'You can't think my dad had anything to do with that? He's been inside for ten years.'

'But he still had plenty of people who'd do his dirty work for him outside, didn't he? That guy Dusty for a start. He was giving you daggers at the party.'

'Don't worry about Dusty. He's a bitter, never-has-been, all piss and wind. I can handle him.'

Emma wasn't sure that was the case. The guy had looked at Harry like he was a piece of shit on his shoe.

'Why do you think my dad would have a policewoman killed?' Harry added.

His question seemed genuine. Did he really not know anything about Laura's connection with Frankie Grant? If not, she wasn't about to enlighten him. The fewer people who knew the better – though there was no doubt that Harry's dad knew, even though he'd been locked up at the time.

'Why don't you drive?' she asked, ignoring his question.

'What? Why are you asking me that now?' She watched his face as he worked it out for himself.

'Fucking hell, Emma, you think I had something to do with it? Why would I run down your predecessor? Because my dad told me to? Is that what you think of me?'

He looked pained.

'If you must know, my brother, Eamonn, was run down and killed on a zebra crossing when I was six years old. He was seven. The only reason I wasn't right beside him was because I'd stopped to do my laces up. I saw the whole thing. It took me years to even get inside a car after that, but I can't get behind a wheel. Believe me, I've tried.'

She remembered his mother talking about a brother when they'd visited her in the care home.

'Does your mum think Eamonn is still alive?'

'Sometimes. Depends what kind of state she's in. Sometimes she thinks I'm him. I don't bother to correct her if she does, what would be the point?'

She shook her head. What a mess she'd made of that. There was no way she could talk about the trafficking now.

'Don't you trust me?' he said.

Her silence was answer enough. Harry shook his head.

'Perhaps this wasn't a good idea. Maybe I should go?'

He'd given her an out and she took it. She needed time to think.

'Maybe you should,' she said.

He was clearly hurt but he didn't say anything, just turned and walked away.

Emma watched him go for a moment and very nearly

called him back but then she turned too and continued to trudge up the hill. She'd done the right thing not telling him about Laura's collusion, even if his dad seemed to know.

But why did she suddenly feel like crying?

## 73

Leon stared at the sightings of Sam Gallagher's car on ANPR, trying to make sense of them. Gallagher claimed that Maria had driven his car away on 31 October but there were no sightings of it at all until three days later when it was picked up on the A720 heading towards Edinburgh airport. Sadly, there was no clear image of the driver.

Later that day it was picked up on a camera on the M8 in Glasgow, then the next day it was caught heading south on the A68 not far from the English border. If Maria Groom had been trying to get away, she had chosen a strange route. Maybe Sam Gallagher was telling porkies – what if it wasn't her driving the car but him? And where did Rob Gibson figure in all of this? How had he ended up driving the same car to his dad's house a few days after that sighting? They'd tried in vain to find an address for him after he'd left Newcastle all those years ago but he seemed to have gone completely off-grid in the meantime. Apparently his dad thought he'd moved to Scotland though so maybe there was a connection there?

He shouted across to Emma, who had only just come into the office.

'Where did you say Sara Quinn lived now?'

'Small place out in the sticks near the Scottish border. Byrness is the nearest place you'll find on a map.'

Leon went on to Google Maps. There was barely a speck where the village was but when he expanded the screen he saw it was on the A68. Was that where Gallagher's car was headed that day? It was too much of a coincidence, surely? And Jack reckoned that Quinn, Maria and Rob Gibson had gone to school together. Was that relevant? Was that where Gibson got hold of the car?

Emma had moved over to look at his screen.

'Do you think that's where Maria Groom was heading when she took Gallagher's car?' she said.

'If she took Gallagher's car. Who knows if he's telling the truth?'

'Or Sara Quinn. She was defensive when I asked her about Gibson. I had a real sense she was trying to steer me down the wrong path. But wasn't Gallagher at work on the days of those sightings?'

Leon sighed. She was right.

'Aye.'

'So we know it wasn't him. But we do know from the fingerprints in the car that both Maria and Gibson have driven it at some point. And in Gibson's case his dad ID'd it as the car he'd seen outside his house.'

Leon was still puzzling over all this when Emma wandered quickly back to her desk and picked up a sheet of paper.

'Brainwave?' he said.

'Maybe.' She scoured the page, running her finger up and down it.

'There's no passport.'

'I'm sorry.'

'This is the list of personal possessions Maria left behind in her house. It includes her phone, her driving licence and even her credit card but there's no passport. We should have spotted that earlier.'

Leon looked back at the screen.

'D'you think she flew somewhere out of Edinburgh? And maybe Gibson helped her and got to keep the car?'

'It's as good a theory as anything else.'

'But we put an alert out to the airports, didn't we?'

'Yes, definitely. I double-checked the other day. But maybe someone at their end missed it.'

Leon shouted across to Clive Andrews, who appeared to be adjusting his Fantasy Football team on his screen.

'If you're not too busy, mate, can you ring Edinburgh Airport and check if they've got any trace of Maria Groom and her son Nicky on their flight lists?'

Clive gave him the finger but picked up the phone anyway.

'You OK?' Leon asked Emma. She had seemed a little distracted when she came in that morning and had barely spoken until she'd come over to see what he was working on now.

'Fine.'

'Really?'

'No, not really. Bit left-field but do you think the Connors are still trafficking girls?'

'Is this because of what Ray found at the post-mortem of that poor woman who was buried at the farm?'

'Aye, I guess.'

'I don't know. I haven't heard anything in recent years and Stevie's been locked up for ten of them. Maybe you should ask your friend Harry?'

'Maybe I will,' she said.

Leon was about to tell her not to when Clive Andrews leapt off his chair and hurried over.

'We've got a bite on Maria Groom. She and Nicky were booked on a flight to Barcelona from Edinburgh on the third of November but they've checked and they didn't get on the plane.'

Leon looked at the ANPR sightings – that tied in to the sighting on the A720.

'If she was driving Gallagher's car that makes sense. It was picked up a few miles away from the airport. But why wouldn't she have got on the plane? It looks like she headed to Glasgow instead.'

'Maybe she had an issue with her passport? There's a passport office in Glasgow, I think,' Clive said. 'My sister had to use it last year when she hadn't realised hers had run out.'

Leon showed Clive the ANPR sighting later that day.

'D'you know where that office is?'

'Aye,' Clive said. 'She's been moaning about it ever since. It's just off the M8 near the city centre. Right there, in fact, almost exactly where the car was spotted,' he added, pointing at the map with a smile.

Leon gave him a quick salute.

'I think you've snatched the employee of the month award, mate. Give them a call as well, will you – see if they've got any record of her. And put some pressure on for quick answers. If for some reason she needed a new passport we need to know what the waiting time is. If it's more than twenty-four hours I reckon it's a fair bet that Maria Groom decided to head to her mate Sara's house to hole out until it was ready for her to fly.'

As Clive returned to his desk, Leon heard Emma's phone buzz. She took it out of her pocket and read the message. He could see she was puzzled.

'What is it?'

'It's Harry Connors.'

'Knob pic?'

'Don't. He wants to see me.'

'Who doesn't?'

'Be serious, Leon. This is work. I haven't mentioned the trafficking but I did tell him that we thought his dad might have been involved in Laura's death.'

'What did he say?'

'He was a bit pissed off, to be honest. I didn't expect to hear from him again. But it looks like he's changed his mind. He says he needs to talk to me.'

She showed Leon the message.

Can you come to the house? I have something for you. It's about dad.

'I should come with you. We could challenge him about the trafficking too.'

'No. You need to explore those sightings a little more. You could be close to finding Maria and Nicky.'

Leon was about to press his case when he noticed Emma's eyes had glazed over – her thinking face.

'That was it,' she said. 'Explore.'

'Explore what?'

'When I was talking to Sara Quinn on the phone that last time she had to turn the TV down.'

'That's it?'

'No, man, I recognised the theme tune of whatever was on, but I couldn't place it. Now I can. It was *Dora the Explorer*.'

Leon shook his head. 'And?'

'It's a kids' show. My sister's kids love it. But Sara Quinn is childless.'

'Maybe she was looking after someone else's.'

'Or maybe Nicky Groom was there. You need to get up there and talk to her.'

'Why me?'

'Because I'm going to see Harry Connors.'

'But—'

'No buts, I'm a big girl. It'll be fine.'

'It's not safe. He's a fucking gangster, Emma.'

'His dad's a gangster, he's a businessman.'

'Jesus, you have drunk the Kool-Aid, haven't you?'

'Not everything's as black and white as you think, you know.'

'Bit racist.'

'That's not even funny.' She was smiling though.

'It's a bit funny. Better than sarcasm.'

'What do you mean?'

'I could have sworn it was you leading the applause when I brought Gallagher in.'

She laughed. 'Jesus, that was ages ago.'

'Yesterday, to be precise.'

'Let it go, man. Look, all I'm saying is that not everything's as clear-cut as you think. Harry Connors might not be a complete innocent but I think, on balance, he's OK. You know, like most people. He has his faults but his heart's in the right place.'

'It's not his heart I'm worried about.'

'What is it with you guys? Jack was the same. Not that it's any of your business.'

'Isn't it?'

'I don't remember signing an exclusive deal with you.'

Leon closed his eyes. He was way out of his league with Emma – his idea of a relationship and hers were miles apart. He was strictly a one-woman man, a serial monogamist if you like. He had no idea if there was a word for what she was.

'For the record, I'm not going to fuck Harry Connors,' she added.

'I know that.'

'Do you really?'

Leon hesitated. She was right. It was exactly what he'd been thinking.

'Yes,' he said. 'I trust you, but seriously, to be on the safe side, let me come with you.'

'No, I'll be fine. You need to find out where Maria Groom

and her son have gone. I think you'll find them at Sara Quinn's house.'

She was right, as usual. She seemed able to compartmentalise her personal and professional lives in a way that he couldn't. Was it a maturity thing? He'd always thought he was quite mature but she made him feel like a child.

'Anyway,' she said. 'It's not like it's the first time I've been to Harry's place, is it?'

'I know, but I've normally been hovering around outside somewhere.'

She laughed. 'You really need to stop that. Though it might help you bond with Sam Gallagher. Maybe you could start a Stalkers Anonymous help group.'

74

Gordon Kemp sat in his favourite armchair. He hadn't taken his eyes off Lee Grant since the pair of us had turned up at his front door. I'd given him some broad-brush details on the phone, not wanting to doorstep him like Gary Coxon or some other pushy journalist might have. It had also given him time to think about his wife, Liz. Only he knew if she was strong enough to deal with this. He'd clearly decided not as she wasn't in the room.

Lee and I were perched on the sofa. Frankie Grant had wanted to come with us but I knew that would be a disaster. I'd managed to avoid telling Gordon the full story about Laura's involvement with Frankie and was still hoping I could keep his knowledge of her treachery to a minimum – especially as she was only doing it to help her dad out of a financial hole. Frankie hadn't been happy but it was either my way or Lee could face the full force of the law so he didn't have much choice. To the kid's credit he didn't fight the idea, he seemed almost relieved to be given the chance to apologise.

'Tell me everything,' Gordon said.

Lee looked at me and I nodded. He turned back to Laura's dad.

'I come from a broken home,' he said, almost whispering.

'You're going to have to speak up, son,' Gordon said. 'My hearing's not what it was.'

'I'm adopted,' he said. 'My biological father – I can never think of him as my dad – had a lot of other women and it destroyed my mam when he eventually left us. She drank herself to death, choked on her own vomit when I was six years old.'

'I'm sorry to hear that, son.'

Lee nodded in thanks but barely paused. I could tell that he had to get to the end of his story before he fell apart.

'I went into a home but got lucky – Mam and Dad, Gloria and Frankie, that is, took me in a year later. I had blond hair and they reckoned I looked like a little angel.'

He attempted a smile but couldn't quite pull it off.

'They've been great parents. I know what my dad does, I'm not saying he's a saint or anything, but he's a good dad, stern but fair.'

I could see Gordon nodding along. He'd been a good dad too, but he'd also had an affair. I wondered if he was thinking about how close he'd come to destroying his own family.

'Go on,' he said.

Lee took a deep breath and carried on.

'I'd never worried about Frankie before but one day, a year or so back, I saw him chatting to this woman in a café, he put his hand on hers and that. It freaked me out. I didn't dare say anything, but I started to follow him sometimes, just to make sure, like.'

'And this was Laura?' Gordon said.

'Aye. I didn't know that at the time though. And I had no idea she was a policewoman at first, I was shocked when I found that out, like. I saw them together a couple more times after that and started to get really suspicious. I nearly said something to Mam but I didn't want to worry her. Then one day I followed my dad to a hotel room, he never saw us, I was good at keeping back. I waited in the foyer and a few minutes later I saw her come in and followed her up to the same room.'

'Hold on a minute,' Gordon said, looking across to me. 'Why was Laura meeting his dad in his hotel room?'

I couldn't tell him the truth. It would have killed him knowing that he was responsible for her working for Frankie Grant.

'She was doing some undercover work.'

'She never mentioned it.'

'That's because she was a professional, Gordon. She would know better than to tell anyone, even her parents.'

The lie seemed to work and, thankfully, even if he knew the truth, Lee was too wrapped up in his own issues to contradict me. Gordon turned back to the lad.

'And that's why you killed her? Because you thought she was having an affair with your father?'

Lee shook his head.

'No, man, no, honestly it wasn't like that. I-I wanted to scare her off. I followed her for a few weeks but she was often in a car so it was difficult. That last time I took my dad's car so I could see where she went and hovered near the police station until I saw her come out with DCI Parker here.'

He turned to me. 'You were driving but you didn't see me following you. I waited around when you went into a building and then afterwards when you went to the pub. I sat in the car outside, thinking it through and then, when you came out and I saw her get in the driving seat, I just acted on instinct.'

Lee had tears streaming down his face now. He turned back to Gordon.

'I didn't mean to kill her, Mr Kemp, swear down. I wanted her to leave my dad alone, that was all, but I lost control of the car. I'd only had a few lessons, just had my provisional licence and that. It was an accident, I swear. I'm really sorry. I can't tell you how much.'

The kid was in bits now. I put my hand on his shoulder to calm him a little and waited for Gordon's response but before he could speak the lounge door swung open and his wife, Liz, stood there, tears running down her face too. She had a large kitchen knife in her hand.

Gordon didn't see her at first, as the door was behind him, but he saw us staring across at her and turned around.

'You heard all that?' he said. I wasn't sure if he'd seen the knife or not.

She nodded but kept her eyes fixed on Lee.

'I was sat on the stairs,' she croaked. 'I heard Jack come in with someone else and knew something was up so I crept down.' She probably hadn't said that much in one go since Laura was killed.

I hadn't seen or spoken to Liz for months and was shocked at how much weight she'd lost. I doubted she even had the strength to stab someone but I edged up onto the balls of my feet in case she tried. She pointed the knife at Lee whose head had dropped completely now. His quiet sobs filling any gap in the conversation.

'Look at me,' she said. Lee lifted his head, barely seeming to register the knife until she pointed it at him. Even then he made no effort to move, unlike Gordon, who flinched and stared at me questioningly. I gestured to him to stay seated. If someone was going to get hurt here I didn't want it to be him. Liz would never forgive herself.

'Are you the one who's been leaving them flowers on Laura's grave?' she said, edging closer to Lee.

Between sobs it was clear that the lad was nodding. He was rubbing the sides of his head as if that would make everything go away. The movements made both his wrists clearly visible and I could see again the scars I'd glimpsed when he'd tried to stop me going into his house the other day. I looked up and could see that Liz saw them too.

'I t-talk to her,' Lee whispered. 'Tell her how sorry I am. I know it's not much but I didn't kn-know what else to do.' He went to stand up but I put my hand on his shoulder to stop him, wanting to keep him away from that knife.

'Why don't you put the knife down, Liz,' I said. She didn't react at all. I'm not sure she even heard me, her eyes still fixed on Lee.

'It always brought me some comfort, seeing that someone else cared,' she said quietly.

I had no idea what was going to happen next and watched in shock as Liz stepped towards Lee. I got to my feet but before I could intercept her she had let the knife fall to the floor and dropped to her knees in front of him, throwing her arms around the weeping kid.

'You poor child,' she said. 'Please don't cry.'

That just seemed to make him worse.

'I'm so sorry,' he wailed. 'I didn't mean to kill her.'

Liz pulled him in tight and patted his back.

'I know you didn't,' she said.

'I wish it had been me instead,' Lee sobbed.

I could see Liz getting a close-up view of the scars on his wrists and shaking her head.

'Don't say that,' she said. 'It's OK now . . . we forgive you.'

## 75

Emma had never driven to Stevie Connors' house before; she'd always been in the back of his chauffeur-driven car, with Micky Chambers, or whatever his name really was, doing the driving, but it wasn't hard to find the house again – head past the airport, take a left at Dobbies' round-about, a couple of zigzags and she'd be there.

As she drove into Ponteland she thought about Maria Groom and her passport issues – part of her hoped the woman had managed to get away. That was the optimistic explanation for Rob Gibson driving the car back down to Newcastle.

The less hopeful version was that whatever issue caused the delay it left her vulnerable to one of several toxic men who seemed attracted to her like she was misogynist catnip. Gibson's reported claim to have killed someone made her fear that explanation was the most likely – and there must be a reason why the man jumped off the Tyne Bridge – guilt seemed to be as likely an explanation as any.

It was easy to forget that the smallest of things could

have the biggest implications. Jack still seemed haunted by Laura's death, knowing that if he hadn't had one drink too many, he would have been driving the car instead of his friend. Then Emma would never have got her job or come anywhere near the Connors family. Maybe that would have been a good thing for all concerned.

She found her way to the long road she was looking for on the eastern side of the town and couldn't miss the large gates that blocked the front of Harry's driveway. She got out of the car and buzzed the intercom, noticing a camera perched on the wall. A few seconds later the gates swung open. Emma got back into the car and drove into the large, tarmacked area in front of the house.

There didn't seem to be a doorbell – she guessed you didn't need one when you controlled your gates. She waited for a second or two, expecting Harry to open the door, then, a little impatiently, banged the large knocker in the centre of the door to speed things up a bit. When it opened, she was surprised to see Stevie Connors standing there, wearing trackie bottoms and a sweat-soaked T-shirt with a towel around his neck.

'I hope you've got a warrant, pet,' he said.

'It's just a social call, I'm here to see Harry.'

'Aye, I knaa. Just pulling your pisser. You could have let yourself in, ya knaa,' he said, indicating a handle on the left of the door.

'Sorry, I didn't see it. Is Harry here?'

'Aye, he's out the back of the house. Apparently I'm his bloody servant now.'

He pulled the door wide open.

'My master awaits you, madam,' he said, bowing extravagantly.

Emma hesitated, remembering Leon's warning.

'Make your mind up, pet, I haven't got all day. As you might have noticed you interrupted my gym session and I've got a bit of a sweat on.' He held his arm up and took a huge sniff of his armpit, grimacing theatrically. 'A wonderful bouquet, if I do say so meself.'

She tried hard to hide her distaste but knew that she was failing.

'Not your kind of thing, eh, pet? Pity. Pretty thing like you would be right up my street.'

In for a penny, she thought. And walked into the house. Immediately she could feel why Stevie Connors was dripping. The house was boiling, a stark contrast to the outside.

'You might want to take your coat off,' Connors said. 'I suppose that's my job as well now I'm me laddo's butler.' He moved behind her and caught the coat as she shrugged it off. The smell of old-man sweat almost made her gag but this time she managed to hide it. No need to really piss him off.

'Where will I find Harry?'

'Don't you worry your pretty little head, I'll go get him. You wait in here.'

He opened a door to a room off the main hallway. There was a drinks cabinet to one side, and a Victorian-looking armchair and chaise longue near the window.

'We keep it posh for visitors,' he said, laughing. 'Help

yourself to a drink if you're thirsty. I'll go and grab lover boy for you.'

Emma chose the armchair, which faced out to the lawn at the side of the house. A lone flag stuck out of the middle and there was a putter lying on the grass. She wondered what Stevie Connors was doing there – surprised that Harry would want to talk about him while he was in the house. Maybe, like he'd said, the old man had lost his edge so he didn't care if he was overheard.

Outside, a lone magpie landed near the putter, eyeing it curiously. One for sorrow, she thought idly, glancing around in the hope of finding a second one to signal joy but with no luck. Emma got up and walked over to the drinks cabinet. There was pretty much every spirit you could imagine. As much as she could do with a drink, it was too early and she was driving so that was a no-no. There was a small fridge beside it where she found some cans of tonic. She grabbed one and poured it into a glass she found in a second cupboard. Once she'd finished that she'd had enough of waiting and decided to go walkabout. She tried the door. It was locked. What the fuck?

'Harry,' she shouted.

Nothing. She banged on the door and shouted again. 'Harry!'

Still nothing. Emma cursed herself for leaving her phone in the car. But then she heard footsteps, the turn of a key and the door opened. Stevie Connors stood there in a white towelling robe. She backed away from him – not because of the robe but because he had a gun in his hand.

'Sorry about the wait, pet,' he said. 'Thought I'd better have a shower before we get down to business. You caught me by surprise coming straight here. Thought you were smarter than that.'

'What the fuck are you doing? Where's Harry?'

'Haven't you heard, love? Three's a crowd. Now come with me.'

Emma didn't move, glancing around the room for a weapon. Her empty glass was still on top of the bar. She grabbed it and pulled her arm back to heave it at Connors' head but before she could let it go there was a huge bang and her arm felt like it had been set on fire. She dropped the glass in agony and clutched her arm, blood seeping out through her fingers.

'You fucking shot me!' she screamed.

'Harry said you were bright,' Connors said, laughing. 'Sorry about that.' He examined the gun as if it was the problem. 'Didn't mean to hit you but I'm a bit out of practice. It's just a flesh wound, mind. Now do as you're told or it'll be your leg next.'

He backed out of the door and beckoned her forward with the gun. This time she did as directed.

'Up there,' he said, moving behind her and ushering her towards a large staircase at the end of the hallway.

'Where are you taking me?'

'Just move.'

As she hesitated, he nudged her in the back with the gun and she stumbled up the steps, her blood dripping down onto the stair-carpet.

'Good job our cleaners know how to get blood out,' he said. 'Keep going. Turn left when you get to the top.'

Emma looked around as she walked, hoping to see something she could use as a weapon, but the landing was bare, no ornaments, not even a painting she could batter him with.

'First door on the right. In you go.'

She stood outside the closed door, fearing what was on the other side, preferring the open space of the landing. She turned around.

'I don't—'

He smashed the butt of the gun into the side of her head, sending her crashing into the wall. She sank to the floor, her head spinning. She heard him open the door himself and felt herself being dragged into the room. She looked up, the light hurting her eyes. Her worst fears were realised. It was a bedroom.

'No!' she screamed.

'Shut the fuck up,' he said, pulling her up by her hair and shoving her firmly onto the bed. She fell face down, crying out as her wounded arm hit the bed frame. Quickly realising she couldn't stay like that, she hauled herself up with her good arm and shuffled across the bed backwards until her back hit the headboard. She grabbed a pillowcase off one of the pillows on the bed and wrapped it around her arm as best she could.

Connors closed the door behind him with his arse, locked it then turned and grinned at her.

'Not so lippy now, eh, missy? I hear you thought I had

something to do with that cop bitch's murder. No one likes a snitch, you know.'

'Did you?'

'As it happens, no, but it hurt my feelings that you'd filled my boy's head with such nonsense. He's always been a soft shite.'

'Does Harry know you're doing this?'

'He sent you that message, didn't he?'

'I think you sent it.'

Connors nodded and bowed.

'Wise after the event, pet. Pity you're not a bit quicker on the uptake.'

The man clearly liked to talk. Maybe she could distract him until she could work out how to get out of there? She took a punt.

'I'm not that slow. I know that you're still trafficking girls.'

He smiled. 'Not me, love, didn't you hear? I've been in prison for a bit.'

'And will be back there soon.'

Connors barked out a laugh.

'I doubt it. Might let my lad take the fall this time. He's the one that's been running the show after all.'

'I don't believe that.'

'They do say love is blind.'

'I think you've let him be a front for the legal stuff but you've had someone else keep the rest of your operation ticking over.'

'You do have your moments then. It's a shame Eamonn

got killed. He was the tough brother, I could have left him in charge of everything if he'd still been around.'

'Instead of Dusty?' she guessed.

'Evan Groom been talking, has he? He's not long for this world. He's been getting above himself anyway. We can't have people damaging our merchandise without our say-so.'

Emma had already met some evil bastards in her short time in the force, but Connors was probably the worst. If she'd had the gun in her hand, she might well have shot him then.

'What do you want with me?' she said.

'You can't be that slow.' Connors patted the bed with his free hand. 'I'd have thought that was obvious.'

'You'll have to kill me first.'

He shrugged. 'I don't really mind which order I do it in.'

Emma actually believed him; she could feel herself going cold all over. Some of that could have been due to the blood loss but more likely it was the fear. She was pretty sure he'd get off on that, so she steeled herself not to show it. Instead, she screamed at the top of her lungs for as long as she could. The only response was Connors laughing mirthlessly.

'There's no one around to hear you, pet, our neighbours know better than to make a fuss, but feel free to tire yourself out. It'll make my life easier. Now are you going to strip or do I have to shoot you again?'

She glanced around the room frantically. There was a bedside table but nothing on top of it. She pulled open its one small drawer but it was empty.

'You're only delaying the inevitable, sweetheart,' Connors

said. 'Why not just lie back and think of England like a good girl, eh!'

Connors untied the belt on his dressing gown and let it fall to the floor. He was stick thin, his ribs clearly visible and he had what she supposed were prison tattoos – given how crap they were – all over his chest. He was naked aside from a pristine pair of white boxer shorts, only marred by the erection she could clearly see poking against the front of them.

'Shall we get started?' he said. 'As you can see, I'm ready.'

He pointed the gun at her.

'Strip.'

'No chance.'

He fired for the second time, blowing a chunk out of the headboard to her left, narrowly missing her good arm.

She screamed despite herself. The echo of the gunshot seemed to fill the room but once it died down, she heard another noise. A door opening. She screamed again.

'Help!'

There was no reaction outside but for the first time Connors looked rattled. Then, in the distance: 'Emma?' Harry's voice, but it sounded a long way away, somewhere downstairs maybe. She screamed again.

'Harry! Help me!'

This time there was an immediate response, footsteps charging up the stairs.

'Where are you?' Harry was much closer now.

'In here,' she shouted.

The door rattled and then something slammed against it.

Stevie Connors moved to one side, his gun still trained on Emma.

'Fuck off, son, leave this to the grown-ups.'

'What are you doing?'

'He has a gun, Harry,' Emma shouted.

The door shuddered again, then she heard a series of kicks, as Harry tried to force his way in. Stevie Connors moved down the side of the bed towards her, but she slid across the covers to the other side.

'Open the fucking door, Dad,' Harry screamed from outside, still battering against the door.

Stevie Connors jumped up onto the bed, closing the gap between him and Emma. He grinned as he neared her. In desperation she grabbed the quilt and yanked it as hard as she could. He stumbled back, falling onto the floor, the gun going off again, taking out half the ceiling light. Harry's assault on the door finally worked as it flew open, crashing back against the wall. He saw Emma crouched down by her side of the bed and then his dad, climbing to his feet, gun still in hand.

'Put the gun down, Dad.'

'Not a chance. I'm not letting this bitch send me back to prison.'

'She won't do that, will you, Emma?'

Emma looked between them. She knew what she ought to say to calm things down but sod that.

'In a heartbeat,' she said.

Stevie Connors turned the gun on her but when Harry took two steps towards him he turned it back on his son.

'Back off, lad, remember where your loyalties lie.'

Harry kept moving. Emma had no doubts that if he didn't stop, his dad would shoot him. She whipped the drawer out of the bedside cabinet and hurled it across the room, hitting the old man on the head and knocking him to the floor. The gun went off again and Harry flew back and slid down the wall, a streak of blood marking his descent to the floor. Stevie Connors climbed to his knees, blood pouring from a gash in his head, dropped the gun and crawled towards his son, who seemed barely conscious.

'Harry?' he said, then louder, 'HARRY!'

Emma saw her chance and scrambled over the bed to get the gun, but Connors saw her coming and reached back to grab it first. They both got their hands on it at the same time and grappled for it. Emma was hampered by her wounded arm but the old man was in a worst state, clearly concussed by the drawer smashing into his skull. She rolled on top of him, clinging desperately to the gun, when it went off again. Connors shuddered for a moment then went still. She thought it might be a trick so she held on to the gun but then she looked up and saw he definitely wasn't faking it: the top of his head was missing.

## 76

*Poisonous masculinity from 11 to 100, perhaps? (5)*

I leaned back in the passenger seat, put the paper on my lap, and closed my eyes, feeling a little queasy. I was still getting used to being a passenger. I could cope with short journeys but the drive up to Byrness was at least an hour and judging by the amount of traffic it was going to be much longer than that. Trying to do the crossword was a rookie error.

'Did you hear anything from Emma?' Leon said.

'Don't think so,' I muttered. Clearly, I wasn't going to be allowed to sleep. I pulled my phone out to check I hadn't missed any messages. 'Nope. Nothing.'

'I shouldn't have let her go to the Connors' house on her own,' Leon said.

'She's been there twice before. Harry Connors isn't going to do anything to a serving officer.'

'It's only two minutes since you suggested he'd killed Laura.'

He was right, though Emma didn't seem to think it was anything to do with him. I sent her a text to check she was OK.

'She practically called me a stalker when I suggested going with her,' Leon added.

'To be fair, you practically are a stalker.'

'I thought you'd be on my side.'

'Why? Because I'm old and clearly think that women should know their place and do whatever it is that I want them to?'

'No! Is that what you think I'm like?'

'You are a bit full on, mate. And keep your eyes on the road, will you? You're making me nervous.'

'Sorry. Shit. What is happening to me? I never used to be like this.'

'At least you have some measure of self-awareness. People like Evan Groom and Sam Gallagher will probably never reach that exalted level. You're nearer to irritating than toxic at the moment.'

Eureka! I glanced down at the crossword clue again to make sure. Then wrote in the answer – a combination of the roman numerals for eleven and 100 and the word *to*.

'So to be clear,' Leon said. 'I'm a better bet than an actual stalker and an illegal drug supplier and probable murderer. Excellent. Gold star for me.'

'Faint praise is better than no praise.'

'Can we change the subject? What do you think we're going to find at Sara Quinn's?'

'I haven't the faintest idea.'

I hoped that it wasn't another body or two. One was enough for this week.

'D'you think I was right not to ring her?'

'Absolutely. Catch her on the hoof, so to speak. No time for her to prepare a story – or even do a runner, if she hasn't already.'

My phone buzzed in my hand.

'That'll probably be Emma now.'

It wasn't. It was Clive Andrews.

'False alarm. It's Clive. The passport office has confirmed that Maria Groom paid for a fast-track new passport on the third of November.'

'Wow. So Evan Groom *was* right all along. She set the whole thing up and put him right in the frame. Then she fled the country.'

'Not quite.'

'What did I get wrong?'

'She never collected the passport.'

I let that sink in.

'Shit,' Leon said, after a moment's thought. 'That's not good.'

'Not good at all,' I said. 'If she didn't leave the country then why would Rob Gibson be driving the car she was using?'

'D'you think she's dead?'

'Who knows? Hopefully Sara Quinn will have some answers for us. Though given that she seems to have been lying through her teeth about Rob Gibson I'm not that hopeful.'

I looked back down at the crossword. Even in the dark my last answer seemed to leap off the page at me: *TOXIC*.

## 77

Harry Connors stared at his father's dead body, shaking his head so hard that Emma feared he might do himself more damage than the bullet wound in his shoulder. Thankfully, the bullet seemed to have gone straight through his shoulder into the wall without severing anything vital. She'd removed a second pillowcase and folded it up for him to hold to help stem the blood flowing out of the wound.

'I need to call this in,' she said. 'You need an ambulance.'

'I'm not the only one,' he said, eyeing her arm.

'Just a flesh wound. Yours is worse.'

'It's not a competition, Emma. And I'll live so hold your horses.' He took a deep breath, clearly in a lot of pain. 'We need to think about this. What were you doing here?'

Emma told him about the text.

'I didn't send that.'

'I know that now. I presume you told him I'd been asking questions about the hit and run.'

'Aye, sorry about that. But I had to know if he was involved.

He took umbrage, obviously, but I didn't think he'd do anything like this. How did he get you up here?'

'He pretended to go and get you but when he came back he had the gun. When I refused to go upstairs with him he shot me in the arm.'

'Jesus. And I thought prison would have calmed the mad bastard down.'

'Maybe it did. I didn't know him before.'

He laughed, a little too hard, apparently, as it stopped with a grimace.

'Will you get in trouble for this?'

She looked back at the body. She'd been avoiding it, had never killed anyone before, but just felt numb.

'Probably. There will certainly be an enquiry and I'll probably be suspended. It won't look good, let's put it like that.'

'What if I said I did it?'

'Why would you do that?'

He gave her a little-boy-hurt look that she found strangely touching in the circumstances.

'It's my fault, isn't it? I shouldn't have taken you to the party, and I certainly shouldn't have mentioned your suspicions to him.'

'You weren't to know.'

'I've known him my whole life, Emma. This probably wouldn't make his top ten of crazy.'

She shook her head. 'It wouldn't work, Harry. The forensics wouldn't back you up. I'll be covered in gunshot residue and his blood is all over me.'

'But we can fuck with that good and proper, can't we.

You know how it all works. I can fire the gun too and we can easily cook up a story that matches the forensics. You were taken hostage and I rescued you. I'll be a fucking hero. The man who saved a beautiful young cop from his crazed father. And you'll be the brave victim who fought off a lunatic after being shot.'

'You think I'm beautiful?'

He barked out another laugh and winced again at the pain.

'That's what you took from that?'

'Naturally.' She couldn't believe she was taking his suggestion seriously, but she was. It could work.

'They'd still charge you, you know.'

'Manslaughter though.'

She nodded. 'For sure.'

'And I'd get off with a self-defence plea when the woman I saved spoke up for me, wouldn't I?'

'What about your family, what would your mum say?'

He shrugged. 'She already thinks he's dead.'

78

As Leon slowed down to turn into the lane that led to Sara Quinn's cottage, I couldn't help but notice the For Sale sign near the entrance. I wasn't entirely surprised. While he waited for a couple of oncoming cars to pass, my phone pinged again. It was a message from Bob Curtis. I read it with growing incredulity as we turned into the lane.

'Fuck me,' I muttered.

Leon looked across at me and could see I was shocked.

'What is it? Is it Emma?'

I nodded. He stopped the car halfway down the lane.

'Is she OK? I knew I should have been with her.'

I held my hand up to give me a moment to read to the end of the message.

'She's OK. Ish.'

'What do you mean?'

'She's been shot.'

Leon's face crumpled but I could tell he was fighting to control his emotions.

'She's fine, she's in hospital but it's just a flesh wound. She's got a few other bumps and bruises but that's it.'

'What about Connors?'

'Which one?'

'I don't know, either, both.'

'Stevie Connors is dead.'

Leon's mouth fell open.

'Did Emma kill him?'

I shook my head.

'Who then?'

'Harry. It would seem he saved Emma's life.'

I let Leon read the message himself. I rang Bob back as Leon tried to contact Emma but understandably neither of them were picking up. It sounded as if there was a huge mess to be sorted out. Leon wanted to head straight back, but it was clear that Emma wasn't in any danger and was getting all the treatment necessary. What she needed now was rest and having the pair of us turning up on the wards wouldn't help with that. Bob would want me on the scene as soon as possible but he also wanted me to try to find the missing kid so he'd forgive me another hour.

I'd expected Sara Quinn to be long gone but when we finally pulled up outside the cottage, I could see there was a light on in the front room. Before we could get out the light went off. Someone was home but it looked like they didn't want company.

Sara's home was a smallholding of some kind. There was a chicken coop behind a wire fence and from the strands of wool floating around I guessed there were sheep tucked away somewhere. An idyllic spot – nice place to raise a kid.

No one answered the door the first time I knocked on it. Or the second time.

'It's DCI Jack Parker, Sara. We know you're in there. We need to talk to you. About Maria. And Nicky. And Rob Gibson.'

The light went back on again. The door opened and Sara Quinn stepped outside, shutting it behind her. She was clearly hiding something.

'It's late,' she said. 'I was just going to bed.'

I looked at my watch. It was barely 7.30 p.m. She could tell I didn't believe her.

'I haven't slept much lately. My best friend and godson are missing.'

'We were hoping you might be able to help us with that.'

'Me? How do you think I might help?'

'Can we come inside?'

She shook her head. A little faster than necessary. It was more of an 'I don't want you to' than a 'no'.

'It's getting a little nippy. Leon here feels the cold more than most. I think it's his West Indian blood.'

'It's true,' Leon said. 'I haven't got the Geordie genes to protect me. And I could murder a cuppa. I don't mind making it.'

'No,' she said, more firmly this time. 'I know the law. You need a warrant to search my house.'

'Who said anything about a search? We just want a chat.'

She didn't respond, simply stared over my shoulder as if she hoped we'd simply walk away.

'And we don't need a warrant if we feel someone's in imminent danger. Did you hear someone cry out, Detective Sergeant Johnson?'

'I think I did, sir, maybe I should investigate.'

'You can't do that,' she said.

'Why wouldn't you want to help us, Mrs Quinn? Your *best friend*'s missing and you seem to be on the verge of obstructing the investigation.' I had deliberately switched to more formal titles, hoping she'd subconsciously recognise that things were getting serious. Leon had followed my lead and done the same. 'I don't want to arrest you, but if I have to—'

'All right,' she snapped. 'We can go through to the kitchen but please be quiet. I have my elderly uncle, my mother's brother, staying with me in my box room. He's recovering from pneumonia and needs all the sleep he can get.'

Leon and I shared a look, both doubtful there was any such uncle.

Sara Quinn opened the door slowly. It led straight into the main living space but she walked through a doorway on the right into the kitchen, turning on the light as we entered it. There was a decent-sized wooden table in the middle and she pointed to the chairs, stopping to put the kettle on before sitting down herself.

'We know that Maria Groom and Nicky came here just over a week ago. A few days after she was last seen at home.' We knew no such thing, but it was an educated guess. One that I knew had been right when her mouth fell open.

'How could you?'

'She was driving Sam Gallagher's car. We have seen them on CCTV at various locations and tracked the car to this address.' It wasn't the exact truth but close enough.

She bowed her head, clearly pulling her thoughts together. I suspected she was pulling them out of her arse rather than her head but was interested to see what she had to say. Getting a suspect to start talking was the hardest thing, once you'd done that you were halfway towards the truth.

'They did come here,' she said. 'Maria was trying to escape from Evan Groom, but she had a problem with her passport and needed a place to hide away for a couple of days.'

'A couple of days?'

'Yes.'

'So she stayed here until the sixth of November?'

'That's right. No. Let me think. Sorry, it's all a bit of a blur. It was the seventh.'

'OK. Where did she go after that?'

'To the airport.'

'Glasgow or Edinburgh? They're about equidistant from here, aren't they?'

She pretended to be considering this.

'Glasgow, I think. We agreed that the less I knew the better. She was desperate to start a new life elsewhere without any of the baggage she'd accumulated over the years.'

'The men, you mean?'

'Yes, that's right.'

'So she and Nicky have fled the country?'

She nodded.

'And she left Mr Gallagher's car at Glasgow Airport, did she?'

There was some hesitation. She'd clearly been lying from the start and had managed to keep it within the realms of possibility but was floundering now.

'I guess she must have. I hadn't really thought about it.'

'And where does Rob Gibson fit into all this? I assume he's part of the left luggage, sorry, baggage. Even though you failed to mention him to my officer when she first spoke to you.'

She was looking at me like I was somehow reading her mind.

'I don't understand.'

'You're not the only one, Mrs Quinn. If Maria Groom left her car at Glasgow Airport on the seventh of November, how was it that Rob Gibson was seen driving it in Newcastle on the ninth?'

Her surprise was clearly genuine this time. I suspected she'd be relieved that she no longer had to lie to us.

'I have no idea.'

'OK. Maybe you could tell me why he told his father he killed someone.'

She shook her head. Whether in disbelief or denial I couldn't tell.

'I'm afraid you'll have to ask him.'

'I'd love to,' I said. 'But unfortunately they pulled his body out of the Tyne two days later.'

Sara Quinn couldn't look at me now. She was shaking.

'Maybe you should make that tea, DS Johnson,' I said. 'Plenty of sugar for Mrs Quinn, please, she's in shock.'

Leon got up and looked through the cupboards for cups and stuff. Sara Quinn kept her head down, her shoulders were trembling. It looked like she was crying. I gave her some space; one way or another I didn't think time was an issue any longer.

Eventually Leon placed two cups on the table in front of us. Sara Quinn barely noticed. Leon caught my eye and pointed at the doorway before quietly disappearing into the front room.

'Tell me about your relationship with Rob Gibson.' I wasn't sure that she'd heard my question but eventually she straightened up. She went to pick up her cup but then realised Leon wasn't where he had been before. She looked around in panic.

'Where's the other one?' she said anxiously, getting to her feet. As she stood up Leon came back into the kitchen with a young child in his arms.

'Look who I've found,' he said.

Sara Quinn jumped up and gently took Nicky Groom out of Leon's arms, cradling the sleeping child tenderly on her shoulder.

'It's not what it looks like,' she said.

## 79

We moved into the front room and waited for Sara Quinn to settle a still-sleeping Nicky Groom back on the sofa next to her before she continued her story.

'When Rob arrived on my doorstep a few years ago he was a broken man,' she said. 'Maria had aborted his baby then thrown him out of their apartment and his dad had rejected him too. He was addicted to cocaine and had no one else to turn to.'

'So he moved in with you?'

'Just for a few weeks, yes. I felt sorry for him. I knew what it was like to want a family and not have one. I helped him get back on his feet. A friend of mine had a house in the village that needed a lot of doing up and she agreed that Rob could live there rent free while he did the redecorating work. He's been living up here ever since, just about making ends meet with a few handyman jobs, amongst other things.'

'Why didn't you tell my other DS all this when she asked you? You pretended you didn't know Rob at first.'

'Because I knew he had nothing to do with Maria's disappearance. He was up here that whole time.'

'And the coke habit?'

'He learnt to control it. And made a few quid selling drugs to some of the locals. He became a bit of a whizz at getting stuff on the dark web.'

'For you?'

'No. I haven't touched that sort of thing for a long time. I like a drink but that's all. Fortunately for Rob, there are a lot of bored soldiers stuck up here with little else to do. Otterburn's not exactly a hive of activity for young men with energy to burn.'

'Is that why you and Maria haven't seen much of each other in recent years, because Rob was here?'

She nodded. 'Partly. She didn't know anything about him being here and I didn't exactly encourage her to visit. I was worried it might set Rob off again if he saw her.'

'And is that what happened?'

'Pretty much. He got off his face and slipped some ketamine into her drink the first night she was here.'

'And is that what killed her?' Leon asked.

Sara looked surprised.

'I'm sorry, I thought you realised. Maria's not dead.'

At first I thought I'd misheard her but I could tell by the look on her face that I hadn't. It took me a moment to recalibrate my thoughts. Leon looked equally dumbfounded but reacted a little quicker than me.

'So where is she?' he said.

Sara shook her head. 'I have no idea.'

I looked across to the sleeping child on the sofa.

'Then what's he doing here?'

'I'm taking care of him for a while.'

'You can't expect me to believe that.'

She looked at the sofa where Nicky seemed to be having a bad dream, muttering and twitching slightly. She stroked his hair and he quietened down. She turned back to me.

'I think you need to speak to Maria,' she said.

It took her a few minutes of texting to persuade Maria to talk to us on a FaceTime call. While we were waiting for her to ring us Sara Quinn told us what had happened before Maria left.

'I'd taken Nicky for a walk while Maria packed. When I got back her car was gone and I thought for a minute she'd left early deliberately – that she couldn't bear to say goodbye to Nicky. But when I got in the house she was lying unconscious on the kitchen floor and there was blood everywhere. Luckily I'd left Nicky outside playing with the chickens so he didn't see her.

'At first I thought she was dead, and Rob must have too, because I found a barely coherent note from him saying he hadn't meant to do it. He was obviously off his face.'

'Have you still got it?'

'Yes. It's in the left-hand drawer in the dresser next to the front door.'

Leon went off to find it.

'Thankfully I found a pulse and managed to get her off the floor and onto the sofa. And the blood mostly came from a cut on her foot. When she came to, she told me that Rob had tried to strangle her.'

'And what did Rob say about that?'

'I never saw him again. Until you told me he was dead I'd assumed he'd fled in panic in Sam Gallagher's car and gone into hiding somewhere. Maybe—'

We were interrupted by two things. Leon returned with the note and Sara's phone rang. She got up and placed it on the table where we could all see it. Maria Groom's face filled the screen. She looked a lot different to the photos I'd seen. Her hair was much shorter and dyed black. She had some obvious signs of bruising around one of her eyes but she was smiling.

'Hello, Maria, I'm Detective Chief Inspector Jack Parker from Northumberland Police and this is Detective Sergeant Leon Johnson. We've been looking for you for quite a while.'

'Well, now you've found me.'

'You've led me on a fairly tortuous journey.'

'I'm sorry about that. But I had to escape from that man and didn't know how else to do it.'

'Would you like to tell me where you are?'

She laughed. 'I don't think so, no.'

'We will find you.'

'Why would you want to?'

I glanced at Nicky who had opened his eyes, probably woken by his mother's voice.

'So that your son here has a mother.'

'He already has one. She's standing right next to you.'

On cue, Nicky Groom held out his arms and Sara gathered

him up in hers. He nestled his face into her shoulder, whether through sleepiness or because he was frightened by the strange men surrounding him I wasn't sure.

'Can you move the phone slightly so I can still see him?' Maria asked. I did what she wanted. 'Ah, what a sweetheart. See how happy he is with Sara,' she added.

I moved the phone back so she could see I meant business.

'You can't just give your son away.'

'Why not? Sara will do a much better job than me. I'm not a good mother, ask anyone. And she's a natural. Has she told you about Rob?'

'Aye, some of it.'

'So you can see the difference between us. I hurt people and she tries to put them back together again. Would you rather Nicky went into care?'

'Obviously not. But what about his father?'

The smile disappeared from her face.

'Aren't you about to charge him with murder?'

It was only a matter of time. We'd released the news of the body being found on the farm and that a suspect was in custody. It was pretty obvious to all concerned that Evan Groom was that suspect and I was certain the DNA results would confirm that he had strangled the as yet unidentified woman.

'I know that you pointed us in the direction of the cannabis farm. Did you know about the dead girl?'

She shook her head. 'No, absolutely not. He'd let slip about the farm when he was pissed but the first I knew about the girl was when I saw the news earlier.'

'Can I ask you something, Maria?' Leon interjected.

She nodded.

'Did Evan ever mention the Connors family?'

'Yes, all the time,' she said. 'That's why I was so scared. That was who he was supplying the weed to. He threatened me with a visit from them more than once.'

'How about Harry Connors?'

She screwed up her face in thought for a moment or two then shook her head.

'No,' she said. 'He was never mentioned directly. The only name I ever heard was someone called Dusty.'

'OK, thank you.'

I could see that Leon was a little disappointed that he couldn't point the finger at Harry Connors.

'So you have no idea who the dead girl was?' I said.

'No, I'm sorry, no idea at all. I wasn't entirely surprised when I heard about her though. Evan was becoming increasingly unhinged. You can see why I had to run. Do you really think he deserves a say in Nicky's future?'

Leon and I shared a look. I could see we were on the same page.

'Maybe not,' I said.

'So what's the problem?' Maria said.

## 80

The taxi dropped me off at the end of my street. We'd gone to the hospital first but Emma was still out cold after surgery and would be for some time. Leon had stayed by her bedside. I had no doubts he'd be there all night.

As I turned onto the driveway I saw Helen sitting on the front doorstep smoking a cigarette which she quickly tried to stub out in the nearby flower bed.

'Busted,' I said, as I sat next to her. 'I thought you'd given up.'

'I had. But I found some tucked away in the back of a cupboard in the kitchen. Must have put them there ages ago.'

I laughed. 'They were Aidan's. I confiscated them off him a few days ago.'

'Little sod told me he'd never do it again last time I caught him.'

I raised an eyebrow.

'Fuck off,' she said. 'My stress levels have been off the scale lately.'

'Work that bad, eh?'

It was her turn to laugh. 'You wish.'

'It's bad for your health, you know?'

'Thank you, Dr Parker. Want one?'

It had been a while for me too but if I'd ever needed a smoke, it was now.

'Aye, why not? I don't think getting cancer is my biggest concern right now.'

She dug into her cardigan pocket and pulled out the packet, removed a cigarette and lit it, taking a drag before passing it over.

'How's Emma?'

I'd rung Helen earlier to let her know I'd be late home.

'OK, all things considered. The doc says she should make a full recovery.'

'That's good.'

'Uh-huh.'

'You OK?'

'Not really.'

'Want to talk about it?'

I did. I gave her chapter and verse on the last thirty-six hours, laying out my mistakes and doubts, barely pausing for breath. When I'd finished, she lit two more cigarettes and passed one over, taking her time to respond.

'Don't be too hard on yourself,' she said, once she'd got about halfway down the cigarette. 'Maria set up a trail and everyone followed it, not just you. It's nothing to do with your condition. And your instinct that Evan Groom was a bad man was spot on, wasn't it?'

'But have I done the right thing in the end?' I asked.

'With Lee Grant or Maria?'

'Both. Either. I'm supposed to uphold the law not be judge and jury. I worry that this thing in here . . .' I tapped my head, 'is affecting my decisions.'

I nearly told her about the headaches, but I'd given her enough problems recently. She took my hand.

'Maybe it is.' I flinched but she held tight. 'But not in a bad way. That "inside man" you're so worried of losing is still holding his own. If anything he's improving, maturing even.'

'Like a fine wine?'

She laughed. 'More like a smelly cheese.'

I nudged her with my shoulder a bit harder than intended but held on to her to stop her falling off the edge of the step.

'You're not just saying that to shut me up?'

'As if that would work. Look, d'you know what they tell doctors when they're starting out?'

'Don't bump into the furniture.'

Her laugh was understandably muted this time.

'Sorry, I thought you said actors.'

'You can't dodge everything with a joke, Jack.'

I nodded. She was right as usual.

'Go on. What do they tell the docs?'

'First, do no harm. I always thought it was a good rule for everyone: politicians, teachers, policemen even.'

I hoped, particularly for Nicky Groom's sake, that she was right. The kid hadn't had the best of starts to life with Maria and Evan Groom. He didn't need any more obstacles to get over. I hoped he'd landed on his feet with Sara Quinn.

'D'you think we're good parents?' I asked.

'I'm not bad,' she said. I nudged her again, more gently this time, and she smiled. 'Sorry, couldn't help myself.'

'Seriously though?'

'Look, Aidan's a good kid compared to a lot of the ones I see at school. He's got a strong moral conscience, he cares about people, and he's relatively polite which, trust me, is remarkable these days. He swears a bit too much but so do you.'

I resisted the obvious response.

'So you think we're doing OK?'

'Better than most,' she said.

Behind us the front door creaked open.

'I couldn't sleep,' Aidan said. 'Thought I heard you out—'

He caught sight of the cigarettes, then saw the packet they came from.

'You hypocritical bastards,' he said.

## 81

*Two days later*

I stood in the doorway of Emma's hospital room watching her sleep. I could see some pretty awful bruising around her left eye and bandages around her upper right arm. The nurse had told me that her cheekbone wasn't fractured, as they'd first suspected, just bruised. From all accounts she'd been lucky to get off so lightly.

I was about to leave to let her get some rest when her eyes flickered open. She yawned, flinching with the pain as she did, and moving her hand towards her cheek.

'I wouldn't touch that if I were you,' I said. 'Might be a bit sore.'

She turned her head slowly towards me.

'Could have been worse,' she muttered.

She was right. I'd gone to the mortuary to hear what Ray had to say about Stevie Connors' death and it wasn't a pretty sight.

'Aye, you should see the other guy. He really lost his head.'

'Please don't try and make me laugh, it hurts too much. Where's Leon?'

'I told him to go and get a bite to eat.'

'Thank God. I need a break from him. He's been lovely but he hasn't let me out of his sight. I could swear he's been pissing in a bottle when I'm asleep rather than going to the bathroom.'

'He feels responsible.'

'Tell me about it. Actually don't, he's already told me . . . a thousand times.'

'We should have been there for you.'

'Not your fault. I chose to go.'

'D'you want to talk me through it all?'

'Should I? Isn't there going to be an investigation?'

'For sure. But it doesn't sound like you have too much to worry about from the IOPC.'

'Really? I'm not sure they'll approve of my relationship with Harry Connors.'

'That's not your problem. I'll take any flak that's going for that. And Harry Connors has made a full confession re the shooting so you should be fine where that's concerned.'

'Though I'll be asked to testify, I'm sure, which won't go down too well. Can't be many times a police officer has spoken up in defence of a gangster who's killed someone.'

'Probably not. I still can't believe he shot his own father to save you.' Emma looked out the window, avoiding my eye.

'Nor can I. He saved my life.'

'Certainly looks that way.'

She turned back. 'What do you mean?'

'I wouldn't have thought he'd have the balls.'

'People are full of surprises.'

That was true. Emma definitely was. The CSIs hadn't yet found anything that totally contradicted the story she and Harry Connors had told us. Stevie Connors lured Emma to the house with the aim of raping and possibly killing her. As she fought him off his son interrupted the assault and, in the struggle to stop his dad, shot him with the man's own gun. Maybe that's what happened. It just all seemed a bit too neat to be true.

'You don't seem convinced,' she said. 'D'you think I might be in trouble?'

'For what? Being taken hostage, assaulted and shot? You didn't do anything wrong, did you?'

'How about consorting with the enemy.'

'Consorting? Is that what you kids call it nowadays?'

'Sod off, Jack. I hadn't fucked him last time you asked and I still haven't.'

'You may have left it too late. You're not looking your best and he's locked up.'

'Never say never. I'll look better one day and there are always conjugal visits.'

It was my turn to laugh.

'I doubt he'll do much time, if any. And I'm not sure Leon would approve of you visiting him if he did.'

'I know he wouldn't. Though it might help his chances of promotion. I assume mine are screwed now.'

'Maybe they've been improved. "Brave hero cop" and

all that. You can wear your medals to the interview. Bob Curtis'll love that.'

'I didn't do anything.'

'Didn't you?'

'You've read our statements.'

'Aye. They match perfectly. All tied up with a nice little bow.'

This time she held my eyes a lot longer, waiting for a question yet to come.

Eventually she seemed to make a decision. 'If you've got something to say, maybe you should say it.'

'One of the neighbours reported hearing six shots.'

'Sounds about right.'

'Your statement said five.'

'Five, six, who can keep count when the shit's going down? Did the neighbour ring the police?'

'Apparently not. Sounds like they knew who lived next door and didn't want to get involved.'

'And how many bullets did they find?'

'Five.'

She smiled. 'What's the problem then?'

'They also claimed the last shot they heard was much later than the others and nearly an hour before you called it in.'

She didn't blink. 'Witnesses are often wrong.'

'That's what the DI in charge of the investigation says.' Because of Emma's involvement they'd brought in a team from Cumbria to investigate the shooting. 'He's old-school. I think he's going to bury it.'

'I like him already.'

'Maybe he's right. Or maybe he wants an easy life.'

'Don't we all? Or do you have a different view?'

'Oh, I don't know, maybe someone, let's call him Harry, realised he needed gunshot residue on his hands to support his story and then removed the other bullet from the scene?'

'I'm not sure he's clever enough to think of that.'

'But you are.'

'What does Leon think? Or Bob Curtis?'

I shook my head. 'I haven't told them. At the moment it's just you, me and the lead investigator.'

I could see that she was mulling something over, not sure whether to go there. Then she did.

'They don't know about your problem either. No one else does.'

I'd been waiting for this conversation for a while. There'd been too many glances, too many hesitations. I knew she suspected something, but I wasn't sure what it was.

'Problem?' I said.

'My uncle had early onset dementia. He tried to change his lifestyle too. Same stuff as you, exercise, diet, those bloody puzzles, Sudoku in his case.'

'Did it work?'

She shook her head. 'Sadly not. He killed himself in the end.'

'That's reassuring. Let's say you're right. Why haven't you told anyone?'

'Because I'm a team player.'

'Me too,' I said.

## 82

Maria Groom's face shone out from the screen on Bob Curtis's desk. Despite her obvious signs of recent injury, she looked happy.

'I'm sorry for leading you on a bit of a dance but I was scared for my life and had to get away,' she said. 'Ever since Evan started selling his cannabis to the Connors gang he'd become increasingly threatening – he seemed to think he could do anything he wanted. Said he had "friends" in the police. I didn't know what to do so when the chance came to escape and point the finger at him, I took it. I genuinely didn't know about that poor woman he kept at the farm but that just shows I was right to be terrified. Please don't try and find me. I'm never coming back to the UK and Evan will be an old man by the time he gets out of prison. Nicky and I are happy and safe here and that's all that matters, surely?'

The video ended. Maria had recorded it for me after I told her I'd do what I could to help her. It was the best I could do to try and cover all our arses.

Bob had no idea that she was being disingenuous and I

doubted he ever would. Sara Quinn was heading for deepest, darkest Scotland where nobody would know her or Nicky and even though the kid's photo had been seen all over, I doubted anyone would recognise him, especially with his new name. Sara had explained that Rob Gibson's one useful contribution at the end had been to leave them all new passports. I didn't press her for the details. As for Evan Groom, I'd decided Maria was right. He shouldn't be allowed anywhere near that boy. It may not be the law but it was the right thing to do.

'It's not ideal, is it?' Bob said, as the recording finished.

'Not at all. But like she says, at least they're both safe. It wasn't looking great at one stage. And Evan Groom won't be seeing the light of day for a very long time.'

We had quickly identified the dead body found at the farm as Iryna Kurkov, a 22-year-old Ukrainian girl who had disappeared from her home city of Kherson six months earlier. Her father had uploaded his DNA onto an Interpol database called I-Familia and the match with Iryna was undeniable. As I'd suspected, Groom's DNA was all over her.

'No one will care whether he sees his son again,' I added, seeing Bob hesitating, 'and there are no other living relatives who might make a fuss.'

Bob sighed and put his head in his hands. This was way out of his comfort zone. He was a black and white kind of guy in a grey world. Until recently I'd thought I was the same, but my diagnosis had made everything in my world a lot less clear than before.

'She really led you on a merry dance, didn't she?' he said.

Bob was right, but I resisted the temptation to remind him that it was him who had urged me to focus on Evan Groom. *Mark my words, Jack, in these cases, it's always the husband.* I knew his memory would be selective on that one, the privilege of rank, I supposed.

'OK,' he said, eventually. 'I'm going to have to pass this upstairs, but I'll recommend that we quietly call off the search for Maria Groom. The press will probably sniff around for a bit but they'll lose interest in it before too long. It might not be the perfect outcome but hopefully the big bosses will see that it's the right one.'

As a summary of how the last few days had gone it was better than anything I could have come up with. Maybe I was finally starting to understand that there was a difference between justice and righteousness. Sadly, we weren't quite finished. Bob turned off his computer and picked up a folder from his desk.

'Which leaves us with the Connors debacle.'

He was surprisingly calm considering he knew I'd disregarded several direct orders and lied to him repeatedly. It was a good job he didn't know the half of it.

'So,' he said, pretending to shuffle around some papers to give me time to stew in my own juices. I could see Emma's statement on top of the folder right in front of him. I couldn't read it upside down but, thankfully, I already knew what it said.

'I take it you knew about DS Steel's "friendship" with Harry Connors,' Bob said.

I nodded.

'And, in fact, actively encouraged it.'

'I wouldn't say that.'

'I bet you wouldn't.'

'I try not to interfere in my team's personal relationships.'

Bob smiled. Not in a friendly way. More like a surgeon with a scalpel that he was looking forward to using a little too much.

'Of course you don't. You're renowned for your hands-off approach. Was she screwing him?'

'I refer you to my previous answer.'

He raised his eyebrows.

'Don't fuck me about, Jack, it won't end well.'

I sighed. 'I don't believe so. She thought that Connors knew something about the hit-and-run that killed Laura and befriended him to pursue that idea.'

'Did he?'

'Probably not.'

'I wonder where she got that idea from, given that she's relatively new here. And why she would take the risk of mixing with a known criminal, especially as she never actually knew Laura. Unlike you.'

I shrugged my shoulders. I had known exactly what Emma's line was going to be, and vice versa. It wasn't the truth, but it was believable enough to get us through this and one she'd clearly started to develop about a minute after she shot Stevie Connors. Ultimately, she and I both knew there was no way they were going to discipline 'the cop hero who took a bullet but still fought for her life', to quote the *Chronicle*'s headline.

'Who can say what goes on in a woman's mind? Maybe she had one eye on the promotion board and wanted to impress you.'

Appealingly to Bob Curtis's vanity never did any harm. Even though he knew fine well that's what I was doing. Now all I had to do was eat humble pie and agree with his conclusion.

'She's certainly impressed the deputy chief constable. She's already mentioned the King's Gallantry Medal,' he said.

'Excellent news for the unit, sir.'

I knew that Bob, despite his absolute knowledge that Emma and I were both lying through our teeth, was already looking forward to bathing in the reflected glory of that award. I also knew that he would have to have the last word. Luckily, I was happy to give it to him.

'Indeed. And it appears that Harry Connors has a cast-iron self-defence case for shooting his father, especially as Emma backs up his story. Given that he's also bending over backwards to help us clean out his late father's stables I suspect that any charges he might have been facing will disappear pretty quickly. We've already rescued several other trafficked girls from properties all over the city thanks to his information. Quite a result, really.'

He closed the folder. The meeting was almost over.

'One more thing.' Here it was.

'I do not want to hear another word about Laura's accident, not even a whisper in the corridors. Whatever off-the-books investigation you lot were running is over. You understand?'

I thought about Lee Grant's meeting with Laura's parents, about the tears that flowed from the kid and Liz, about Gordon's quiet acceptance and his arm around my shoulder as he walked me back down their path. He may have been a little bemused about the outcome of the kid's confession, but he'd already lost his daughter and until that moment had felt his wife slipping away too. Maybe it was the first step to getting her back. I had no intention of getting in the way of that. And I knew that after recent events both Emma and Leon would be more than happy to drop our off-the-books investigation.

'Completely,' I said.

Bob looked a little surprised. He'd clearly expected some pushback.

'Then we're done,' he said, taking the folder and putting it in his out-tray. 'Case closed.'

# EPILOGUE

*One month later*

'Last question. Where do you see yourself in five years' time?'

Deputy Chief Constable Barbara Shearer sat forward in her chair as if this was the most probing question she'd ever asked. In contrast I sat back, glad that we'd reached the end of the final interview for the DI post. I glanced along the table at Bob Curtis who was already making notes on his scoresheet even though I was sure he'd already made his mind up.

Across the table from the three of us, Emma Steel smiled. I had no doubts this was one answer she'd already prepared. It was pretty much guaranteed for every organisation with an HR department to throw it in, along with 'what's your biggest weakness?' How this was supposed to help us decide anything was a mystery to me.

Emma had dealt with the latter question neatly, first with a gag – 'I'm not great at dodging bullets' – and then, more seriously, but equally pointed: 'I used to rush in where fools fear to tread but I've now learned the hard way to prepare for every eventuality before I commit to an action.' She knew how to play the game.

As she was pretending to consider her answer to the final question, I could hear a couple of drunks singing 'Fairytale of New York' as they walked along the path outside the building. They may have been noisy but at least they had good taste. I wondered if the NYPD went through the same rigmarole as we had to when promoting officers. Somehow, I doubted it.

Emma finally committed to the answer she'd probably been practising half the night. She made sure to look straight at me when she delivered it.

'I hope that I will have done this job so well and picked up enough experience of working with the best that I'll be a shoo-in for the DCI's position next.'

The other two panel members laughed and I pretended to join in.

'They'd be big boots to fill,' the DCC said. 'What do you think, Jack? Will you be ready to step down by then?'

'I've already been checking out fishing rods, ma'am.' Cue more laughter. It was as false as my answer. I wasn't planning on going anywhere just yet – though the Alzheimer's gods may have already decided differently.

'OK, thank you, DS Steel,' the DCC said. 'Obviously we'll be taking some time to discuss the situation. There have been some excellent candidates so it may take a while.

We'll let you know our decision as soon as we've made it, Monday at the latest.'

Emma climbed to her feet.

'Thanks for the opportunity, ma'am,' she said, clearly having watched too many episodes of *The Apprentice*, before turning and leaving the room.

'Bright girl,' the DCC said. I had no doubts that she would be on Team Emma, a view which she almost immediately confirmed.

'Now that we've managed to ensure a strong female representation in the senior management it would be nice to match it on the ground, don't you think?'

She was slightly understating the case. As well as herself, the chief constable, the mayor, and the police and crime commissioner were all women. Fortunately, they were all good at their jobs, even though, in the case of the latter two, I still didn't like having civilians in charge of the police force.

Bob Curtis surprised me by taking a different view. I'd always had him marked as a 'yes man' but he made it clear he was leaning towards Leon.

'That's true, ma'am, but the black community are hugely under-represented at every level and if we're serious about diversity then we have to consider Detective Sergeant Johnson. He's got more experience than DS Steel by some distance and has had some great results in recent years.'

He had a point. Leon was one of just two black faces on the police side of our operations. We had one or two civilians too but if you were talking boots on the ground then we were well below the national average.

'You're right, obviously, and Johnson spoke very well too,' the DCC said.

I agreed, not least because I'd given him a bit of a coaching session the previous day, to give him a fighting chance. As a fast-tracker, Emma was much more used to the interview process. There were also two external candidates but neither of them were as good as my two detectives.

An hour later we were still debating the pros and cons of our final two. The externals were in the bin but we were finding it hard to separate Leon and Emma.

The DCC checked her watch – it was almost 6 p.m. on a Friday, the witching hour in Newcastle when the streets started to fill with hen nights. It would be nice to get away before that happened.

'I'm supposed to be at the Northern Symphonia concert in an hour,' she said. 'Shall we take a vote?'

Bob Curtis nodded and I followed suit.

'I suspect you already know that I'm going to go for DS Steel,' the DCC said. 'I scored her at 78 while Johnson was 74. And while the numbers don't always tell the whole story, the optics will be perfect and it sends a message out to anyone who thinks they can have a go at the police. She's a great role model for other women too.'

'I'm going for DS Johnson,' Bob Curtis said, confirming what I'd guessed before the last question had been answered.

'Very close though, 75 to 73. I think he has all the attributes to make an excellent detective inspector.'

They both turned towards me.

'That gives you the casting vote, Jack. Which only seems fair given that you will have to work with them.'

I had been hoping it wouldn't turn out that way; that I'd have been outvoted whichever way it went so I wouldn't have to make a decision between my two junior colleagues. I tried to focus on my notes but my headache had got progressively worse as the interviews had gone on. I knew I'd scored them equal anyway. They both deserved a promotion but there was only one job, and I didn't subscribe to the tokenism that my fellow interviewers seemed to. I couldn't care less about race or gender, I just wanted the best DI I could get.

I tried to think back over what they'd both done over the last few months, how they'd supported me in my search for Laura's killer. How they'd helped to cover up some of my indiscretions, but mostly, selfishly, I thought about Emma's knowledge of my condition. If that came out, my career could be over in weeks.

My headache was the worst one so far. I wished to God it would fuck off so I could think straight. I remembered my consultant mentioning brain bleeds. Was that what was causing them? I rubbed my temples as if that might help.

'Well, Jack?'

I looked up. Bob and the DCC were both staring at me with concern in their faces. Had I zoned out for a minute there? Was this another step on the slippery slope?

'I'm sorry?' I said.

The DCC laughed.

'It's been a long day, Jack, and we're all tired but try and stay awake. I said, "Time's up, who's it going to be?"'

# ACKNOWLEDGEMENTS

Dementia is now the UK's biggest killer, outstripping both lung cancer and Covid in recent years and accounting for more than one in ten of the deaths in this country.

And if the cases of this pernicious and, frankly, terrifying disease keep increasing at the same rate, one in two of us will be affected by 2030, either by caring for someone with the condition or suffering ourselves – or, in the worst case scenario, both.

Alzheimer's Research have been incredibly helpful in my research for these books, in particular a big shout out to Fiona Burrell and Sara Grix for all their support. It is a charity that is working incredibly hard to find a cure for dementia and a breakthrough is getting ever closer but it's an expensive business and it needs all the help it can get. If you can afford to donate then please do. There's a link here: https://www.alzheimersresearchuk.org/campaign/for-a-cure.

As usual I'd also like to thank Team Quercus, my fabulous editor, Jane Wood, and her colleagues, Stef Bierwerth, Ella Patel, Elizabeth Masters, Beth Wright, Charlotte Gill and

Florence Hare. Thanks also to my copy editor Liz Hatherell, who I can always rely on to improve my books no end. And a big nod of gratitude to Andrew Smith for designing the latest in a series of great covers featuring the mighty Tyne Bridge.

The brilliant David Nellist, who has narrated all my books bar one, brings his dulcet Geordie tones to the voices of Jack and others. Hearing him read a chapter from *The Silent Killer* at my Goldsboro Books launch last year was spine-tingling.

Another shout out to my fantastic agent, Oli Munson, there is no better man to have beside you in the publishing trenches.

I have so many other writer friends to thank, too. The D20s – a group of writers who teamed up when they realised they were about to have their debut novels published in lockdown – remain a constant source of support, a particular round of applause this time to Nikki Smith and Frances Quinn for their emergency feedback when I needed it most. My Newcastle-based writing group have also continued to offer considered, constructive criticism of my work. Many thanks to Simon Van der Velde, Karon Alderman, Ben Appleby-Dean and Roz Wyllie. I must also again mention my ever-supportive fellow Northern Crime Syndicate writers, Robert Scragg, Rob Parker, Jude O'Reilly, Fiona Erskine, Adam Peacock, and Chris McGeorge.

A huge cheer too for all the booksellers, readers, bloggers, reviewers and friends who have supported the books to date. If I haven't bought you that pint yet, I will hopefully catch up with you in one of my Bars of the World soon.

You couldn't write a police procedural without asking a policeman for help. Big thanks to Graham Bartlett for his invaluable assistance. All mistakes are mine to own.

If you wish to learn more about the effects of dementia, then I can recommend further reading. All of these books have been invaluable in my research for this series: *A Tattoo on my Brain* by Daniel Gibbs, *Somebody I Used to Know* by the late Wendy Mitchell, *On Pluto* by Greg O'Brien and, in the fictional world, the brilliant *Still Alice* by Lisa Genova.

Last, but obviously best, huge LOVE to my fabulous family, Pam and Becca, my harshest critics and (sometimes) biggest fans. Not forgetting the furry boys Dexter and Leo who rightfully prefer my lap to anyone else's.